"I found *The Albatross* to be a very interesting book, and I am glad that I read it."

— *Captain Al Haynes, pilot of United 232, which crash-landed in the cornfields of Sioux City, Iowa, in 1989 after losing not only an engine but the entire hydraulic systems that controlled the airplane. His heroics saved 184 of the 232 passengers onboard.*

"Gerry does a superb job of showing how airplane crews actually think, work together, and react to the unexpected. It is a great story and I truly enjoyed reading it."

— *Jerry Davis, former FAA Flight Standards Manager, pilot, author of* The Air Carrier Inspector's Handbook, *consultant to Airbus Industries Flight Safety Program, and one of the recipients of the Robert J. Collier Trophy housed in the Air and Space Museum in Washington. It was awarded in 2008 for his contributions to the CAST, the Commercial Aviation Safety Team, which was credited for reducing the risk of future fatal airline accidents by 83 percent.*

My very best to you
Blue Skies!

THE ALBATROSS

A novel

GERRY HAWES

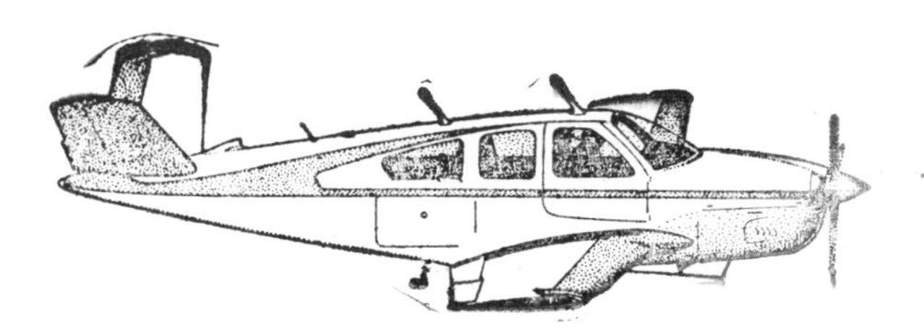

The Albatross

ISBN: 978-1-940244-73-0

This is a work of fiction. Names, characters, businesses, places, events and incidents are either the products of the author's imagination or used in a fictitious manner. Any resemblance to actual persons, living or dead, or actual events is purely coincidental.

Cover photo "Thalassarche bulleri in flight 1 - SE Tasmania" *by*

JJ Harrison (jjharrison89@facebook.com)

Designed and Produced by

Indie Author Warehouse

12 High Street, Thomaston, Maine 04861

www.indieauthorwarehouse.com

Printed in the United States of America

FOREWORD

The Albatross is a novel about an ordinary man, his life, and his loves—his love of his family, his friends, and the special world that hides in the vast blue sky above. It is the story of an airline pilot—his successes, his failures, and his struggles to cope with events that altered his life and haunt his memory daily.

The Rime of the Ancient Mariner

(Excerpts)

By Samuel Taylor Coleridge

And I had done a hellish thing,
And it would work 'em woe:
For all averred, I had killed the bird
That made the breeze to blow.
Ah wretch! said they, the bird to slay,
That made the breeze to blow!

Nor dim nor red, like God's own head,
The glorious Sun uprist:
Then all averred, I had killed the bird
That brought the fog and mist.
'Twas right, said they, such birds to slay,
That bring the fog and mist.

The fair breeze blew, the white foam flew,
The furrow followed free;
We were the first that ever burst
Into that silent sea.

Down dropt the breeze, the sails dropt down,
'Twas sad as sad could be;
And we did speak only to break
The silence of the sea!

Ah! well a-day! what evil looks
Had I from old and young!
Instead of the cross, the Albatross
About my neck was hung.

PROLOGUE

Friday, August 4, 1989

Aboard *Otter*, a 43-foot Shannon Ketch sailboat

Position: The North Atlantic Ocean—140 nautical miles west of Santiago, Spain and 850 nautical miles northeast of Horta on the Azorean island of Faial, their next destination. Kevin O'Connor was sitting in the swivel chair at the navigator's station, his elbows on the slanted table, his thumbs supporting his chin, and his eyes staring straight ahead. On the surface, he was a ruggedly handsome forty-six-year-old Army retiree. His towering frame he inherited from his father; his golden locks, swept back in a ponytail, from his Swedish mother. He rather liked his hair on the long side, which was probably a carryover from the military buzz cut that he had had to endure during his four years as a cadet at West Point. But that was twenty-four years in the past, a long time ago, as were Ranger training and two tours of duty in Vietnam. His chair was uncomfortable to begin with because the lumbar support was designed for a much smaller person, but he had pulled his back out slightly the day before by tripping on a line on deck, and this made the matter even worse. But he had no choice.

His wife, Jenny, was standing behind him looking over his shoulder. "What do you think is wrong with it, Kevin?" she asked.

He was worried and he looked tired—he was not the free spirit that he normally was. "I don't know, Jen."

"What *could* be wrong with it?" she asked.

Kevin was frustrated and became sarcastic. "What kind of stupid question is that? What could be wrong with it?" he barked. "It's broken. We're out in the middle of the Atlantic Ocean and we don't know where the hell the monster storm is!"

Jenny drew closer and began to massage his shoulders. "You know I'm only trying to help, and your shoulders are as tight as a knot. You've taught me a lot of mechanical lessons over the years, admit it. I've helped you solve some of the problems in the past, haven't I? Haven't I?" she repeated.

Kevin sighed. "Sorry I was short with you, Jen, and yes, you have, but I just have no idea what's wrong with this stupid weather fax. It just doesn't work!"

"You were the one who told me that salt air and electricity are not very good friends. Did you already try cleaning the ground connection?"

"Yes, I did."

"The antenna connection?"

"I did that, too."

"Wait a minute, Kev. Didn't you say that the radio transceiver hasn't worked for two days?"

"Yeah. We haven't been able to make or receive any radio transmissions since...well...two days ago."

Jenny began to nod her head. She was onto something. "So, don't you think it's odd or maybe improbable that two different radios that both use the same HF range of frequencies both quit at the same time?"

"I see what you're saying, and you know, this happened before, over a year ago, but we were in port and it didn't really matter. And I think it was about the same time of the year, too, when there was all that solar activity, sunspots, and all that stuff. I remember that it shut down all HF radio traffic everywhere for a couple of days. You're right, Jen, that could be it. And I sure hope so."

Kevin was scared. He normally didn't hide unpleasant facts from his wife, but here he was in a small boat in a big Atlantic Ocean with the remnants of Hurricane Felix approaching, and he didn't know exactly where it was and how to avoid it. He thought about sharing his fears with her but decided that it wouldn't serve any purpose other than making Jenny even more upset than she already was.

"Are you frightened?" Jenny asked slowly.

"Wrong word. *Concerned* is a better one. Look, we both have our Coast Guard captain's licenses. We've been sailing for twenty-five years and have already crossed the Atlantic once successfully. The boat is seaworthy, and we just had another survey done before we left Malaga, and best of all, it's a Shannon 43 Ketch, which has more successful circumnavigations than any other sailboat in the world. So, am I scared? No! Concerned? Yes. We have to make some contingency plans, that's all. So we can't talk to our meteorologist, Jim Breaugh, and we can't get our weather maps and forecasts. We'll just have to play it by ear and plan it very conservatively. We'll be okay, Jen. Don't worry. I just don't like not having all the facts in front of me, that's all."

"Well, your shoulders are loosening up a little."

"I know, thank you." He reached up across his chest and squeezed her hand.

Kevin lifted the hinged chart table and retrieved a folder that was stored inside. It was the weather prognoses—or progs—that they had received two days earlier, actually fifty hours ago. "Here are the notes that I took while talking with Jim. Forecasts go out ninety-six hours in advance, and Jim said that there were three different computer models for the remnants of the hurricane that he was looking at as it moves up the East Coast. Two probably would not affect us. The third one would, and that's the one I want to know more about. So, right now, we're in limbo."

"Should we have waited in Malaga a few more days to see what was going to happen before we left?" Jenny meekly asked.

"No, that's pure hindsight. Storms in the U.S. don't normally affect Europe or the Eastern Atlantic, but I guess this one isn't really normal. Again, we have a seaworthy boat and we are an experienced crew, and if we know where the storm is going, we could try to distance ourselves from it."

"Don't we have two more days of validity for the weather forecast? You said we had ninety-six hours forecast from him two days ago. That leaves two days forecast in the future, right?"

"Yes," Kevin said, nodding his head, "that's good thinking! The only hang-up is that Jim thought that the present forecast was going to change when it came out the next time, which is every six hours, and that's when we lost the contact."

"So, what's our plan then?" Jenny asked, still standing behind him.

"Well, we'll go with the info we have. We will plan our course using the 'One, Two, Three' plan for hurricane avoidance. We'll have the storm jib on the forestay, the storm trysail on the mast instead of the reefed main, and a reefed mizzen. I thought that we could preposition the parachute drogue and lash it down by the bowsprit just in case, but I doubt that we'll need it. But, better safe than sorry. Can you think of anything else?"

"Well, I know that we have a checklist for heavy-weather sailing. Why don't you review it while I throw something together for dinner?"

"Okay. It'll be dark soon. Let's have a glass of wine on deck and watch the moon again. Wasn't that spectacular last night? And it's not even completely full yet."

Kevin rose from his navigator station chair and reached for his inflatable life vest and jack-line tether lying on the rear quarter berth.

"Do you really have to clip onto the jack line if we're only going to be out there for a few minutes?"

"Jenny, it's starting to get dark, and we're not on a lake. You know the rules," Kevin replied. He put on his red personal flotation device and ascended the main hatch ladder with Jenny following.

Sitting on a pair of white floatable seat cushions on the forward-most part of the port coach roof, they sat in silence looking out at the sea, the stars, and the moon.

"You know, Kev, it doesn't feel like there's a storm out there, does it?"

"Well, it's at least about six hundred miles away. The barometer is already falling, although nothing drastic."

"Oh, six hundred miles away? When do you think it will reach us?"

"Storms in the Atlantic usually only travel about ten or fifteen miles an hour. That's about fifty-three hours. That's more than two days. We'll have time, Jen, and we'll be ready."

Kevin was truly treasuring this moment—there they were, both tethered to the jack line, both attached to each other hand in hand. He could feel the boat slicing through the waves with a soft and steady *whoosh, whoosh.*

Below decks, the mellow glow from the brass trawler lamp swinging gently on its chain created a visual rhythm of light on the paneled wall of the ship's salon. You could imagine a cat watching a bird on a swing with its eyes and its head going back and forth like a metronome.

"Seems like the sea is picking up," Kevin nonchalantly mumbled as his right hand rose to steady the swinging oil lamp.

"Do you always talk with your mouth full, Kevin?"

"Don't be a wise guy," he retorted as a slight smile overcame his faux sternness. "And the answer is yes." It was a broad grin now, so wide that his handlebar mustache seemed to change directions on its ends.

"Honey, I know that you like it, but the swinging of that lamp is talking to my stomach. Would you please attach a tether? Thank you. And I'll tell you what, I'll do the old dishes in the sink if you go topside and assess things and see if we should shorten sail together before you nod off."

The warmly lit cabin with its two oil lamps and one candle was by no means bright, but it seemed that way in contrast to what greeted Kevin as he climbed the six rungs of the cabin ladder and stepped out onto the cockpit. There was a huge full moon—the August Sturgeon Moon. There were stars everywhere. While he was standing in the cockpit and looking around, he thought he saw something out of the ordinary. "Honey!" he suddenly yelled. "Don't turn on the spreader lights just yet, and bring me the binoculars."

"What do you see?" Jenny asked with her head poking out of the hatch opening.

"Come on up here. Tell me what *you* think."

Off in the distance—way, way off in the distance on the horizon—there was a light, a very bright, twinkling light. "What do you suppose it is?" Jenny asked.

"Well, it must be a ship with a searchlight looking for something."

"Well, like what?" she asked.

"I don't know."

"Yeah. You're probably right. What else could it be? But it looks weird out here. What does it look like through the binoculars?"

"Here, you take a look." He handed her the glasses and walked back the twenty feet to the cockpit, then to the hatch, before disappearing below.

"Where are you going?"

As he got to the bottom of the cabin stairs, he turned around and called out of the hatch, "I'm turning the VHF radio on to channel sixteen, the emergency frequency, to see if I can raise him." He had another thought as his hand rose to the bookshelf behind the radio. He grabbed the ship's log, put it down on the map table, and opened to the page with the paper clip. As his watch ended, he wrote the following entry:

Date: 3 August, 1989. Time: 0153 Zulu (GMT)

Sea Condition: force three; gentle breeze; large wavelets; scattered whitecaps

Position: 41 degrees 56' 04" North; 023 degrees 40' 02" West

Bearing to light: 249 degrees

Message: Unusual bright light observed above the horizon appears to be moving, getting larger, hard to tell; twinkles similar to that of Venus; too high above the horizon unless there is an ocular bend in the light due to the atmospheric range. Will try to raise the subject on the radio.

"Kevin!" Jenny shouted. "Kevin, come up here! I don't think that's a ship!"

"What?" Kevin asked as he walked over and came closer to the cockpit hatchway. "I can't hear you!" he yelled.

"I said I don't think it's a ship! The light is too bright, and it seems to be moving too fast. At least, it appears that way through the binoculars." She was talking into the wind, and her last words were unheard. "Oh, it has to be a ship or a star or…." Her words trailed off. "What else could it be?" She was talking quietly to herself now. "Well, it's changed just in the time since you've been below." Her voice was much louder now. "I don't think that it's a ship."

"Will you just wait a minute, please?" Kevin asked.

"Kevin! Kevin, come up here! Come up here *now*!"

"Okay. All right. What's going on?" he asked as he hurried up the ladder out into the cockpit, out to midship. Jenny was sitting on the coach roof.

"Here, you take a look!" she said.

"What the hell? You're right, I don't think it's a ship, either."

"Well, what do you think it is?"

"I don't know—"

"Maybe it's an airplane."

"An airplane?" Kevin asked. "We're out in the Atlantic Ocean.

We're days away from the Azores."

"Well, maybe it's a Navy patrol plane—you know, like they have up at Brunswick Naval Air Station, a P-3 anti-sub or something."

"Well, you might be right. It might be a military operation or something. But to me, it's really spooky seeing that. Well, we'll know soon. It looks like it's heading our way."

"Are you scared?" Jenny asked somewhat timidly.

"About what? About a light? No! I'm very curious, though." He paused. "Why? Do *you* think there's something to be worried about?"

"I don't know—I just don't like it. I feel very vulnerable out here in this small boat."

"Well, *Otter* is forty-three feet long, and she's a Shannon."

"Yes, forty-three feet is big on Loon Pond, but not out here," Jenny quipped.

"Okay, let's not get into another argument about the size of the ocean versus the boat, okay?"

"Sorry!"

"I'm sorry, too. I didn't mean to bark. I'm going to try the radio again."

"Kevin, why don't you stay here just for a minute? It's getting bigger."

"I'm going to get the other binos. I'll be right back." Kevin scampered back to the cockpit down the companionway and was back in thirty seconds.

Now they both sat, eyes glued to the binoculars, trying to stay focused and aimed at the light on the horizon as the ship's bow gently rose and fell gliding through the black Atlantic waves. Suddenly, after about ten seconds, the light disappeared, and they just sat there, sitting on the coach roof of the boat, looking and wondering.

"Well, it probably *was* a military operation, Jen. But it looks like it's gone now. Anyway, let's go below and brief the changing of the watch."

They went back to the cockpit, pushed back the storm hatch, and descended the ladder to the salon. After about five minutes, Kevin went topside to check on the light again. The moon was still there, but not the mysterious light. He came below and sat down on the settee behind the chart table.

Jenny rubbed her temples, trying to put the unusual light out of her mind. "Well, I guess it's time to come up with something to eat, make it, and then tuck you in. It's my watch coming up. We have to stick to the schedule, right, Love?"

"Absolutely," Kevin agreed. "Tell me what I can do to help. How about dried pasta with canned tomatoes tonight?"

Suddenly, a deafening, thunderous roar shook the boat, the vibration rattling the dishes and pots and pans that were in the galley shelves. Jenny and Kevin's lungs felt as if they were bouncing around inside their rib cages.

"Kevin, Kevin!" Jenny screamed.

"What the hell?" he yelled.

The event was over almost as fast as it began. They both looked at each other in complete shock, then hurriedly made their way to the companionway ladder and up to the cockpit outside. There was a gentle breeze topside, Beaufort force three, scattered whitecaps with seven to ten knots of wind, just enough to cause a whistling sound in their ears and affect their hearing.

"Kev," Jenny exclaimed, "Do you see anything? What the hell was that?"

Kevin strained his eyes looking into the black sky. "I don't see it, but I hear something, and it's fading fast. But it had to be an airplane—what else could it have been? And, do you smell *that*?"

"Smell what?"

"The exhaust fumes in the air. Those are from a jet engine—I *know* that!"

"*How* do you know that?"

"Don't you remember when we used to fly down to the Caribbean? At those small airports, the jets would start their engines and taxi away, blowing their exhaust behind them into the waiting area. That's the smell of a jet engine, I'm sure of it."

"Okay, well, if it is a jet, and it *was* a jet that we saw with that light in the distance before, what do you think it was doing?"

"I don't know, but I'm going to record our position and time, and if we ever get our HF radio back, I'll call on the emergency frequency and report it. It's probably nothing, but it is highly unusual and might mean something." They lingered in the cockpit for a few minutes, and then descended the companionway ladder to the cabin below. After making an entry in the ship's log, Kevin began to help Jenny gather ingredients for their meager dinner. As Jenny grabbed two dinner plates, she happened to glance at the navigator's station.

"Kevin! Kevin!" she excitedly announced, "there's a piece of paper sticking out of the weather fax machine. I think it's working again!"

CHAPTER ONE

Saturday, September 8, 1962
Miami, Florida, 9:35 p.m.

Captain Jack Rheinstrom moved the tiller with his left hand, and the nose wheel of the Baker Mercury 100 turned to the right as he taxied the airplane onto the active runway and aligned it with the centerline of runway nine left.

"Trans Ocean three three," came the voice from the Miami tower, "you are cleared for takeoff on nine left. Maintain runway heading, climb and maintain three thousand, and contact departure on one two six point five when airborne."

"Roger, Miami. Cleared to go nine left, up to three, departure twenty-six five, TO thirty-three."

Jack looked to his right at the copilot with his eyebrows raised. "Ready to go?"

"Yes, sir!" came the reply, as Jack slowly but surely pushed all three throttle levers forward to the approximate takeoff setting. Copilot and first officer John Battagliola, aka Batman, leaned forward from his right seat and fine-tuned the throttles to their exact takeoff EPR setting.

It was night, and the cockpit was dark except for the background lighting on the round dial instruments on the forward instrument panel. After announcing, "Before-takeoff check complete," second officer Ron Kerley swung his seat around from its previous position of facing the flight engineer's panel. He was now facing forward, sitting directly between and behind the two pilots, intensely watching the engine instruments during the critical takeoff roll.

When his airspeed indicator reached the correct speed, John announced, "Eighty knots!" at which time Captain Rheinstrom removed his left hand from the tiller and put it on the left horn of his yoke.

The airspeed continued to increase, and when it reached the calculated takeoff commit point, John said, "V-1." Seconds later, he called out, "V-2! Rotate!"

Jack slowly pulled back on the yoke and the three-engine Baker Mercury lifted off into the black Miami sky, its altitude increasing all the while. When the vertical velocity indicator and altimeter both confirmed the climb, the first officer had another announcement to make: "Positive rate."

"Gear up!" Jack announced.

John repeated the command and reached forward in his seat to raise the landing gear handle. The three components of the landing gear system—the nose, the left main, and the right main—began their coordinated ballet, eventually nestling themselves into the belly of the wings and the fuselage.

The airplane was now at approximately one thousand feet, and the flap retraction schedule began, having been set at fifteen degrees for takeoff.

"Flaps five!" called Jack.

"Flaps five," responded the first officer as he moved the flap handle.

"Flaps two."

"Flaps two," John repeated.

"Flaps up."

"Flaps up."

"Climb power," said the captain, and soon the response followed, "Climb power set."

It was now time for the copilot to call departure control. John reached his hand to his right and instinctively found the mike that was hanging by its cord on the side window latch. When he called departure, Ron slid his seat backward and sideways to once again face the flight engineer's panel of aircraft system monitors and silently perform the called-for climb check.

They had just entered the overcast, a cloud deck that was forecast to extend to at least six thousand feet, when a red light and loud bell changed the entire night for the crew. The piercing ring was sharp and startling. Accompanying it was a steady bright light inside a red plastic handle mounted on the front glare shield. It was the fire light, labeled for engine two. The fire-detection system had detected an intense heat or fire that had burned through somewhere on a continuous loop wire that surrounded the hot section of engine number two, the engine that was incorporated in the vertical stabilizer of the tail section.

Jack quickly looked to his right and barked to the copilot, "You silence the bell and fight the fire with the engineer. I've got the airplane and the radio. We're going back!"

John vigorously nodded his head up and down, and Ron swung his seat around once again so he was facing forward and could help the pilots run the engine-fire checklist.

Captain Rheinstrom called out, "Departure, this is TO thirty-three. We've got a problem here—indicated fire on number two. Declaring an emergency and requesting clearance for a short approach back to Miami. Requesting fire equipment standing by!"

"Roger, Trans Ocean thirty-three. Turn left to a heading of two seven zero, maintain three thousand. This will be vectors for an ILS to runway nine left. Do you want the weather again? And state number of souls aboard, Captain."

"No, a little busy right now! Uh…stand by…we have one hundred and ten passengers and a crew of eight." Jack looked to his right again. "When you're finished with the checklist, uh—"

The first officer immediately interrupted him. "Captain, we've fired both fire bottles and the red fire light is still on!"

"Okay, John, I'm going as fast as I can! Brief the senior that we'll be evacuating on the ground as soon as we land—but *not,* I repeat, *not* until my 'Easy Victor' call over the intercom. Okay?" Jack paused. "No, wait a minute—you do that, Ron—John, you help me get ready for this approach."

In four minutes the airplane smoothly touched down and was in the landing rollout phase at approximately sixty knots. A hand in the aft section of the cockpit reached up and pushed a small yellow button labeled *Motion* on a panel that was mounted there on the wall. A voice announced, "Okay, guys, I've got it. Motion is coming off. Good job!"

The simulator stabilized itself in a perfectly horizontal position and began to slowly descend hydraulically the five or so feet until it settled on its base with a gentle *ka-thump.*

"Okay, guys," the instructor pilot said, "let's take fifteen for a quick pit stop and get strapped back in here again. All we have left is three approaches for the first officer and then we'll be done. Overall, very good crew coordination, good flying, and good job. And, Jack, congratulations on your first captain checkout! Okay, let's break."

The crew of three and the instructor, Captain Dave Pratt, walked through the door of the Mercury 100 simulator at Trans Ocean Training Headquarters, up the stairs, and into the lobby.

As they were walking down the corridor, Jack turned to his copilot with his arms spread out like a bird. "Yeah, I guess *I* could use a pit stop! Look at my shirt! The armpits are completely soaked. Man, I was humping!"

John looked over at Jack and smiled. "Yup! Did a good job, *Captain* Rheinstrom! Very good job, Jack!"

"Could not have done it without your support, Kid, thanks. Glad that you were with me today!" He glanced backward. "You too, Ron! You too!"

The rest of the simulator ride was uneventful, and after the debriefing by Captain Pratt, who lived locally and departed soon afterwards, the crew of three was left standing in the Hartley Building lobby together contemplating their next move.

"What time do you have there, John?" Jack asked. "My watch stopped after your last, uh, *landing.*"

John looked at Jack with a wry smile. "Busting my chops are you, Captain? Now that you don't need me anymore to carry you through the check ride on my back!"

"Very good, John! Touché. Anyway, I have a blinking low-level beer light right now, and we need to take corrective action. I think that Big Daddy's across the street is open until 0100, as I remember. So, I think that this new captain should take care of his crew that took care of him. A flagon or two and a bite to eat! What do you say?" Jack asked, looking around at his men.

It was an easy sell. Soon, the three of them were sitting in a booth across the street at Big Daddy's.

"Where do you guys live?" Jack asked.

John Battagliola went first. "New Jersey. Up on the shore in Bricktown with five other guys."

Jack nodded. "Sounds like college days, doesn't it? Part two."

"Yeah. Well, it's fun being on the shore, and the other roomies are either airline or Air Force stationed at McGuire about thirty minutes away. So, we all get along."

"Do you have a boat on the shore?"

"Well, you kind of have to, or at least have a friend who has one. All five of us own a share of a twenty-one-foot fiberglass runabout, a Zephyr. Three guys like to runabout and two of us like to fish, so it all works out."

"What about you, Ron?" the new captain asked, putting his empty beer mug down and catching the waiter's eye.

"I live in New Hampshire. Up in Seabrook, actually along the evacuation route from the nuke plant there."

"What? That sounds rather precarious."

"Well, I guess it makes a good story. Actually, it was somewhat intimidating when I was first in the area, but after a while you get used to the signs, and if you think about it, it does make sense to have everyone aware of what to do and where to go if something happens. I equate it to living in San Francisco. You just don't think it's going to happen to you, so you just go about and live your life."

"You sound like a wise man of many years," Jack said. "How old are you, Ron?"

"Twenty-six. In fact, I just got off probation. So, I've only really been here at Trans Ocean for a little over a year and a half. This was my first real annual check ride since I was hired."

John interrupted with a sideways look and smile to his ex-roomie sitting next to him. "Ron here used to be one of us until he went out and got married, but we forgave him. We were all stationed together at McGuire flying C-54s. But I'm a couple of years older and had already been there for a while when he showed up after Air Force pilot training."

"So where are you guys based?" Jack asked.

"I'm in New York, and Ron is out of Boston," John replied.

"Great, Ron, because I'll be based up there too once I go through language school and learn how to say *lobstah*!"

John nodded and smiled slightly. "What about you, Captain Rheinstrom? What's your story?" he asked, wiping the beer foam from his mouth with the back of his hand.

"Well, I'm a lucky guy. I grew up in a suburb outside of Cleveland, and our next-door neighbor worked for the state government; I forget what capacity. Anyway, he watched me grow up playing with balsa wood gliders, the ones powered by rubber bands. I remember they were called A-J Hornets. How's that? Anyway, my dad was away a lot, and Mr. Berline took an interest in my love of airplanes. Long story short, he got me into the Ohio Air National Guard just out of college. I spent a year at Reese Air Force Base in Texas for training, then just part-time flying in the New Jersey Air National Guard so I could apply to the airlines. No five years of active duty for me like you guys had to do; just one year, and I was out and off active duty. Consequently, I got on with Trans Ocean early, age-wise, and I made it to captain in just seven years. Some of the guys at Reese had never even *heard* of the National Guard. In fact, I wouldn't have been there either had it not been for Mr. Berline. So lucky, lucky me!" He raised his glass mug with an outreached hand across the booth toward Ron and John, his two newest friends. "To Mr. Berline!" Three outstretched hands with their accompanying mugs met in the middle of the table with a resounding *clink*. "To Mr. Berline."

Even though seven years represents an early rise to captaincy in the airline world, it could not have come any sooner for Jack Rheinstrom. He had been waiting and dreaming about this career for as long as he could remember. His father was, as they say, a traveling man; he was always coming to or going from somewhere in his early career. He had been hired in 1935 in one of the first groups of employees for American Airlines. The airline industry was in its infancy then. It was an exciting and dynamic career, to say the least. It planted a seed in Jack that drove his aspirations and ambitions for the rest of his life.

His mother was intelligent and well-read, and, as was the custom at the time, a full-time, stay-at-home mom. She had been raised in a one-time wealthy family until the Depression hit, but she considered the real wealth to be education, and much more important than tangible assets measured in dollars. She also imparted in her young Jack a sense of empathy and sensitivity that could sometimes break through as a moist eye in certain circumstances. He earned his nickname early as "Scrappy Jack" for his refusal to ever back down from a fight, a trait that he developed when he was very young and undersized compared to others in his age group.

"Hey, Ron," Jack spoke up, "I need to figure out a place to stay in Boston. I'm not the commuting type. I already tried that—too many missed flights at the last minute and too many wasted days getting into position for a trip. You've obviously found your place in New Hampshire. Where would you suggest I start looking?"

"Well, to tell you the truth, Jack, I kind of miss the shore. We're in Seabrook because that's where Harriet was living, and her family is near us right now; funny how that works out, isn't it?" Kerley rhetorically asked. "An awful lot of crews, single ones, especially the stews, live in either Marblehead or Salem—you know, the *witch* capital. But, if you go there, you'll have to learn how to pronounce it correctly."

"Pronounce what?" Jack asked.

"Well," said Ron, smirking, "it's not *Marble*head, it's Marble*head.*"

"Oh, I see! It's Marble*head.* How's that?"

"Great! You'll fit in just fine," said Ron with a laugh, raising his mug to his lips.

CHAPTER TWO

"I'm a docent," Andrea Summers was saying to Jack Rheinstrom with a smile.

"You're a *doe send*?" asked Jack confusedly, struggling with the accent. "What do you do?"

"I work, if that's the correct word, at the Gardner."

"You work at the garden and you're a doe send?"

"Yes. That's what I just said, didn't I?" Andrea looked puzzled about his repeated questioning.

Now Jack looked puzzled. "Let's start over, shall we? My name is Jack Rheinstrom, and I've been in Boston for a total of—" he paused to look down at his watch, "a total of eight daylight hours now. And I'm sorry, but I don't know anything local. Which garden did you say that was?"

A broad grin enveloped her face. It was a kind smile exposing a perfect set of bright white teeth, albeit with a slight space between the two front ones. The effect was not homely in the least but rather slightly mysterious and becoming. As she smiled, she slowly and steadily moved her head back and forth. "Oh! Here comes Packrat now!" she said, looking behind Jack to the area just to the side of the long bar at the rear of The Black Rose.

Did she say here comes *Packrat* now? Jack thought to himself. He turned around and watched a very attractive woman with short brown hair in her early twenties, wearing khaki slacks and a white short-sleeved blouse, approach the area where the two of them were standing. They could have been sitting if they chose to, as there were six portable bar stools located there. The seats were in front of a four-foot wall with a long wooden counter on the top, and it separated the bar area in the back from the eating area and the live music stage in the front by the main entrance.

Andrea began, "Patty, I want you to meet my newest friend, whom I have known all the way since you went to the loo." She looked to the right with raised eyebrows. "Patty McGrath, meet John Enstrom."

"*Rheinstrom*!" Jack chortled.

"I'm sorry, John Rheinstrom!"

"Nope, *Jack* Rheinstrom."

"I'll get it yet! Jack Rheinstrom."

Patty appeared slightly wary and hesitant. After looking at him, then at Andrea, then back at Jack, she extended her hand and said in a very soft voice, "Hello."

"Hello, Connie," was Jack's reply, which was absolutely perfect. In an instant, and amidst their shared laughter, the three of them morphed from complete strangers to potential new friends.

"May I buy you two ladies a drink, perhaps?" Jack asked.

"Oh! You don't have to do that!" said Andrea.

"I know, but I'd like to."

"Well, that would be nice! Thank you."

"And what will that be?" he asked, looking at one then the other.

"A white wine please," said Andrea.

Jack then looked at Patty McGrath.

"A Harp would be great, thanks."

Jack was still struggling with the accent. "I'm sorry. A hop?"

"An *H-A-R-P*. A Harp beer," she clarified, amused.

"Okay, a Harp beer and a white wine—I've got it. I'll be right back." Jack then left to put in his order and waited in the queue at the bar behind them.

"Who is this guy, Andy?" Patty asked.

"I don't know. I just met him while you in the john. I was standing here and my sunglasses fell off the counter. He was standing nearby, saw it, and before I knew it, he came over, picked them up, dusted them off with his handkerchief, and gave them back to me. I just said 'Thank you,' and he turned around and went back to where he was standing before. So, I went over to him and said, 'That was very nice of you.' He pooh-poohed it, and we started a small-talk conversation then you returned."

"Well," Patty said, "he seems like a nice enough fellow. I mean, after thirty seconds anyway, but you never know."

"I don't know anything about him other than he's been in Boston for less than a day. He doesn't know very much about the city, doesn't even know what a docent is, and he thinks that I work in a garden."

"What?" Patty asked. "You're kidding, aren't you, Andy?"

"No," Andrea said, shaking her head. "I really am not."

The two drinks and Jack arrived. He put them on the long counter in front of them and turned around.

"Where's yours?" Andrea asked.

"I'm sorry, but I have to meet someone in ten minutes at some place around here, and I am not sure where it is," Jack said.

"Where are you going to meet them?" asked Andrea.

"The Union Oyster Club is the name, I think."

"Oh! You mean the Union Oyster *House*!" Andrea said.

"Okay. Do you know where that is?"

"Yes. You go left out of here and across the street until you see Faneuil Hall. Then turn right, and you can see it down the street on the right. It has an old-fashioned sign hanging outside that you can't miss. It's a very old and neat restaurant. It has a cozy oyster bar."

"Fanny Hall?" asked Jack.

Andrea sighed. "Patty, do you have a pen?" She took a coaster from the counter, and in the blank space on it not occupied by the word *Guinness,* she drew Jack a map and spelled out the word *Faneuil.*

"Thank you, Andrea," said Jack. "This will really help." He continued, "The tab has been paid, and I think I'd better leave. Way too short. I've enjoyed your company; my best to you both." He smiled momentarily, grabbing an imaginary hat brim with his right hand, turned around, and left The Black Rose.

"Phew! That was fast," said Andrea.

"Yeah. Not the typical guy that you normally meet around here. Kind of a gentleman, wasn't he?" asked Patty.

"Yes. And he didn't even come on to either of us at all."

"Of course," said Andrea, chuckling. "There certainly wasn't much time, so we will forgive him this one time. Anyway, that's our enigma for the day! Now, tell me how your day went." And the two old friends from high school picked up where they had left off some ten minutes prior.

* * *

Mac McCarthy was sitting at the rounded zinc-topped oyster bar when Jack Rheinstrom walked in. He had been watching the front door in anticipation of Jack's arrival, as Jack was fifteen minutes late for the planned rendezvous.

Jack walked in and immediately saw his friend. "Mac! It's so good to see you!"

They approached each other meeting halfway, smiling and shaking hands.

"Same here, Jack! Here—I saved a seat for you at the oyster bar."

Mac turned around, and both of them walked back to the two open stools that looked directly into the oyster-shucking pit. The view beyond the restaurant's large multi-paned windows looked out onto the picturesque sidewalks of Union Street in Boston, Massachusetts.

Jack was the first to speak. "How long has it been, Mac?"

"I don't know, five, maybe seven years? I remember you had just been hired by your airline, and it was your first Boston layover, I think, Jack."

"Oh, yes! I remember that. You took me pub-crawling and we ended up at a neat old place called Sullivan's."

"Oh yeah, Sullivan's. That was an old Boston Irish haunt that's not here anymore. It was a good time, Jack. And now you're going to be based in Boston and living around here. That's great news, man. Great news. Kess was happy to hear the news, too. She'd be here, but she had to work this afternoon."

"Work? Kess works?" Jack asked. "I thought that you were a successful heart surgeon. What, does she want to be out of the house or something?"

"Take it easy, Jack! She doesn't really work; she volunteers once a week serving as a docent at the Gardner."

Jack's eyes widened in recognition. "I don't believe it! I just had the exact same conversation with a woman half an hour ago at The Black Rose about the same subject. And what the hell is a doe send, anyway? And what's the 'gahdnah'? Isn't that where the Boston Celtics play?" implored Jack.

McCarthy threw his head back and laughed out loud. "The Gardner is not the Boston Garden basketball arena. It's a very fine museum, The Isabella Stuart Gardner Museum in downtown Boston. And a docent is a volunteer guide, unpaid but highly trained in the field of art appreciation and details of paintings on display there."

"Oh, no!" Jack's face reddened. "Boy, do I feel stupid."

"Hey, don't beat yourself up, Jack! I didn't know before Kess came up with the idea."

"Well, the girl I was talking to must have thought I was a clod. She was a docent there, also."

"What was her name? I am sure that Kess would probably know her."

"Let's see. I am trying to remember…I talked with her for only a few minutes. Her friend kept calling her Sandy. Or was it Andy? Andy. Maybe it was Andrea. I don't know."

"Okay. I'll ask Kess tonight."

Then the two old friends, fraternity brothers and roomies from Denison University some fourteen years prior, began to peel back the years since their last time together.

* * *

Jack was standing by the office door waiting for the secretary to return. After about three minutes, Mary Keegan returned to her desk. As she was sitting down, she noticed Jack standing there off in a corner. "Hello. May I help you?" she asked.

"Hello. My name is Jack Rheinstrom, and I'm new here in Boston. I'm wondering if it's possible at all to speak to the chief pilot."

"Well, welcome to Boston, Jack Rheinstrom," Mary said. "I was actually expecting you sometime soon. I just placed your name on your mailbox."

"Oh! Where is that?"

"Here, let me show you. Follow me." She got up from her desk and walked down the hall a short way and into the mailroom. "You are…there!" she said, pointing to a vertical pigeonhole arrangement on the back wall. "And, as you can see, your mail from JFK has caught up with you. Looks like you have some chart revisions to do by the looks of all those pink envelopes in there."

"Oh, goody," Jack murmured sarcastically.

"Well, there he is. He just walked by."

"Who?"

"The chief pilot, Captain Lou Cusimano. Wait here a minute and I'll find out if he can see you now." Mary quickly left the mailroom and walked down the hall in pursuit.

"This is a small base, Jack," Captain Cusimano began, once the pair was settled in his office. "It is somewhat akin to a family. We all look out for one another, and we all, believe me, pretty much *know* everything about one another. And that is good, but sometimes not so good."

Jack nodded, shifting his crossed legs from left to right.

"I hope that you'll like it here," Cusimano continued. "We have lots of good people here. Good workers, reliable, and some real characters, too. You'll see. It sounds standard, I know, but I have an open-door policy. Please, please come see me if you think there is anything I should know about. I don't like surprises. Okay?" Cusimano asked.

"Sure, of course!" said Jack, nodding in agreement.

"I see that you're a brand-new captain. Do you have any previous command experience, Jack?"

"Well," he began, "I had five years in the Air Force flying interceptors down at McGuire Air Force Base while I was in the New Jersey Guard, and the only crew I had was *me*."

"Not really a very large crew," Cusimano commented.

"Well, when you're the only one in the cockpit and things get tight, there's no one there to help you. So you just have to be very thorough to begin with and then not make any mistakes."

"Point well made," Captain Cusimano said, nodding in agreement. "I see that you've been in all three seats on the *Mercury*—flight engineer, copilot, and now captain. As a new captain, Jack, you'll discover that there is a world of difference in the three feet that separate the two front seats, first officer and captain. Before, you had to be prepared and obedient, and also a psychiatrist at times. Now you have the buck-stops-here responsibility for many, many lives and some very expensive equipment. In the past, you just more or less did what you were trained to do and didn't question it. But now you're the one who must ask the questions, and you're the one who must answer them. You're the one who must decide. It's a heady experience, Jack, but one that you'll grow to love. We are lucky men to have these jobs. I mean that. I can't think of anything else I'd rather do. Can you?" he asked.

"Absolutely not, Captain Cusimano. Absolutely not."

The chief pilot stood up from behind his desk and asked Jack to accompany him to visit the various departments in the Trans Ocean office in Boston's Logan Airport—manpower, crew scheduling, maintenance, operations and dispatch, the cafeteria, and finally, the ready room, otherwise known as the crew lounge. After the tour, Captain Cusimano thrust his hand forward and gripped Jack's hand in a firm handshake. "Welcome to Boston, Captain Rheinstrom."

"Thank you, sir," said Jack, looking directly into the chief pilot's eyes. He nodded and replied, "I love it here already!"

On his way out, Jack stopped to talk with Mary again. Mary was a very attractive woman. She was neat, well dressed, and she had a kind of built-in smile that suggested that she knew something that you didn't know. She seemed perfectly suited for the position of executive secretary. She appeared to be in her early forties, and since the placard on her desk just said *Mary Keegan,* Jack wasn't exactly sure how to address her, so he guessed. "Mrs. Keegan—"

She looked up from her typewriter and firmly said with a smile, "Mary, please."

"Okay. Mary. Just one last question, if you don't mind."

"I don't mind."

"Do you know anyone in real estate, uh, in the Marblehead or Salem area?"

"Yes I do!" Keegan replied and stared at Jack.

Jack stared back and after a few seconds said, "Well...good," and turned around to leave.

"Hey, Jack, come back here," Mary barked with a broad grin. "How far were you going to go just now?"

"Well, about three more feet," he said, returning the smile.

"We have a stewardess, Amanda Beesley, who works for an agency in Salem part-time when she's not flying—she's a really nice person and sharp as a tack. I can drop a note in her mailbox with your name and number or ask her to RSVP in your pigeonhole. How's that?"

"That would be great, Mary—that would work. Where's her mailbox?"

"Oh, they have their own mailroom. Follow me again."

* * *

Jack closed the hallway door to the office section behind him and was now standing in the baggage room. It had a large concrete floor with a footprint of six normal-size garages and was the terminus for little tugs that pulled the luggage-laden carts from the incoming airplanes parked at their gates.

It was between arrivals. The large overhead doors to the outside tarmac were open and in the up position. It was quiet because there was no one around. Even the conveyor belts that delivered the bags to the baggage claim carousals on the other side of the wall were stopped. In a matter of minutes, however, this could become a very busy place with lots of people, lots of baggage carts going here and there, and lots of noise. Jack noticed a stack of newspapers by the door he had just closed. It was a new edition of the company newspaper, *The Falcon*. He grabbed a copy, something to peruse while having lunch in the cafeteria, which was exactly where he was going.

"Hey, Batman! Over here!" Jack called out, with his arm high in the air. John Battagliola, who had just walked through the door from the outside ramp and had just taken off his uniform hat, turned and looked around, then waved back.

"May I join you?" he asked in a raised voice from his position on the other side of the cafeteria. Jack nodded and beckoned him, motioning enthusiastically.

"Are you coming or going?"

"Well, I'm kind of in between," John replied as he pulled the chair out from the table and began to sit down. "I was a little short on time this month. Only scheduled for seventy hours flying credit, and a shuttle trip was open for today so I bid it and got it, and here I am."

"Did you come from Newark or LaGuardia?"

"LaGuardia. You know, for a change of pace, flying the shuttle is kind of fun. For a day, that is. I don't know how some people can fly it all of the time. It would drive me nuts!"

"Well, I think that some of the people," Jack said, "especially the back end, the cabin staff, like to sleep in their own beds at night. But I think that you're right. It really isn't very exciting."

After going through the cafeteria queue, John came back, put a bowl of chowder on the table and sat down. "So, Captain Jack, how do you like it so far?"

"Well, I really haven't done much of anything yet since I saw you in Miami on the check ride. I had some days off. They gave me some travel time because I'm changing bases, and I showed up in Boston yesterday. I just now met chief pilot Lou Cusimano. Do you know him?"

"No. Remember, Jack, I'm really junior, just three years on the property."

"Well, anyway, he seems like a good man. First impression, you know. I've got my IOE, my Initial Operating Experience phase, coming up in a few days—Boston to JFK, San Juan and back with Captain Peter McCullough as instructor pilot. Do you know him?"

"Oh, yeah. He's based in New York, too. I just flew a two-day trip with him a couple of months ago, I think. Nice guy, but I'm sure he doesn't remember me."

John looked at his watch, gulped down the last of his coffee, and reached for his uniform hat saying, "Tick tock, tick tock. Got to run, Jack! Good to see you again. Good luck on your IOE."

"Same here, Batman! Blue side up," encouraged Jack. John walked out the door, out to the ramp, and over to gate 12. He climbed up the Jetway stairs and was in his seat and in place for the Trans Ocean shuttle "prime" to La Guardia at 1:00 p.m.

* * *

"I know you said you were an aircraft commander before, albeit on a crew of one in the Air Force, and you've worked with crews before but not as a captain. Jack, this is about people, lots of them, and it's about airline operations. This is my standard new-captain spiel, so I'm not talking down to you at all, I just need to cover all the bases and hit the important parts, okay?" Captain Peter McCullough asked as he unfolded an aero-navigation chart on Trans Ocean 87. He was sitting in his copilot seat, bound for New York's Kennedy Airport.

It was 10:25 a.m. on Friday morning, September 16th. "If *I'm* brand new on a route," McCullough went on to say, "I'll probably do this at home the night before. Otherwise I'll show up early in flight planning and do it then. I have highlighted the route in yellow. See here?" He pointed to the map with his pencil. "And here on the chart, also in yellow highlight, are the alternates that dispatch has selected. Usually there's just one for the destination unless the weather is forecast to be marginal. In that case, there will be two listed. Why do I mark these on the chart? I know that the names and locations are listed on the flight release papers in English with distances and weather forecasts provided, but I'd like to see from a bird's-eye view where exactly they're talking about. Again, I don't do this every time I fly, but I do it with routes that I'm new on and unfamiliar with. It's a big leap from the right to the left seat. I know that you've been a first officer for a while. How long?" Captain McCullough asked.

Jack thought a minute. "Well, let's see, I was an engineer for two years after I was hired, and I've been in the right seat ever since. So, for seven years now."

Captain McCullough nodded. "Okay, during this time when you were a 'first' and you were on, say, a trip like this over water many hours in length, and you were sitting in your seat, what were you thinking about?" He paused. "Excuse me," he said, raising his right finger in the air, "let me answer this first. New York, this is Trans Ocean eighty-seven, go ahead."

"Trans Ocean eight seven, New York, contact Miami on one two four point five at intersection Bozo."

"Roger, twenty-four five at Bozo, TO eighty-seven, so long."

McCullough put the mike back in its holder on the cockpit wall. "Let's see. Where were we? Oh, yes, a typical trip. What were you thinking while you were flying along? The upcoming position report? The how-goes-it on the flight plan? The motorcycle that's in pieces in your basement?"

Jack couldn't help but laugh out loud. "How did you know?"

McCullough continued. "Maybe the dinner party scheduled for later on? Or maybe the last date you had with what's her name? The point is, Jack, that when you are in *that* seat," he paused and pointed to Jack's seat for emphasis, "you may actually be thinking the same thoughts, but that's only in the background. You must *constantly* be thinking about the what-ifs. You always have to know what you would do in any number of contingencies ahead of time. Where would we go if we lost an engine? What about a cabin fire? What about a psychopath with a knife or a gun or a bomb? You don't just pick up the mike and call company dispatch and ask them for advice. If you declare an emergency with air traffic control, the very first thing they'll ask you is 'What are your intentions, Trans Ocean eighty-seven?' and you don't say, 'Well, I don't know. I really haven't thought about it.' No, you have to be able to say, 'I want to do this, and this, and this, and I want to do it *now*!' It's called situational awareness, and that is why, Jack Rheinstrom, they are paying you the big bucks."

Jack nodded his head vigorously. "I see what you mean, Captain McCullough. I see what you mean."

Trans Ocean 87 from New York's JFK Airport pulled into Jetway 14 at Logan, the same Jetway from which it had left two days prior. The parking brake was set, the engines were shut down, and the before-leaving checklist was completed.

"Well, Jack," Captain McCullough began, "I will be very blunt with you."

Jack slowly turned his head to the right to meet Captain McCullough's eyes straight on.

"The announcement that you thought you were giving to the passengers but in fact were giving to San Juan Center about their wonderful city was the most informative, if not hilarious, PA that I've ever heard! But, overall, good job, Jack," laughed McCullough, "Good job, Captain Rheinstrom, good job."

With a slap on Jack's back, he led the procession out of the cockpit, into the Jetway, and down its stairs to operations. The trip was over. They were home and, for Jack, the wait was over. It was no longer a dream. The brass ring was on his finger.

* * *

The next day, Jack met with his new real-estate agent, Amanda, at a cozy coffee shop right in the middle of the old town called Buzzy's. "So, how did your check ride go?" Amanda asked, putting her cappuccino cup back on its saucer.

"Great. No hitches. Nice IP, Captain Pete McCullough from New York. Do you fly San Juan very much?"

"I used to. I kind of got tired of all the layovers there."

"At the Holiday Inn?"

"Yeah."

"Ever been there on Thursday night?" Jack asked.

"Oh, you mean the Manager's Special night?" Amanda asked.

"That's what I mean," said Jack, smiling.

"You mean the night where all the senior pilots at whatever position bid the trip in order to be there?"

"That's what I mean," said Jack, still smiling but now slowly shaking his head.

"You mean where all the old captains are lined up against the wall with drinks in their hands dressed in their leisure suits like penguins, and the first officers are over at the Ron Rico rum reception table seeing how many of the free piña coladas they can pound down their throats before the reception is over, and where the second officers are hovering directly over the steaming trays of Swedish meatballs with toothpicks in their hands like they were at a fishing hole, stabbing the meatballs and stuffing them into their mouths while standing there? Is that what you mean?" Amanda asked.

"Yes, that's exactly what I mean," exclaimed Jack.

"No, I haven't, Jack."

Now both of them were laughing and shaking their heads in disbelief. "I think that if I were an artist, I'd like to paint a caricature of that—unbelievable on one hand, but on Thursday night, oh so true. You had to be there," added Jack, "you really had to be there. Do you want another cup, Amanda?"

"No. I'm fine, thanks. So what do you think of what you've seen so far? Does anything really interest you or jump out at you?" Amanda asked.

"Well, no, not exactly. Nothing except the old sea captain's house in Newburyport. But that's going to take so much work and money that I'm rather hesitant to jump in. At least right now, I don't want to. You know, Amanda, I was kind of thinking about renting for six months or a year so I can snoop around and get used to the area. If I find something, then I can call you and we can go investigate. What do you think?"

Amanda nodded in agreement. "That makes a lot of sense, Jack. In fact, I know just the person to get in touch with! There's a stewardess, Janie Kaiser. You said that you liked the old sea captains' houses. Well, she has one just like that and she rents out rooms, mostly to crew members. It's a big white colonial and it's old, and there's even a widow's walk on the roof. You can climb up there and look east beyond Marblehead Neck toward the open ocean, or you can look at all the sailboats on their moorings in Marblehead Harbor. You can see Rockport or even Boston if the weather is nice. Yeah, I've seen many a sundown up there. Neat place and I think it's just now opened up. I'll give her a call for you!"

CHAPTER THREE

"Is this Laurie Mills?" a woman's voice on the other end of the telephone began.

"Yes, it is."

"Hi, Laurie. This is Peggy in crew scheduling. We have a trip for you, but we don't have much time."

"We don't have much time?" Laurie asked, sounding worried.

"No. There was an accident about an hour ago, and we just received word that one of the crew members on the San Fran flight was injured. Luckily, not seriously, but she won't be able to make the trip. It leaves in an hour and a half."

"An hour and a half?" Laurie exclaimed, her voice rising. Her eyes were now wide open.

"Laurie, how long will it take you to get to the airport?" Peggy asked. "You're the only reserve on call that can do a three-day."

"Well, I just got back from jogging, Peggy, and I'm covered with sweat, and I'm not packed, and...." Her breathing rate began to increase noticeably. "And I live in Marblehead, and, and, and I'm on probation, and this is my first trip since graduating, and—"

Peggy stopped Laurie mid-sentence. "Laurie, calm down a minute. This is a late callout, and the plane will leave when it leaves. This kind of situation happens. Not a lot, but it happens, and the show will go on. We don't need another accident today, so *don't* kill yourself. This is a non-stop to San Fran. We're not talking about missed connections. So a couple of people will be a little late. It could have been a mechanical or a thunderstorm moving through. Get there when you can, okay? I will advise operations that you will be there in...in...well, give me a guess with a lot of padding," Peggy said.

"I, uh, I, uh...." Laurie looked at her watch, her eyes darting back and forth. "I think maybe in an hour and a half. Would that be okay?"

"That will be just fine, Laurie. I will tell them to plan on two hours. Calm down and don't worry about the probation thing. This is a good company, especially in the flying side. We take care of our own. So have a good trip. Let me hang up so you can get ready, okay?"

"Okay. Thank you, Peggy." Laurie hung up and her personal whirlwind began.

Fortunately for her, it was between rush hours, and the traffic to Boston was light and in her favor. The employee parking lot at Logan was multileveled, covered, and just a short walk across from the Terminal A building and ops—a five-minute walk, or in this case, a three-minute canter. You wouldn't want to be in her way.

Inside the terminal, just past the revolving baggage carousel was a security door into ops, the offices, and crew scheduling. The door had a lock with buttons with numbers on them. Laurie put her suitcase down, set her matching travel bag on top of it, and opened the zipper pocket on the side.

It wasn't there. It wasn't there! The small memo pad where she had written the security code was not there. She intently stared at the floor. In her mind, she retraced the steps she had taken two days prior when she remembered writing all the important numbers down on the pad. Where did I put it? She thought as she raised her left arm and looked at her watch. She took a deep breath, exhaling through her pursed lips. She thought of something. I can ask a baggage agent!

She looked to her left, but there was no one at the counter. There was no one there! She quickly turned her head to the right. No agent was there. There were just some people milling around waiting for their bags to arrive.

I know, she thought. She left her bags by the door and went outside to the curbside skycaps.

"No, ma'am. I don't know it. Maybe he does," the first one said, pointing down the curb a bit.

"No, ma'am. I'm sorry, ma'am, we're not allowed back there," the second skycap apologetically answered. "Why don't you call your office?"

Laurie looked at her watch again. "A good idea. Do you have their number?"

"No. I don't. Don't you?"

"It's on the same piece of paper as the door code," she said. Her voice was rising along with her blood pressure. She went back to the lost baggage office, and finally she could see that there was someone standing behind the counter. She hurriedly walked in and noticed with a sinking feeling that her suitcase and travel bag were missing. They were not where she had left them, next to that obnoxious door! She shook her head as she kept walking. What else? What else can go wrong today?

As Laurie stormed into the office, an agent now sitting at a desk looked up and asked, "Are those yours?"

There were her bags. "Oh, thank God. Thank God. I thought someone had stolen them."

"No. The other agent saw you leaving your bags there and thought that they should be secured, so she brought them in for you."

"Oh, thank you, thank you. I'm late for my trip, and I'm new, and I forgot the combination...."

Sensing her angst, the agent got up from her desk. "You get your bags, and I'll open the door for you."

"I owe you," Laurie said hurriedly.

"Ha, don't be silly! Have a safe trip."

The door closed with Laurie safely on the other side.

* * *

"Where did you say you live?" Jack asked.

"Portsmouth," replied the first officer Dick Walter as the two of them went through the door with their suitcases and flight bags in tow. They were walking from ops into the baggage room, which then led to the ramp. They were awaiting the arrival of the Mercury 100, Trans Ocean Flight 59.

"Are there a lot of—" Those were the only words that Jack was able to get out of his mouth before *wham,* he was hit with what felt like a small speeding truck, and he toppled over. It was right at the corner of the small corridor where the security door joins the baggage room. The "truck" went down too, and she was now sprawled on the floor, crying. Jack quickly got to his feet, helped by Dick's strong hand.

Immediately, he went over to the woman, now sitting up, braced by her outstretched right arm, her legs folded behind her. Her crying had stopped and was replaced by heavy breathing.

"Are you okay, miss? Are you okay?" Jack asked, standing over her, extending his hand.

She was staring at the floor and just nodded her head. Her body language suddenly changed. The nodding head going up and down slowly began to move left, then right, then left again.

"Are you hurt?" Jack asked again.

Finally, an answer. "No, I don't think so." She struggled to get to her feet by herself but Jack and Dick had to help her. Once standing, she blurted out, "I'm late! I'm on probation! This is my first trip! I hit you! I'm so sorry!" The tremors in her voice rose with each couple of words.

"Hey, slow down a minute! Everything's going to be okay." Jack's voice was slow, calm, and reassuring. "Are you sure you aren't hurt?" he asked.

Laurie looked down at her right knee. It was bleeding. "No, I'll be okay. I've got another pair of stockings in my suitcase. I'll be okay, but I am late. They're waiting for me," said Laurie, looking down at her watch again.

"You're not heading to San Francisco, are you?" Jack asked.

Laurie picked up her suitcase and handbag that were lying on their sides. She nodded. "Well, yes I am."

"Good," Jack continued, "that's great news, because so are we, and we're not leaving without you." He nodded to Dick. "Go ahead out there without me and get things started. Let the senior know that the reserve girl is finally here and will be coming along shortly. Get the clearance going and as much of the checklists done as you can without me." He turned back to Laurie. "Here, put your bags over here with mine." Jack dropped them into the corner where the company newspapers always were. She followed his lead. "Okay, let's get you checked in, Miss...."

"Mills, Laurie Mills."

"Well, hello, Laurie Mills. My name is Jack Rheinstrom." He opened the door to the hall that led to operations and crew scheduling. "Hi, Tia!" he suddenly exclaimed.

Tia looked up from her desk and winked. "Hey, Jack, how's it going?"

"Tia, this is your call-out for the San Francisco flight, Laurie Mills. I just plowed into her in the hall and knocked her down. Could you put a note into her file about the knee that she fell on, just in case it turns into something later on? We've got to run to the plane now 'cause we're late."

"Got it," Tia said. "Are you sure you feel okay for the trip?"

"Oh, yes," Laurie replied, smiling faintly, "I'll be fine."

"Great! Have a safe flight, guys!"

The two of them turned around and went back down the hall. Jack turned to Laurie. "Tia is a wonderful person. You'll really like her—everyone does. I got to know her in New York. She just transferred up here last month."

* * *

"Well, there it is, Dick. There's the ship," said Jack, pointing and looking at his copilot in the right seat.

"The ship?" Dick asked.

"Yeah. Ship Rock, over there. I can see it now. There's no mistaking it for anything else; it really sticks out. See? It looks like an old sailing ship with sails, in the middle of nowhere, and it's over sixteen hundred feet high. If we can see it, we must be on course on our way to California. That's a relief," said Jack, smiling. "Every time I fly over Monument Valley or the Ship Rock or the Grand Canyon, for that matter, I look down and say to myself, 'I have to take the time to go there, and drive around in a car seeing this beautiful country from ground level, sometime.' You know what I mean?"

"I sure do," Dick said. "All this time off that we supposedly have, but there's always something that comes up and gets in the way."

"Yup," Jack said. "Life is what happens when you're out making other plans! Someday...someday." They both continued to gaze out their cockpit windows upon the wonderland beginning to unfold beneath them amidst the background of the shadows and the slowly setting sun.

* * *

The temperature was just right, especially if you were just completing a forty-five-minute jog, and the last leg was mostly uphill. The day was cool with sunny skies and a cloud here and there, and the aroma of the sea was in the air. It was a perfect San

Francisco afternoon. Jack slowed down and walked the last hundred yards to the hotel, cooling down while wiping the sweat from his brow with a washcloth that he carried with him from the room. He walked into the lobby of the historic Canterbury Hotel and passed the reception desk. The counter there was unusual and reminded him of a cubbyhole in a small, rural post office, maybe a telegraph office from long, long ago. He then noticed Laurie Mills sitting by herself over in the corner of the lobby. He walked up to her. "How's your knee?" he asked.

Laurie looked up from the postcard that she was writing. "Oh, it's fine, Captain Rheinstrom. I have a little Band-Aid on it now," she said, looking down at her leg. "But, how about you? Did I injure you at all? And, by the way, it was very kind of you to say that you plowed into me—because, as you know, I blindsided you. And, again, I am very sorry."

"Let's not argue," Jack said with a grin. "You didn't hurt me. Anyway, how did the first day on the job go? Did things settle down at all for you?"

"Well, yes, and what a wonderful crew. Everyone was so nice to me, including the passengers. I know it won't always be like this, but it was especially nice the way it started. This was a special day."

"Good," Jack said. "Is the crew planning to go to dinner tonight?"

"Dinner? I don't know. No one asked," Laurie said with a slightly puzzled look.

"Hmm," said Jack. "Maybe Boston crews are different from New York crews, but that's standard operating procedure normally." He glanced at Laurie, who was looking slightly disappointed. He was disappointed himself; he had always pictured his first layover on his first captaincy flight with his first crew as a very special event, a lifetime event. He had been looking forward to it for a long, long time. Oh well, he thought, we'll do it next time. "Let me ask you this—have you ever been to San Francisco before?"

"No, I've only read about it."

"Well, I have an idea, and you kind of owe me anyway. But if you'd like to join me, I would love to show you some of the best spots of my favorite city."

Laurie's eyes twinkled. "Are you asking me out for a date?" she asked with a smile, her eyebrows raised.

"No—not really a date. Let's just look at it like we kind of ran into each other. And I mean literally. Ha! Anyway, I'm off to shower, but I'll meet you here in the lobby at 5:30. How does that sound?" asked Jack.

"Sounds like a plan, Captain!"

* * *

"I love it," hooted Laurie as she turned her head around to face Jack, who was seated on the cable car behind her. Her hair was blowing back into her face. "I absolutely love it!"

"Laurie," said Jack nervously as he reached forward, "let me just hold onto your forearm." Laurie was standing on the running board in the very front of the cable car, leaning forward, somewhat resembling the maidenhead on an old clipper sailing ship.

"I'm holding onto the bar, Jack. I'll be okay."

"Just in case, Laurie! You're kind of hanging out there a bit."

"Oh, you're just like my older brother." She turned around again, facing forward. Her hair, now off her face, was blowing directly backward in a snapshot of motion if captured on a camera.

The cable car's bell sang as the car now headed down the steepest hill on Hyde Street, with the majestic Aquatic Park and San Francisco Bay in view at the bottom. When they stepped off the car into Ghirardelli Square, Laurie was still beaming.

"Where are we headed?" she asked excitedly.

As they began walking, Jack playfully asked, "Does this look like a commercial area to you, Laurie?"

Laurie shrugged. "It looks like a neighborhood. Why do you ask?"

"All I'm going to say is that the restaurant where we're going—I'll even give you the name, it's called The Brazen Head—is on this street and is within the next two blocks. I'll buy you dinner if you can find it. Is that a deal?"

"Yeah, you're on, Captain!" And so the hunt officially began.

The special intangible is experienced by most people in their lifetime—usually, if they're lucky, a couple of times over—and it defies description. It is that certain *aha* moment when you become connected and comfortable with another person's character and personality. In this instance, it occurred almost simultaneously to the two crew members from the Trans Ocean flight from Boston, and it happened that evening as they were walking along Buchanan Street in San Francisco.

"You lost it, Kiddo," said Jack.

"Lost what, *Kiddo*?"

"Your free dinner."

"What do you mean, I lost it?"

"The restaurant was two blocks ago—you walked right past it."

"I couldn't have!" Laurie protested.

"Okay, let's retrace our steps, and I'll even feed you some hints along the way," Jack condescendingly offered.

"Oh, no! I don't need any of your charity, Jack. I'll find it on my own—you wait and see. In fact, if I don't, then I'll buy *you* dinner."

"Okayyy," said Jack, eyebrows raised, looking up at the evening sky.

"I don't like the way you just said that, Jack," Laurie announced. "Very patronizing!"

Jack shook his head and smiled. "Okeydokey—is that better?"

Laurie smiled. "It's perfect."

"Ahem." Jack cleared his throat. "Ahem." Jack cleared his throat again even louder and stopped in his tracks twenty steps past the intersection of Greenwich and Buchanan streets.

Laurie looked at Jack, and then turned around. "What? Do you mean that? That's a restaurant?" She went over to the windows of the ordinary-looking brick building in question, and as she got right up next to them, she could see through the small venetian blinds a very cozy setting—people eating, low lights, and candles on small tables. Behind the tables, she could see a horizontal curtain suspended on a long brass rail about four feet high that separated the bar behind from the seating and dining area nearest to her.

"Don't feel too badly, Laurie—dinner is still on me. The first time that I came here, I took a cab from the Canterbury that dropped me off at the corner, per my instructions, and it still took me five minutes or so, walking both sides of the streets, to find it. Like you, I had to look through the blinds to confirm it. Now, let's go in and say hello to Eddie. He's the bartender and owner, too." Jack pushed open the side door and held it open for her.

* * *

"He sure seemed like a nice fellow, Jack, and it looked like he was really glad to see you," Laurie said.

"Well," Jack said, taking the napkin off the table and placing it on his lap, "I've been coming here for the past seven years pretty much every couple of months or so, and we've become good friends. In fact, I came here on my very first layover at Trans Ocean. It was just after I got out of 'new hire' school as a flight engineer—kind of like someone else I know sitting at this table."

"Well, I'd like to come back here again sometime—it's very cozy. How is the food?"

"Continental, as they say, but a pretty good and varied menu, and cooked extremely well. You'll see."

"Oh, Jack, here comes our waitress now, coming up behind you."

A delighted voice drifted down to their table. "Well, hello there, Scrap."

Jack turned around to his right and began to stand up. "Hey, Liz, good to see you! How have you been?"

"Oh, Jack, don't be silly—sit down!" Liz insisted.

And as he did, he motioned across the table. "Liz Kennedy, I'd like you to meet a new friend of mine, Laurie Mills, who's actually on her very first layover ever at Trans Ocean. It's kind of ironic, isn't it? I was on my first layover too when I first met Liz many moons ago, back in '55, I think."

"Very pleased to meet you, Laurie. I'm sure that Jack will help you select a wonderful meal." Liz smiled and handed her a menu. "You don't want one do you, Jack? Don't you just want the regular?"

"Liz, why don't you give me one just so that I can go over it with her."

"Sure, here it is, and I'll be back in a jiffy. Nice to meet you, Laurie."

"Same here, Liz." They both smiled, and Liz walked back to the kitchen.

Laurie leaned forward and looked at Jack questioningly. "What did she call you, Jack?"

"What do you mean?" said Jack, looking at Laurie and putting his menu down.

"It sounded like she called you, excuse my French, 'Crap'!"

Jack smiled as he looked at the table. "No, she called me Scrap, short for Scrappy, which is a nickname that some of my friends use."

"What does it mean?"

"Well, it comes from childhood. I was small for a kid. I really didn't start growing until I got to high school. Anyway, some kids thought that it would be easy to pick on me, which they did successfully until I came home one day in tears and told Mom what had happened. Well, she, of course, told Dad that evening about me being bullied. Funniest thing—the exact same scenario had happened to him until a friend of the family took him aside one day and taught him how to box. He became very good at it; in fact, he actually won a Golden Gloves one year. I became good, too, and the bullies, after the first couple of 'counseling' sessions, suddenly wanted to be my friends. I don't think that the experience affected me in a bad way. I mean, I don't think that it gave me a chip on my shoulder or an attitude—it actually gave me a sense of relief and, of course, confidence. Anyway," Jack concluded, "the moniker goes back a long way."

"This is so much fun talking to you, Jack—or may I now call you Scrappy? I feel as though I'm really getting to know you and we're becoming friends. 'Scrappy Jack Rheinstrom' even has a kind of melody to it!"

Jack was smiling, slowly shaking his head. "Yes, you may if you must, but, hey, I've been doing all the talking—tell me something about yourself, okay?"

Liz returned and took their orders as the dinner and the evening unfolded.

"Can I get you guys anything else?" Liz asked. "An after-dinner drink? A dessert? We have apple crumb cake tonight, Mr. Rheinstrom!"

"No, but thank you, Liz. But everything, everything was great, as usual."

"Yes, it really was," Laurie chimed in.

"Good. I'll be right back with your check and your sandwich, Jack."

"You're still hungry, Jack?" asked Laurie.

"No, I thought that was a great dinner, especially the roasted garlic on the toasted bread and just the right amount of everything.

Why do you ask?"

"Well, Liz just said that you ordered another sandwich—to go, I guess."

"The sandwich is not for me," Jack said somberly.

"It isn't? Well, then, who is it for?"

"I don't know yet. I don't know if you noticed this morning on the way in from the airport, Laurie, but there is a pretty big homeless population here in San Francisco, especially in the Mission Bay area. During the seven years that I've been flying here, it seems to have only gotten worse. The city doesn't seem to be able to solve it. I'm only one person, but a couple of years ago, I started giving a sandwich away to someone that I saw on the street that looked hungry. I'm not talking about the hard-core winos, but rather like a runaway kid that looked frightened or out of place."

"Whatever gave you the idea to do something like that?" asked Laurie with a puzzled look on her face.

"I had a trip out of LaGuardia a few years ago with a captain named George Theall—nice guy. We had a layover somewhere down in Florida, maybe it was West Palm or Daytona, but it doesn't matter. Anyway, we picked up some sandwiches at a deli and were going to eat them, but we ended up going into a bar first instead. There was a young girl sitting all by herself at the bar and she looked like, well, she looked like she didn't belong there, if you know what I mean. She was cute, but she was way too thin and she looked scared. Anyway, I watched as George looked at her. He suddenly went over to her as a father might and asked her to accept his sandwich as a present. You should have seen the look in both of their eyes. It was a very tender and special moment for them, I'm sure, but it was for me, too. Later, I found out that his daughter had run away from home one time. I have never been a witness to a vignette like that before, and I feel very lucky to have actually seen it, because I don't think I ever will again."

"What do you think, Jack?"

"What do I think? Well, that is kind of a leading question and I'm not really sure what you are asking about, but I will tell you what I'm thinking right now—and it's all about sharing. There are so many fortunate people in this world that have caught the brass ring, and they take it and they put it in their pocket and move on with their own lives, never thinking about the ones left behind them on the very same merry-go-round that reach for the same ring but come up empty. Sorry, Laurie, I didn't mean to be so serious or even maudlin—it's just that life puzzles me sometimes."

"You seem so prescient, so wise, Jack, older than your years."

Jack smiled. "My dear Laurie, I am thirty-two years old and have been flying all over the world, taking notes, if you will, wherever I go. You are eleven years younger and your note-taking is just beginning, believe me, it is just beginning. And you will do well." They looked at each other, nodded, and then both looked away, lost in thought.

"Well, here is your check and your baggie, Jack," Liz said as she put a large paper bag down on the table. "And you've got some extra veggies in there, too."

"That's great, Liz. Say, can I use your pen for a second?" He returned it after quickly jotting the letter *B* on the top of his left hand, the part of the skin where the thumb and the index finger join. Liz watched, took the pen back, turned around, and left.

"Do you always write on your hand?" asked Laurie.

"Not daily, I would say, but every once in a while, so I guess the answer is yes—actually ever since UPT, Undergraduate Pilot Training in the Air Force."

"Do a lot of Air Force pilots do that?"

"Well," he said, pausing to think for a moment, "not a whole lot, but it's not unusual. I remember watching my instructor do that one day when I was flying Tweets—T-37's—and then I started doing it. It happened before a training flight one day. We walked up to the assignment desk where we learned that we had been assigned tail number, say 385, and it was on, say, Foxtrot 3 parking space on the ramp. Lieutenant Moynihan pulled out a pen from the pocket on the sleeve of his flight suit and wrote it on his left hand. I watched and concluded it was brilliant! Why carry a scratch pad around with you when there's already one attached to your left arm? Anyway, that was a long time ago."

"Did you like pilot training?"

"Laurie, it was the most exciting time in my entire life, I would say. It was magical, absolutely magical. I still pinch myself thinking about how lucky I was to get there."

"What did you write on your hand just now, Jack—it looks like the letter *B*."

"Well, you are absolutely correct there. It's *B* for Bartholomew!"

Laurie's head snapped back, and her eyes changed. They were no longer glinting and cheerful, and they now looked down directly at the tablecloth.

"Yep, *B* for Bartholomew—that's my brother, and it's his birthday today. I can't forget to call him." Jack looked up from gazing at the *B* on his hand and peered at Laurie. Her head was bowed, and a tear had traveled halfway down her left cheek and was about to drop onto the table.

"What?" Jack asked passionately. "What did I say? What happened?" Laurie abruptly stood up and asked where the ladies' room was located. Jack stood up too and pointed in the general direction. Laurie hurriedly walked away and passed Liz, who was clearing a table nearby.

"What was that all about, Jack? I thought you said you barely know the girl, and now she just ran away from your table crying like you just broke up with her or something!"

"Liz, dear friend, you have to help me here. Please." Jack recalled for her the steps that led up to Laurie's sudden departure. Liz sat down at the table across from Jack and stroked her chin with her left hand. She sat there for a minute thinking.

"Well, from what you've told me so far, Jack, there is probably someone, somewhere whose name is Bartholomew who is or was very important in her life, and you reminded her of him when you talked about your brother. It must have startled her into thinking about that someone whom she didn't want to think about."

"Wow," Jack said, shaking his head back and forth, "women are amazing. I never cease to be amazed at how different we all are wired. It would have taken me a long time to come up with that theory."

"Oh, really? I don't think so. You just have to hear the facts like I did from another person and you would've come up with it, too," Liz said, slowly nodding her head.

"Liz, what do I do now, when she comes back? I don't know how to react or what to say to make her feel better," Jack pleaded.

"Well, I'll tell you, Jack, I don't think that you *can* help her. You don't know her, and as you just said, you really don't know anything about her. She needs the comfort of her best friend or her sister's shoulder and ear, and I'm afraid you don't qualify. So when she comes back, what are you going to do? That's the question. I guess what I would do is apologize for saying something that upset her and take her back to your hotel. Wait, no, I've a better idea—offer to get her a cab so that she can go back to the hotel alone. I think that she probably embarrassed herself and would prefer to be alone. Anyway, that's what comes to mind to me."

"Thank you, friend—and you are one, a good one," Jack said as he stared intently at her.

Liz got up and put her hand on Jack's shoulder as she left. "Fair skies, Jack. It's always good to see you. And I'm going to order a cab now. You can give it to her and catch another one later if need be." She then disappeared behind the chest-high curtain that separated the dining room area from the bar. Liz had been right, as Laurie did accept the offer of a solo cab and waited for it just outside the restaurant door while Jack sat inside at the bar across from Eddie.

* * *

The next morning was stiff at best, as Jack waited for everyone to get on the limo minivan before he boarded. Laurie had arrived first and was sitting all the way in the back with her sunglasses on. Jack sat down in the front. As the limo was approaching San Francisco International Airport, the right hand of the senior stewardess reached over the back of Jack's seat and held out a multi-folded piece of paper. Jack turned partially around but couldn't see who actually gave it to him. He took it and looked at the paper for a few seconds before he opened it to read the following: *Jack, I'm very sorry. I owe you an explanation, but I can't talk about it now. Please understand. —Laurie*

The flight back to Boston was uneventful and quicker than normal by almost thirty minutes, aided by a sixty-knot tailwind, which was stronger than normal for a summer weather system. Jack didn't see Laurie in the limo, in the plane, or in operations in Boston. Whereas the outbound flight was full of excitement and anticipation for Jack, the return trip was just the opposite—flat and full of questions.

CHAPTER FOUR

"This is great, Janie, absolutely great! I don't really know how I fell into such a good deal, but I'll take it," Jack said, excitement in his eyes. He had just completed his tour of Dodge House and was completely taken with the historical charm and beautiful architecture. Not to mention he would be renting the best room in the house.

"I'm glad that you like it, Jack, and I think that you'll really enjoy the other guys and gals here. There are a total of five including you, and they're all crew members. And I know that you said that you've been flying into Boston for the past seven years, but the Boston base, you will discover, is different from all the others. There is a very strong sense of family here, and that spirit of the base spills over to all of the crews that live here. Yes, I think that you will like it here."

"Maybe we could fly together some time?" suggested Jack.

Janie shook her head and laughed. "Not unless you like to only fly round-trips to LaGuardia—I am a shuttle queen. You can have all the exciting trips and the jet lag. I like it here, and I like sleeping in my own bed."

"Well, to each his or her own, I guess." Jack shrugged and started writing out the check for his next month's rent.

* * *

"What kind of beer is this, Janie? It has kind of a different under-taste to it."

"It's a 'Gansett. Do you like it?"

"What's a 'Gansett?"

"Boy, you really aren't from here! It's 'Gansett as in Narragansett—you know, from Rhode Island?"

"Gotcha. Well, it's obvious that I have a lot to learn. A 'Gansett, huh?"

Janie nodded. "So, how was your latest trip, Captain?"

Jack and Janie were relaxing on the widow's walk of the Dodge House, drinking beer and soaking in the late afternoon sun.

"The trip went fine, Janie, my third one. The first officer was Nick Vislocky. Do you know him?"

"Oh, everyone knows St. Nick—funny guy and quite the ladies' man, I hear."

Jack let out a belly laugh. "I did appreciate his loquacious and unsuccessful attempts to squire a particular young lady onto the dance floor one night." Jack was on his second 'Gansett, and he was becoming very relaxed talking to his new friend, landlord, and fellow crew member. "Janie," he began, "I don't know you all that well. Wait a minute, let me try that again. I haven't known you for very long—that's better—but I feel a good comfort zone with you. I have a favor to ask, and *no* is a good answer."

"Well, the answer is yes, Jack. And now tell me, what's the question?"

Jack smiled at Janie, his cheeks flushed. He then began to recount the evening with Laurie Mills at The Brazen Head in San Francisco, beginning with their head-on collision in the baggage room. When he had finished his story, he pensively looked at the floor.

"What do you want *me* to do?" Janie asked.

"Well, I really don't know if there is anything to be done, anything that either you or I can do, and I am not, believe me, I am not looking at this girl as a potential dating partner. I had offered—without being asked, I might add—some friendly advice on a bunch of topics to her. She said that I reminded her of her big brother, but she didn't have one. Anyway, I know what it's like to be the new kid on the block and not know anyone, but, then again, I'm thirty-two years old and I know my way around the airline, the airport, and I have lots of friends scattered throughout Trans Ocean. But she, on the other hand, is just twenty-one years old, and a rather young twenty-one at that. She's on her first-ever job at a new base with no one really to turn to if something is terribly amiss in her life, which appears to be the case."

"Well, I haven't known you very long either, Jack, and I like a man who's sensitive, but I think that maybe you're being too sensitive in this case. Maybe she's a very emotional person and just had a spat with her boyfriend, and maybe his name is Bartholomew and she overreacted to you mentioning his name."

"Well, you're probably right. I think that maybe I was the one who overreacted. So I guess that I'll just butt out—or rather, I won't butt in. It's just that I feel so sorry for the girl, and maybe everything is just fine now after all. Anyway, Janie, you passed your first test—thank you for listening." Jack smiled again and reached for his beer on the table beside him. "I can't believe the view up here—the setting sun, the harbor, the ocean, Boston over there in the distance. I am one lucky pup, a very lucky pup, Janie."

Janie looked thoughtful. "Let me do something for you. I will talk with Dee Sietz, who is head of in-flight in Boston—I know her pretty well. Since this Laurie girl is not only new to the base but also new to the company and on probation, Dee will have been keeping close tabs on her anyway. And I'll have her find out if any of her classmates from new-hire school are based here. I'll just see, in a very light-handed way from afar, if there are any red flags that jump out. But, hey, it's very nice of you to show compassion for someone you don't even know very well. And I'm thinking that part of the problem might be that you, as the captain, feel responsible for someone who is on your crew."

Jack nodded—Janie had hit the nail on the head. Jack was really getting into his new position of being a captain. Sure, the airplane flew just the same as it had before. He had had to get used to changing hands for the yoke and the throttles when he switched from the right to the left seat, but that didn't take him very long at all. And the aircraft systems all worked the same as they did seven years ago when he was a new-hire flight engineer on the very same plane. The main difference was the mindset and the ultimate responsibility involved in being captain. The responsibility for hundreds of lives that Jack was accepting every day that he flew was heavy. But he knew that he had accepted it, and to Jack it felt good, almost as if it were a reward. He considered himself a very fortunate man. He loved being up in the air, he loved to fly, and he was living his dream.

* * *

"Captain Rheinstrom?"

"Yes, Jimmy, what is it?" Jack answered, turning around in his seat.

"Can I give this to you before we land so I don't forget about it?" Jimmy Clark, new-hire second officer on his first trip since his initial check ride, handed a company form to Jack.

"Oh, yes, I remember these," mused Jack, looking over the white piece of paper. The title at the top of the page was written in heavy black print—*Probation Progress Report.* Jack looked it over for a minute. "Now, Jimmy—"

"Yes, sir," was the instant response.

Jack corrected him. "Thank you for the title, Jimmy, but it's just Jack."

"Yes, Jack," was the response this time.

"Now, Jimmy, have you been a good boy?"

Second officer Clark sensed the levity creeping into the conversation and instantly felt more relaxed.

"Jimmy, I'm sure that you've made mistakes, many mistakes, on our trip together today, but I'm willing to overlook these shortcomings and give you a glowing report if you do one thing for me."

"Yes, sir, uh, yes, Jack. What is it?" asked Jimmy.

"A cup of black, if you don't mind." Jack looked over at his copilot, Rusty Hay. "Rusty, do you want anything?" Getting a negative nod in return, Jack continued. "And when you're back there, Jimmy—what's the senior's name, Betty? Betty, that's right—tell Betty that because of the tailwind we have today we're going to be about twenty-five minutes early and we're about to start down pretty soon. So she should probably think about terminating the meal service and begin putting things away if she hasn't done so already. Do you think that you can remember all those things, new hire Clark?"

With a broad smile and a sharp "Yes, Jack," he pushed his movable seat back, stood up, looked out the peephole in the cockpit door, then opened it and went aft. When he returned, Betty was right behind him and sat down on the jump seat just behind Jack.

"Thanks for the heads-up about the early arrival, Jack. I'm sorry that I didn't get a chance to come up and see you guys on this leg. We were busy with some passenger issues—nothing major, mind you, but it gobbled up my free time. And oh, Mr. Engineer, we'll be needing two wheelchairs in Boston, okay?"

"You bet," said Jimmy.

"Betty, can I ask you a favor?" said Jack, partially turning his head around to the right.

"Of course, Jack, what is it?"

"I've pulled something in my neck, again! I have a chiropractor in Boston who helps me out time and time again by grabbing my head with both hands and suddenly twisting it, and then everything is okay. May I ask you to do that for me, Betty?"

"Sure, Jack, I feel your pain. I've pulled my neck a bunch of times myself." Betty rose to stand behind the captain's seat to get a better grip and more leverage for the procedure. "Are you ready?" she asked as she put her two hands on both sides of Jack's head.

"I'm ready."

As soon as Betty twisted Jack's head to the left, there was a very loud, sharp, audible cracking sound coming from Jack's seat, simultaneous with Jack suddenly groaning loudly and Betty exclaiming "Oh, no!" All three of these alarming sounds soon morphed into broad laughter in the cockpit as Jack, smiling, held up a large empty plastic water bottle from his lap that he had squashed completely at the exact right moment to make the startling sound.

"Jack Rheinstrom, I will warn the others in Boston about you!" Betty cried, and still laughing, she turned around, looked out the peephole, and said, "Gotta go, see you on the ground," before opening the door and leaving.

Still laughing, Rusty turned to Jack. "How in the world did you ever come up with that?"

"I didn't think it up. I was a copilot on a trip maybe five years ago, I think, when the captain did it. It was funny then, too, but only after the fact. I didn't know that it was coming and it really, really startled me at first."

"Well, I can vouch for that," Rusty conceded, smiling and nodding his head.

Suddenly they heard, "Trans Ocean six three nine, New York, descend and maintain one five thousand and contact Boston approach on one twenty-nine point seven."

"Roger, New York, down to fifteen, Boston on twenty-nine point seven, six thirty-nine, so long."

* * *

After leaving the Jetway, Jack checked his mailbox on the way to the luggage room to drop off his brain bag. He found a couple more monthly revisions to his Jeppesen aeronautical charts, an internal memo to all Boston-based pilots about the employee parking lot, and a legal-size white envelope addressed to him. This had all accumulated there since he checked the mailbox three days ago before leaving on his trip outbound. He stuffed the revisions and the memo into his bag and decided to attend to the updating process later, in a couple of days. He looked at the letter, and from the style of the fancy and flamboyant handwriting, he guessed that a female must have written it. He stood there in the mailroom and opened it. He was right. The body of the letter was short and to the point. It read *Jack, I don't know when you will be coming back to the Dodge House, so give me a call as soon as you can. Thanks, Janie Kaiser.*

"Hmm," Jack said aloud to himself, then continued walking. He dropped off his flight bag and left the terminal.

* * *

"Trans Ocean seven five, Boston Tower, turn left to one four zero, climb and maintain three thousand, contact departure on one thirty-three point zero; you are cleared for takeoff runway two-two left."

"Roger, left to one forty, up to three, departure on thirty-three point zero, cleared to go on the left, TO seven five."

Jack looked back at the engineer, then to his copilot on the right. "You guys ready to go to Tampa"?

"Yes, sir," replied the second officer.

"Yup," said the copilot.

Jack nodded, and with a gesture of flair reminiscent of the barnstorming pilots of yesteryear, grabbed his black tie with his hand and threw it over his right shoulder, where it remained during takeoff. He pushed the throttles forward to the approximate takeoff position, released the brakes, and then removed his right hand temporarily from the throttle quadrant. "Your throttles," he said, and first officer Fred Robinson leaned forward from his right seat and fine-tuned throttles to the exact takeoff EPR setting.

"EPR set," Fred stated.

Jack's right hand returned to the throttles. His left hand was on the nose wheel tiller or steering wheel, guiding the now rolling Baker Mercury down its path on the centerline of runway two-two left.

"Eighty knots," Fred announced.

"Checks," said Jack.

"V-1. Rotate."

Jack slowly pulled the yoke back toward his lap, and the silver bird responded. As its nose began to rise, the nose wheel was the first to break contact with the runway, followed shortly by the mains a second or two later. The bird returned to the skies and was climbing homeward. It is a very special event in the cockpit of an airplane to witness the now common, everyday occurrence of a takeoff. One minute you're crawling around on paths of cement like a car or a bulldozer, and the next minute, you're flying like a bird. A pilot, no matter how old or experienced, never tires of this metamorphosis, the caterpillar to the butterfly. And this transition is only part of the theater—the landings are always a challenge. One must work constantly to attain consistent good ones. But the landing means that the flight is now over and the bird no longer exists. The magical world that you looked down upon just a few minutes prior has suddenly disappeared and now sits and waits for the next takeoff. The world from the air is not the same as the one on the ground. The difference is basic—and stark.

"About our flight tomorrow, have you ever been to Mexico City before, Captain Rheinstrom?"

"As a matter of fact, Fred, I have—and you can just call me Jack. Yeah, it was about five years ago and I was a novice sitting in your very seat. And that was a trip that I never will forget."

"You won't? Why is that?"

"Have you isolated the appropriate Jeppesen charts for Mexico City yet, like some guys do, or are they still buried in your books?" asked Jack.

"Well, they're still in the books. I'm rather new as a copilot, and I was about to tell you that when we got to cruise altitude."

"Well, we're just about there. Give me a minute here." After the cruise checklist was completed, Jack turned to Fred. "Here, take a look at mine—I have them handy and arranged in alphabetical order for the airports on our trip."

"That sounds like a good idea. I think that maybe I'll start doing that," Fred conceded. Jack then handed him six separate pages; three were precision instrument approaches for the runway at destination; one was the airport diagram with the runways and taxiways depicted including various tower, ground control, and clearance delivery radio frequencies; and two were for instrument arrival procedures.

"Here, Fred, take a look at the Chapultepec One arrival and tell me what you think about it."

Fred studied it for a few minutes. "Boy, that's rather complicated, isn't it?"

"Yeah, it sure is, and did you notice the minimum safe altitudes that are printed on the page?"

"No, I wasn't paying that much attention to that. Let me look again."

Jack waited for his copilot studying the page to respond. "Let me ask you this—you said that you were new in the right seat. Have you been into this airport as an engineer, or are you familiar at all with the topography around Mexico City?"

"No, about the only thing that I know about Mexico City is that it's in Mexico," Fred said with a laugh, "and it has one of the largest populations in the world."

"Well, pardner, you're in the exact same position that I was in five years ago when I first went there.

I was new, very new in the right seat and really wasn't that comfortable yet in the airplane. I didn't know the captain other than the fact that he was supposed to be a loner, didn't talk very much, and reportedly drank a lot—an awful lot. So, here you have the picture—it's night, we really haven't talked about the airport, the arrival, nothing, and we're coming in at say, I don't know, flight level two six zero, something like that, when we were handed off to approach control. That's when things really got interesting. First of all, I couldn't even tell if approach was speaking English or not. You know what it's like when you get an ATC clearance for your flight. There's a lot of information transmitted in a very short time frame, but you know, at least, the sequence of what you are about to hear—for instance, the destination, the altitude, the procedure, the transponder code, the radio frequencies. So when you hear all that stuff being transmitted to you from clearance delivery, even when it's rattled off quickly, it all makes sense to you and it's not that hard to get it right. But that night it was tough. I couldn't understand the controller other than the 'Cleared Chapultepec One arrival,' and we weren't even expecting an *arrival.* I had to ask the controller to 'say again' three, count them, three times to get it right, and then there was an altitude that we were cleared to that I couldn't understand, and I had to request that he 'say again' two more times. And I'm supposed to be helping the captain get things set up for the arrival. We're in the weather, can't see out, and there are mountains in the nearby vicinity. Mexico City is a little over seven thousand feet altitude, and there are three granite clouds at thirteen, fifteen, and seventeen thousand feet surrounding it. We're changing headings, trying to tune in radio frequencies, and then the controller wants us to 'expedite our descent.' We turned our cockpit lights on to full bright to make sure that we were reading the arrival procedures correctly and also seeing exactly where those mountains were. There were charts and maps all over the place, and with the cockpit lights full on---well, there goes our night vision for at least thirty minutes Anyway, that was my introduction to 'being prepared' in preflight planning and learning to talk about the upcoming airport arrival ahead of time—not in the damn descent. We were expecting just radar vectors to an instrument landing system. Never again, as the saying goes, *never again.*"

Fred just sat there the entire time glued to every word that Jack offered, sometimes shaking his head. "Wow, there were a lot of lessons in there—thank you for passing that on. I will be ready when we get there, you can count on that."

"I told you this because I feel that it's my duty. I remember when I first got my silver Air Force wings after undergraduate pilot training. I thought that I was a real hotshot; I thought I knew everything there was to know about flying. I was a Second Lieutenant in the United States Air Force, and wow, it just doesn't get any better than that. And that was just my first year. You know, it was my second year in the Air Force when I really learned how to fly. Why? you may ask. Well, it was listening at the bar at the various officers' clubs around the world, learning from the old guys recanting their tales and horror stories about flying. I was almost aghast at some of them, but there was always a lesson in the stories that were passed down to me, and now, Fred, to you."

"You know, Captain Rheinstrom, I'm new here, I'm younger than you—I'm only twenty-six—and I've only been at Trans Ocean for four years, but this is the first time, the very first time that I have felt that someone, the captain, even the first officer, was interested in handing something down to a newcomer. I said 'thank you' before—well, I really mean it."

"Well, you are more than welcome. That means a great deal to me. I feel very fortunate that I was born in this country, that my parents instilled certain values in me, that they sacrificed things so that I could go to college, and I was physically qualified to enter Air Force pilot training. And I'm lucky that I ended up in the airlines. None of that stuff had to happen—but it did, it just did. And there are a lot of our brothers out there who have similar stories but they only accept the facts, they don't treasure them—they take everything for granted. As you pointed out, you're new here. You'll find in the coming years, and you have a lot of them in front of you, you'll find some real jerks sitting in this seat, guys that think that they were born with their seniority number, like a kind of birthright, and they care only about themselves—not the passengers, not the stews, not the cockpit crew, not the company—only themselves. And that might not come as any big surprise to you, but it always does to me. We have a very unique fraternity here, Fred, and a very special set of skills, and we must never forget how truly lucky we really are. I thought that I was finished, but I want to say one more thing—and again, none of this is gospel, it's just how Jack Rheinstrom looks at things. When you look at the plane today, it's not *the* plane; no, it's *your* plane. Those people in the back are *your* passengers, and it's not *the* crew, it's *your* crew. Everything in life is special; you only have to come to realize that. There, I'm done! I'll get off my soapbox and you can forget everything that I just said."

"No, Jack, I don't think so. In fact, I know so." Fred paused for a moment, then asked, "Are you married?"

"Married? No, why do you ask?"

"I don't know. I was just thinking that someday you would make a great dad."

* * *

"How did you find all of this out about her, Janie?" Jack asked with consternation written all over his face.

"Please don't press me on that, Jack—it doesn't matter how I found out, just believe me that what I told you is true. I can't tell you the source because they told me in the strictest confidence and it can never, never get back to them that I broke my word."

"Okay, I understand. It's just hard for me to believe that a man could be that mean, that insensitive, that cruel."

"Well, Jack, there are a lot of them like that out there, believe me."

"I mean, to not even tell her in person? What kind of man is that? Did she have any clue at all that this was coming?"

"I don't know. I don't think so, but looking back, I think that this explains why she suddenly broke down in front of you that night in San Francisco. The actual event was supposed to be that very next weekend. I mean, the invitations had been sent out way before, family travel plans and reservations had been made, and presents had been received. It's just really, really sad."

Jack and Janie had once again taken their posts on the widow walk of the Dodge House, and Janie had just informed Jack that Laurie Mills had been dumped at the altar by her fiancé, a man named Bartholomew.

"Kind of a hard thing to recover from, wouldn't you say, at least in the short term? I sure hope that she has a good support network around her. Do you know if that's the case?" he asked.

"No, I don't, and I'm not really sure how I would find that out, but I'll try. Apparently Trans Ocean wouldn't even give her any sick leave when it happened. According to my source, she's still a mess. And get this—from what I hear, her parents are blaming *her* for this debacle. Can you imagine that? As I said, this reads almost like a Greek tragedy, don't you think?"

Jack didn't respond. He just sat there clutching his frosty beer, looking off into space.

* * *

The doorbell rang, and Kess McCarthy smiled at her husband, John. "I'll bet it's Jack, right on time!"

Kess opened the front door of a small clapboard cape on Emerson

Road in Wellesley, Massachusetts. "Well, hello, Jack, please come in."

"Hi, Kess, you look great!" Jack said as he opened the door and came in, sideways, holding a bouquet behind his back.

"Oh, Jack, you shouldn't have. They're beautiful!"

"Well, Mac told me that I had to."

"Mac said what?" she exclaimed.

"Just kidding, Kess," he admitted as he closed the door behind him.

"I did what?" asked Mac as he came around the corner from the kitchen.

"Brother McCarthy!" Jack's hand went out.

"Brother Rheinstrom!" A firm handshake and slight body hug ensued, complete with backslapping. "Well, we have a lot of catching up to do, even though you're not the guest of honor here tonight. Here, Jack, come this way." The three of them walked to the living room. Jack took in the baby grand piano, a fireplace, and then finally, a woman sitting on a sofa. She rose as they walked into the room.

"Andrea Williams," Mac began, "do you remember my old friend Jack Rheinstrom from your brief encounter at the Black Rose a while ago?"

Her face lit up with a bright smile, exposing her perfect and very white teeth with the little space in the middle. She answered with a simple "Hi."

Jack looked back at her with a look of surprise. She did look familiar, but she sure didn't look like the woman he had met at the Black Rose that night. The woman standing in front of him now with her hand extended looked like she just stepped out of a Hollywood screen test.

"You must be a docent," Jack began with a knowing smile. He was impressed with her right away—the handshake was very firm, and she looked him directly in the eye. Jack took instant notice.

The evening was a roaring success both from the hosts' point of view and also from Jack and Andrea's. There were lots of laughing and lots of memories shared between the two fraternity brothers. By the end of the evening and two bottles of wine, the new couple on their surprise first date seemed the most animated and outwardly happy—just as Mac and Kess had hoped for.

* * *

"Hi Betsy, it's Jack," the telephone call began.

"Hello, sweet brother. How are you, and where are you?"

"Well, I just got back from a trip, San Francisco again, and I'm up here in Boston, or shall I say Marblehead, at my Dodge House digs. And I'm just about to go upstairs and have a sundowner on the porch of the widow's walk. It is a simply gorgeous summer evening up here. I tried you at your apartment in New York but no answer, so I figured you were 'on island' at the Vineyard."

"And you were right! You're so smart," Betsy remarked.

"Yes, yes, please go on. Anyway, I just wanted you to know that I might be progressing to the next stage of my relationship with a girl that I've been dating."

"Oh, Andrea? So you think that it's getting serious, do you?"

"Well, it's funny—I guess that I should know something like that, but let's just say that I'm thinking about it. How's that?"

"Well, you know what Dad would say if he were still here: 'Pay attention, be careful now, watch what you're doing.'"

Jack laughed into the telephone. "Now I know why I called you! You're perfect, Sis, just perfect."

* * *

The days stretched into weeks, weeks stretched into months, until finally, one day, Jack popped the question. When he woke up that morning, he didn't realize that he was actually going to do it, but by the time he picked Andrea up that night, he'd pretty much made up his mind.

The next time they visited The Black Rose, it was as an engaged couple; the fact that they had met there made the visit all the sweeter. "This place looks kind of familiar, doesn't it?" Jack asked when they arrived. "In fact, you were standing right over *there* when you threw your sunglasses onto the floor."

"I did what?" asked Andrea with a surprised look on her face.

"It was a trap. I know that it was a trap. You saw this good-looking guy standing over in the corner all by himself and you thought that you could nab him by making him feel like a gentleman by picking up your 'dropped' sunglasses."

Andrea's mouth was open, and her eyes were as big as saucers. "You've got to be kidding! Are you serious?"

Jack just shook his head and laughed. "Yes, I am kidding, and no, I'm not serious. Man, are you easy! Come on Andy, loosen up."

"Well, back to your original question, you asked if I was surprised. Well, yes. I guess because as much as we had dated and talked about mutual interests and laughed together, we never broached the subject of marriage. And I wasn't going to be the one to bring it up. I was wondering how you saw this relationship ending up, so when you asked me for my hand that night, I thought that you were talking about me helping you with one of your many, many projects—like saying 'give me a hand with putting on the new roof.'" They both laughed. "It took me a minute to realize that you were serious and serious about *that*. I really wasn't hesitating about answering, Jack, honest, I was just kind of confused. And now, I'm truly on cloud nine."

Jack nodded, thought for a minute, and regarded Andrea with a very serious look. "So, you *will* help me with a new roof?"

Andrea shook her head and smiled. "Jack Rheinstrom!"

* * *

The honeymoon in Bermuda was perfect—the flight, the hotel, the weather, the motorbike, and the trip to the local market for the wine, bread, and cheese. Even the problem at the end of the trek on the deserted beach turned out okay when Jack realized that if he put a stick through the neck of the upended red wine bottle, it would hold the pushed-in cork back far enough so that wine could dribble out. He had remembered the wine, the cheese, the bread, and the beach blanket, but not the corkscrew. The very next day Jack bought a Swiss Army knife that he carried with him for the rest of his life.

Back in their room at the Grotto Bay Hotel, they sat on their balcony sipping their special bottle of Veuve Clicquot Ponsardin that they had bought at duty-free in Boston and looking out at the reflection of the moon on the ocean. Andrea was wearing a short white peignoir with satin straps, made from a silky, almost gossamer, fabric. Jack was wearing a white hotel terry-cloth bathrobe over his birthday suit. Jack's flute was still almost half-full when he stood and spoke.

"Andrea...?"

"Yes?" she answered softly.

"Come here."

It was cloudless that night in Bermuda and the moon was not only full, it was much larger and brighter than normal. It was a once in a three-year cycle occurrence, known as a supermoon. Andrea stopped about five feet from him and stood in the middle of the opening by the French doors that led to the balcony overlooking Grotto Bay.

Jack had looked forward to this night for a long time, as he had been rather old-fashioned in his desire to wait for the honeymoon to actually make love. He wasn't positive that he would have been successful had he tried, but he hadn't wanted to press it with Andrea. He had wanted the nuptials to be special—he wasn't planning on being married more than once. Jack was not a virgin by any means, but he was a hopeless romantic. He had planned the night's progression carefully. He would be strong, and he would go slowly. But then her peignoir suddenly fell to the carpet, landing in an almost perfect circle on the floor around her ankles. She was standing facing him, directly next to the open French doors leading to the balcony. The light from the supermoon shone in so that only her right side was illuminated. Jack felt as though he'd seen a ghost—he'd never seen anything this beautiful before in his entire life. Her very blond hair wasn't blond anymore, but rather took on the appearance of a sparkling silver waterfall, cascading softly off her right shoulder. He could see the silhouette of her right arm hanging down by her side, the outline of her thigh, and her entire right leg. The only other thing he could see was the right side and outline of her large breast, which actually cast a shadow upon the other one. Jack's robe was of such heavy material that it made a sound as it fell to the floor and lay next to her peignoir. They softly kissed and both slightly moaned. Jack's plan was progressing well, but when he felt the tip of her warm tongue searching for his, the plan went out the window. The stars never shone more clearly, the moon was never so bright, and their bodies were never more perfect than they were that night—day one of their voyage together.

Three hours later, Jack was standing in front of the balcony. He couldn't see in the darkness so he held the champagne bottle up to the light of the moon to see if any remained. He quietly cleared his throat but not quietly enough. Andrea heard him.

"Are you okay, Jack?" she asked.

"Oh, yeah, I was just in the powder room for a moment." The

moonlight revealed that the bottle was still half full. "Do you want any more, Andrea?" Jack asked.

"No, Tiger, let's just wait until tomorrow."

He turned to see her lying face down on the pillow, then chuckled to himself. "Okay, Hon." He returned to bed and was soon sound asleep.

* * *

It was August of 1963 when the handsome newlyweds returned to Boston after a week in Bermuda and began to settle into their new life together. Andrea continued her Thursday docent role at the Gardner, but scaled back her involvement as an interior decorator at Warwick's, becoming more of a consultant than an active employee. And Major Jack Rheinstrom found it less and less compelling to drive the six and a half hours down to McGuire Air Force Base to fly for the New Jersey Guard and to attend the meetings and training there. It was great, he thought, when he was single and lived in Bordentown, but now the landscape had changed dramatically. He was thirty-four years old now and had thirteen years of credit toward a twenty-year requirement to qualify for a pension at age sixty. If he could only hang on for two more years, he could then transfer to an inactive status and perform alternate service, like correspondence courses. But most important of all, he could be home. He had passed on the purchase of a ship captain's house when he had first arrived in Boston a year prior. Now, he and Andrea found the home of their dreams in Salem—a 1780 colonial that supposedly, according to some, was haunted by the ghost of its builder, Captain Obadiah Brewster. It was a project for sure, but to the optimistic Jack Rheinstrom it was definitely worth it—in fact, he considered it a steal. The fact that Andrea cooled on the idea shortly after moving in did not diminish Jack's enthusiasm about the place, for he was sure that she would eventually change her mind.

* * *

The scene was once again San Francisco, and two best friends found themselves together on a layover at one of their favorite haunts. They walked into The Brazen Head and were shown their table. "Okay, now," Jack began as he held the chair for Laurie Mills and then proceeded to his seat on the opposite side of the table, "let's try this again."

No sooner had he sat down than Liz Kennedy appeared at the table. "Hello, stranger," she said, addressing Laurie first. "What did you think of the Black Horse Saloon? Did you go?"

"What a neat place, Liz. It was a hoot! I got to know Joe the bartender, although it's kind of hard not to in a place like that. Who would've thought that a room that small could be a successful bar? Oh, and I made friends with a nice couple from Sausalito who even asked me to come visit them on my next trip. And I guess it is a saloon, but that name doesn't do it justice. Anyway, thanks for the tip. And Joe said to say hi to you when I saw you next."

Liz looked down at Jack. "Hello, Scrap."

"Hello, Liz. I guess you guys are friends now, huh?"

"Yeah, we're buds, thanks to you," Liz said and placed two menus on the table. "I'll give you two a few minutes," she said and walked away toward the kitchen.

"Yeah, Jack, she's a nice person, a very nice person. I've gotten to know her—I must've come here at least ten or more times since you first introduced me to The Brazen Head, and that was a while ago. And I know that you know because I've said it to you so many times, but your support for me has been above and beyond."

"Wait a minute, Laurie—what I did for you is something that you would have done for me, right? I'm just glad that I could help and that you're back flying and living your life again."

"What I'm trying to say, Jack, if you'll stop and listen to me, is that I couldn't have done it without you, and in clear words, I want to thank you."

Jack looked down at the table. He couldn't bring himself to say something sterile like "You're welcome," so he gently nodded his head, and still looking down the table, quietly muttered "Okay."

"And I just love San Francisco. Every time I see it on the open board, I put in for it. But the trip is too senior for me to hold it as a monthly pattern, so I just get the trip every now and then when there's an opening. Anyway, a lot has changed since we sat here for the first time. Here you are, married and settling down, and here I am, not married and settling up." They both laughed, and almost simultaneously, their glasses were in the air. They met in the middle and clinked. They were both now on a roll.

* * *

It was the Fourth of July, 1967, and just hours before, Jack had been pinching himself, life was so happy. Now he was sitting in a chair in a hospital ward, stifling the urge to scream and remembering how things had all started eight months ago. He had just driven home from Boston to Salem. It was a beautiful summer day, not too hot and not too cold, with low humidity and perfect visibility. It was about four o'clock and the shadows were beginning to lengthen—his favorite time of day. He remembered it like it was yesterday, getting out of his car in the driveway, getting his suitcase out of the trunk and heading for the side door of his home. He saw Andrea coming out the front door, so he dropped his bag where he was standing and cut across the front lawn to meet her. There was something about her that looked different, he thought to himself. As he came closer, she appeared as if she had something to say. Not wishing to distract her, he said nothing, and they finally came face-to-face. He was right.

"Jack," she said, pausing ever so slightly, "Jack...I'm pregnant!"

Jack's eyes popped open widely and then they closed as he threw his arms around her. His body was trembling and sobs spilled out of him.

Andrea pulled her head back and looked at him. "Jack, I thought that you would be happy!"

Jack struggled to regain his composure. With tears rolling down his cheeks, he finally smiled. "Andrea, I am, I am, you wonderful creature. I'm so happy I can't even tell you!"

But that scene seemed light years away, and that complete sense of happiness and exhilaration was now gone. Now, here he was in Boston Children's Hospital, and things were different, very different. His face was splotchy and speckled, his eyes puffy and full of tears. He could not comprehend or believe what he had just heard.

With shock and horror, Jack tried to process the fact that there had been major complications in the delivery of his and Andrea's stillborn child, and it had been necessary for Andrea to undergo a complete hysterectomy at age twenty-nine.

The actual physical recovery for her and the adjustment for them as a couple were not easy. The burial of their son Matthew was devastating for both Andrea and Jack. Jack loved his son so much, yet he had never even gotten a chance to hold him in his arms, only in his heart, only in his mind. The fact that his only son—in fact, the only child ever in his life—had died was a sobering thought that tormented Jack on a daily basis. And the pain never dulled, never went away.

For Andrea, facing a life without her newborn was crushing. She was struggling through her own grief, coping the best way she knew how. Her doctor tossed around terms like *postpartum depression,* and Jack did all he could to research the condition and find a solution to help her. But she was mourning not only the death of her baby boy, but also the fact that she would never have children, ever. The hysterectomy had changed everything, and Andrea was despondent.

* * *

"Didn't you just have one of those damn military exercises last month?" Andrea asked angrily. "And didn't you say about four or five years ago that you were going to quit the Guard?"

"Are we going to argue about this again, Andrea? How many times do you need to have this explained to you?" Jack's voice was changing in tone.

"Well, you're always away. Why don't you ever stay home?" Andrea shot back. "And I hate this house, I just hate it! I hate it!"

"Listen," Jack's voice became louder, "the reason I leave home is to make an income for our family!"

"We don't have a family!" Andrea shouted back.

Jack stared at her in surprise. "What do you mean we don't have a family?"

"Well, we don't. Do you see any little kids running around here?"

"Why do you keep doing this to me, Andrea?" Jack asked, his eyes welling up. He violently shook his head, stormed out the front door, got into his car, and sped out of the driveway.

Hours later, Jack parked his car in the lot of the Corinthian Yacht Club. It was now dark, and the moon shining brightly in the evening sky was reflected on the water in the bay at Marblehead Neck where Jack was standing. He looked across the water and noticed that there were lights on at the Dodge House. He paused and just stood there for a few minutes, remembering how happy he was and how perfect his life had been back then. His heart was now so heavy. He wondered what he had done wrong, and what, if anything, he should do now.

My dearest Andrea, the letter began. It was difficult to write on the bench where he was sitting because the only light besides the moon was from a street lamp on the other side of the street. And the words were blurry from the salt in his eyes.

Later that night, when he arrived home back in Salem, he decided he would pack for his upcoming trip in the morning, as he would have plenty of time. He went down to the basement rec room, found the blanket in its regular place in the closet next to the TV, sat down on the sofa, and turned out the light. He lay on the couch in the dark with his eyes open until eventually he fell asleep.

Thursday was Andrea's day to be a docent at the Gardner, and she had already left the house that morning when Jack climbed up the basement stairs. After he packed, he took the envelope and placed it on her pillow. He stood there for a moment gazing at the bed. He turned around to leave and noticed her pink slippers on the floor by the bathroom door. One was pointed one way, the other in the opposite direction. He picked them up, walked over to her closet, and neatly arranged them on the floor side by side, both now pointed in the same direction. With suitcase in hand, he walked out the front door and slowly closed it behind him. He paused on the front step and put the suitcase down. He stood there and thought for a minute, then picked up the suitcase, walked to the car, and drove to Logan Airport.

CHAPTER FIVE

Before starting the descent into Boston, second officer Jeff Johnston called forward from his flight engineer's table where he was completing entries into the aircraft logbook for the day's flight from Phoenix. "You guys have any write-ups up there for the log?" he asked. The two pilots look at each other and shrugged.

"Nope," said Jack. "How about you, Jeff?"

"Just the rain repellent reservoir—the site gauge shows that it's a little low."

"Oh my God, man!" Jack exclaimed. "You're kidding! We must declare an emergency!" The three crewmembers chuckled.

"Well, actually," Jack began, "has anyone ever seen that stuff being used?" Jeff and the copilot shook their heads. "Well, if you want to hear *my* war story, I'll pass it on before we start down. I haven't detected any aroma of perfume emanating from the first-class lav, so I think that I'll have time. Those stews are amazing, aren't they? They always know when the descent clearance is coming, even before we do. Ever notice that?" Jack asked.

"Oh, please tell us your story, dear Captain," joked the copilot, Don Guarino.

"Well, if you insist," said Jack, smiling and nodding. "I was brand-new in the right seat, and it was my leg going into Raleigh-Durham. The weather forecast was calling for a frontal passage about the time of our arrival, with gusty winds and heavy rain. But that didn't seem to bother the captain—Waldo Harrington was his name. Anyway, we're on approach and I was hand-flying the ILS, and I was really humping. I don't know why I didn't hook it up to the autopilot, but I didn't. I was sweating and getting a little concerned about whether or not I should be the one shooting the approach. So I asked him that, since I was brand-new in the right seat, if he should be the one flying the ILS. 'Nope, you're doing fine, Kid.' I'm not sure that he actually said 'Kid,' but it helps the story. Anyway, I was on instruments but below the cloud deck, and I could see that there were approach lights up ahead of us. The windshield was just a complete blur—I couldn't make out anything. I asked Waldo to turn the wipers on, which he did, on *high*. And I don't have to tell you, or do I, how noisy and distracting the Mercury wipers are?"

Both men nodded, riveted.

"Well, if it's really noisy on medium, you guessed it—on high, you can't even hear yourself think, and they deliver a sense of upcoming doom in their rapid screaming chant of *roing! roing! roing! roing!* The speed of their cadence was almost as fast as my heartbeat. Looking up from the instruments, I still couldn't make out the airport. Then Captain Waldo calmly turned to me and said, 'Do you want some repellent?' 'Sure,' I said, not knowing what to expect. He reached up and pushed those two little buttons, and presto—I could instantly see and was able to ask for the wipers back to medium, which not only slowed them down but also my heart and the noise level."

"And how did the landing go?" Don asked.

"Well, it was heavy rain and we were being buffeted around quite a bit, so the hell with a perfect landing—I just planted it. I was thinking, let's just get this hummer on the ground and start getting it stopped. The thought of hydroplaning was very much on my mind."

A voice from the radio interrupted Jack's story. "Trans Ocean four four, Boston Center, descend and maintain flight level one nine zero, and contact Boston approach on one twenty-three point seven."

"Okay, Boston, down to nineteen, and approach on twenty-three seven, TO forty-four, so long." Jack again addressed the men in the cockpit. "Well, that was pretty good timing. I'll finish the other story another time. Let me give them a call and check in, and then let's run the descent checklist, okay?" Jack reached up behind his head to grab the two retracted shoulder harness clips and pulled them down over his shoulders to the waiting buckle apparatus on his lap. "Boston approach, this is Trans Ocean four four."

A sudden persistent dinging caused Jeff to look up at the blue cabin call button, which was blinking on and off, on and off. "That sounds urgent," Jack said, glancing backward at the second officer. "Answer that for me, will you, Jeff?" Jeff reached forward to the back of the center radio console and picked the phone up from its cradle.

"Hello, engine room here."

The voice on the other end of the intercom was harried and in no mood for light banter. "Cockpit, this is Lead. Get back here as fast as you can—there's a fight going on back here with a bunch of GIs. Paula almost got hit in the mouth! Hurry, please!"

Jeff told Jack what the call was about, got up, and was about to open the cockpit door when Jack stopped him. "Jeff, put on your jacket and hat—you want to look the part of an authority figure. And let me know what's going on ASAP!" He turned to the copilot. "Don, you've got the airplane. I'm going to talk to approach and tell them that we might have a problem here."

Don nodded. "Roger, I have the airplane."

When the second officer got to the scene of the skirmish, the fists were no longer flying, but the tension was palpable. "You!" Jeff pointed at a young baby-faced Marine, a shorthaired boy of about nineteen. "I want you to sit in one of those three empty seats over there!" The Marine obeyed and thus left the vicinity of the two Army privates who were sitting together. "And you two, stay where you are and stay seated!"

Jeff then went back and huddled with stewardesses Paula Gilman and Barbara Berger. "Okay, guys, who started it all? What happened?" He spoke in hushed tones and kept an observant watch over the seated and now passive soldiers. "And is that guy, the sailor over there in the white uniform, is he involved?"

Paula spoke first. "No, he wasn't involved at all! He's a sweet guy. Anyway, I'm one lucky girl, I tell you. When the pushing and shoving began, Barbara and I went back to investigate and try to settle things down. Then, when we got there, that's when the fists began flying, and I swear, one of them missed my chin by an inch. An inch!" Paula continued. "Well, the two Army guys were in the last row on the left, over there and across from the lav. The Marine was sitting a few rows up, all by himself and also on the left side. Anyway, the Marine went back to use the lav and shut the door behind him. But he didn't lock it, or maybe he closed it incorrectly, because it opened by itself and revealed the guy, standing there in front of the toilet, peeing, I guess."

Barbara chimed in. "I was standing in the aft galley and I didn't want to embarrass the guy and close the door myself, so I said to the Army guys sitting there, 'Could you please close the door for your buddy?' Well, one of the Army guys got up and went over and shut the lavatory door, but he must have said something insulting to the Marine first—I think that maybe he called him an 'animal'—because when he came out, you could tell that he was, excuse the pun, pissed!"

Jeff nodded. "Well, guys, keep an eye on them, and let me know if you sense anything brewing, okay?"

"We will, Jeff, and thank you for coming back," said Paula.

"Sure thing. See you in Boston—we're about to start down."

Jeff looked at his stewards again, then went back to the cockpit, recounting the details for the captain and first officer when he got there.

"So, you think that the situation has been diffused?" Jack asked his second officer.

Jeff looked thoughtful. "Yeah, I think so."

Jack then picked up his mike and called Boston approach, reassuring them that everything was now stable and under control. "Okay, Jeff, let's get that checklist out of the way," he continued.

"Roger, in-range checklist," the second officer announced, and before he could get the first checklist challenge item out of his mouth, the overhead cabin call button light illuminated, accompanied by multiple chimes. Jeff grabbed the intercom phone with his left hand, and at the same time, he unbuckled his seatbelt with his right hand and pushed his seat back on its tracks with his legs.

It was Paula's voice. "They're at it again, Jeff! Hurry! Hurry!"

Jeff skipped the coat and hat this time and rushed out the cockpit door. He didn't even pause to look out the peephole to check that no one was waiting on the other side. He scanned the rows of seats, both on the left and the right, as he hurried back. Nobody in first class...keep going...there's one, he thought. He suddenly stopped in the aisle. "I need your help in stopping a fight, sir. Will you help me?" he asked, bending over aisle seat 10C and talking to a broad-shouldered, clean-cut, twenty-something young man, named Thomie Dombrowski, who was wearing a Texas A&M sweatshirt and looking very much the part of the college linebacker or wrestler.

"Sure!" the man said, and he immediately dropped his magazine and stood up.

"Good! Find two more like you and meet me in the back, ASAP!" Jeff hurried down the aisle, all passenger eyes on him as he approached, and all those behind him turned around in their seats to watch. He could see, from about mid-cabin, that there were two male figures wrestling on the aisle floor and another one standing nearly over them, occasionally kicking one of them in the head. By the time he got to the actual scene, one of the Army privates had the Marine in a headlock, and the other private was trying to position himself for more selective kicks.

Jeff's voice was so loud that it could be heard all the way up in first class. "Stop! Stop it *now*!" he boomed. "And I'm not asking you anything, boy, I am *telling* you—*stop*!" Jeff was now just three feet away. He looked behind him and was relieved to see that there were now three bouncer-quality young men standing there, all with a question in their eyes. The actual wrestling had stopped, but the Marine was still in a headlock and he lay on the aisle floor, motionless. All of the passengers were glued to the drama playing out before them, their eyes wide open, with some gasping in fear.

Jeff looked at the lone standing private and walked up to him, standing very close to his face. "You're going to go," he said, turning around to see the selection of empty seats. "You're going to sit *there*, and you will sit with my Aggie friend, and you will not move for the duration of this flight. Do you understand me, soldier?" The second officer was beginning to ease into his new role as drill instructor. He then bent over this seeming still life of two men lying in the aisle. "I'm going to tell you something, and I'm only going to say it once so you'd better listen up, because you guys are in *deep serious*. Your commanding officer is not going to be a happy camper when he hears about this. And it's only going to get worse unless you both disengage and get up and go to opposite sections of the plane. And each of you will sit with one of my deputies here." Jeff then hand-signaled the other two volunteers to come forward. "And you will not move from your seat until we land. Do you read me, soldier?" Jeff's voice was still booming. "Do you read me?" Jeff suddenly stood upright as he felt the speed brakes extend on the wings. He quickly found an empty row of seats and looked out the window. "Christ, we're getting close," he muttered under his breath.

Once the "deputies" and their quarry were sufficiently settled, Jeff ran back to the cockpit and got there just as the plane was intercepting the glide slope and Jack was asking for the landing gear. The second officer quickly sat down, explained the now stable situation, ran through the remaining checklists, and called the company radio to find out the Jetway parking assignment. "Jetway 12, Jack," he called out.

"Yes, I already know that, Jeff. When you left, we declared an emergency, and they cleared us for *any* approach that we wanted, switched us over to tower on their same frequency, and even gave us taxi clearance as well, all while we were still in the air. What service!"

"Okay," Jeff continued, "did ops tell you to make an announcement to the passengers that when we get to the Jetway, everyone should remain seated and not to get up?"

"No, they didn't, but I will. Thanks."

The senior stewardess, Mary Alice McCullough, was standing at her assigned position by the front entry door, 1 left. She heard a knock on the door, and since she had already disarmed the evacuation slide, she responded with a thumbs-up signal that could be seen from the outside through the door's inspection window. The large, almost three-foot door handle subsequently swung its arc, the massive door unlocked, and it slowly swung open. The three cockpit crewmembers stood in the open cockpit doorway and watched the ensuing spectacle develop.

"You know, I'm not exactly a small guy," Jack quietly commented, "I'm six foot two, but those guys are huge!"

With their knee-high black leather boots and jodhpurs, and their holstered guns and billy clubs, four Massachusetts State Troopers in their blue uniforms and *fifty-mission crush* wheel hats entered the Baker Mercury and began marching down the aisle. In addition, for good measure, there were also two white uniformed EMT personnel in tow, complete with their suitcase-sized medical kits. The passengers had all turned around in their seats, watching the theater and wondering what was going to happen next. In just a matter of minutes, the direction was reversed, this time with the accompaniment of the Marine, the two Army privates, and the one lone sailor—each with a large hand clenching his shoulder.

"Well, that's a first," said Jack.

"And I sure wouldn't want to be in their shoes," commented Don.

"Me neither," agreed Jeff.

* * *

Jack Rheinstrom answered the ringing telephone to hear his sister's voice.

"Hello, sweet brother!"

"Oh, hi, Bets. How are you?"

"We're doing great, Jack. I just wanted to talk to you before your trip in case you got stuck out. Did you get my package yet?"

"I'm not sure. I just got back from a two-day, and I'm going out again on Tuesday to Mexico City, so I haven't checked the mail yet. Did you get mine?"

"Yes, we did, and thank you very much. I'm so sorry that we didn't get together on the vineyard this summer—with all the houseguests and your crazy schedule, it just didn't work out. I'm sorry."

"Not to worry, Betsy, we have the wintertime, and we'll work harder on it next summer."

"How are things with you, Jack?" Betsy asked in a serious tone.

"Oh, fine, same old, same old."

"What I mean is, are you ever going to go through with the divorce and break the tie? I mean *she* was the one who originally filed for it and said that she was so unhappy. It seems to me that she has all the bennies of being married to you and you have nothing in return—except the bills. And she's not even really very nice to you, either. Or am I just being a protective big sister?"

"Well," Jack began, "as I've mentioned to you before, Andrea is not well. She has a hard time coping with life—she's very fragile—and is much different from the spark plug that I first married. If I dropped her and basically cut her off, number one, that might be her last straw, if you know what I mean. Number two, this way she still has my insurance coverage, and, believe me, she has a lot of medical bills. But I guarantee you it *will* end, sooner rather than later."

"But how long has it been though, Jack?" his sister pressed.

"Well, let's see here—about two years, I guess."

"Well, you said that you were dating before—are you playing the field, or is it just a sporadic date here and there?"

"Well, Sis, I have met some interesting ladies these past couple of years, but there is one in particular, a very special person, that I want you to meet. I can fill you in on everything at Christmas when I arrive for your feast. Luckily, I was able to put these two trips back-to-back so that when I land on Christmas Eve, I'll have nine straight days off, including Christmas and New Year's. So the hard schedule is well worth it."

"Oh, good!" Betsy replied. "We'll have lots to talk about for the New Year—1970. Nineteen seventy! Doesn't that sound weird? I just got used to putting in 1969 on my checks. Well, as you said, same old, same old. Anyway, it was great to talk to you, little brother. Fly safely and we'll see you soon."

"I can hardly wait! And I read you loud and clear, Sis—you take care of yourself and hi to Davis. Love you. Oh, and Merry Christmas."

"Love you, too, Jack, and Merry Christmas to you. Bye."

Jack put the phone back on its cradle and went to look for his mail, waiting for him somewhere in the Dodge House, his new "old" home since the separation.

* * *

"Have you ever seen sword-swallowers or fire-eaters before, Marshall?" Captain Rheinstrom asked as he turned toward his first officer. Marshall Hewitt looked puzzled. "Wait a minute, Jack, a minute ago we were talking about the Boston Patriots' season and Gino Cappelletti, and now you're suddenly asking me about sword-swallowers? You are rather odd, Captain Rheinstrom, rather odd indeed."

"I also asked you if this was your first time into Mexico City, did I not?" Jack retorted.

"Yeah, so?"

Jack smiled. "I have an idea. Let's, all three of us, get out the approach plate and go over the Chapultepec arrival, okay?" And the three crewmembers were indeed ready when the Baker Mercury descended for landing at Mexico City's Benito Juarez airport one hour later.

Before long the crew members were sitting in their limo, stopped in traffic, waiting for the light to change and watching an unusual spectacle unfolding on the traffic island just five feet away. "Weird, man, totally weird!" exclaimed Marshall. "Well, we're not in Kansas anymore, are we, Captain Toto? What you were saying before now makes sense, and I'm glad you didn't give it away because I love surprises. I must say—this is a first for me! A sword-swallower and a fire-eater all in one night! I wonder how they do it?" The whole crew agreed it was truly an amazing sight as the limo resumed its trip to the layover hotel.

Jack turned around in the front seat of the limo so that he could address the whole crew. "Have any of you ever been to the San Angel Inn?" he asked. His question was met with silence. "Well, if you want to join us, because the three of us are going, I'll buy the first round of margaritas."

"What's it like? Is it a restaurant or just a bar?" came a voice from the back.

"Well, it's an old hacienda, converted from a Carmelite monastery. There are beautiful gardens outside and you can eat there, or you can go inside and eat under magnificent high ceilings in the dining rooms. It's a little pricey, but you don't have to order the most expensive thing on the menu—just stick with the Mexican dishes, not the lobster ones. So, what do you guys think?" he asked again.

The crew let out a cheer from the back of the limo. They were already in a holiday mood—it was going to be Christmas in just three days.

* * *

The flight from Mexico City to Atlanta on December 22, 1969, was the best that one could hope for—it was routine. It was night, and they were over the Gulf of Mexico. "Trans Ocean nine three, this is Mexico Oceanic, do you read?"

"Mexico Oceanic, this is TO ninety-three, go ahead."

"Trans Ocean nine three, contact Houston on one thirty-three point seven. Good night and Merry Christmas to you."

"Thank you, sir, and the same to you," Jack replied. He was handling the radios, as it was Marshall's leg to fly. The Christmas spirit was alive and well in the United States that evening as evidenced by the radio exchange with Houston air traffic control: "Good evening, Houston, this is Trans Ocean nine three, flight level three three zero."

"Good evening to you, Trans Ocean ninety-three, ident." Jack looked down to his right for the transponder on the center instrument panel and pushed the little *ident* button.

"Okay, ninety-three, we've got you in radar contact two hundred eighty miles southwest of Port Arthur, Texas. Tell you what, ninety-three, if you can name the Three Wise Men for me, I will clear you 'present position direct Atlanta.' What do you think about that?"

Jack had no clue, but he thought about this lonely air traffic controller stuck somewhere in Texas late at night with nothing to do, just trying to have some fun. Why not? His thoughts were suddenly interrupted by the voice of second officer Jesus Cruz, who was a nice guy, professional crew member, and more importantly, a devout Catholic from Puerto Rico.

"I know!" he blurted out. "I know, Jack!"

Jack turned around in his seat and looked at him.

"They are Gaspar, Melchior, and Balthasar!"

Jack shook his head. "That's great, Jesus, good job." He then grabbed his mike with his left hand and sat up very straight in his seat. "Sorry for the delay there, Houston, but the Three Wise Men were Gaspar, Melchior, and Balthasar."

"*Bingo*, ninety-three, congratulations! You are cleared present position direct Atlanta. And Merry Christmas, guys."

Just then another flight called Houston.

"Houston center, this is American one four three."

"Go ahead, American."

"Hey, we know the names of the Three Wise Men, too—can we go direct Chicago?"

"Nice try, American! Continue on present flight plan."

Just that little banter of silliness brought grins and good feelings to the crews on two airplanes and the guy on the ground—a strong sense of fellowship at a very special time of year.

* * *

It was the morning of Christmas Eve, and Jack Rheinstrom stood in front of the elevator of the Crowne Plaza airport hotel in Atlanta, Georgia, and looked up. One elevator was on floor fourteen and wasn't moving, and the other one had started down and was just leaving floor six. He stood there in front of the doors, just thinking during the time it took for the elevator to reach the lobby floor. The two doors retracted to their sides and revealed two occupants who both looked pleasantly surprised at seeing their lobby-floor greeter. Marshall spoke first. "Hey, Jack, good morning."

Jack smiled. "Hi, Marshall, Jesus. Are you guys coming down to breakfast?"

"Yup," Jesus responded.

"Great. I have to go up to the room for a few minutes, but if you'd like to join me, I'm the table for four on the left with a cup of coffee—cold by now, I'm sure—and a paper on the placemat."

"Sure, sounds good," Marshall said, as the two of them walked out of the elevator.

When Jack returned, he picked up his napkin from the table and sat down. "Did you guys order yet?"

"No, just coffee—we were waiting for you," Marshall replied.

"Well," Jack began, "I was just talking to dispatch."

Marshall Hewitt's ears perked up. "Did they call? Has our trip changed? Are we going to deadhead home?" he asked.

"No, I talked to dispatch, *not* crew sched."

"Well, why did they call?"

"They didn't—I called them."

"You called them?" Marshall asked. "Why?"

"Because of *this,*" Jack said as he handed him *The New York Times.* Marshall read the headlines with Jesus looking over his shoulder.

"And who is the guy," Jack asked sarcastically, "who asked in Mexico City the other day, 'Why can't we have some snow for Christmas for a change?' Huh? Well, it looks like you got your wish!"

"So, how bad is it going to get?" Jesus asked.

"Well, it depends. Ever heard that one before?" Jack asked. "It depends on the track of the storm, but the least amount of snow will be a lot, and the most will be paralyzing, according to the paper. It will be a nor'easter, that's for sure! It's kind of funny because when I was talking to the dispatcher about the winds coming out of the east, she said that 'the only good thing that ever came out of the east were the Three Wise Men,' which made me laugh remembering our fun over the Gulf of Mexico yesterday."

"So, what's the game plan, Jack?" Marshall asked.

"Well, first of all, we might be load-limited out of here due to our weight. We're going to have to take max fuel because the storm system is so big and the alternate airport is so far away. I mean, we're going to be flying two and a half hours from Atlanta to Boston, plan for two hours of holding, and then, if we divert, we're going to have to fly all the way back to Baltimore! Can you believe that? And Baltimore isn't 'severe clear' either, but its forecast conditions qualify it for use as a weather alternate."

"I'm supposed to be at my father's for our family's annual Christmas dinner tomorrow night," Marshall whined.

"And I'm participating in the service at Mass tonight," added Jesus.

"Yeah, well, I have an important date, too, guys. Believe me, we will make max effort to get there, but only safely. If we can land, we will, if we can't, we won't—it is what it is. I know the prospect of not getting there for a once-in-a-year Christmas is very disappointing, but you guys know the game," Jack said. "We'll make the best of it, guys. Don't worry, things will work out. They always do, okay?" Jack looked around the table, receiving two affirmative nods from his seated compatriots. Thus the day began with excitement, consternation, and resolve.

* * *

"Ladies and gentlemen, good afternoon, this is Captain Rheinstrom from the cockpit. On behalf of Trans Ocean, First Officer Hewitt, Second Officer Cruz, myself, and the entire Boston-based cabin staff, I offer you a very warm welcome on board. I'm sorry that I wasn't able to personally greet you as you boarded, as I wanted to show you my new Christmas tie with the reindeer on it, but seriously, we've been kind of busy up here. I don't know if you've been watching the TV news or have read today's newspaper yet, but there is a large storm system developing in New England today that will adversely affect all forms of transportation up there. I'm going to be perfectly honest with you so that you can make your personal decision *now* rather than halfway through the flight when you really can't. Our arrival time is approximately three and a half hours from now, and—excuse me, folks, I just got a call from the company. I'll be right back."

Two minutes passed but the passengers all stayed alert, waiting for Captain Rheinstrom to return. They didn't read newspapers or books or even fidget around in their seats—they just sat there, waiting. The most common activity in the cabin was trading concerned glances with the other passengers within close proximity.

"I'm sorry, I'm back with you now," Jack continued. "Let's see, where were we? Oh, yes—arrival about four hours from now. The problem, you see, is that the weather forecast is just that—a forecast of what might happen or what probably will happen. The degree of accuracy of a weather forecast is...well, I don't have to tell you. The facts are that it is snowing heavily now, and it's supposed to snow even heavier during the next six to eight hours with increasing winds, a typical nor'easter. Now, if there is any airport equipped to handle snow, it's Logan—that's a given. Another given is that this airplane and this crew are very qualified and very capable of safely, and I will repeat the word *safely*, flying in any kind of weather. If it's not safe, we won't do it, period! So, here it is in a nutshell. We have more than enough fuel to fly to Boston, hold—in other words, make circles in the sky for two hours while waiting—and if we still can't get in, fly to our alternate airport. The problem with that is that this system is so large, that we'll have to fly all the way back to Baltimore, Maryland to find an airport that has good weather. That will take another two or so hours. So, this being a very special two days, Christmas Eve and then tomorrow, do you want to—and please don't tell the company that I offered you this option—do you want to get off the plane now and have a controlled Christmas Eve here in Atlanta and try your luck tomorrow, or do you want to come back with us to Boston with the possibility that you will end up in Baltimore late tonight? But you will have to decide pretty soon because we have to push back in ten minutes."

There was a GI in the back of the plane that day. He was seated in the very last row, a Seaman second-class, wearing his white bell-bottoms and sailor hat. He had possibly been drinking before boarding the flight, because as soon as Jack finished his talk on the PA, he stood up from his aisle seat at 34C and unabashedly, loudly bellowed out, "I'm with you, Captain!"

All the passengers in front of him turned around to see what the commotion was all about. He shouted again, "Who's in?"

Probably fueled by the spirit of fellowship that the Christmas holidays always bring, a sudden feeling of camaraderie spread throughout the entire passenger cabin and all seemed to agree—one for all, all for one. They were all along for the ride. Unanimous applause rippled from the galley in the back all the way up to first class.

The two stewardesses standing in the back galley looked at each other with total surprise. "Ever seen anything like that before?" one asked. The other shook her head and smiled. "Nope!"

* * *

Trans Ocean Flight 66 taxied out for takeoff on runway eight right at Atlanta's Hartsfield Airport. When they got to the runway holding point on the taxiway, they requested from tower to turn off onto the waiting area for a few minutes to talk to the company.

"Dispatch, this is flight six six, over," Jack spoke into his mike.

"Sixty-six, this is Bob Rensalear in dispatch, go ahead."

"Hi, I just talked to you guys about an hour ago on the landline. Any updates, anything new in Boston? We are number one for takeoff here in Atlanta and are about to launch. I thought that I'd call you before we became airborne."

"No, Captain, nothing new, but let me read you the latest field condition report for Boston. Runway four right is one hundred percent covered with packed snow over ice, and braking action is fair, as reported by the latest aircraft, a 727. They've been closing the runway about every three hours so they can plow the runway a hundred feet wide and keep ahead of the snow accumulation. So obviously, we have holding delays. But so far, everyone has been able to get in. Any other or specific questions?"

"Yeah, how long have the holding delays been?"

"About forty-five minutes when the approaches are active, and obviously longer when they close the runway for plowing—that shuts everything down for about half an hour. Anything else?" Rensalear asked.

"Yeah, how about the winds and any forecast change in them?" Jack pressed.

"Well, let's see here…right now they are zero nine zero at eighteen gusting to thirty knots. Looks like they've been pretty much the same direction for the past hour, and no changes in the forecast. The visibility has been ranging from a half to quarter mile, ceilings running from four hundred to two hundred feet."

"Well, that sounds just ducky!" Jack said.

"Yup. Anyway, let me know if I can get you anything else, otherwise, I have a bunch of calls waiting. It's pretty busy down here tonight."

"No, thanks for your help. We'll be taking off momentarily. Merry Christmas."

"Yeah, you too, sixty-six. Dispatch out."

Jack looked to his right and nodded his head at first officer Marshall Hewitt, who then picked up his mike. "Atlanta Tower, Trans Ocean six six is now ready."

"Roger, Trans Ocean six six, following the departing National Airlines DC-8, you are cleared into position on runway eight left and hold," the tower responded.

"Roger, position and hold on the left, TO six six." Jack advanced the throttles slightly and moved the nose wheel tiller, maneuvering the now rolling airplane onto the runway and aligning it with the centerline markings. When stopped, he pushed on the toe brakes on his rudder pedals with his feet and set the parking brake by pulling up on the small lever on the center console. He then turned to Marshall again and announced, "You've got it!" It was Marshall's leg to fly today.

"Roger, I have it," Marshall replied, his left hand now resting on the three throttles on the center console.

Jack turned around in his seat and eyed his crew. "Everybody ready?" he questioned. The copilot and engineer both nodded. Jack turned back around in his seat, now facing forward, and waited.

Fifteen seconds later they heard, "Trans Ocean six six, Atlanta Tower, winds are one zero zero at five. You are cleared takeoff on runway nine left. After takeoff, climb on runway heading until reaching three thousand feet and contact departure on one two nine point seven. And Merry Christmas."

"Cleared to go on the left, up to three, and departure on twenty-nine seven. And a very Merry Christmas to you, too, sir, sixty-six."

After putting his mike back in its holder, Captain Rheinstrom again depressed the toe brakes on his rudder pedal, thus releasing the parking brake, and as the first officer pushed the throttles up to their approximate takeoff EPR setting, the Mercury 100 began to roll. At eighty knots indicated on his airspeed indicator, Jack took his left hand off the nose wheel steering tiller, announced "Eighty knots," and then placed his right hand on the throttle quadrant just behind the throttles.

Five seconds passed. "One hundred twenty knots."

As the aircraft reached takeoff speed, Jack announced, "V-2, rotate twelve degrees."

First officer Hewitt then gently pulled back on the yoke until the attitude indicator showed twelve degrees nose up. The Mercury lifted off from the Atlanta runway and was once again airborne. The rate of climb indicator pointed up to eight hundred feet per minute as the altimeter readings increased.

"Positive rate," Jack announced.

"Gear up," responded Marshall.

Captain Rheinstrom leaned forward in his seat to grab and lift the landing gear lever to the *up* position. The nose and main gear retracted and slowly nestled into their respective wheel wells. The flaps were retracted on schedule, and Flight 66 was on her way—back to Boston, a nor'easter, and Christmas Eve, 1969.

The crew was settling in for their three-hour flight when a blue light, accompanied by a ding, illuminated on the pilots' overhead panel.

"I'll get it," Jack said. "Hello, hello, who's this?"

"Hi, it's only me, Nancy Bell, your faithful sky slave. Do you guys want anything up there before I start the meal service—coffee or water maybe? And also, tell me when you want me to throw your crew meals on."

Jack looked around the cockpit. "You guys want anything? Hungry?"

The rest of the crew shook their heads. "No takers, Nancy. But thanks, and of course, I will keep you informed of anything new about Boston."

"Okay then, see you later."

"Jesus?" Jack asked.

"Yes, Captain?"

"On your hourly position reports to the company, please request and record the weather for Boston and our alternate Baltimore, okay?"

"Sure thing, Boss."

Jack turned to his right after pushing his seat back and putting his feet up on the horizontal bar above the rudder pedals. "You know, Marshall, I was thinking about our fuel load for today, and all those calculations are based on a best-case scenario for the divert—you know, getting the altitude that you'd plan for, no unexpected delays en route, no unplanned snafus at the landing airport, no mechanical irregularities, no drastic changes in the weather. I'm going to add five thousand pounds to our fuel reserve—'for Mom and the kids.'"

Marshall looked back at him. "Well, the decision is yours, obviously, but it sure makes a lot of sense to me."

"Well, someday, Marshall, you'll have the fun of worrying all the time about things like this. How far are you from checking out?"

"Well, if they keep hiring, or they buy some more planes, I could be captain as soon as next year. And then I would have to decide if I wanted to do it and be on reserve or not. I rather like being senior, even if I have to stay in this seat. Also, the opening would have to be in Boston. I tried commuting once before, and it sucks."

"Roger that," Jack heartily agreed, nodding his head.

Jesus handed a piece of paper forward to Jack. "Here's the latest."

"Thanks," said Jack as he took it, turned on his overhead reading light, and sat back upright in his seat. "Looks pretty much the same, Marsh," he said as he handed the paper to his copilot. "We shall see what we shall see, but I have a good feeling that we will get in tonight. But with those gusty crosswinds," Jack continued, "and the snow and ice on the runway, Marshall, I'm thinking that—and I've only done this once before and it has nothing to do with you—but I'm thinking about taking the approach and landing at Boston myself. That is, if we don't have to divert. If anything happened at all—sliding on the ice, thrust reverser failing to come out, weathervaning into the wind, going off the runway—I'd want it to be on me. Do you understand?"

Marshall Hewitt grinned back at his captain. "Jack, I think that's a wonderful idea. I honestly wasn't looking forward to it anyway. So, yes, I completely understand."

"Trans Ocean six six, New York...."

Marshall looked to his left. "Jack, let's swap duties *now*. I'll take the radios back and you take back your bird."

Jack agreed. "Okay, I've got it."

Marshall picked up his mike. "New York, TO sixty-six, go ahead."

"Trans Ocean six six, just as a heads-up, it looks like things are backing up—they're holding over Providence right now. Contact Boston approach on one three two point seven. Merry Christmas to you."

"Roger, Boston on thirty-two seven, TO sixty-six, and a Merry Christmas to you, too."

Indeed, the approaches into Logan were backing up. Holding over Providence was much farther south than normal, and it was only the first in a series of two holding points.

After holding for an hour and a half at Providence, Trans Ocean 66 was finally cleared to hold at the final pattern at "cricket," a holding fix on the aeronautical chart.

"Jesus," Jack said, turning around in his seat. "what do we have for fuel right now?" After receiving the information, Jack turned back around forward and began stroking his chin. "Well," he said, turning around again, "at this fuel burn, we'll either be landing at Logan in thirty minutes or we'll be going to Baltimore." Jack had been keeping the passengers informed all during the flight and made one last PA that night to sum it all up. "In thirty minutes, we'll know…."

Exactly twenty-five minutes after Captain Rheinstrom had declared a thirty-minute decision time, Boston approach called. "Hey, Trans Ocean six six, I have good news—at least for you, that is. Three flights below you in the stack just declared minimum fuel and diverted to their alternate. So, you are number one and are now cleared to descend to three thousand feet and fly heading three five zero. This will be vectors to intercept the localizer ILS four right. Contact approach on one two four point nine."

* * *

On this particular Christmas Eve, Alphonso Barba was working the tower. Alphonso had been with the Federal Aviation Administration for thirty-eight years. He'd been working Boston Tower the entire time and was indeed the very symbol of that organization at Logan. Even though he was number one in seniority and could easily have picked any schedule that he desired at the tower, here he was working on Christmas Eve and was scheduled to work on Christmas day, too. He was a widower living in nearby Winthrop. So nearby, in fact that the planes virtually flew over his house when runways two seven and nine were in use. He had lost his wife ten years ago, and his children were grown and settled with their families on the West Coast. He volunteered to work these shifts so that some of the younger tower staff at Logan could be home with their families on these very special days. Alfonzo was that kind of guy. And that was only one of the reasons why his peers held him in such high esteem.

"Boston Tower, Trans Ocean six six, outer marker inbound, ILS four right."

Alphonso pressed his mike button and responded, "Trans Ocean six six, winds are zero nine zero at eighteen gusting to thirty, ceiling reported two hundred feet, visibility is RVR twelve hundred in moderate snow squalls, braking action reported fair to poor by the previous landing 727. You are cleared to land on four right. Due to the snow and low visibility, you will not be visible from the tower, so call when you're on the ground."

It would be the last voice that Jack heard for many days.

CHAPTER SIX

Jack Rheinstrom was lying on his back. He was just emerging from a very deep sleep and a weird dream about submarine warfare and the use of sonar in their detection. His dream had lots of *pings* in it—he was remembering that strange sound that sonar makes when the signal makes contact with a metal hull. His eyes were still closed as he slowly drifted into consciousness. He heard another *ping* again and wondered if he was still dreaming. He was confused and wondered why he felt so sluggish and why it was taking so long to wake up. He felt as if something was stuck in his throat! He forced his eyes to open but only the right one obeyed. He grabbed for his mouth to pull whatever it was out of his throat, but his arms only struggled, they did not move—his wrists were restrained by gauze straps that were tied to the side rails of his metal bed. He heard another *ping* and the sound of something like a small vacuum cleaner turning on, and then turning off: *click...pssst...click.* He tried to think, but he couldn't and fell back asleep.

After a while, he thought that he heard a female voice say, "Mr. Rheinstrom, Mr. Rheinstrom, can you hear me?" It wasn't a dream—he had heard a voice, a real voice. He heard the *ping* again and then the vacuum cleaner, and then felt that thing in his throat again. His right eye struggled to open. There was a woman bending over him. He could barely make her out, her features were so fuzzy.

"Mr. Rheinstrom, my name is Margy Goodman. Can you hear me? But don't try to talk, because you can't—right now, that is. There are some tubes going down your throat, and I'm sorry, but they have to be there. They're there to help you breathe. If you can hear me, blink your right eye, or if you can, squeeze my hand."

His right eyelid remained closed, but then it slowly opened so that he could see her, a little better this second time. She was a very attractive middle-aged woman with long blond hair in a ponytail. She had very soft eyes and a warm smile, and was wearing light blue scrubs. "You probably want to know, Mr. Rheinstrom, where you are and why you're here. If you want me to tell you now, I will, but maybe you're tired and want to go back to sleep. If you want me to tell you now, blink your right eye."

Jack's right eyelid closed and stayed that way—he had fallen back asleep.

* * *

The next day Betsy Bowne stood patiently at Nurse Station 3B at Massachusetts General Hospital, waiting for one of the obviously busy nurses to take notice of her. She stood there for about four minutes. Finally, the one closest to her put her phone into its cradle, looked up, and inquired, "Can I help you?"

"Yes," she began, "I was told early this morning that I might be able to see my brother who is a patient here."

"And what is your brother's name?" Nurse Margy Goodman asked, looking down at the clipboard that was now in her hand.

"Jack Rheinstrom," she said.

Margy instantly looked up. "You're Rheinstrom's sister?" she asked as she stood up.

"Yes, that's what I said."

"Well, you can peek in and see him for just a bit, but he's not conscious. He has been in a drug-induced coma pretty much since he was brought in on Christmas Eve. Please come this way," Margy said as she stepped away from behind the counter. "It's just down the hall."

They both walked into private room 327 with the nurse leading the way. Jack's sister stopped after only a few steps. She had braced herself for this moment, not knowing what to expect. When within earshot of the room, Betsy could hear strange sounds emanating from inside. There were pings, beeps, and a rhythmic whooshing noise that all heightened her anxiety of actually seeing him. She stood there at first just watching. There was a body form under the bed sheet that looked like a gauze-wrapped mummy with wires and tubes attached everywhere. The only part of her brother that she recognized was Jack's nose. It was a proud "patrician" nose, just like his father Gordon had sported.

"The reason that he's in a coma," Margy continued, "is because his ICP, his intracranial pressure, was too high, the result of his head injuries. So we purposely slowed his body down. Basically, they drilled a little hole in the back of the skull, and a catheter was inserted into the lateral ventricle of his brain. That area contains the cerebrospinal fluid. If there is swelling of the brain in a TBI, excuse me, a traumatic brain injury, they can modify the amount of fluid in the skull to compensate for any brain swelling. The tube in his nose is an NG, or nasogastric, tube. It's a liquid feeding tube placed in the nose, and it goes down through the throat and into the stomach."

"What is that clicking and whooshing noise?" Betsy asked.

"That's the bird," Margy said.

"The bird?"

"Do you see that little green box over there, the one attached to the mouth tube, that has dials and gadgets on it?"

"Yes."

"Well, that's the ventilator that helps him breathe. We call it 'the bird' because of the man who invented it—that was his last name."

"Well, nurse—I'm sorry, I forgot your name...."

"Margy."

"Thank you, Margy. I have to ask you...." Betsy paused and took a deep breath. "How bad *is it*? Do you think that he'll live?"

"Well, as you know I'm a nurse, not a doctor, and only he can give you his opinion. But just let me say that when they brought your brother in on Christmas Eve, he was not expected to live through the night. And here we are now two days later and he's still improving. In fact, he actually opened his eye momentarily yesterday and looked at me. Let me give you his doctor's phone number. Your brother is lucky to be alive, and he's also lucky to have Dr. Norton Levine looking after him. He's a crackerjack, one of the best brain surgeons in the United States, and he also teaches at Harvard, which says a lot." Margy pulled a pen out of its holder that was hanging around her neck on a lanyard. She looked at the clipboard at the foot of the bed. "Here's his number. Give him a call—he's a very kind and thoughtful person, and very approachable. You'll feel better after you talk to him."

"Thank you," Betsy replied, taking the piece of paper from the nurse's hand. "What about his other injuries?"

"Well, he has burns over thirty percent of his body, and his lower spine has been compressed. We won't know more until he's conscious, and he has a broken left arm, wrist, and femur, just above the knee. All of those should heal over time—but the brain and the back? It's too soon to tell. Any other questions?"

"Yes, who else has been here to see him?"

"Only you. You are his only kin, correct?"

"Well, we lost our younger brother in Vietnam a few years ago but he has an estranged wife—she hasn't tried to see him?" Betsy asked.

"No, and she hasn't called to inquire either, to my knowledge. There have been no visitors allowed, not even the immediate family until today, so no one else could have seen him. Oh yes, there is a female coworker who came in the past two days and sits in the ICU waiting room. She stays there until there is an update after the doctors' first rounds, then she leaves."

"Is she still there, I mean, today?"

"I really don't know. There was an update issued this morning after the first rounds, but I don't know if she left after that or not. Maybe she's still there?"

"I will check on my way out. Do you know her name, by chance?"

"Lauren or something like that, I think, but I'm not sure. That's all I remember."

Margy nodded. "I think that we have to leave now. I'll give you the inside phone number for the ICU nurse's station, and I'll let the others know that you'll be calling for updates."

"Thank you, Margy—may I touch him before I leave?"

"Of course you can. His left fingers are sticking out from the cast, so that might be a good place."

Betsy slowly walked over to the bed and put her hand around Jack's left index finger. She closed her eyes and prayed for about a minute before loosening her grip on his finger and wiping the tears from her eyes. Then she turned around and walked out of the room, her head down, looking at the floor.

* * *

The Boston Specialty and Rehabilitation Hospital was on River Street in Mattapan. Jack Rheinstrom was never a patient there.

However, his alias, Jack Harkness, was. While Jack had been recovering from his injuries at Mass General, he saw only three visitors: his sister Betsy; his lawyer, Steven Lattimer; and a fellow named Finn Nielsen, the lead investigator for the National Transportation Safety Board, who was looking into the crash of the Trans Ocean flight on December 24th. After five weeks of medical care at Mass General, it was deemed that the next phase of recovery for Jack should be at Boston Specialty and Rehabilitation Hospital. His transfer to this new hospital was not under the public eye due to the successful efforts of his attorney. Jack's last name was changed to Harkness and his address was now "C/O Lattimer and Howland, Attorneys at Law, Wellesley, Massachusetts."

Jack's bones were mending, as was expected, the herniated discs in his lower back were responding well to the surgery, and the swelling in his brain was slowly abating. Jack's physical condition was definitely improving—but his mental state was a different story. He spent most of his waking hours just trying to remember. And it was always the same. He remembered hearing the clearance from Boston tower and the voice of his copilot, Marshall Hewitt, on the radio: "Wilco, Boston, TO sixty-six, cleared to land." He thought about what could've happened, what he might have done, and what he might not have done. And he thought about his passengers, all the people who trusted him to do the right thing that night—trusted Jack Rheinstrom with their lives—and how he had let them down. There were 132 men, women, and children who had been killed that night, and the 12 who had actually survived had had their lives forever changed.

* * *

"First of all, what you describe to me, Ms. Bowne," said Dr. Levine, "and what you are concerned about does not surprise me in the least—in fact, it's quite common in a TBI. A brain injury doesn't heal like a normal physical injury, like say a broken bone or a laceration. The brain is a very complex organ that we are just really beginning to learn about. So, when I project the possibilities of something in the future about your brother, I do that not by reading a special gizmo 'brain meter,' but by referring to analyses of past medical histories of patients under similar circumstances. I think that it would be a good idea for your own benefit, unless you have already done so, to go to the library and do some research on a TBI. But in a nutshell, you are looking at—and all of this with varying degrees according to the individual case and what location of the brain was traumatized—you are looking at possible confusion, anxiety, depression, memory loss, and anger. Now, I am talking about a stand-alone TBI case. Your brother's circumstances are more complex and, I suspect, will increase the likelihood of more severe symptoms. Why do I say this? Notwithstanding the TBI, he has a lot of serious issues to confront, the most obvious being his involvement in an accident that took over a hundred lives. How do you deal with that? And how do you deal with something like that if you can't even remember how it happened? And then there's the matter of the investigations that have already been launched, the FAA, and the NTSB, and I think that you can almost hear the circling sharks of the legal profession. I mean, this is a real mess and a real shame, because what I'm hearing from a bunch of sources is that your brother Jack is an exceptionally fine person and doesn't deserve any of this. And it worries me what you said about him cutting off all ties with his previous life. You mentioned that his divorce was about to be finalized and that you are his only family. But you live in New York, and now he has cut off all contact with his previous friends who were local. So basically, at this most critical—and I mean critical—time in his life, he has no caregiver, no advocate, no safety network of friends to help. Talk about making things more difficult!" Dr. Levine paused. "I've talked to you so many times in the past five weeks that I would like to call you 'Betsy'—may I do that?"

Betsy was still trying to process the onslaught of information from the doctor. "Of course, Dr. Levine."

Dr. Levine nodded. "Now, Betsy, what I'm going to do, based on our conversation today, is recommend that your brother be seen by a very trusted colleague of mine who also teaches at Harvard. His name is Dr. Claes Bernhardson. He and I go back a long way, and he is very well respected and a renowned psychiatrist. I think the sooner that we do that, the better it will be for your brother. What you think about that?"

"Oh, I agree, of course. You're the pro—let's do it. I'm just a worried older sister…."

"No, you're more than that. You are his family, and his only family. You're very important in all of this. Don't forget that, Betsy. Okay?"

"I won't," she replied softly.

* * *

Christmas Eve—1970

"Hi, Mom, I'll call you tomorrow and let the kids talk to you on the phone, but looking at the calendar just now, I realized that it was exactly a year ago that it happened! How is Uncle Jack doing? Do you know?" Nicky asked.

"Well, Nicky, I really don't know for sure. I get reports from two of his doctors and they say that he continues to improve, but he never communicates with me—I always have to call *him.* And I always just get his answering machine. Sometimes he calls me back, but never on the same day, and usually not even in the same week. And he always sounds so sad and distant. The NTSB final report just came out two weeks ago, and it's not good, not good at all."

"What did it say?"

"It said that he was at fault. It said that he lost control of the aircraft at a critical time and he was negligent in attempting the approach if it was beyond his capabilities."

"But wasn't there an airplane that landed just before he did?"

"I know, I know—but this is terrible news and he's going to take it very badly. And then there is all this talk about suing the company and conjecture that he might even be fired. This is not the right time to talk. I don't want to spoil the Christmas spirit for you and Mandy and the kids, but my heart just aches for Jack. He has suffered so much, so very much."

"I'm so sorry, Mom. I didn't mean to upset you."

"No, no, Nicky, it's been on my mind daily since the report came out. And Jack won't answer my calls. But, honey, he is living his life and while we must help him as best we can, we all must live our lives, too. I'm glad that you called—I actually feel better just being able to talk to you about it. So, hang up and get back in the spirit, and don't worry. Keep your uncle in your prayers, as I do...and enjoy life, dear son. It flies by a little faster than you think, each year. Love to Mandy."

"Bye, Mom, I'll call you tomorrow. I love you."

"I love you too, Nicky. Good night."

CHAPTER SEVEN

It was an early Monday morning in November of 1987 when the phone rang in the Federal Aviation Administration Headquarters in Washington, D.C.

"Good morning, this is Dan Beaudette, Flight Standards."

"Hi, Dan, it's Chuck Beattie."

"Hey, Chuck, how's it going?"

"Oh, fine, but it's Monday—what can I say?"

"Yeah, I know," Dan agreed.

"Look, Dan, something very interesting just came across my desk, and I want you to see it. Please give me your fax number again."

"The last four numbers are 3019," Dan replied. "What's it about?"

"If I remember correctly, didn't you know that guy, the captain of the Trans Ocean flight that crashed on Christmas Eve way back in '69, up in Boston?"

"Yes, Jack Rheinstrom. We were in the Air Force together. What brought that up?"

"Well, I'll send this over to you right now—read it and get back to me right away. I want to know your take on it, okay?"

"Wow, what a mystery. I'll be waiting. Talk to you soon." Dan got up from his chair and went over to check the fax machine. Yes, the green light was on.

Chuck Beattie's phone rang fifteen minutes later—it was Dan Beaudette.

"Have you talked to Legal yet?"

"No, you're the first person that I've talked to about this."

"You know what this means if it can be substantiated, don't you, Chuck?"

"I certainly do!"

"Who sent this info, and how did you get it?"

"Well, I got a call from a good friend over at the National Transportation Safety Board, Charlie Hire. Do you know him?"

"No, I just know who he is—a good man, supposedly."

"Yeah, really top-notch. Anyway, the NTSB has already launched an investigation into it. I don't know who the anonymous whistle-blower is, but he either has a very strong sense of ethics, or was seeking revenge on the company—maybe he was fired or passed over or something like that, because a scandal like this will not go over well with the honchos at Baker Aircraft. Can you imagine what it will be like when the lawyers get a hold of this, assuming it's true...are you still there, Dan?" asked Chuck.

"Yeah, I'm here. I was just thinking about Jack Rheinstrom. Chuck, let's back up a minute here. The sequence as I remember it, and I will have to review the case again, but as I recall, the NTSB ruled that the accident was avoidable and that the pilot in command mismanaged the approach—at least the landing part, and that he was solely responsible for the crash. You made a good point in your fax just now, about the NTSB not being able to retrieve all the information from the flight data recorder because it was damaged by being run over by a fire truck, of all things, and that's why they sent it to Baker Aircraft, for them to try to extract the info in their more sophisticated labs. Now, what this whistle-blower from Baker is saying is that in their investigation, they found an uncommanded input from the rudder servo control that caused a sharp lateral movement at two hundred feet above the ground, resulting in the left-wing hitting the ground and the resulting cartwheel. And now this part, which is beginning to really piss me off, that they, Baker Aircraft, concealed these findings, so that now, some poor schmuck like my friend Jack can take the full blame, saving Baker millions in lawsuits. Am I getting this all right, Chuck? Is that how you see it?"

"Yeah, Dan, that's the way I see it, too. You know about the rudder modification don't you, Dan?"

"No—what rudder mod?"

"Well, I looked into it while I was waiting for your callback. Baker sent a communiqué to us, and we consequently issued an Airworthiness Directive ordering the replacement of the main rudder power control unit servo valve in all Baker Mercurys. This was six months after the crash, and two months after the initial NTSB findings came out blaming your friend. No one connected the dots of the crash to the AD because a 'hard over rudder' was never in any of the possible crash scenarios."

"Wow," replied Dan, slowly shaking his head. "Unbelievable."

* * *

On a chilly December day in South Freeport, Maine, Jon Brewer climbed the wooden steps that led to his waiting office. He heard his phone ringing so he quickened his pace, taking two steps at a time. Standing at his desk, he picked up the phone and said breathlessly, "Hello, Brewer's Boatyard."

* * *

With an air of resignation, Jack took a deep breath, leaned back until his head was resting horizontally on the cross bar, put the flashlight in his mouth, and pushed off the wall with his feet. He didn't have far to wiggle, and soon his head, then his shoulders, then his chest, made their way into and through the small opening. It still wasn't right, so he took another breath and rolled slightly sideways, pushing again against the wall. His right hand released the toolkit that he had dragged with him and then reached to his mouth for the flashlight, still shining on the panel above.

Jack was in the middle of listening to a National Public Radio program about the accidental shooting down of an Iranian airliner by a U.S. Navy cruiser in the Persian Gulf when he felt a knock somewhere on *Raccoon*'s hull. As he extracted himself again from the engine access cubbyhole in the aft cabin quarter berth, he looked at his watch—it was 8:45 a.m.—and wondered who would be calling on him so early in the morning. As he sat up from the prone position prior to standing, he could hear a voice calling "Mr. Rheinstrom? Mr. Rheinstrom?" from the stern area of the boat. He climbed the cabin stairs and walked through the cockpit to the aft deck. Jack peered down the ladder that was propped up, leaning against the stern rail. "Good morning, Kristin," he said.

"Good morning, Mr. Rheinstrom. Jon Brewer asked me to deliver this message to you—he said that it was important," she said, standing on the ladder, extending her right hand.

Jack reached down and took the envelope. "Thanks, Kristen."

"When was *Raccoon* built?" she asked as she descended the ladder.

"1937, prewar."

"Well, she's a beauty!"

"Thanks. Lots of history here."

Jack turned his attention to the envelope and squinted at the letter inside. *Jack, all is well, but call me as soon as you can. We need to talk. —Boo.* Dan Beaudette's phone number was listed on the bottom of the page.

Since 1971, Jack had been living on and restoring a fifty-three-foot Elco Cockpit motor vessel. It was a classic boat, made of wood, and a lot of its structural members were full of rot. She was a beautiful boat and had turned many heads over the years when she steamed by, or even when she was sitting on a mooring or waiting at the dock. On board, Jack's living arrangements were basic by any measure, and there were tools everywhere. There was a kerosene stove and cook top, a small refrigerator, an electric heater, and a little TV, the electricity being supplied by a very long fifty-amp yellow shore power cord plugged in at the marina. The century-old, shingled mast storage building on the marina yard had a toilet and a shower and was only a short walk away.

Jack's divorce from Andrea had not been contested, and there was no alimony involved. When he had been fired from Trans Ocean, he had lost his pension, a sizable hit. His earnings from being a freelance salvage diver, a part-time scalloper, and a temporary yard worker at Brewer's was only enough to keep his head above water. Luckily, before the crash, he had acquired enough points in the New Jersey Air Guard to qualify for a small pension available at age sixty. But more importantly, he had acquired a retired reserve ID card that enabled him access to the commissary for groceries and the Base Exchange, a small department store, at nearby Brunswick Naval Air Station, a mere twenty-minute drive away. He had zero social life, other than occasional boat-related conversations with the workers at the yard. However, he wasn't overly upset about the situation, but rather resigned to his life of self-imposed exile. He thought about the misguided trust of his passengers almost daily—the scar was very deep and would never heal. And the guilt of his actions was only part of it. The other belonged to another kind of guilt, the question of why he was alive and they were not. He tried and tried to remember what happened that night, but his memory always stopped at the same place: "Trans Ocean six six, cleared to land."

* * *

Well, there's the huge Indian he was talking about, Dan Beaudette thought as he glanced at the forty-foot-high statue rising out of the parking lot in front of the Casco Bay Trading Company in Freeport. He turned right from Route 1 onto S. Freeport Road and pushed the reset button on the car's odometer, trying to refresh his memory from the notes he had scribbled on the back of a laundry receipt that was in his jacket pocket. "Let's see now," he said aloud, "it's two miles to the mom-and-pop store and the post office on the right, then a stop sign. Turn right until morning." That sounded like a long time, but he had been friends with Scrappy Jack Rheinstrom for many years and knew that what he said was sometimes the exact opposite of what he meant. "Just wanted to see if you're listening," Jack would normally respond when challenged, with a satisfied grin on his face. But that was the old Scrap, Dan thought. He really hadn't seen *that* guy in a long time, not for seventeen years. It had been three years since Dan had seen his best friend. And all told, Jack had only allowed a total of five visits over the years. It hurt him that Jack could be so reclusive and standoffish to him, but deep down inside, Dan knew that it hurt Jack, too—but maybe that's what he really wanted.

Upon arrival at Brewer's, he parked his car and got directions to the *Raccoon*. When he got there, he walked over to the ladder and climbed halfway up. He knocked on the hull and shouted, "Anybody home? Jack, you onboard?" Jack suddenly appeared, walking aft through the cockpit.

"Permission to board, Captain?" Dan formally asked, his back arched straight as a board. The only thing missing was a U.S. Navy uniform and a crisp salute. Jack granted it and Dan subsequently climbed aboard. They shook hands, looked each other directly in the eye, and embraced in two long bear hugs.

"How's Suds?" Jack asked as he broke the hug and stepped back.

"Oh, she's fine, Scrap, and sends her love. She's visiting her sister in Fernandina Beach right now and was sorry that she couldn't come."

"Where's that?"

"Amelia Island, Florida. It's right on the ocean, just north of Jacksonville."

"Never heard of it."

"Well, it's really neat—laid-back, beautiful beaches, old historic downtown. Susan grew up there and goes back there at least once a year."

"All right, Boo, sit down here in the cockpit. I'll grab a couple of Heinekens and you can tell me about this mysterious message that you sent."

"You're on," said Dan as he sat down on the blue cushion on the starboard settee of the cockpit. Jack came back with the two bottled beers and sat down across from his friend._

"Jack, if I weren't ninety-nine percent positive of the outcome, I wouldn't be getting your hopes up. But what I'm about to tell you is *big*!" Dan paused, and Jack stared at him curiously. "Someone, and it appears to be a former employee at Baker Aircraft, has been sending anonymous, inside, and official confidential reports, including substantiating data, about the flight data recorder findings on flight sixty-six to the NTSB!"

Jack's stare became intense.

Dan cleared his throat and went on. "And what these reports indicate is that there was a major rudder malfunction on your flight, on final, at exactly one hundred eighty-five feet above ground level."

Jack put his beer down and inched closer to the edge of his seat. Dan continued. "This information was not made available to the NTSB nor the FAA, Jack, because it was suppressed by someone at Baker Aircraft. I don't know if you remember or not, but Baker had the flight data recorder in their possession because it was sent to them by the NTSB. They felt that Baker was the only one that had the equipment sophisticated enough to retrieve the data. Recall that the flight data recorder had been damaged in the crash when one of the fire trucks ran over it on the way to the crash scene."

Jack gazed out into space, blinking his eyes and furrowing his brow, then returned to stare at Dan. "What are you saying, Dan?"

"What I'm saying Jack, is that you were driving a dead pony, it was going to happen, and you just happened to be there at the wrong time. You were only along for the ride, Jack, and it wasn't a good one."

Dan was now standing in front of Jack, looking down at his seated friend, his right hand resting on Jack's shoulder. Jack lowered his head and just stared down at the cabin sole.

"You know, Scrap, this is pretty heavy stuff that I just hit you with, but I had to tell you as soon as I thought that it was safe to do so. It's going to take a while for all this to sink in, so I'm going to go for my daily jog and leave you alone for awhile. We can talk more when I get back. Okay? Okay, Jack?"

Jack looked up at his friend with a faraway look in his eyes and slowly nodded, then nodded again. Dan went down the ladder, changed clothes in the mast shed, and jogged slowly up the Town Landing road. He headed toward the South Freeport Cemetery, per Jack's suggested route. When he returned, he took a shower in the mast shed and then headed back to *Raccoon*. He climbed the ladder once again and sat down across from Jack, who was sitting in the same place as when Dan had left. They sat together in silence for about three minutes.

"Tell me about the rudder, Boo," Jack began.

"Well, interestingly enough, Baker just 'happened' to come out with some information that led the FAA to issue a mandatory Airworthiness Directive on the rudder system exactly six months after the crash, which was two months after the preliminary NTSB findings came out—the ones blaming you *completely* for the accident. It turns out that the airplane you were flying, and all Baker Mercurys out there, for that matter, had a faulty design in the rudder system. They still don't know what sets them off, but the servo- motor would suddenly command a rudder movement in the completely opposite direction. You put in right rudder, and it goes completely 'hard over' to a full-blown left rudder position. So on sixty-six, you put in some *right* rudder, and it went full *left*! Your left wing went down instantly, it dug in, and you cartwheeled. At that point in the approach, there was nothing, absolutely nothing that you could've done. I feel certain that the NTSB findings will be overturned and you will be exonerated. Consequently, you can have your FAA Air Transport Pilot rating reinstated, subsequent a successful first-class physical exam if you feel like flying again. Jack—and this is so important that I'm going to say it very slowly—it wasn't your fault. *It wasn't your fault*!"

Dan had thought a lot about this moment and hadn't been sure what kind of reaction he would get when he told his friend the good news. Would he get angry? Would he be mad? Would he cry? Would he be ecstatic? He was therefore slightly confused when there was no reaction whatsoever—Jack just continued to silently sit there with a blank look on his face, looking off into space.

* * *

Wednesday, January 11, 1989

Attorney Steven Lattimer was sitting in the waiting room of the Legal Affairs office at Baker Aircraft and Engineering Company at their corporate headquarters in San Diego. He had an appointment scheduled for ten o'clock, which was an hour and thirty minutes ago.

A secretary stepped into the room. "Mr. Lattimer?"

"Yes?"

"Mr. Waite will see you now."

Steven stood up. "Is it normal to wait this long for a scheduled meeting?" he asked.

"Mr. Waite is a very, very busy man."

"I see."

The secretary opened the door to the office, and he followed her in as she announced his presence. She then turned around and closed the door behind her as she left. A couple of things are out of order, Steven thought to himself as he stood there in the middle of the room. First of all, it was highly unusual and unprofessional for a scheduled meeting to be delayed by this much without so much as an explanation, a rescheduling, or an apology. And secondly, his appointment was to meet with a one Mr. Parker Waite, not an apparent tribunal of lawyers, all strategically perched behind a long formal table, in front of which was a lone wooden chair that had no arm rests. No one rose to greet him, no one extended his hand. His greeting consisted of "Please sit down, Mr. Lattimer." The interrogation will now begin, he mused to himself. He knew how this meeting was going to go, and inwardly he welcomed it because it meant that the gloves were now officially off.

"Let me get right to the point, Mr. Lattimer. We don't want to waste your time," Waite began.

Don't want to waste my time? Really? Steven laughed to himself.

"We have received your proposal and have given it our utmost attention and consideration. Unfortunately, our findings are that your request is completely unacceptable."

There's a surprise, Steven thought silently.

"It is not Baker Aircraft's fault that the NTSB found your client responsible for the accident, nor is it our fault that the FAA chose to revoke his license, which prevented him from flying again. And Trans Ocean Airlines has every right to hire and fire employees at their company pursuant to their behavior. As for suggesting and fabricating this story of a cover-up by our company, you have no proof, only pieces of paper that could be manufactured in any number of ways. Anonymous tips and rumors carry very little weight in the legal world—you should be aware of that, Mr. Lattimer. So in essence, we really don't have anything more to talk about, don't you agree?"

Steven leaned forward in his "interrogation" chair, his right index finger and his thumb now cradling his chin. "Mr. Waite, you leave me very little choice. If you want to be unprofessional and rude to me, as you have succeeded in doing so far, great! Bring it on! I can play rough, too. Before I walked into your cozy little nook here, I was proposing only that Baker Aircraft take responsibility for my client losing his job and his profession and cover his loss of paychecks for the past seventeen years. You know that it was not his fault. You know that it was a malfunction of the Mercury's rudder system. You hid this intentionally, and you also withheld information related to a federal investigation that not only affected its findings and conclusions, but affected the safety of the flying public—and that's not just here in the U.S., for, as you know, Mercurys are flying all over the world. No, your arrogant attitude and your egregious behavior have just changed my client's demands. We now want not only his lost paychecks, but a letter of disclosure, a formal apology, and damages in the amount of ten million dollars for mental cruelty—for hanging my client out to dry, forcing him to live a life of hell ever since Christmas Eve, 1969, with the lives of one hundred forty-four people hanging around his neck and buried in his heart and soul. I look forward to the trial—and there *will* be one. I must go now," he said, standing up and gathering his papers into his briefcase. "But I will leave you with one name, and you might want to write this down. The name is Walter Dawson. He's a previous employee of Baker and was the assistant manager to the project head engineer, Jasper Sneed."

Steven stopped halfway to the door and turned around. "Oh, and one more thing," he continued, eyes flashing. "While you're busy checking things out, you might want to look up Lattimer and Howland, Attorneys at Law in Wellesley, Massachusetts, and peruse our gone-to-trial record—it might be interesting to you. And by the way, I only take cases that I believe very strongly in, and in this case, well...good day, gentlemen."

* * *

Seven days later, the interphone buzzer sounded on Steven Lattimer's desk. He pushed the button. "Yes, Penny?"

"There is a Mr. Waite from Baker Aircraft on the line—do you wish to speak with him?"

"Sure, put him on."

In a few seconds a familiar voice was on the line. "Mr. Lattimer, this is Parker Waite, Baker Aircraft. We met about a week ago here in San Diego."

"Yes, Mr. Waite, I remember you well."

"Well, first of all, may I call you Steven?"

"I don't mind."

"I have to be perfectly candid here, Steven. I find that I'm personally and professionally embarrassed as a result of our first meeting."

"Really?" Steven said, leaning back in his chair.

"Steven, when you left the office after our meeting, we were perplexed. The four of us all thought that you appeared very upset when you first entered the room. We called our secretary in after you left and asked if she could shed any light on our perception. It was then that we realized that we had unintentionally left you hanging for an hour and a half in the waiting room for our scheduled appointment. Sparing you the details, we screwed up! Royally! Our appointment calendar was changed weeks before you arrived, and the ball was dropped because you were never notified. The appointment secretary stated that she was planning to call you or leave a message on your machine to that effect, but when I asked her if she actually did, she admitted that she was distracted and never followed up on it. I think that I would be steaming, too, if I had flown all the way from Boston to LA and then to San Diego and that had happened to me. Do you have some time for me right now, or shall I call back later?"

"No, I have about a half an hour before I have to leave," he replied, glancing at the regulator clock hanging on the office wall.

"Good. Well, I didn't call just to set the record straight—I called because I feel that we have some very important items to discuss. And I'm not going to ask you to come all the way out to San Diego again, so I am offering to fly to Boston for a face-to-face meeting, and at your convenience, of course."

Steven sighed. "I think that we both know where the other stands, unless there is some new revelation—"

"Actually there is, Steven, actually there is."

"Okay, I'll bite. What's new?"

"Well, I'm going to be candid with you here, Steven, and I'm not going to withhold any information from you, even if my 'lawyer' side thinks that it might be dangerous or disadvantageous for me to do so. On your suggestion, we talked to our hydraulics project manager, a Mr. Sneed, who is also the division manager in the flight control and engineering department. We asked him if he had worked on the data retrieval of the flight data recorder that the National Transportation Safety Board originally sent to us. He said yes, that he and his assistant manager had retrieved all the data that they could from the damaged box. When queried about rudder and aileron data, his response was that the only control surface activity that the FDR recorded was the elevator and that appeared as normal activity—the rudder and aileron data was missing. When I mentioned that reports had surfaced concerning a 'hard over' rudder reversal that might have caused the accident, he said, and these are his words, that it was 'preposterous, totally absurd,' and he then walked away."

Mr. Waite paused, but Steven remained silent. "I thought that quite odd—an overreaction by any measure. You know, Steven, when you ask your kid a question and you get an answer and you just know that he's not telling the truth? Well, there was just something about the way he answered the question that sent me in another direction. We tried contacting his assistant, who was also involved with the FDR data retrieval project, the fellow that you had mentioned when you were in our office. We discovered that he resigned from Baker about sixteen years ago, and we had trouble trying to locate him. Anyway, an associate of mine came to me one day recently with an idea. Baker Aerospace has a data research and storage facility in Long Beach. Dealing with so much technical information that is so crucial to our design and engineering departments and, not the least, to our company's future, Baker began an information duplication process for almost everything that we create. I sent one of my assistants over there, and you know what he found?"

Steven was now sitting erect in his chair. "No, what did he find?"

"He found the original FDR printout—and that printout displayed all three control service inputs, the elevator, the ailerons, and most importantly, the *rudder*."

Steven couldn't believe what he was hearing. Was this guy truly giving him everything he needed, and more?

"Mr. Sneed had covered up important information that could be personally damaging to his career and also to Baker Aerospace. We believe that he acted alone. His assistant, the Dawson fellow, was finally contacted and confirmed what you and we had suspected. To his credit, Mr. Dawson is on record urging divulgence of the FDR data but was overridden by his superior, Sneed. It is because of Mr. Dawson that we have, or will have, closure on this very troubling chapter at Baker. I know, Mr. Lattimer, Steven, that you have done your due diligence concerning Baker, and I have no doubt that you uncovered what has been evident for the past sixty-five years—that we have been a leader in our chosen field, in aviation, in our community, and in labor-management relations. The company has always been a family, and that is why this is so disturbing. I gave you a lot of sensitive information just now, Steven, information that you could easily crucify us with, but I hope that you and your client will see the true spectrum of what happened and that we can come to a settlement without having to go to court."

Steven was stunned, his mouth hanging open. "Parker, I have to tell you, I've been practicing law for over thirty-five years, and this is truly the most bizarre and unique case that I have ever seen. I have a question for you—what motivated Dawson to come out with this evidence against his boss? It sure looks to me like a one-way ticket to getting fired."

"Well, you are partially correct on that, because he *was* fired, and fired on trumped-up charges. However, and this might interest you, he was fired way back in 1970!"

"He was fired eighteen years ago and is only *now* coming forward with this? Why?"

"Well, it appears, and this is only hearsay, it appears that there was a nasty divorce at one time."

"So?"

"Well, he didn't take it very well and hired a detective to check on his ex-wife, albeit many years later."

"And?" Steven's eyebrows were rising.

"She was having an affair with none other than his boss at Baker, Sneed—make that his ex-boss, because he had been fired six months prior!"

"I thought you said that he had resigned?"

"Well, that was the story that we were originally given, and that was from his ex-boss."

"So, what you're saying is that the truth probably wouldn't have come out at all but for the actions of a wayward wife?"

"It appears that way."

Steven shook his head. "I'll say it again—this is the most bizarre case that I've ever seen!"

"Well, that's the background, Steven, and I've told you all this sensitive information in hopes that you'll see Baker's side of the story and that we can come to an amicable settlement."

"Parker, it sure has changed the battlefield, I would say. So, what are you proposing in return for my client?"

* * *

A meeting was quickly arranged. Jack listened intensely as Steven relayed the new facts in the case.

"You know, Steven," Jack began, "the details of this thing changes my feelings about it."

"Continue," Steven urged.

"I'm happy just getting my back paychecks. I'm not a vindictive person—I don't need any 'damages' money, and I don't need a letter of apology. The rest of the company didn't know anything about this, so let's just settle for the lost income."

"Are you sure?"

"Yes, very sure."

"Jack, then there's the subject of Jasper Sneed—he's the one who is culpable. Baker's attorney, Waite, suggested to me that they would gladly testify on our behalf if we went after him for damages. What you think about that?"

"Steven, I don't take it personally what this guy did. He's a pretty poor excuse for a man, I would say, but I can see why he did it. I don't like it, but, hey, life's not fair sometimes. But you're right, we do hold a trump card here." Jack paused. "I was just thinking...."

Steven looked up. "Yes?"

"That Sneed guy really is a prick, isn't he? Not because of what he did to me—hell, he didn't even know who I was—but to his assistant, that Dawson guy. First he gets him fired on a made-up charge, and then he steals his wife! I mean, that shouldn't go unpunished, do you think? And if Dawson hadn't come forward, I would still be in my hellhole. So, what do you think about contacting Dawson and seeing if he would have any interest in suing that guy, Sneed? We might be able to do Dawson a favor, you know? He certainly has done one for me."

"You sure, Jack?"

Jack thought for a minute. "Yeah, Steven, I'm sure."

"Okay. Now let's get back to our next agenda—Trans Ocean. Jack, the company you knew seventeen years ago isn't the same company now."

"How do you mean?"

"Well, you generally described Trans Ocean as a pioneer airline that forged a lot of new routes, innovations, and aviation milestones over the years. That part, its history, hasn't changed. But you also indicated that the traditions and employee-friendly management were part of its ethos, its culture, going all the way back to when the company was founded by a group of barnstorming World War I pilots. That's not what I found when I talked with their human resources department recently."

"Well, what *did* you find?"

"There appears to be a lot of young MBAs in management now, and the so-called 'bean counter' philosophy prevails. You've been out of aviation for good while, Jack, and I have to tell you the landscape has changed, and has changed dramatically."

"Like how? How has it changed?"

"Well, let me tell you about the education that I received when I spoke with Trans Ocean."

"Your education? What do you mean, 'education'?"

"Well, this twenty-year-old twerp—maybe he was thirty at the oldest—proceeded to tell me the ABC's of airline management. I'm sixty-three and halfway intelligent—no comment, please—but he treated me like I was an idiot. And the reason that I'm going into so much detail is because I want to show you why I think that we have a battle on our hands trying to get your job back. Anyway this kid, a Mr. Monroe, spelled it out for me in very basic terms—the deregulation act of 1978 and how it changed the playing field. He said that the law deregulated the airlines' fare structure, but it did not deregulate labor costs. And now everything, and I mean everything, every aspect of costs, has to be put through a test to see if it's worth it. If it's not a surefire profit enhancer or at least a breakeven one, they won't even touch it."

Steven peered at Jack, waiting for the information to sink in before continuing. "When I said that you wanted your job back, Mr. Monroe sounded surprised and asked why. I said because you were robbed of your profession and have spent years in hell, feeling guilty for something that you didn't do, and that you deserve to get your job back now. And then the mantra of Baker Aerospace reared its ugly head again: 'We weren't the NTSB, we weren't the FAA, and we had no choice. Besides, it's very expensive to train a pilot, and who knows if he can still fly, and furthermore, after all the expensive training, we'd only have his services for less than a year—so it's completely absurd, no way.' I asked him to talk to his superiors, that we were not going to go away. I said that reconsideration is the good-faith response to my request that I expected. I have a lot of thinking and a ton of research to do, like precedents and stuff like that, but I think that I might just have an idea that could give us some ammo in the standoff." Steven took a breath and looked at Jack. "You still with me, pal?"

"Yeah, I'm still with you, Steven. It's just kind of sad, like losing an old friend."

"I know, Jack. And I'm sorry. You've had more than your share of disappointments. But look at it this way—you can't change the way it is, but they can't take the good times and the friends and memories away from you. You just have to press on. I know you—you won't quit, and we'll win. I really believe that we'll win, Jack, you'll get your job back, and you'll have the last laugh. And then you will fly off into the sunset. You wait and see, my friend, you just wait and see."

* * *

It was a few days later when Steven Lattimer received a call directly from Trans Ocean Airlines.

"Mr. Lattimer," the caller began, "this is Roger Jamieson, legal counsel for Trans Ocean Airlines. You recently spoke with Lester Monroe, our Vice President of Human Resources."

"Yes, I recall speaking with Mr. Monroe. How can I help you, Mr. Jamieson?"

"Your request was passed on to me. We have reconsidered all the pertinent facts in the case; we had our top-level managers for operations, legal affairs, and the executive office all meet to discuss this rather unique situation concerning your client, Jack Rheinstrom. And I must be candid with you, Mr. Lattimer, we have genuine sympathy concerning Captain Rheinstrom's saga, and we don't want this to turn into a fight in the public arena—God knows he's suffered enough. So as a goodwill gesture, we're offering to, assuming he can pass the company physical and interview, we're offering to welcome Captain Rheinstrom back to his 'family' here at Trans Ocean so that he can finish his career here and segue into this well-earned retirement."

Steven heard the omission and instantly responded. "I noticed that you didn't mention anything about training or returning to flight status."

"No—that would be impossible. Captain Rheinstrom will be benched."

"And what exactly does 'benched' mean?"

"That means that we will pay him his salary based on the equipment he can hold according to his seniority—and that, specifically, is the highest-paid position there is at Trans Ocean, the Boeing 747. But as far as returning to flying, no, that is not in our offer, which we think is more than fair."

Steven bristled. "Well, Mr. Jamieson, thank you for your call and for your offer. I will pass it on to my client, but to be sure here, he won't be satisfied, nor will I, until he returns to active flight status, however short that might be."

Mr. Jamieson seemed to remain unmoved. "Well, that's all we feel that we can offer Captain Rheinstrom. If you have any more questions, my extension is thirty-seven hundred. It's been nice talking to you, Mr. Lattimer."

"And to you, too," he replied as he put down the receiver and then immediately picked it up again, dialing Jack's phone number.

* * *

The next time Steven Lattimer talked with Mr. Jamieson, almost two weeks had passed, and he had only become more determined than ever to help Jack get his life back. By the time he got Mr. Jamieson on the line, he was ready to get right to the point.

"Good morning to you, Mr. Lattimer. What's on your mind?"

"In my last letter to you, Mr. Jamieson, I stated that my client feels that he has every right, if qualified, to resume his career in the cockpit, albeit short in duration. You have stated that Trans Ocean does not agree. I understand your position but don't agree with it. Therefore, if we cannot achieve the desired outcome amicably, then we will pursue it through the legal process. I would like to interview your vice president of aircraft maintenance. Dun & Bradstreet lists a Mr. Steve Barlow—is he the current VP?"

"And why do you want to speak to him?"

"Just to ascertain some relevant facts."

"This is not a trial, Mr. Lattimer. I find this very unusual. You are being decidedly vague and mysterious, and I wish that you would just get to the point," Jamieson said in an irritated tone.

"I have documented proof in my possession that Baker Aerospace sent your Trans Ocean's engineering and maintenance division an SAIB concerning the rudder system on all Baker Mercurys. There were actually two SAIBs sent to you via the FAA, one in December 1968 and one in July 1969. Both bulletins were sent well before the Boston Christmas Eve crash in '69. I would like to talk to Mr. Barlow and see if Trans Ocean, in fact, received the notices and if they acted upon them, and if they did not, then why not?"

"And just what exactly is an SAIB?" Jameison demanded.

"A Special Airworthiness Information Bulletin."

An awkward silence lasted for about five seconds before Jamieson continued. "And what is your source for this information that you are alleging?" he asked.

"The FOIA."

"The FOIA?" asked Jamieson. "What's that?"

"The Freedom of Information Act, that's what!"

Another pause. "Mr. Lattimer, I'm going to have to call you back."

CHAPTER EIGHT

It was a beautiful June day when Jack Rheinstrom entered the Trans Ocean Airlines Headquarters in Miami and rode the elevator to the sixth floor. When he found room 6B, he walked in and sat down on a swivel seat behind one of the thirty-foot long tables, choosing the one in the last row. He was fifteen minutes early, the first one to arrive that Monday morning, and as he looked around, he suddenly remembered—this was the very same room that he had been in for his first ever ground-school class as a new hire. And then it all came back to him, his career in a nutshell. He quizzically shook his head slowly, took a sip from the white Styrofoam coffee cup that he had brought with him, and then opened his new notebook to the first page.

The other students eventually showed up, and class officially began. During the first fifteen minutes of the ground school, the syllabus was explained and handouts covering the various Boeing 747 systems were distributed to the class of ten. Present were four captains, three first officers—copilots—and three second officers—flight engineers. A few things had changed over the years, but basically the entire course was just a review for Jack, since he had attended the very same course when he was a copilot back in the sixties. But again, that was more than twenty years ago.

It was an odd feeling though for Jack—two weeks into the course, he still didn't recognize one face in the cafeteria, where all the students and instructor personnel met for lunch. It was kind of like transferring high schools in the twelfth grade—no one knows you and vice versa. But Jack was just happy to be there and decided not to dwell on the past.

* * *

July 21, 1989 was a big day for Jack Rheinstrom—it was simulator ride number 7, his check ride. He had gone through the first six sims with the same copilot and they worked well together, which pleased Jack. But there would be extra pressure put on him today. Not only was the FAA going to be present as his ultimate evaluating observer, but the FAA was also going to be administering a check ride to the Trans Ocean candidate to be an FAA check airman designee. This aspiring designee would be giving Jack his actual official check ride. Jack wondered to himself if this seeming double jeopardy was a coincidence or just another "gift" from the new Trans Ocean. It doesn't matter, he thought. It is what it is.

John Battagliola was having an early lunch in the cafeteria. He sat in his chair over in the corner because he wanted some time alone, to think and plan his upcoming week in Miami working in the training department. He jotted down some notes, looked at his watch, and stood up to leave, dropping off his cafeteria tray on the stack on his way out. He walked outside across the campus to the Hartley Training Building and into the scheduling office. "Hey, Tammy, how are you?" John said with a smile, standing in front of the 747 simulator scheduler.

"Hey, Johnny B, good to see you again! Looks like you'll be here with us for a week—cool! I got a call from Estophan White that he wants to see you in his office before the sim. Looks like you'll have plenty of time for that."

"Wants to see *me*? Sounds ominous."

He left the scheduling office and climbed the stairs to the second floor, exchanging greetings with other instructors that he had known and had worked with over the years in the training department. He walked down the hall and stood by the entrance door of the B-747 fleet manager's office. He could hear Captain White inside, on the phone, so he stayed out of view and waited. After five minutes, the conversation ended and John moved forward a few feet so that he would become visible.

"Hey, John," Captain White announced, "come on in. Hope that you haven't been waiting long—I didn't see you out there until just now. Take a seat." He gestured to a couch in the corner of the office. "I wanted to talk to you about your check ride tonight—the one that you'll be giving and the one that you'll be getting. There are a lot of firsts here tonight. The FAA guy, Kevin McCann, was just assigned to us as our new principal operating inspector. As you've probably heard, the previous inspector just retired, so I'm hoping to get off on the right foot with his replacement. You should know that you come highly recommended! But complicating the check ride tonight is the captain that you'll be evaluating. His name is Jack Rheinstrom—do you know him?"

John's eyes widened. "Yes, I sure do! I was his copilot for his first captain's check ride—has to be more than twenty-five years ago. I also know that he was the captain on the Christmas Eve crash."

"Yes, and he's been out of the cockpit, 'off the property,' for twenty years now. It was a messy episode for the company, but now he's back and wants to return to the cockpit and ride out the next six or so months until his retirement at age sixty. So, he's presently a very high-profile pilot, for not only us, but for the FAA, too. I've gone over his training records and talked to the instructor who took him through the first six rides, but this is different today—there will be a lot of pressure, not only on him, but on you."

"Me?" John asked.

"Yes, you, John. Look, all I'm saying is just do your evaluating job as you have in the past—don't do anything special. What I mean is that I don't want you to give him any extra slack because you know him and maybe feel sorry for him, and on the other hand, don't be too hard on him because the FAA is looking at you and him."

"I see your concern, Captain White. The rumor mill has been working overtime the past few months with Rheinstrom stories, but I will be fair and I will be consistent. It's really quite straightforward what he has to do for a successful ride, and I won't get cute with any ad lib surprises."

"Good, you're saying all the right things. And one other thing—please come up and see me as soon as the ride is over. I'll be eager to know your impressions. Well, now I'm off for lunch. Good luck. I'll see you later."

They both stood up and shook hands with Captain White following John out the door. The captain's rating ride was scheduled for an 11:30 a.m. "show" in the briefing room and then a 12:30 p.m. "go" for the simulator phase. The first two hours would be Jack's check ride, then a fifteen-minute break, and then the second half would be the first officer's turn.

Jack was the first to show up—he was early, as he always was. Then, first officer Bryan Carpenter walked into the room, followed shortly by the company's pilot designee candidate.

"Batman!" Jack exclaimed with relief as he stood up, finally recognizing someone.

"Jack, I saw your name on the schedule—boy, it's good to see you!" The two stood in front of the blackboard, vigorously shaking hands and smiling.

"John, do you remember the last time we flew with each other, here in Miami? It seems like just yesterday, but it was 1965, my initial captain check ride—and now here you are, an instructor on the '74. Wow, time flies, doesn't it? Say, do you know the fed who'll be watching the both of us tonight?"

"No, I don't know him, yet. His name is Kevin McCann and he's new, at least to Trans Ocean as a POI, so there aren't any real reports on him. We'll see." Just then, POI McCann walked into the room and the official check ride began.

* * *

Check airman John Battagliola finished his debriefing in the presence of the FAA observer, signed the necessary paperwork, and went upstairs to talk to Captain White, who was eagerly awaiting his report.

John sat down on the couch in the corner and leaned forward. "Well, Captain White, do you want the good news first or the bad news?"

Captain White thought for a few seconds. "How bad was it?" he burst out. "All right, give me the bad news first."

"Well, the second officer got a 'down.'"

"Continue."

"The first officer did okay and he passed."

"Yes."

"And Jack Rheinstrom...." John began.

"Yes?"

"You may know," John went on, "that Rheinstrom had the reputation, and I think totally deserved, of being one of the most professional and consummate pilots around. That being said, I can't believe that he hasn't flown for twenty years. You know how we teach our new captains that it's no longer enough to be a team member, that now they have to be the quarterback, too? Well, tonight this guy was not only the quarterback, but he was the linebacker and the tight end, too. And he did it all with a certain amount of class. I told you that the second officer busted his ride tonight. I looked at his training folder—solid past performance, no flags. I think that he just got spooked by the fed being there. We'll just give him another training ride with a recheck at the end. But what significantly happened tonight was that on two separate emergencies, one an engine fire and the other an electrical fire, the second officer skipped an item, and a very important one, on the checklist that he was reading. Rheinstrom, in a very calm and cool way, realized this and mentioned that maybe they should just go back over the checklist again and make sure that they hadn't missed anything. The omissions were not lost on the FAA inspector, because I noticed that he was taking notes on the procedure even before Rheinstrom corrected it. Anyway, while Rheinstrom was turned around in his seat, working the electrical emergency with the engineer, the first officer, who was the primary pilot flying the airplane, was given directions by ATC to hold on a radial of the Miami VOR. Well, anyway, the first officer turned *left* to enter the hold, which Rheinstrom immediately noticed, and he had him correct the turn to the standard right-hand pattern. So, all in all, complete situational awareness. Any worries that the company has about Rheinstrom losing it after all these years couldn't be farther from the truth."

Captain White nodded. "Great news, John. I will pass this on upstairs, and I guess we'll just have scheduling set him up for the last phase, his Initial Operating Experience. Oh, and one last thing—what is your take on our new FAA inspector, McCann?"

"Well, he seemed like a nice enough guy. He didn't talk too much in the debriefing. I think that he'll be okay."

"Good. Anyway, thanks for the details and your thoughts. And welcome aboard, Check Airman Designee Battagliola!" They both stood and shook hands, after which John left the office to go back to find Jack in the cafeteria.

* * *

It was a beautiful July afternoon in Boston, with temperatures in the seventies. The drive into the city on Route 93 South through the Callahan Tunnel to Boston Logan Airport was surprisingly uneventful. Boston always seems to have more than its fair share of traffic, so to be prudent, you have to always add extra time for the "somethings" that would almost always occur, and Jack Rheinstrom had. Just before he turned off the expressway at the Callahan Tunnel exit, he looked to his left and could see the Bunker Hill Monument, the obelisk commemorating the famous battle of the Revolutionary War, the white oilcan spire of the North Church of "one if by land" fame, and the old stone buildings of the Charlestown Navy Yard. "Old Ironsides," the *USS Constitution,* was sitting at her berth, her three masts pointing majestically upward, and just beyond her, Jack could see many groupings of small sailboats at play with the zephyrs blowing in Boston's Inner Harbor. It looked like a postcard.

His arrival was rather early, but that was the plan. So after finding a parking spot in the employee's lot, he got out of his blue-and-white 1970 Land Rover, picked up his suitcase, and walked over to the waiting shelter for the employee bus. He put his suitcase down and took a slow, deep breath of the warm summer air, noticing the strong hint of salt water and fish. Ah, the Atlantic, he thought, exhaling completely and smiling to himself. He changed his mind and decided not to wait. He picked his suitcase up again and started the twenty-five-minute walk to the terminal.

Boston's airfield was started in 1923 as a fifteen-hundred-foot cinder runway built by the U.S. Army on 189 acres of tidal flats. The first commercial airline service began four years later, between Boston and New York. Almost four thousand acres of land were reclaimed from Boston Harbor, and in 1941 it officially became General Edward Lawrence Logan Airport.

Jack Rheinstrom had walked this route many times during the past thirty-three years. But this time, it was different—he was fifty-nine years old now, and with only four more months to go until his mandatory retirement, his career was coming to an end. However, he didn't see it that way, but was undecided about how he really felt inside. He had become a very pensive, inward, and complex man these past twenty years. But he did know one thing for sure—that the man he had *become* over the years since the crash was not the man that he *really was*. He now saw the possibility of a new beginning, one that could possibly reset his life. For once in a very long time, he was thinking of himself and not about the 132 people who died that night, the 69 men, the 53 women, and the 10 children who had appeared in his dreams so many times.

The firehouse near the Trans Ocean terminal had been blocking his view of runway three three left, but as he walked a little farther, it was now in full view. He watched as an Air France 747 was touching down, its dangling landing gear probing the air below, trying to find the concrete that was that flight's destiny. He stopped and gazed but did not put his suitcase down. He saw an airplane that was landing and that was it. He didn't see billowing smoke, he didn't see twisted metal and debris, or lifeless or writhing bodies—no, he didn't see any of those today. He watched as the nose gear was lowered to the waiting tarmac, he watched as the spoilers sprang up on the wings, he heard the engines roar into reverse, and then he continued his walk. Inside the terminal, he walked by the luggage carousels to the lost baggage office and then to the white security door waiting just beyond.

He sighed as he struggled to find the right combination for the door. "Excuse me," he said to the agent behind the counter, holding out his employee ID badge for inspection, "could you give me the combo for the security door? My numbers aren't working."

As there were two passengers inside the office looking over the mass of lost bags for their own, the agent scribbled the numbers on a small memo pad and handed it to him.

"Here, Captain, and have a safe flight."

Jack smiled and thanked her, then returned to the white door. As he punched in the correct numbers and opened the door, he looked behind him before entering the hallway. He closed the door slowly to make sure that it locked securely and turned to his left to head for the bag room, a corral that held all of the pilots' flight kits, aka brain bags. These small, boxlike black briefcases carried important reference material necessary for a safe flight. In addition to the Jepps—Jeppesen Publishing Company's editions of high and low altitude navigation charts, detailed information about each airport, and approach charts used to navigate precisely to the runway in poor visibility—there was a book for Federal Aviation Regulations, company procedures and regulations, and an airplane specific operations manual, describing in detail, normal, abnormal, and emergency operations. Also in the brain bag was a toolkit, a hand-manipulated computer, earphones, pencils, and more. They tended to be heavy, especially if you were walking very far.

Before entering the flight planning room, Jack stopped off at the mailroom and checked his pigeonhole mailbox, removing and sorting the dozen or more different pieces of paper. After reviewing the Jepp revisions, he realized that they didn't affect either Logan or Charles de Gaulle airport in Paris, so he could attend to them later. And he didn't care about the upcoming parking lot repaving or the change in location for the post-flight drug testing. There was also a large brown manila envelope that was sealed via a piece of red string that wound around a button on the front of the envelope. It was a company mail envelope, and it had seen many stops along the way: Los Angeles, Atlanta, Miami, San Francisco, Honolulu, and New York, and it had just now arrived at Boston.

Hmm, Jack thought as he propped his right leg up on top of his brain bag and opened the envelope. There were two letter envelopes inside. He reached in and pulled out the first one. It was addressed to Jack Rheinstrom, C/O Trans Ocean Airlines, JFK International Airport, New York, New York. It had a return address printed on it: Bill Bausch, 15 Winthrop St., Newton, MA 02458. He was slightly curious as to who this unfamiliar person might be and why he was writing to him until he saw at the bottom left of the envelope—*Flight 66, seat 22A.*

Jack felt his heart go *thump* and was suddenly terrified to open the envelope. He put his leg back on the floor and walked the fifty or so steps it took to reach the men's room down the hall. He walked into the largest stall and locked the door behind him. He stared at the name, then stared at the seat number—22A. He didn't recognize the name from the class-action suit filed against him and the airline; that had only contained six names, exactly one half of the number of the actual survivors. He could feel his heart pounding—in fact, he could actually *hear* it. He knew, he always knew, that this moment would come someday. He wondered what Bill Bausch had looked like before the flight, and what he looked like now. Had he actually looked him in the eye when greeting the passengers during the boarding process that day, which he always made a point to do? *Welcome, it's good to have you on board; Good afternoon, ladies, hope you enjoy the flight; Hi there, Pardner, what grade are you in?* On arrival, after engine shutdown, he would scramble out of his left seat to assume his pastor-like, post-sermon position at the entrance to the cockpit door, telling the first officer and flight engineer to finish the engine-shutdown checklist without him.

Who is Bill Bausch, and why is he writing to me? Why now? Perspiration beads began to appear on Jack's brow; he was suddenly very warm. He pulled out a white handkerchief from his back pocket, took off his hat, hung it on the stall door, and patted his forehead dry. Seat 22A—that was a window seat on the left side of the Mercury, just aft of the wing where the fuselage had its main fracture before the fire erupted. He couldn't go back and revisit the grisly details of that night because his memory was blank from the last part of the approach to the heavily drugged days at the burn center at Mass General. Well, he thought, here goes. He pulled out his red Swiss Army knife and slit the envelope open. The letter was handwritten and had the unique signature of a fountain pen.

Dear Captain Rheinstrom, it began, *I had pretty much put December 24, 1969 behind me. I really hadn't thought about it for probably ten years—until I watched Channel 5 news the other night and saw the piece about the Christmas Eve crash and the report of you returning to work and the cockpit after two decades away. From a personal point of view, that night changed my life, but not as you might have first thought. It was not in a negative way, but rather in a positive one. My life at that time was all about me, all about making money, all about getting ahead no matter who got hurt; "damn the torpedoes," you know. I don't know why, but I was lucky that night. Not only was I not severely injured, but I didn't lose any loved ones or friends. After a few weeks, I returned to work in the financial sector, but not for long. Something was wrong, something was out of whack, something didn't taste or smell right. Long story short—I returned to school, received a graduate degree in education, and am now a counselor for emotionally challenged kids in a large New England school system. I really don't know why I am writing to you about this—I guess that I just share a happenstance bond with you through that night. I don't know your particulars, I just wish you well. Sincerely, Bill Bausch, Newton, Massachusetts*

Well, that was not what Jack had been anticipating when he first opened the letter. His angst subsided, the perspiration began to evaporate, and he no longer felt overheated. His heartbeat returned to normal. He glanced down at his watch and realized he should head over to flight planning. Deciding to read the other letter later, he slipped the papers back into the large envelope, grabbed his hat from the hook on the door, and left the men's room.

He was walking down the hall, still reeling from the surprise letter, when he heard a female voice behind him. "Scrappy?" the voice asked quizzically.

They both stopped. It had been a period of twenty years, but Jack would know that voice anywhere. He turned around to see Laurie Mills with wide eyes and outstretched arms twenty feet away and closing fast. They were alone in the hall, but it wouldn't have mattered to either of the two old friends if they had been on a subway or in a crowded theater.

They pulled apart from their embrace a little, and then both slowly shook their heads, beaming. They both began talking at once.

"Scrappy, I—"

"Laurie, I…so much to say, so much to say." He paused and looked at her warmly. "You're not on flight thirty-eight, are you?"

"Yes, yes, are you?"

"I sure am. So, tomorrow in Paris, we'll catch up, or shall I say, begin to catch up. Twenty years is a long time." A sense of serenity, of natural calm, had arisen in both their hearts. They had once shared a very special bond for many, many years. But that had been lost by a stroke of Providence. Now, it had been unexpectedly rekindled.

"What to say? I still can't believe it. Laurie, I don't have much time right now—I'm getting ready for my IOE with a check airman. His name's Jerry Black. Do you know him?" Jack asked.

"Oh, do you mean Johnny Love? Yes, he's God's gift to women, didn't you know?

What do you mean IOE? Are you checking out in a new plane?"

"Laurie, it's a long story that I'll share with you later; let's just say that I haven't flown in a while. Johnny Love, huh? Interesting."

Again, another smile, another slow shaking of heads, and then they both turned around and went to their destinations on opposite ends of the building.

* * *

Behind a huge desk almost the size of a ping-pong table stood Mike Smith, flight planner. He was leaning over the table working with a long straight edge, about a yardstick long, and was marking navigational tracks on the Atlantic Oceanic chart. When he finished the plots, he colored the lines with magic markers of red, yellow, and green, and then assigned a name to each—Alpha, Bravo, and Charlie, in that order, depicting them as *A, B,* and *C* on the actual chart. He was the only one in the room at that time and looked up as Jack Rheinstrom walked in.

"Captain Rheinstrom," he exclaimed as he rose from the table.

"Mike Smith!" came the retort. They had last spoken to each other on Christmas Eve, when Flight 66 was inbound; *in range* was the airline term. They had been talking on the company radio frequency, where the details of the flight's arrival were being discussed—ETA, ramp conditions, gate number, wheelchairs, and any special requests. Mike and other coworkers at Logan had tried to visit Jack when he was at Mass General, but burn victims are not usually allowed visitors, and anyway, Jack didn't remember the first few weeks that he was there at all.

"I was so surprised and happy when I heard that you were coming back. Silly question, but how you been, Jack?"

"I'm doing okay, Mike, thanks. Tonight is part of my IOE, and I get my check ride on the leg coming back from a second Paris trip later. How have you been? How's Debbie?"

"Oh, she's fine. She's a stew—, uh, excuse me, flight attendant with Pan Am now out of Kennedy. She flies international, and the commute isn't too bad."

"Good, glad to hear it. My regards, of course. I could never figure out what a beautiful woman like that was doing with a railroad man like you! And, on top of that, one from Amherst."

"Very funny! I see that your sense of humor hasn't changed very much. But, hey, welcome back—we can use a little levity around here. Where are you off to, Jack? Well, our next flight is in two hours and that goes to Paris, so that must be you. And who are you flying with?" He paused. "Wait a minute, I wasn't expecting you tonight, just hopefully sometime. Let's look at the crew list...there you are. Let's see, the second officer is Gary Wagoner, and it shows here that there is an instructor on the flight, a Jerry Black."

"Nice guy?" Jack offhandedly asked.

"You mean Johnny Love?"

"That's the second time I've heard that today, Mike. Laurie Mills said that to me just fifteen minutes ago."

"He's all right, I guess. His father is big in management, and he was hired very young—at the absolute minimum age, I believe. I think that he gets a lot of flak for being a *boy* captain."

"What about the flight engineer?"

"Oh, Bear Wagoner? Top-notch. Everyone likes him."

"Why did you call him *Bear*?" Jack asked.

"He's a big guy, you'll see." Mike then added, "A gentle bear, though."

"I'm a little early, Mike, but I think that I'll start now," Jack said as he walked over to the back of the room to a desk that had a bank of four direct-line phones to dispatch and picked up the closest one.

"Dispatch, Brubaker."

"Hi there, this is Captain Rheinstrom on thirty-eight to Paris tonight."

"Standby a sec, I'll get the paperwork. Okay, let's see here—departure, climb out, good. And en route, I see no problems on Nat Track Bravo. However, right about thirty west, there's a little disturbance, but we have you initially at thirty-three thousand feet, and you should be climbing to thirty-seven before that. And it should be below you, probably max thirty-five. Flight forty-two to Heathrow is two hours ahead of you, so we'll have him and meteorology watching it before you get there. There are just isolated thunderstorms anyway, no front or squall line or anything like that. As I said, you should be above it all. Now, when we look at Charles de Gaulle, that's a little more interesting. They're calling for a warm frontal passage right about your time of arrival in the morning, 0700. The problem is that right now, and it's forecast to stay that way, right now they're experiencing record lows—can you believe forty degrees in July? Anyway, if you have cold ground and then add warm air, bingo—you have the possibility, or shall we say the probability, of fog. How much, how thick, how long? Well, it depends. Heard that one before? Anyway, the UK will be clear and visibility unlimited, so depending on if there are other diversions, if you divert, you're looking at probably Gatwick, because they have the space to accommodate you, followed by Heathrow or even Amsterdam, but that last one, Amsterdam, might be iffy since they're on the same European continent as Paris. No turbulence is expected en route. You'll probably want extra fuel in case you have to hold for Charles de Gaulle, but I think that by the time you make landfall over the UK, the flight plan with the best tailwind has you coming over Lands End, and we should have a pretty good idea of the big picture. En route emergency diversions for the Atlantic, since you'll be taking the northern tracks, will be Gander, Newfoundland; Keflavik, Iceland; and Glasgow, Scotland. There are no anticipated departure or ATC delays. Any questions?"

"No, good briefing. Oh, yes—is Al Burnett still working in dispatch?"

"Yes, but he's off tonight. Shall I relay anything?"

"No, thank you, though—just an old friend that I haven't talked to in a long time. I'll catch him later."

"Okay, great. Have a safe flight, Captain."

Jack was just putting the phone down when Jerry Black walked into the room. Jack had never seen the fellow, but somehow, he just knew that this must be Johnny Love. The new entrant took off his hat and walked over to the long table that had four separate stacks of maps and paperwork. He looked over each one until he found Flight 38, picked it up, and went to the end of the table where it was clear and uncluttered. Jack went over to his chair with an outstretched hand and introduced himself. "Captain Black, I'm Jack Rheinstrom, and I'll be with you tonight on thirty-eight to Paris."

Captain Black didn't look up, but continued writing something down in a small appointment book. "I'll be with you in a minute," he said. Jack continued to stand there, and then slowly dropped his right hand back to his side.

Hmm, he thought to himself, this is not starting out very well, you rude little twerp.

A number of seconds passed, but it seemed much longer. Black finally looked up, after proving who was really in charge, and said, "Hello, I'm Captain Black. I'll be the instructor for your IOE, and if all goes well, we'll make the last leg of this four-day trip, the Paris to Boston leg, your check ride. And if that goes okay, I'll sign you off and you'll be back in business."

Captain Black? Not Jerry? Is this guy for real? Jack thought to himself. He was quite familiar with the positions of flight instructor and check airman, as he had been one himself on the Lockheed Electra, the Douglas DC-9, and the Boeing 727. He'd always been aware of the power of the position and made a point to go out of his way in making his students feel comfortable and relaxed, with a shared sense of mission and camaraderie. Yes, I know what the drill is—do I look like a new hire to you? Jack seethed inwardly. But Jack's emotion was invisible. He remained cool, nodded his head, and smiled slightly. "Right." He was going to discuss what he had learned from dispatch, but now decided that it would be pointless. He just watched as Black got up, walked over to the bank of phones, and duplicated Jack's previous call.

"Hello, this is Captain Black. Who is working 38 tonight?"

When the briefing was complete, and the phones were put back in their cradles, dispatcher Brubaker pushed back from his table and let his chair coast a few feet and reviewed his past half hour. "Two captains, two flight briefings, same flight--- what was that all about?" He stood up, went over to the coffee pot, and poured himself another cup. His shift was only half over. Soon Black came back to the table where Jack Rheinstrom was studying the map.

"Pretty routine, maybe some low vis, (visibility) on arrival; we'll keep an eye on it."

That's it? Jack thought. He recalled his earlier conversation with dispatch. Nothing about possible turbulence at thirty west if we can't get our desired altitude assignment? What about the entire European continent and fog? What about a possible divert to the UK? And which airport? I'm not going to play this game. And I sure hope this gets better, because if it doesn't improve, I might just ask for another check airman when we get back to Detroit. But I *will* make the best of it, he finally said to himself.

Just then, none other than Bear walked through the doorway. Maybe he wasn't actually a bear, but the moniker sure seemed to fit. The strapping young man in his twenties, with a smile as broad as his shoulders, stood six-foot-four and probably weighed in at a good 260 pounds. "You're Captain Rheinstrom, aren't you?" he said as he walked up to Jack, his hand outstretched. "I'm Gary Wagoner. My dad is Ollie Wagoner. He used to fly with you—I've heard a lot of stories about you, all of them good, I must say. And it's a real pleasure to meet you."

"I'm going to brief the flight attendants," Black commented as he walked out of the room, completely ignoring the third member of his crew.

"Who was that?" Bear asked.

"He's the guy giving me my IOE and check ride—Captain Jerry Black. You don't know him?"

"No, Captain Rheinstrom, I don't. I've only been based in Boston for four months now. I'm about to go out to the bird and preflight—the TV screen says that it's on Jetway 3A. Anything that I should know about the flight?"

"Well, I didn't see if he changed the fuel, which he might have, since there is a weather question at de Gaulle, but the flight plan originally called for a fuel load of two hundred thousand, including holding and possible divert to Gatwick."

"Okay, Captain Rheinstrom, see you out there," replied Bear as he walked out of the flight planning room. Since Captain Black was giving a pre-departure briefing to the flight attendants, Jack picked up the route map and papers, folded them very neatly, and put them in the correct order on his aluminum clipboard. Then he went back to the bag room for his suitcase and brain bag and proceeded to operations. To get to ops, he had to transit the ready room of the baggage handlers and maintenance crews. He inserted the code into the door lock, opened it, and walked past the rows of lockers, past the picnic-style tables with assorted lunchboxes scattered about on the top, and then in front of the dozen or so ground crew in waiting. They were sitting in cafeteria-style chairs and on benches, all watching the Red Sox and New York Yankees game on a TV mounted on the wall.

"What's the score?" Jack asked as he walked by.

"6 to 5, in the ninth—Yankees," came the solemn reply.

He continued on through another door and entered the world of operations, normally a beehive of activity even when the day was slow. He approached the counter and smiled. "Hi, thirty-eight to Paris."

"Hi there, Captain. We have the updates, the new weather—they just came off, and the new release reflecting the changed fuel load. It's the first stack of paperwork over there," the man said, cocking his head and pointing to a desk in the corner of the room. Jack looked at the papers, and then replaced them in the stack, awaiting Captain Black's arrival. He started toward the door that led out to the ramp and the waiting B-747 on Jetway 3A. Just then, there was a loud rhythmic thumping that could be heard and felt through the walls as loud cheers and yelling arose from the TV waiting room next door. Above it all, a loudspeaker announced that Flight 130 from Miami had landed and was now approaching Jetway 2B. The baggage handlers and aircraft marshallers, a group of six, piled out of the ready room and noisily shuffled past the open ops doorway on their way to the outside ramp. Everyone in operations stopped what they were doing and looked at them. Corky Sullivan, a red-haired young man from South Boston (who looked like a Corky Sullivan from South Boston) walked by, grinning, his left thumb held high in the air. He turned to his new audience and exclaimed in a loud voice, "Jim Rice—homer in the tenth, with Boggs on first. Seven to six, Sox. Go Sox!" Everyone nodded, smiled, and went back to what they were doing before. All was well in Red Sox Nation.

Jack picked up his clipboard. "Captain Black will be along shortly to sign the release." Then he smiled. "Go Sox."

"Safe flight, Captain."

"Thanks, see you in a couple days." Jack walked out onto the ramp, pulling his wheelie behind him, suitcase and brain bag attached. There was only one B-747 out there at the time, so he felt confident that lugging the two heavy bags up the long outside Jetway stairs one at a time was a sound decision. He had, several times in the past, albeit many years ago, climbed the stairways, secured his bags in the cockpit, assembled the paperwork, and sat down in his seat to "make a nest," only to wonder at the lack of activity—no flight attendants, no maintenance personnel, no fueling, no catering. Of course, he was on the wrong airplane! Not the wrong airplane thirty minutes ago, or even fifteen, but wrong now because usually due to a maintenance problem, the company had swapped tail numbers and had assigned a different airplane to the flight.

He climbed the Jetway stairs with his suitcase, and it seemed seemed as steep as a ladder. During the second time, with his brain bag in tow, he paused to look around and did a once-over of the plane sitting on the ramp. The team was in place and everyone was doing their part. The fueler was standing in his raised caged platform under the starboard wing, plugged in and pumping fuel; the baggage handlers were loading the metal LD-1 baggage containers into the cargo hold with their specialized pallet-loading platforms; and the catering trucks, two of them, had parked in position and raised their bodies to the waiting aircraft galley doors—one aft, one forward—almost twenty-five feet in the air above the ramp. Once inside the airplane, Jack looked around. The cleaners were busy as bees, cleaning up the litter from the inbound flight and primping the interior, the trays, the pillows, and the blankets for the flight to Paris.

He approached the first flight attendant that he saw. "Hi, I'm Jack Rheinstrom. Have you seen Laurie Mills, by chance?"

"Oh, hello, Captain—Laurie is right over there," she said, gesturing.

Laurie smiled as she saw Jack approach. "Well, hello again, Jack, and by the way, your cohort seems like a real doozy."

"Say again?"

"I had only heard about Jerry Black—bad news seems to flow with him. Anyway, his briefing at in-flight was unbelievable."

"Why was that?"

"Everyone was turned off. I don't know, he's very unfriendly, very authoritative, condescending, not a team spirit builder...more like a drill instructor and maybe a German one at that. Anyway, Scrappy," she continued with a wink, "what can I get you?"

"Thanks, Laurie, but I'm fine now. I just wanted to meet the purser before we get busy."

"Oh, she's over there, talking to the agent. Jane Farnsworth is her name. I have flown with her many times before. She's top-notch, easy to work with, and lots of fun."

Jack walked over to Jane and waited for her to finish her conversation.

"Hi, Jane, I'm Jack Rheinstrom, and I'm the other guy on our flight tonight. I just wanted to introduce myself to you before we got busy up there."

"Thank you, Captain, I appreciate that. Captain Black briefed us about the flight. As far as the back end goes, we're pretty full today, but there are maybe ten to fourteen seats open, so the pass riders should be able to get on. I have no special-needs passengers that I know about, and we do have an interpreter tonight, which is good, because there's been a system-wide shortage of them lately. I'll bring the meals up after we finish the beverage service, if that's okay?"

"Of course, Jane, that'll be fine. It was a pleasure to meet you." Jack left and returned to the front of the airplane to begin his second ascent up another set of stairs—this time, the spiral staircase that went from the main to the upper deck and the access door to the cockpit. The second officer was doing his cockpit preflight check.

"Hello again, Captain."

"Hello again, Mr. Engineer," Jack said as he stowed his suitcase in the back of the cockpit and placed his brain bag to left of the captain's seat on the floor. "How's the bird? May I see the logbook, please?"

The second officer nodded. "Pretty good, nothing substantial. There are a couple of things on the minimum equipment list, but nothing much at all. The instrument lights on my engineer's panel are either on or off, so you can't dim them."

"Well, Bear, that's a biggie, but I think that we're going to have to go to Paris anyway."

"I guess so, Captain. I'm going to run out and do my walk around. They delivered the bottled water for the crew over there," he said, nodding his head to the left. "Do you want any coffee on my way back?"

"Nah, but thanks anyway."

Bear dug a large flashlight out of his brain bag, left the cockpit, hustled down the spiral staircase, and went outside to descend the Jetway stairs.

Jack heard a ding and looked up at his overhead panel. He saw the blue flight attendant button illuminated. He picked up the intercom phone and answered, "Engine room."

"Is this the engineer?"

"No, this is Captain Rheinstrom. What's up?"

"Hi, this is Jane. Well, they shorted us two liquor kits, and we still need seven more first-class entrées, and we only have fifteen minutes to pushback."

"Okay, Jane, thanks, I'll let them know." Jack switched the radio mixer switch to VHF radio number three and relayed the information to operations on the company frequency. Jerry Black arrived in the cockpit and placed his suitcase in the storage area. He dropped the additional paperwork on the center console between the two pilot seats, put his brain bag on the floor to the right of his copilot seat, and then, without a word, left the cockpit.

Jack sat in his seat, thinking. Maybe this guy was just having a bad day, or a bad week, or a bad divorce settlement, Jack didn't know. But he did know one thing—this was the strangest feeling of crew incompatibility that he had ever experienced in his career, and it wasn't just because he'd been away for twenty years. Of that Jack was positive.

Bear came back into the cockpit and sat down in his chair facing the flight engineer's instrument panel. This was located behind the copilot's right seat and was situated lengthwise, along the fuselage wall.

"Well, it's all there!" he remarked.

"What's all there?" Jack asked.

"The airplane—the tires and the engines, they're all there! I'm ready, let's go to Paree."

"Well, Bear, you've done an absolutely wonderful job out there. I agree, Paree it is."

Captain Black came back into the cockpit, a single coffee in his hand, got into the right seat, and began to strap himself in. Jack looked at his watch—thirteen minutes to the pushback. He glanced at the door light annunciator; the forward, mid, and aft cargo doors were all still open.

"Do we have all of our fuel?" he asked Bear.

"Well, they just stopped pumping. We have two hundred and ten thousand pounds on board. Is that the final fuel load?" asked Bear.

"Yup."

"Well, then, we have all of our fuel. Forward and mid-cargo door lights out, Captain," he announced.

"Okay," acknowledged Jack.

"Hi, Captain," said the gate agent, who suddenly appeared in the cockpit, reams of paper in her hand. Rheinstrom and Black both turned around in their seats. "All the passengers are on board, the cabin has their shorted meals, and they're loading the last two LD-1 baggage containers in the aft. Here is the latest weather; we might even be able to get you guys out of here a few minutes early."

"Thanks for the good work," Jack acknowledged. "See you in a few days." He glanced at Black. "Did you get the clearance yet?"

"No."

"No?" asked Jack.

"No, I was waiting for you to ask for it."

What a jerk, Jack thought. "Never mind, I'll get it myself."

Boston Logan departure ATIS information Delta; winds three three zero at one five, visibility one zero, few clouds at two five thousand, temperature two five Celcius, dew point five, altimeter three zero three four, ILS runway two seven in use, departing three three left, heavy bird activity in all quadrants. Advise on initial contact that you have information Delta. Second officer Wagoner wrote it all down on a piece of paper, leaned forward, and placed it on the front pedestal between the two pilots.

Jack looked at it, picked up his mike, changed the frequency on VHF radio 1, and made a call. "Clearance delivery, Trans Ocean three eight to Paris, Charles de Gaulle, with ATIS Delta, requesting clearance."

"Roger, standby...Trans Ocean three eight, you are cleared to Paris, Charles de Gaulle, via radar vectors, flight planned route. Climb and maintain eight thousand, squawk three four four one, Boston departure on one three three point zero. Read back."

Bear could see very well what Black was doing, which was as little as possible—resulting in, effectively, a team of one. "I just got a call from Jane Farnsworth, the purser. They're ready in the back," he announced.

Jack looked back at the second officer's panel. "Okay, all cargo door lights out, cabin door light is out." He could feel the ground crew connecting the tow bar to the nose wheel below. Looking to his right, he told Captain Black to get the pushback clearance. Black didn't return the look or verbally acknowledge the command, but instead just picked up his microphone and called ground control.

"Boston, Trans Ocean three eight, at three bravo to pushback," he said.

"Thirty-eight, do you have information delta?"

The captain and second officer just looked at each other. Black had omitted a required step in the process.

"Yes, Boston, we have the information. Sorry."

"Okay, thirty-eight, you have a Northwest DC-10 at your six o'clock passing left to right. When clear of him, you are cleared to push, tail west." By this time, the ground crew had hooked up the tow bar from the tug to the nose wheel and checked in on interphone.

"Hey there, Captain," said someone from the ground crew, "tow bar connected, nose gear pin removed, steering disconnected. Brakes off?"

"Brakes off, cleared to push, and tail west after a Northwest DC-10 taxis by," said Jack.

"Okay, tail west—here we go." The 747 began its backward push.

"Mr. Engineer, a reading of the scriptures, please," Jack requested.

"Roger that," answered Bear. The team commenced with the before-start checklist.

"Okay, Captain," came a reply from the ground crew, "tow bar is disconnected, steering pin installed, nose wheel steering is reconnected. You are cleared on all four engines. Have a safe flight."

"Okay, thanks, see you in a few." Jack addressed his crew members. "Okay, guys, let's crank 'em!" One by one, from number one to number four, the engines were started and the big sleeping bird was now awake, eager to stretch her wings and get back into the air.

There was a sudden crescendo of noise both inside and outside the airplane cabin, and even though the airplane did not really bolt from its standing position, the power of the four engines, each developing over forty-six thousand pounds of thrust, was clearly evident. The airplane had come alive, and it was growling like a twirling German shepherd that suddenly sees his master with the leash in his hand. The bird seemed to be saying, "Come on, hurry up, let's go, let's fly!"

As the speed increased and the plane hurtled down the runway, the passengers looking out the side windows could see that the wings, which were almost two hundred feet long, tip to tip, were beginning to change their shape. They morphed from drooping whales beached on the runway under the weight of two hundred thousand pounds of fuel tucked inside and became straight as an arrow as the lift increased. Then, when the aircraft nose was rotated to a fifteen-degree takeoff attitude and the airplane became airborne, the wings changed again—the tips now bent upward. Not only did it look like the wings of the airplane were flying, but all those onboard could feel it in the seat of their pants. As the airplane broke ground and the wings assumed command, the g-forces increased and pushed the passengers deeper into their seat cushions. The bird was flying—and she was happy.

Back in the cockpit, the crew could see that they were airborne, but abiding by company procedures, they needed to verify the fact by their instrument readings. The pilot not flying, first officer Black, watched as the altimeter showed an increase in height, a climb indication. "Positive rate," he called out.

"Gear up," said Jack.

"Gear up," repeated Black. The climb continued. The speed and altitude increased; they turned to a heading of 010 and began the flap retraction schedule.

Once the after-takeoff checklist was accomplished, the airplane eventually leveled off and Jack made the standard obligatory briefing to the passengers.

"Ladies and gentlemen, good afternoon and welcome on board. We have just leveled off at an intermediate altitude of twenty-eight thousand feet. The ride is expected to be smooth, so I will turn off the seatbelt sign and you are free to move about in the cabin. However, we recommend that you keep your belt fastened when you're in your seat, just in case we run into any unforecasted bumpy air. The entire flight, from takeoff to touchdown in Paris, is just a little over six hours, and since many of you will be taking a nap this evening, I will save any further announcements for when we are approaching France. So please, sit back and relax, and let some of Boston's finest attend to your every need. If there is anything we can do to make your flight more enjoyable, please let us know. Again, welcome on board."

The Boston-to-Paris flight was now on a direct course to Gander, Newfoundland, which would be their coast-out point—where the overwater portion of their flight would begin. It would terminate when they coasted in over the shores of the British Isles, just south of Lands End, England.

* * *

The crew was beginning to settle into their routine. The only thing left to be done was to get their oceanic clearance from the next ATC controller, which would be Gander Oceanic. They were anticipating clearance on the flight plan that they had originally filed, but they also had two alternate routings on two other North Atlantic Tracks in case there was a change. The fuel load that they had requested back in Boston was based on all three possibilities. Often times, the flight in front of you will get the route or altitude that you were going to ask for. Why? Because he got there first and he requested it. The moral of the story is that you have to be flexible.

With a ding, the overhead blue flight attendant call button illuminated.

"Engine room," answered Bear after he picked the interphone up from its cradle.

"Hi, this is Jane. First of all, it's too warm in the aft section. Second of all, I've got a couple of minutes free and I wanted to know if I could get you guys anything to drink."

"Okay, Jane, I'll cool down in the back, and please stand by." Bear swiveled his seat to the left and leaned forward. "It's Jane, and she's taking drink orders."

"I'll have a black," said Jack.

"Make that two," murmured Black.

"It looks like just three blacks, Jane."

"Okay, I'll be up momentarily." Three minutes later, Jane opened the cockpit door with her cockpit key and entered, holding a tray with three black coffees and three tiny bowls of mixed nuts. "These kind of fell off the first-class tray somehow," she said, smiling.

"What kind of crowd do you have back there today?" asked Jack.

"Oh, nothing special. Nice people, no problems."

"Good, let's keep it that way. As I mentioned before, Paris weather is kind of iffy. We'll stay on top of it and will be talking to dispatch when we coast in over England. You'll be the second to know."

"Okay, Captain Rheinstrom, thank you. And I'll be bringing the meals up after we finish the beverage service. And we have something new and different tonight for you guys."

Bear's ears perked up. "You do?"

"Yup—Lobster Thermidor or prime rib," Jane said.

"You're kidding, right?" the second officer said.

"Yup."

"Yup, what? Yup lobster, or yup you were kidding?" Bear pressed.

"I'm sorry, I was kidding. It's same old, same old—leather or feather."

Jack turned around in his seat. "Jane, you are one mean woman." He looked around the cockpit. "Okay, what do you guys want?"

Captain Black jumped in first. "I'll take the steak."

"Well, Captain Rheinstrom, I really don't care," Bear graciously said.

Jack regarded him thoughtfully. "Choose."

"Okay, then, I guess I would like the steak also."

"Jane, then I'll have the chicken."

"Okay, guys, I'll see you in a bit, and Mr. Engineer, it's still too warm in the back."

After the purser left the cockpit, Black moved his seat back and started to unbuckle his seatbelt. "I'm going to hit the lav," he announced. "I'll be back before we have to call in the next position report to Gander." It was one of his responsibilities, being the pilot not flying. As he got up and began to walk toward the cockpit door, he turned around and sternly asked Jack, "Aren't you going to put on your oxygen mask?"

"No, I'm not going to 'hang the hose' because the second officer, our third in command, will be sitting in your seat until you return." Bear stood up and nimbly climbed into the right seat. Black just looked at them both, then turned around and left the cockpit.

Settling into his new seat and fastening his seatbelt, Bear turned to his left and addressed Jack. "May I ask you something, Captain Rheinstrom?"

"Sure, Bear, go ahead, but I think I know what you're going to say—and it's *Jack*."

"Okay, Jack, I've only been with the company for six years now, but I've never flown with anyone like this before, ever! Is he always like this, or is he doing us a favor?"

Jack chuckled at his last bit of sarcasm. "Well, you know, Bear, I don't know what his story is—just be glad you're not married to him. And I'm thankful that you're along on this flight. You not only make it bearable, but enjoyable, too." He paused and Bear groaned at the pun. "It's just you and me, babe. Anyway, someday we'll look back and laugh about it. But here's what I suggest—what he does is his business, and what we do is ours. I'm not going to have some arrogant, self-important dork determine how I'm going to act or react. We'll just do our job like we always do, and this trip will be history. But, as I said, I'm truly glad that you're along for this ride."

"Yeah, Jack, I see what you mean. And, yeah, me too."

As the captain was making some annotations on the flight plan attached to the clipboard, second officer Wagoner, now first officer, looked around and announced, "You know, I like the way this feels!"

"The way *what* feels?" Jack asked.

"The feel of sitting in this seat—of being a seven forty-seven first officer."

"You said before that you fly the C-141 in the Air Force Reserves at McGuire; are you in the left or the right seat on it?"

"Left seat—in fact, I'm an instructor—but it's not the same. There's a difference between being a military pilot and an airline pilot, or maybe it's just the way I'm wired. The military was always the means for me to get here, to learn how to fly and get the job I've wanted ever since I can remember. My dad was a pilot, and I grew up always around airplanes and airports. I just love flying, and I can hardly wait to get into this seat."

"Well, Bear, I don't have any kids—in fact, I'm not even married—but I am old enough to be your father. I know you didn't ask me, but because I like you, I'm going to say this anyway. You're a young man with your life ahead of you. Don't wish for time to speed by any faster than it already is. Enjoy every moment! It sounds stupid when you're twenty-eight or twenty-nine years old, but when you're fifty-nine, stopping and smelling the roses makes a lot of sense, an awful lot of sense."

"I see what you mean, Jack, and I'll try. Thanks."

"You're welcome." They both glanced at each other and exchanged a small but earnest smile.

The moon was only days away from being full, and it majestically spread its brightness and magic over the entire night sky. As he looked out his right window to the stars above, to the illuminated towering cumulonimbus clouds a hundred or so miles distant to the south, and to the speckled silver Atlantic Ocean thirty-five thousand feet below, the new first officer mused, "It's mystical, isn't it, Jack?"

"What, the moon?"

"Yeah, the moon, the stars, the clouds, the ocean. It's all so special. Makes you feel...*spiritual* I guess is the right word."

"I never get tired of it, Bear. It's always like a first-time event for me. Sometimes, I kind of feel sorry for the landlubbers, for all that they've missed."

"Looks like we have some traffic up there, Captain."

"I haven't heard anyone on frequency."

"Well, it looks like we're following *somebody*—maybe they're on the same Nat Track? I can't tell if we're following him at the same or a different altitude, can you?"

"Where are you looking?"

"Right there, straight ahead, or maybe a little at one o'clock."

Jack leaned forward and looked, then sat back in his seat. "You think that's an airplane?" he asked.

"Well, yeah, I can see its rotating beacon blinking on and off, red. I'm sure it's a plane."

Jack knew but was waiting to respond. "Well, let's just keep an eye on it for a while, shall we?" A few minutes later, he asked. "How's that other airplane looking now, Bear?"

"Same position. We must be at the same speed and the same altitude, Jack."

"What would you say if I said that it isn't an airplane?"

"Well, I can see the flashing rotating beacon—it's an airplane."

"What would you say if I said that it's a planet?"

"Then I would say that it's an airplane—I'm looking right at it," Bear confidently stated.

"How about a beer on that, Mr. Copilot?"

"Right on! In fact, let's make it two beers. Or why don't we make it a dinner, Jack?"

"No, Bear, I'm not going to steal from you. I'll just let you buy me a beer."

Bear studied the blinking light for another few minutes. "You say that you think that it's a planet, not a plane?" he asked again.

"It's the planet Venus—you know, the evening star."

"Well, I've seen Venus before many times in the early evening sky, but it was always a white, bright object, not a blinking red one," Bear countered.

"That's because you were looking pretty much straight up, and here, at cruising altitude, you are looking sideways *through* the atmosphere, with all its pollutants and impurities. That's what gives it the red, pulsing appearance."

"*Really*?" the first officer said, turning his head to look at his captain.

"Really, Bear. Hey, I've had this discussion before, many moons ago, and I was taking your side of the argument. And I lost some beer on it, too."

Just then, Jerry Black came back into the cockpit and stood there with a solo cup of coffee in his right hand. Bear slid his seat back, unbuckled his seatbelt, and retreated to his engineer's panel. During this time, Jack held his sweep-on oxygen mask in his right hand, resting it on his lap. Black sat down and strapped in, and Jack returned his mask to its straphanger. Jack turned to his right and handed the clipboard with the flight papers on it to his returning first officer. "You just missed the last position report to Gander. Next one is at thirty west to Shanwick." Black took the clipboard from Jack but made no comment.

Bear stood up. "I'm going back for a minute, anybody want anything?" Again, Black didn't say anything.

"No, I'm fine, but thanks for the offer," Jack said, glancing at Black. The two captains sat in the darkened cockpit alone for about ten minutes, Jack monitoring the engine instruments and occasionally gazing out the window at the theater of light that the soon-to-be supermoon was providing, and Black examining paperwork and scribbling on the computerized flight plan. Not a single word was exchanged while the second officer was absent. Bear reentered the cockpit with a cup of coffee, looked around the cockpit, glanced at his instrument panel at the flight engineer station, and sat down.

With a sudden dinging, the yellow selcall light blinked on and off, on and off. This indicated the selective calling feature on the long-range HF radio. Black reached up with his left hand and pushed the lighted knob in to cancel the alert. And with his right hand, he reached for his hand mike that was dangling on its cord, wrapped around a knob by the copilot's side window. He brought the mike to his mouth and pressed the transmit button. "Trans Ocean thirty-eight, answering selcall."

"Trans Ocean thirty-eight, standby for a phone patch from company."

"Roger."

"Trans Ocean thirty-eight, this is New York Dispatch, do you read, over?" Black turned around in his seat to look at the other two crew members. With his left index finger, he tapped his headset's left ear. They in turn flipped up the wafer switch on their individual radio control panels so that they could all monitor the possibly important call.

"Affirmative, TO thirty-eight, go ahead."

"Roger, this is dispatch. I've just been talking to the meteorological department, and there are some contingencies that we need to talk about. Even though it doesn't even open for another four hours, at 0600 local, Paris de Gaulle is presently WOXOF." Those in the cockpit all recognized this aviation meteorological term for an airport's existing conditions—indefinite ceiling, vertical visibility zero, sky obscured, horizontal visibility zero, fog. "Metro doesn't think that will improve until at least noon. And that's the optimistic view. Pretty much all of that area in central Europe, France, Germany, and Spain are in the same weather pattern. That's the bad news. The good news is that the UK is clear and visibility is unlimited, clear as a bell, so presently we are planning for you to divert to London Gatwick where you will land and, subsequently, run out of crew duty time, assuming the original forecast for Paris holds true. Now, normally, we would put up the passengers in hotels for the night, if they so choose, or protect them on another airline's flight later in the day. And we would rest overnight the crew because you would now be illegal. You would continue tomorrow to Paris, your original destination, a day late, pick up your originating passengers there, and continue back to Detroit as scheduled, basically swapping your layovers, i.e. London for Paris. Now, here is where it gets dicey and we need to play Let's Make a Deal. The weather for Paris tomorrow is not looking good either, so I see a scenario where you are delayed tomorrow getting out of Gatwick and delayed again getting into Paris, and running out of crew availability again, since you're a basic crew, not augmented, and the whole thing could end up taking more than the limiting twelve hours. We have a situation in Paris where there are literally thousands of people potentially affected and stranded for the next few days. We are thinking about sending some of the passengers up to Amsterdam via train and flying some of them out of there, since, because of a mechanical, we have an extra plane and crew there, and for some reason, the weather is better, at least for tomorrow. But the trains are running out of seats, if you can believe that, and on top of that, the train union, CSFN, is suddenly talking about slowdowns because of their stalled contract talks. But that is neither here nor there for you. Here's the deal—we want to get the airplane to Paris tomorrow, even if you have to fly over there and hold for eight hours, then finally sneak in an approach and landing. You would layover in Paris for that night and continue on the next day when the weather is expected to break. So, your trip gets extended one day, or hopefully, not at all, in rather unusual circumstances. By contrast, you could say "No, deadhead us back to our next scheduled layover after Paris, Detroit, from Gatwick, and we'll continue our month from there, as scheduled." But we are hoping that you don't do that. And there is one very important catch, here—the entire crew has to agree to this manipulation of the contract, because we can't afford to have someone walking out at the last minute, or have a grievance filed in the future. Now, this is an important question—did you possibly get all that?"

The three crew members sat and looked at one another. Jack acted first by pointing to himself with his right index finger and the back of the plane with his thumb. He slid his seat back and unbuckled his seatbelt. As he started to stand up, he looked at the other two. "I'm going back and talk with Jane. I'm assuming that you two are okay with this." With a boyish grin, Bear nodded his head emphatically. Black just shrugged his shoulders.

"Dispatch, yeah, we got all that. The front end is okay with the plan, and Captain Rheinstrom is headed back now to talk to the flight attendants. We'll call you back." Black rewound the mike cord around the window knob, reached for his sweep-on oxygen mask, then pulled it over the back of his head and covered his mouth.

Laurie Mills and Jane Farnsworth were on break and were standing in the first-class galley. "Have you ever flown with that guy, before?" Janie asked.

"Who?" said Laurie.

"The jerk."

"No, but I've heard about him, and it seems that all reports are pretty accurate, except…."

"Except what?" Janie asked.

"Except that he seems rather inward and reclusive, not the extroverted 'Johnny Love' who hits on anything that wears a skirt."

"Who is that other guy? The other captain?"

"Oh, Jack Rheinstrom?"

"Yes, he seems like an awfully nice person—rather handsome, but a little shy."

"Well, I've known Jack for over twenty-six years."

"Really? I've been here at Trans Ocean for over twenty years and I've never seen him before—and I think that I would have remembered a guy like that! What's he like?"

"Well, he's one of a kind, he really is. We were very close at one time—not romantically, but he was like a big brother to me. I could tell him of my life's trials and tribulations, and he, being older and wiser, would tell me the ways of the world for free—well, almost free. There was usually a beer fee attached. But I haven't seen him for twenty years or so."

"You haven't seen him for twenty years? That's strange. What, did you have a fallout?"

"Janie, you said that you were hired twenty years ago—what month?"

"What month? It was February 1990—February twenty-first, I'll never forget the date. Why do you ask?"

"Well, this happened a couple of months before you were hired.

Do you remember the Christmas Eve crash in Boston in '69? The plane that crashed on approach in a snowstorm and killed one hundred thirty or so people?" Laurie asked.

"Yes, I certainly do. I had my interview down in Miami a week before that. I remember reading about it after it happened and wondering to myself if I actually wanted to fly for a living and expose myself to something like that. It was scary—still is, sometimes. I mean, it doesn't keep me up at night. Not always anyway, only when there's a crash and I can see myself in that position. But, I think that's normal and healthy, don't you? Don't you ever wonder about fate, about being in the wrong place at the wrong time?"

"Well, Jane, yes and no. I lost two friends on that flight. One was only an acquaintance, but the other one was my roommate at new-hire school. I miss her to this very day. So the fate thing bothers me a little because it's kind of like why her, not me? I spent a long time after the crash imagining every minute of her life on that flight, up to the second of the crash. But other than the personal loss, I guess I'd have to say that I'm somewhat fatalistic. You know, Jane, it's kind of funny—you and I, well, the passengers too, for that matter, are really powerless. When there's a crash, you think about it and you dismiss it because you just have to, or it would eat you up inside. You dismiss it by being fatalistic about it, whether the cause was human error, or weather-related, or just plain happenstance. But pilots are different. They're intensely interested in *every* accident, not because they're morbid and enjoy reading about tragic events, but so they can learn from the mistakes of others and avoid repeating them. I know a lot of pilots, and not one of them is fatalistic about a crash. They look at an accident and the details, and they say 'Well, that wouldn't have happened to me because I would've done this and not done that.' In other words, their fate is in their own hands. But as far as you and me and all the peeps go, I'm afraid that we're all just along for the ride."

"You knew didn't you, Jane, that he was the captain on that flight"?

Jane grimaced—a sudden look of pain and sorrow on her face. "Boston? No—no, I didn't."

Just then Laurie looked up and watched as Jack Rheinstrom descended the spiral staircase from the top deck. She beamed at him, and Jack responded with a smile. He gestured for her to approach him.

"So how's it going, Scrappy?" she asked.

"The flight, or him?"

"Him."

"I was telling Bear, the engineer—who really is a good man—that this guy's a jerk, but he is in control of this check ride and we can't change that. So who cares? Press on. Hopefully you'll never have to fly with him again. But that's not why I came down to talk to you—we have a situation"

Laurie raised her eyebrows and wrinkled her forehead. "What do you mean, situation?"

"I wasn't there for Black's briefing because I was preflighting. How did he describe the weather at Charles de Gaulle to your group?"

"Well, he didn't! Why? I assume that it's not very good?"

"No, it's not good. The forecast is making it impossible to land. There is zero, I mean *zero*, visibility. What is your crew like? I mean, do you know them? Because crew scheduling has offered us a pretty good deal, *if* we agree to change our monthly forward schedule. Another thing, it's a little bit of a stretch of the contract. So everyone has to agree to it unanimously—there will be no walking if someone changes his or her mind."

"Well, what exactly is the deal?"

"Laurie, let's get the lead purser into the conversation. This has to be a crew decision." He gently touched her arm and led her the ten or so steps to Jane Farnsworth.

"Hello, Captain Rheinstrom."

"Hello, Jane. How's the flight going so far for you guys?"

"Pretty much routine, which is actually fine with me. How about you?"

"Well, funny you should ask, because we need to have a powwow."

"Oh?" Jane said, a worried look on her face. "Is everything okay? Is anything wrong?"

"No, nothing's wrong with the airplane. The airplane is fine." Jack then proceeded to explain the situation and the options available. Both flight attendants listened intently, occasionally nodding their heads in understanding and approval. After he finished, he moved closer to the galley. "Could I get a black, please?" Laurie was the first to move and poured a cup from the carafe that was being heated in the coffeemaker machine. "Thanks," Jack said, "and I don't need the crew answer immediately. I know that there are some taking a nap on their break, but I do need an answer within an hour, okay?" He looked at them both, nodded his head saying "Ladies," almost clicking his heels at the same time, and proceeded up the circular stairway back to the cockpit.

Although most of the passengers were asleep, or at least had their eyes closed, there were enough of them awake, either reading or fiddling with their computers, that Jane decided to proceed through the cabin and individually explain the situation and options to the crew, avoiding the potential of alarming the passengers with a large en masse crew briefing. All in the crew seemed happy and excited with the advent of a London layover and the guarantee of a full credit of eighty hours for the month, even if they were previously short of that number. All but one, Molly Maloney. About ten minutes after she received her individual briefing and the purser had completed talking with all the other flight attendants, she approached Jane in the first-class galley, where she was standing alone doing paperwork.

"Jane?"

"Yes, Molly, what's wrong? You look upset!"

"I don't know what to say. The whole crew is so excited about the idea of a London, plus a Paris, plus the bonus of full month—and they're going to hate me."

"Hate you? Why?" said Farnsworth, putting down her papers on the galley countertop and removing her glasses.

"They're going to hate me because I'm going to spoil their good deal. I feel horrible."

Jane softly took Molly's arm and gestured her over to door one left. "Molly, let's just slow down a minute here—a deep yoga breath, okay? I assume you're saying this because you can't stay out an extra day, am I right? Hey, if you can't stay out an extra day, you can't stay out an extra day. I'm sure you have a valid reason."

"I do, I do," she exclaimed fervently, but in a hushed and guarded voice.

"Wait a minute, Sweetie, we need another yoga breath. Here, I'll do one, too, okay?" They both closed their eyes and took a long, deep breath, exhaling slowly. "Okay, Molly, continue."

"Jane, if we stay out an extra day, I'll lose my mammogram appointment!"

"You'll lose your mammogram appointment?"

"Yes, and you know how hard it is to get another one soon, if you cancel. I had to wait a month once, even when I told them I had a lump!" she explained.

"Molly, it sounds to me like you need to find a more accommodating practice—that's not right, not right at all."

"And the thing is, Jane, I lost my mother to breast cancer, and now my sister has been diagnosed with stage one and I…I…." Her head was now bowed down, her right thumb and index finger reaching for her closed eyes, her thin frame shaking. She was trying to suppress a cry. "I, I have fibroids, I always have lumps, and I'm always scared when I go in."

"Molly, Molly, look at me. Look at me." Molly took her hand away from her eyes, took another deep breath, and slowly looked up. "I feel a little like a mother here because our ages are so far apart, but tell me, how old are you?"

"I was twenty in April."

"And when were you hired?"

"In April."

"Well, let's get some perspective here. Number one, your health, physical and mental, is more important than any layover—and believe me, there are many, many more of those to come. And number two, what makes you think that your crew won't understand? You are new to this airline and you are new to the concept of crew, but it's a synonym for *team*, and that's what we are—a team. We work together, we play together, and you know what? Just like the passengers that we have here on this plane tonight, we depend on one another for our lives. Think about it. I would be very surprised, no make that flabbergasted, if one of our crew didn't understand. And if they didn't and if they gave you a hard time, I, along with everyone else on this crew—people that I have worked with and known for many, many years—would rip them a new one, if you will excuse my French."

Jane reached out, took Molly's hand in hers, and gently squeezed it. "Molly, I'm the lead on this flight. There are two open seats over there. I designate an extra thirty-minute break for you. Take it easy, girl, and think about what I just said."

"Thank you, Jane. You don't know how much that means to me," she said, her speckled face slowly returning to normal.

In the cockpit, Jack looked up and saw the blue flight attendant call light illuminated on the overhead enunciator panel. He picked up the hanging phone from the center pedestal and said "Hello, cockpit."

"This is Jane. Is this Captain Rheinstrom?"

"Yes, Jane, it is."

"Can you break away, or do you want me to come up there? We have come to a crew decision about the offer from crew sched."

"I was just about to come down there and stretch my legs anyway. I'll see you in a couple of minutes." He slid his seat back and unbuckled his seatbelt, just as Captain Black put on his oxygen mask. As he left the cockpit, as he always did, he asked, "Does anyone want anything?" Black just moved his head from side to side, while Bear thanked him and said that he was fine. As he descended the spiral staircase, he saw both Jane and Laurie standing in the first-class galley. The purser saw him first and approached. "I'm sorry, Captain Rheinstrom, but we can't get a universal agreement on the plan. There is one on the crew who has a very important medical appointment that she can't afford to miss, and she would if she was out an extra day. The poor thing is very sorry and feels badly about it, worried that she's being a spoilsport for the rest the crew. I told her that she was being ridiculous, that the crew stood behind her, and that she has to prioritize things in life. But she still feels a little down; she's rather young and new to Trans Ocean."

"Well, tell her," Jack said, "that the front end supports her, too. There will be other such offers from crew scheduling in the future. We've all been through Chinese fire drills like this before. I will let them know our decision and get back to you with the details as soon as I get them. Okay?"

"Great, Jack, thank you." She reached up and put her hand on his arm and looked at him. "And thank you for your support, too."

Jack turned around, gave a thumbs-up signal, then went over to talk to Laurie.

"It looks like we'll be laying over in Brighton," Jack explained, "then deadheading back to Detroit the next day."

"What day is it, Jack?" Laurie suddenly asked.

"Now, or when we get there? It's Wednesday right now, but when we arrive, it will be Thursday morning."

"Thursday, that's great!"

"And why is that great?"

"Why? Because it's the most senior trip in all of Europe!"

"What is, Laurie?"

"A Brighton layover at the Metropole on a Thursday—it's *pound night*!" she exclaimed.

"Pound night, what's that? Never heard of it."

"Didn't you ever fly Europe way back when?"

"Yeah, I did when I was in the right seat on this, but we stayed in London, not Brighton. Let's get back to 'pound night'—what is it?"

"Well, Scrap, there's a waitress in the hotel main dining room named Maggie, and she knows all the airline crews. There must be five or six airlines, maybe more, that lay over there. I don't know how, but she knows them all and we all love her—she's a real mother hen. She fusses over us all the time and makes us feel very special and welcome. Anyway, she convinced the Metro, as we call it, to open up a special room for airline crews on Thursday night and cater it with snacks and beer and waitresses from eighteen hundred to twenty hundred. And all it costs you is one pound! One pound plus a tip, of course."

"Wow, no wonder it's such a senior trip! Are you planning to go?"

"Well, I am, if you take me—and the night is on me, Scrap!"

"Well, my friend, you drive a hard bargain. But I'll make it up to you someday, you'll see. Jack looked down, then up, then down again. He put his hands in his pockets, slowly took three steps away, and then returned. "You know, Kiddo, we used to be pretty close—well, change that to very close. I know that you know what happened to me, or at least the basic facts surrounding flight sixty-six, but there's a lot more to the story than meets the eye. I can tell just by the way that you look at me that you want me to open up and share my feelings with you, but you don't want to pry, don't want to push. I think you're eager to be a listener and act as a friend, just like you always have. I don't know where or when I will start, Laurie—maybe tonight, maybe back in Boston, maybe sometime on this trip when we're together alone. The time has to be right. I will let you in, okay?" He looked at her with the warmest, sincerest eyes she had ever seen in her entire life.

She stared back at him, her eyes a little full, and smiled. "You bet, Jack, of course."

The divert went smoothly, and the weather at London's Gatwick Airport was uncommonly good. Temperatures were in the seventies, and there was only a scattering of light, fluffy cirrus clouds, also known as mares' tails. The sky was blue, and Londoners were in an exceptionally good mood, as were these particular passengers. They seemed understanding, given the inconvenience of an unplanned stop, the extra hours, and an overnight lodging at a yet-to-be-determined hotel. The only problem was access to the terminal. There were so many flights diverted to Gatwick that there weren't enough parking spaces to accommodate all the planes. This led to confusion and delays and short tempers, in some cases. Once the conga line of elephants, with their engines still running, were assigned places to park, usually on remote areas of the field, the problem changed to how to transport all the extra people to the terminal without the luxury of a Jetway. This was essentially solved by using portable air stairs and buses, but there were only so many to go around. Thus, a large amount of time was spent just waiting—and waiting. And once the passengers finally did get to the terminal, the customs, agriculture, and passport control personnel were completely overwhelmed. The unlucky passengers endured up to a six-hour delay from aircraft to cab, train, or local hotel.

* * *

As the unmarked silver Mercedes-Benz bus pulled away from London Gatwick Airport, its cargo of flight crew from TO 38 were making their nests and getting settled for the approximately one-hour drive to Brighton, sometimes referred to as "London by the Sea." Most of the crew of twelve were sitting in the first third of the bus. Captain Black was sitting by himself in the second-to-last aisle in the back. He pulled out a dog-eared copy of *Field and Stream* from the zippered back pocket of his suitcase and began flipping the pages in search of the perfect article to read. Jack Rheinstrom was in the back row of the large crew grouping in the front, sitting at the window next to an empty seat. Laurie Mills was in the identical seat in the next row, right in front of him, and Bear was in a seat across the aisle from Jack. He was the first to speak.

"What a zoo!" he began.

"Well, Bear, it could have been worse," Jack offered, "a lot worse. I'm just happy that we had our own crew bus that picked us up right on time, and that we had our crew-only line for passport control, customs, and agriculture. That was a walk-through. The only headache that I saw was sitting there in the conga line, inching along, wasting all that fuel with the engines running, even though we did have the inboards shut down. Did you see the passenger lines at passport control? They'll be there for hours. Yep, it could've been a lot, lot worse."

Laurie turned around in her seat, sat up on her knees, and leaned over the seat back to talk to Jack. "So, what do you have planned for your layover, Jack? I mean, after the emergency nap."

"Well, my plans for Paris aren't really going to work now, are they? No. Well, you tell me—I've never been to Brighton before. I had plans for the Cornish coast some twenty-odd years ago, but then things changed," he said, pausing and looking away briefly.

"Well, after we nap—and if you like soft, not hard beds, you'll love the Metropole Hotel—anyway, after we nap, the crew usually walks along the promenade by the beach and the piers, ending up in The Lanes. It's a very old area of town, with lots of little cobblestone alleys and funky shops. We window-shop there and usually meet around happy hour at a neat little pub on Southwick Street called the Ship Inn. There's a big painting of an old square rigger on the marquee sign hanging outside like the old shops used to have, and it's only about a ten-minute walk from the Metro. You can't miss it if you want to join us there. Then, since it's Thursday, we'll probably meet back at the Metro after The Lanes for Pound Night. Anyway, since you've never been here before, you might want to think about visiting the Royal Pavilion."

"What's that?"

"It used to be the royal residence of George, Prince of Wales, back in the seventeen hundreds. It's really neat looking, like some of the old buildings in India, not the normal English seaside architecture. I think that you'd like it. Anyway, Scrappy, I just like being near the English Channel—there's just so much energy there. It's exciting being on the coast, just walking along the beach, looking out at the water. And did you notice, by the way, that I am somewhat of a romantic?"

"Nope, never. I never noticed it at all." The two looked at each other and smiled. "Well, Laurie, I'm not really in 'jetlag shape' yet. I don't know if it's the age or the fact that I've been up all night, but I think that I will take my mandatory, not-over-four-hour nap, and just stroll around to get the flavor of the place. And then I'll meet you guys back at the Metro for Pound Night. How does that sound?"

"Sounds like a winner, Jack, and remember—I'm buying tonight." Laurie turned around and plopped down in her seat. She unzipped a large pocket on her suitcase, retrieved a black inflatable pillow, and began to blow air into it.

Jack was tired, very tired, as he hadn't closed his eyes at all on the flight that night. But he found the bus ride through the English countryside so fascinating that he just sat there in his seat awake, occasionally yawning or rubbing his gritty eyes, watching it all just roll by the window. It had been almost an hour since they had left Gatwick, and the silver Mercedes bus was now making its way through the outskirts of Brighton. Soon, Jack could see a glimpse of water ahead, and suddenly there it was—a boulevard, and beyond that, the beach, and the English Channel.

The bus stopped at a red traffic light and Jack looked down from the bus window at a cluster of shops on the corner to his left. In front of one shop, Benny's Money Shop, there stood a young woman with dishwater blond hair drawn back in a tight ponytail, wearing a worn red jacket and faded blue jeans. In one hand, she held a cigarette, and in the other, the hand of a small blond girl, maybe six years old, dressed in a little blue jumper. He couldn't see their faces, only their backs. The pawnshop was dark, and the lights were off. The two were standing in front of the large storefront glass window and they appeared to be looking at an object inside the store located in the front row, next to an oil lamp and a blue Wedgwood vase. What they were apparently gazing at was a large stuffed rabbit, grayish in color, probably white at some point in time, and in obvious used condition; one ear was up, one ear was down. And it was huge, almost as tall as the little girl. Laurie, awakening from her nap and now yawning, looked out her window and softly muttered to herself. "Oh, there they are again."

Jack heard her and leaned forward over the back of her seat. "Again?" he queried. The light turned green, and as the bus began to move Jack turned around in his seat, still trying to see what they looked like, but the bus turned the corner and they were soon out of sight.

* * *

It was eight o'clock in the morning, and there was a queue at the reception desk at the Metropole Hotel. There were many people standing in line waiting to check out. And there was a flight crew of twelve waiting to check in: to get their keys, trudge to their rooms, lie down, and finally go to sleep in a real bed. On this particular morning, there was a flurry of activity in and around the reception area, the main restaurant salon, and the nearby bar area. Jack looked around at the mysterious groups of people going to and fro and others just milling around. He saw several boys sporting recent bowl shaped haircuts—they all appeared spiffy, but were wearing ties that were way too long for them and suits that were slightly too big, some too small. There were little girls also, with questionable fitting clothes, and women with heavy makeup in bright colored dresses many with ruffles, and they were wearing lots of gold. When they walked by, they looked uncomfortable in high heels. It was an odd scene in the Metro that morning. In the bar area, there were three tables that were full of men sitting around in their chairs, smoking cigarettes, some wearing gold earrings, drinking whiskey, and playing cards, their collars open, the loosened ties hanging from their necks.

An Englishwoman in her seventies, smartly dressed, was waiting to check out. She was standing just behind Jack, who was the last in the line of flight crew queue. When she saw an opportunity to talk to him, she blurted out in her heavy cockney accent, "Oh, you should have been here last night, you should have…it was a beautiful sight to behold, it was!" She paused as Jack looked at her questioningly. "We had a gypsy wedding here last night, we did!"

Jack glanced around the area again, nodded, and smiled slightly. "That explains a lot."

Jack's four-hour nap began the instant his head hit the pillow, and before he knew it, he was back at the reception desk in another line—but one much shorter this time.

"Hello, luv, how can I help you this morning?" asked the perky receptionist with beautiful blue eyes and a smile to match.

"Hello, I'd just like to drop off my room key, please. This attached brass ornament must weigh two pounds, and I have nowhere to put it."

Her right hand shot out from behind the counter. "Oh, wonderful, it will be waiting for you upon your return. Have a good run, luv!"

He started to walk away, then returned to the counter. "Oh, excuse me, miss, but I seem to be missing a washcloth in my room. There are big towels, small towels, but no washcloths."

"I'm sorry, sir—a washcloth? What is a washcloth?" she asked.

"By your question, I guess that you don't have them over here."

"No, I'm very sorry, sir."

"Oh, it's okay, thank you." Jack walked out through the revolving brass doors to the waiting sea and salt air of the English Channel. He looked around up and down the boulevard, reconstructing the arrival route of the crew bus earlier that morning. He wasn't the only jogger out that day, but most of them were down near the beach. Jack was running on the sidewalk, which was occupied by strollers, but was not by any means crowded. After jogging for about fifteen minutes, he recognized the corner. He stopped, caught his breath, and walked into Benny's Money Shop. He was only sweating slightly, as the sea breeze had kept him cool.

"Hello, Mate, what would we be selling today?" the shopkeeper began.

Jack looked down at his running shorts and shoes and understood the question.

"Actually, sir, I'm here to buy."

"Oh, brilliant. What's on your mind?"

"I would like to buy the rabbit in your front window."

"You want to buy the big stuffed rabbit?"

"Yes, how much is it?"

"Well, it's very unique, you know. You won't find a rabbit like that, like him, anywhere else."

"Yes, I'm quite sure of it. How much do you want for the rabbit?"

"Well, I won't take less than ten quid for it. It really is quite a unique rabbit, one of a kind, you know."

"Yes, I know," Jack said again. "Okay, ten quid."

"Smashing! I think that I have a large box in the back that it will fit into, or do you want me to put it into a large bag?"

"Thank you, but I'd like you to keep it there in the window and give it to someone."

"How's that?" the shopkeeper asked with a puzzled look on his face.

Jack continued, "Have you ever noticed a young woman with blond hair and a small child about six or so in front of your shop, looking in?"

"Oh, do you mean Cricket?" the shopkeeper asked.

"Cricket—is that the woman, the mother?"

"No, that's the child."

"Oh, do you know them, then?" Jack asked.

"No," the shopkeeper said curtly.

Jack paused. Clearly the shopkeeper was familiar with the woman and her daughter, although he didn't want to admit it. "Well, the next time you see them," Jack said, "I'd like you to give the little Cricket girl the rabbit. Please look out for them." Jack pulled out his wallet from his fanny pack and started counting money.

The shopkeeper thought for a moment. "What will I say, what will I tell them your name is and why you're doing this?" he queried.

Jack looked thoughtful. "Do you have any ribbon?"

"Ribbon?" the shopkeeper asked.

"Yes, ribbon, like you wrap Christmas presents with."

"Oh, I imagine I do, somewhere in the shop. Why?"

"Well, and I'll pay you extra, I'd like you to wrap the ribbon, hopefully a red one, around the rabbit's neck and attach a sign to it that says 'Please take care of me.' And if you would, I'd like you to tell the little girl that you've run out of space in your shop and that you would be grateful to her if she would take the rabbit home with her and take care of it."

"That's it?" the shopkeeper asked.

"That's it," Jack replied. "Do you think that you can do all of that?"

"Yes, I think that I can do all that," he replied as he watched Jack counting out the bills from his wallet and putting them into a small pile on the display case.

"And this is little extra—for you," Jack said.

"Thank you, Mate. I appreciate it."

Jack put out his hand, and the shopkeeper did also. They shook hands, exchanged a nod, and then Jack turned around and walked out of Benny's Money Shop onto Southwick Road. He lingered outside the storefront window for a moment, looking at the rabbit and wishing that he could have at least gotten a glimpse of the little girl's face. He began jogging again, this time in the opposite direction back toward the Brighton Piers and the Metropole Hotel.

Jack returned to his room and looked at the bed. The sheets and the bedspread were rumpled from the haphazard way that he had made the bed just hours before, but it looked so incredibly comfortable and inviting. Can't do it, he thought, can't do it. So he continued his post-shower toilette, placed the razor on the sink, and unpacked the rest of the suitcase. He set aside his socks and underwear for the next day, unfolded his uniform shirt, installed the shoulder epaulets, and hung it in the closet next to the uniform jacket. He buffed his black shoes with his dirty socks and packed away the pair of running shoes in his suitcase, each in a zippered exterior pocket, one on each side. The original forecast for Paris had been calling for evening temperatures in the seventies, so he hadn't brought a jacket or a sweater, leaving more room for presents that he might find roaming around the local Paris neighborhoods.

Satisfied that he was sufficiently organized, he made his way out of his room. "London by the Sea" was much cooler and damper due to the moisture of the Channel, but at least he didn't have far to walk. He made his way to the receptionist counter in the lobby of the hotel.

Holding an outstretched hand, he began, "Well, hello there, you're still here!"

"And hello to you Captain. Here, I'll take your key."

Jack moved closer to the counter—"Tell me, Miss Edwards," he began, eyeing the woman's name tag, "can I please get a wake-up at zero seven forty-five?"

"Brilliant," she retorted, her smile as fresh as it had been in the morning when he had checked in.

Jack smiled back at her and also to himself. What was so brilliant about asking for a wake-up call? But he loved the Brits; he loved their stiff upper lip when it was needed, and he loved how they seemed to always celebrate the occasion, whatever it was, large or small—or in this case, trivial.

* * *

The sun was now setting on this late July summer day. Various groups were still on the beach, the families with their sun umbrellas and children, the young men showing off their athletic prowess, and the young women getting the most of the sun on this rare cloudless day in England. There were men with their long rods, fishing near the pilings of the old pier. There were a few brave souls actually out on the water in their small, brightly colored sailboats, some blue, some red. They were for rent and patiently waiting for their patrons, all of them lined up neatly side-by-side in a perfect row on the sandy beach.

Jack crossed the boulevard from the hotel side to the beach. For about five minutes, he just stood stationary on the wide sidewalk, looking down at the beach, at times breathing deeply, inhaling through his nose. It was a lot like Marblehead, Massachusetts, he thought to himself, the smell of the salt, the sea, and the fish—but there was a hint of another scent. He tried, but couldn't put his finger on exactly what it was. He just knew that it was there, and it was different from back home. He descended the stone steps that led to the beach and stood in the sand about forty feet behind the nearest beachgoers. He looked left, which was east, to a distant marina that he could barely see; only the miniature masts were visible, all pointing up to the blue sky. He looked to his right, or west, down the beach to the two giant steel erector sets, stretching their arms out into the sea. One was a beehive of activity, a mini amusement park with flashing lights, carousels, a small roller coaster and other rides, concessions, and throngs of young people going to and fro, having the time of their lives.

The other steel pier was a ghost—a dark, foreboding, rusting derelict, which had once hosted revelers and fun-seekers in a different time, many years ago. She had served Brighton well since being born in 1823. Originally known as the Royal Suspension Chain Pier, she had been built intending to service the packet boats to Dieppe, France, across the Channel. Jack walked toward the piers. The soft, coarse sand under his feet made the hike feel somewhat awkward and slowed his progress. *DANGER, NO TRESPASSING* read the sign, ten feet high, written with bold red block letters. It stood before the gates and was erected to block entry to the main concourse of the crumbling yet still proud relic.

Jack stopped at a bench and sat down. He stared at the aging dinosaur. He was fascinated by it—its shape, its size, but most of all, its aura; it was history. He grew inward and lost awareness of his actual surroundings. He thought that he could almost hear the sounds and see the sights that the pier had seen in her life of 166 years. Especially foremost in his thoughts were the images of young soldiers from the Great War who were home on leave for just a few days. They were back from the trenches and the horrors of war, and were now almost within sight—right across the Channel from France and Belgium—of where they had just been, and where they were soon to be again. What was the unreal part to them, he wondered, playing a game in the arcade and drinking a pint with friends, or going back to the slaughter in the next day or two? Jack sat there on the bench for at least ten whole minutes and thought about nothing but that.

* * *

"Miss Edwards?"

"Oh, it's you again, Captain Rheinstrom. What is it now?" She smiled, raised one eyebrow, and cocked her head, her arms folded in front of her in mock anger.

"Well, I only have one left," he said, reaching into his pocket and displaying a pound in his open right palm. "And I wanted to donate it to pound night, if you would be so kind as to tell me where it takes place."

"Absolutely," she replied and proceeded to tell him that it was necessary to go out the hotel entrance door, down the stairs to the sidewalk, take a left, walk for about thirty paces, descend another flight of stairs on the left, go under a canopy, then open the door. "And, spot on—you'll be there!" Those were her final words, with a smile, of course.

Jack found the door, walked in, and looked around. There were maybe ten tables, each with four to six chairs. The room was cozy. A huge mirror hung on the wall on the left side, and on the right was a smattering of framed posters, including one of the HMS *Sparrow*. There were about thirty people present, all crewmembers from three different airlines, and all laying over at the Metro. There was Jack's crew from Trans Ocean, one from South African Airlines, and one from Qantas, the Australian airline. He noticed two tables pushed together over in a corner and recognized Jane, Laurie, and some of the other back-end crew.

"Jack, Jack, over here!" called out Laurie, whose voice was barely audible over the simultaneous claps of laughter arising from the Qantas table. "You found us," she beamed as Jack approached. "Jack, there's an extra chair over there—grab it before someone else does." Jack did, pulled it up to the table between Laurie and Janie, and sat down.

"Here comes Maggie now with another round. I'll introduce you," said Laurie, as the woman approached. "Maggie, this is a very good friend—a dear friend—Captain Jack Rheinstrom."

Jack stood up, as a proper gentleman would always do, and accepted Maggie's hand when she extended it.

"Pleased to meet you, Captain Rheinstrom," Maggie said.

"Maggie, the pleasure is mine. I understand from Laurie that this was your idea, and I would just like to say, as one of the crews that you look after, thank you very much."

"It's a lot of fun, Captain. I have to do something for all these chicks that are away from their homes, the mother hen that I am. I have to deliver these pints to our Aussie friends over there, but can I fetch a pint for you after that?"

"That would be great, Maggie."

"Now, Captain, what would you like—a Carlsberg, a Foster's, or a Kronenbourg?"

"Make it a surprise, Maggie, make it a surprise."

After listening to the review of the previous day's flight and the post-nap Brighton shopping activities, Jack started to feel as though he was wasting his time sitting there at the table. He had just finished his second pint of Kronenbourg and was feeling quite relaxed and comfortable. When Janie looked away and was talking to another flight attendant, Jack leaned over toward Laurie and softly asked, "Laurie, do you want to know?" She started to say, "Know what?" but the serious look in his eyes stopped her.

"Yes, Jack, I want to know. Let's walk over to The Ship. They have booths there, and pretty good fish and chips, too." They stood up, excused themselves, said good night to the crew and Maggie, and left Pound Night.

* * *

Jack Rheinstrom had been standing outside a short distance from the hotel entrance, watching the passersby and thinking about the upcoming day. The past few days had gone by in a blur, and now here he was in Detroit. He waited for everyone to board the crew bus before he did. Captain Black boarded the bus first and sat alone. He brought a cup of coffee from the hotel and was looking out the window at the traffic in the back row. The flight attendants and Bear were bunched in the middle seats, rehashing their dinner at Fishbone's in Greektown the night before. Jack sat all alone in the front. As the bus pulled away from the Renaissance Hotel, Laurie looked around the bus, got up, and walked forward. She plopped down next to Jack and looked over at him. "So, you're a slam-click now, huh?"

"Hey, Laurie, good morning. A slam-click? No, I don't think so. I'm just not used to the time zone stuff yet. Let me get my sea legs, okay?"

"Sure, I know, it's just that after our great reunion and pow-wow in Brighton, I thought that we were back to being best friends, and then you didn't show at crew muster last night. I was really looking forward to your company for dinner last night."

"Well, guess where I was for dinner last night?"

"Where? The hotel bar and restaurant?"

"No, I was in bed. I skipped dinner and went to bed at seven o'clock and slept straight through to wake up. I don't know if it's flying with Black, not being used to the international flying, or getting older, but the fact is that the bed felt awfully good last night. I didn't really stand you up—I think that I said that I wasn't sure that I could make it—and we *are* best friends again. Laurie, we always have been! Anyway, you have a dinner date tonight with me at La Polidor in Paree.

"The what?"

"La Cremerie-Restaurant Polidor. It's an old bistro near the Luxembourg Gardens. I was there a bunch of times many years ago, and I loved it. I want to see if it's still there. It used to be like the old Paris of the forties and fifties."

"Is it formal? Do I need to dress up? Because I really didn't bring any fancy clothes."

"No, it's a bistro, very local. In fact, Hemingway frequented the place—that is, when he wasn't supposedly catching pigeons to eat in the Luxembourg Gardens."

"Really?"

"I don't know---that's just what I've read. Anyway, we have a date."

* * *

All preflight duties were accomplished on time and the plane was pushed back from the gate. After ten minutes of taxiing the blue and white 747 stopped and switched the radio from ground to tower frequency. It was now sitting at the number one position for takeoff, ninety degrees to runway two two.

"Metro Tower, Trans Ocean four zero is ready," said Black.

"Trans Ocean four zero, following the departing Northwest DC-10, line up and hold runway two two." At that exact moment the overhead cabin call light illuminated accompanied by rapid multiple *dings.*

"Get that for me Bear, will you?"

Wagoner picked up the intercom mike, "Cockpit here."

"Gary! Gary! This is Jane—we have a fire in the first class galley—come quick! The smoke alarm is screaming so loud I can't even think!"

"I'll be right there!"

"Jack, there's a fire in the first class galley—I'm going back!"

Jack picked up his mike—"Metro Tower, Trans Ocean four zero, we have a reported fire in the galley—I don't know the status yet. I am going to hold my present position and get back to you in a minute."

"Roger, Trans Ocean, I will notify the fire department and standby for your intentions."

"Bear, let me know ASAP—I need to know if we should evacuate or not."

Gary unbuckled his seatbelt, slid his seat backwards, and bolted out the cockpit door bypassing the normal protocol of first looking out the peephole. He ran back the entire length of the upper deck much to the astonishment of the gawking passengers, descending the spiral staircase two steps at a time, the distinct smell of smoke getting stronger the closer he got.

"Over there Gary!" Jane Farnsworth yelled over the scream of the alarm, "Over there!" The fire was indeed real and appeared to be in or behind one of the convection ovens that were preheating the passengers' meals. Wagoner opened the oven door and black smoke billowed out into the entire galley area. He momentarily tried to pull on the multi-tiered container that held the meals but it wouldn't budge—it was too heavy and the metal frame was very hot from the preheating. *I can't pull it out—too heavy—gotta make it lighter.* His decision was made. He put the asbestos glove that was sitting on the galley counter on his right hand and reached into the oven grabbing each tin-foiled entrée and rapidly flinging them out onto the galley floor with some of the round potatoes and green peas actually rolling into the first class passenger area. Between the shrill of the alarm, the dark smoke wafting out of the galley, and the bizarre behavior of the engineer heaving food onto the ground, the first class passengers, who were the only ones that could see this drama unfold and whose eyes were now the size of saucers, became very alarmed. That was especially the case of a pregnant women sitting with her husband in the last row of first class, the row closest to the galley and the fire.

"What the hell is going on, Bob?"

"I don't know—I've never seen anything like this before!" Being a volunteer fireman from a small town in New Hampshire, his second nature kicked in.

"I'm going to ask them if I can help," he said as he rose to stand up.

"What? Are you crazy? You will do no such thing," she said grabbing on to his left arm. "They are trained for emergencies. Look, the flight attendants are standing by with fire extinguishers! And if it gets worse, we only have to go fifteen feet to get to that exit door over there."

After three full trays of meals had been extracted, Gary once again tried to pull the container out, this time with success. He quickly dropped it onto the galley floor and peered inside the oven. There, through the smoke he could see the flames and could make out the telltale blue print title of a burning USA TODAY. He thought for a split-second—*it must've been sitting on the galley counter and the caterers didn't see it, they heaved the heavy meal container up onto the counter and on top of the paper, then pushed it into the oven—what an innocent but dangerous mistake that was.* No time to lose—he reached into the back of the oven, grabbed the burning newspaper, and hurried into the first class lavatory ten feet away. Visibly wincing with the pain in his ears from the loud alarm only inches above his head, he held the burning paper under the faucet and turned on the water, eventually extinguishing the flames.

"Quick Jane, call Jack and tell him there's no need to evacuate, that it was a small paper fire, and that it is extinguished, and there is no damage. And maybe he should say something to the folks." After two minutes the smoke dissipated and the alarm fell silent. The engineer emerged from the galley area on his way to the spiral stairway back to the top deck. He glanced at the first class section only to see thirty-six eyeballs trained directly on him and all of them looking very much relieved. He wanted to apologize to them for the circus that they had just been subjected to but he was unable to because in the middle of his first word to them they all stood up and enthusiastically began clapping; their hands raised high in the air. He couldn't see it because they were standing behind him, but the flight attendants were clapping, too. True to his nature, the strapping engineer shyly looked at the floor, nodded, and scurried up the stairs. Halfway up he stopped, turned around, and asked Jane if she could clean up the mess as best she could.

"What do you think that we're going to do, Gary?"

"We'll probably go back to the gate to have maintenance check out that there isn't any damage, get more meals, and try it again."

Back in the cockpit, Wagoner debriefed the entire episode as they taxied in.

"Well, Gary, it sounds as though you are the man of the hour. Good job, Bear."

"Thanks, Captain Rheinstrom. But can you imagine if this had occurred one minute later than it did, like right after liftoff?"

"Yeah, that would have been a hell of a different scenario. I think guys, that we really lucked out on this one."

* * *

Once finally airborne, the actual flight from Detroit to Charles de Gaulle was routine, uneventful, and unremarkable. No weather problems, no passenger problems; in fact, the flight even had an early arrival. When Trans Ocean 40 landed, they turned off the runway at the taxiway nearest their stopping point, switched radio frequencies, and contacted ground control.

"De Gaulle Ground, Trans Ocean four zero, clear of runway nine right."

"Bonjour, Trans Ocean four zero. Your company says that your gate is not yet ready; you are cleared to Romeo one two eight."

"Roger, cleared to Romeo one two eight."

Jack was busy taxiing the airplane to the terminal complex. Second officer Wagoner ran the after-landing checklist and used his number three radio to contact company operations, informing them that they had landed and were taxiing in.

"Captain Rheinstrom?" Wagoner asked.

"Yes, what is it?"

"There's a plane still at our gate since we're early, and that flight is supposed to push off the Jetway in five minutes. I was looking at the parking spot chart near our terminal—I see Romeo Row, but not Romeo one two eight. It only goes up to number twelve."

"Thanks, Bear. Let me get a clarification." He turned his attention to the radio and asked for confirmation from ground.

"Trans Ocean four zero, that is affirmative. Taxi to Romeo one two eight."

"Well, we see Romeo Row on our chart, but the positions are only numbered one through twelve. We don't see Romeo one two eight—can you give us progressive taxi to get there?"

"Trans Ocean four zero, that is parking spot Romeo *one—to wait* for your gate!"

"Oh, got it now! Thanks. Sorry."

"*De rien,* Trans Ocean, it's nothing. Welcome to Paris." All three crewmembers looked at one another, shook their heads slightly, and smiled. The Boeing 747 taxied into Romeo one, stopped, and Jack applied the parking brake. Only three minutes passed before ground control called and cleared them into their gate.

"Is the APU up?" Jack asked the flight engineer.

"Yes, sir, up and running."

"Okay, I'm shutting 'em down." Captain Rheinstrom reached down to the middle console between the captain and first officer seats and pulled the start levers back to the shut-off position. Engines one, two, three, and four spooled down, the auxiliary power unit assuming the aircraft's electrical and air-conditioning loads. Both crews performed their post flight duties, grabbed their bags, and trundled out the Jetway on their way to Customs.

The bus that arrived that morning was small—a minivan with just enough capacity to accommodate the whole crew. The driver was busy piling their suitcases and brain bags on top of each other into the rear compartment as the queue of the crew slowly boarded and found their way to a seat. The captain and the flight engineer ended up sitting together.

"You know, Jack, we could be out there right now taxing around in circles still looking for that infamous Romeo one two eight. That was funny!

"Kind of reminds me of Japan," Jack said, nodding.

"What reminds you of Japan?"

"Not completely understanding a foreign language when you think that you do—and we're only talking about English here."

"Well, why does this remind you of Japan?" Bear reiterated.

"Do you remember when Pan Am sold their Pacific routes to United Airlines a number years ago? They were in their death spiral, selling off their crown jewels—Pacific routes to United, European routes to Delta. Anyway, United was the newbie, the new guy on the block in the Pacific, and they were just feeling their way along on this new route, San Francisco to Tokyo's Narita airport. Maybe it was the crew's first flight there, I don't know. Anyway, as the story goes, a United 747 had just been given a clearance by Tokyo control: 'United so-and-so, you are creared direct to the Meron intersection.' United came back on the radio: 'Roger, United two-five, cleared direct to the Meron intersection.' A minute or so passed by, and United was back on the radio. 'Tokyo, United two-five, please confirm that we are cleared direct to the Meron intersection.' Tokyo answered, 'Loger,

United two-five, you are creared direct to Meron intersection.' United came back again, 'Thank you, United two-five cleared direct to the Meron intersection.' Another minute passed by, then, 'Hey, Northwest, are you still on this frequency?' Northwest answered, 'Yeah sure, United, this is Northwest one six, go ahead.' 'Thanks, well, we've just been cleared to a Meron intersection. Our Jepps are all up-to-date, but for the life of us, all three of us cannot seem to find the Meron intersection anywhere on the bloody chart.' There was a pause, then, 'Well, it's called Meron intersection as in watermeron!' 'Oh, *Melon* intersection—there it is! Got it! Well, that's something. Thanks, Northwest.' 'You bet.'

Jack continued the thread—"The point, Bear, is that communication is so important out here when we're flying these things, that sometimes you really have to work hard to get it right. And flying to other countries where English is not their first language—well, you just have to be aware of all the traps. And that works both ways—remember the Columbian 707 that went down near JFK last year?"

"I remember that there was pretty lousy weather involved, that it crashed and that there was no fire because it ran out of fuel but what does that have to do with what you are talking about?"

"Well, there was miscommunication on both sides and not only between the crew and the controllers at Kennedy, but between the cockpit crew themselves. Everyone flying into there had been delayed with multiple holding patterns and was worried about fuel reserves. The captain, who I believe was the weaker of the two in English, kept on telling the first officer to tell the controllers that they were getting dangerously low on fuel, they didn't even have enough to get to their alternate, Boston and that they were in an emergency situation. The first officer *did* announce that they were getting low on fuel but he didn't use the called for *exact* term *Emergency Fuel*, which would have set off alarm bells giving them immediate priority. The traps are out there and they are plenty. Once again, that *SA*, situational awareness, is so critical."

After an hour ride from the airport in the morning Paris rush hour, the crew bus pulled up in front of the Holiday Inn St. Germain des Pres on Rue de l'Abbé Grégoire. The interpreter departed the bus first and instead of waiting for his fellow crew, made a beeline across the street, dodging the morning traffic, and headed straight toward the hotel entrance. "What's his problem?" Jane asked Laurie, watching the interpreter depart.

"I don't know. He's in a snit about something. Ginny noticed him during the breakfast service. I've flown with him before. It's always something with him."

"That's too bad. Kind of makes you not want to fly with him, you know?"

"Yup."

Jack and Laurie got off the bus together, one behind the other, and pulled their wheelies across the street to the hotel, making sure to avoid the early morning flush of water down the gutters on either side of the Paris streets. "Jack, over here, there's a little bridge in the pavement over the water." Jack nodded and followed her lead. When the crew checked in at the reception counter, to their surprise and delight, all the rooms were ready, which wasn't the normal routine. After they all had their keys, they queued up in front of the two elevators in the hotel lobby.

"Now, Jack, you're not going to stand me up again, are you?"

"Hey, come on Laurie. I didn't stand you up, and if you're not down here at fifteen hundred—that's six hours from now—I'll be knocking on room 304. You see, I noticed your room assignment when you checked in."

"Very observant! See you down here at fifteen hundred. That is all, Captain." They entered the elevator together and then went to their individual rooms.

Emerging from the shower after his nap, Jack walked back into the bedroom wearing the fluffy white terrycloth robe that had been hanging on the inside of the bathroom door. He noticed that the telephone was still lying on the floor from when he had knocked it off the table during his wake-up call. He picked it up and put it back on the tabletop. What to wear, he asked himself as he rustled through his suitcase, picking out his change of underwear and white uniform shirt for the flight tomorrow. He walked over to the window, opened it, and looked down at the street below. People were wearing normal summer clothes, and he couldn't see any humid mist in the air. He stuck his head partially out the window and took in a deep breath. I think that I'm in luck, he told himself. This smells like a beautiful summer day.

* * *

"Morning, Jack."

"Good afternoon, Laurie," he said as he pulled up a stool and sat next to her at the small bar just off the hotel lobby. "How's the espresso?" he asked.

"Perfect, just like everything in Paris."

"Oh, are you a Francophile?"

"If that means that I like everything in France, then yes, I'm a Francophile," she said, flashing a smile.

"Well, I rather like the place myself. I really don't know where the French got their bad reputation that they have in the States, because about the worst thing I've ever encountered here is an impatient waiter, and that's about it. How did you sleep?"

"Are you kidding? Like a rock. So what's your plan for today?" she asked, sipping her espresso.

Jack paused. "Well, whenever I'm in Paris, I mean, whenever I *was* here, twenty years ago, I always made a point of going to Notre Dame and just soaking it in. I would go inside to sit and just...think."

"Think? Think about what?"

"Well, Notre Dame is just so old, built in the eleven hundreds. I'd think about all of the things that happened right outside its walls, and inside them, too; what the people, what Paris, went through during the Black Plague, the fact that the third Crusade actually launched from there, from Notre Dame. I'd look at the stained-glass windows in the main church, and, well, it's just spiritual to me. All the history, the crowning of kings and queens, all of the wars, all the suffering over the ages, and the changes in European society, in civilization—I find it all, well, mesmerizing."

"Well, I'm up for it," chimed Laurie. "I've probably had twelve or more layovers in Paris, and I've never been inside Notre Dame. I've always been deterred by the big line out front just to get in. So yeah, let's go!"

"Great." Jack stood, put five francs on the bar top, and the two of them departed the hotel. The metro station was less than a four-minute walk from the hotel, and in the blink of an eye they were descending the steps of Metro St. Placide toward the platform that was labeled Clignancourt and metro train number 4, which headed north into the heart of Paris. As they stood there on the subway platform, they looked across the tracks to an identical platform and to the people that were waiting for *their* train to arrive, which was headed in the opposite direction, south to Orleans.

"Kind of funny, isn't it?" asked Laurie.

"What?"

"Oh, you know, looking at those people over there is like looking at yourself, which is kind of hard to do, if you know what I mean."

"Yeah, I *think* that I do," Jack said. "Observant yet introspective. And what is your conclusion—that is, after looking at those people who are probably a lot like us?"

"You know, Scrappy, I don't have a conclusion. I guess that I just find people-watching in Paris a giant step above what I normally see, and being in this business, you and I see a lot of people."

"Laurie, I don't know if it's just the fact that Paris is known for its haute couture and is so important in the fashion world, but my observation as a normal, healthy male—no comment, please—and don't call me a sexist, is that the Parisian women above all others that I have observed exude femininity. They dress and act like a woman *all* of the time. They take pride in their appearance and there is definitely an air of mystery about them. Do you agree, or do you know what I mean?"

"I think that it's kind of funny that you said that. I just read an article in *the New Yorker* magazine that had an interview with a middle-aged Parisienne, and she said that even if she went out into the backyard to deposit a bag of garbage in the trashcan, she would always make sure that she was dressed 'presentably.' When asked why she went to the extra effort, she replied 'One never knows!' Now, does that sound American to you? I don't think so."

The two of them could not yet see the headlight of the approaching train, but they knew that it was coming, first by the rush of air that suddenly blew their hair back and sent dust into their eyes, then by the hint of a distant sound that was getting louder and louder. The silver train, maybe six cars long, came to a smart stop just in front of them. The double doors slid open, three per car, and people scurried out. Laurie and Jack waited on the platform for them to disembark, then hopped on and found two open seats at the very end of the car near a designated open space. It had four vertical metal poles to hold for balance, reserved for those who were standing. After about thirty seconds, there was a long toot over the PA system, and the doors subsequently closed. The train began to move down the tracks, away from the light of Saint-Placide station, and into the dark tunnel toward its next stop, Saint-Sulpice. In just a few minutes, the routine was repeated—the stop, the sliding doors, the people, the toot, the closing doors, and then they were off again to Saint-Germain-des-Prés and then finally to Cité.

Just as the doors were about to close at the Saint-Sulpice station, a man about forty years old jumped in at the very last second. That was okay, it happened all the time. But this time it was a little different. He was well dressed and had the look of familiarity, of someone that you might have actually known. He began speaking as soon as the doors slid closed, right after the toot. His voice was clearly audible in the entire car; it undulated up and down, all the time making his point of view and appealing to his captured audience. He was emotional, but not theatrical, and his audience put down their newspapers and correspondence, looked at him, and listened. The train ride only lasted for about four minutes, and just before it was over, he came around to each row with his beret held upside down while passengers reached into their purses or pockets and, without any eye contact, gave him a coin or two. And then when the next stop arrived, he hopped out, never to be seen again, at least for this particular audience.

"What do you *think*?" asked Jack.

"About what?"

"About *him*?"

"I don't know. I'm so tired of beggars coming up to me and asking for money wherever I go, out on the streets of wherever."

"No, Laurie, what did *you* think about *him*? Did you believe him?"

"That's an interesting question, Jack, I don't know. Did you?"

"Well, I don't speak or understand French very well, especially when it's spoken that fast, but yes. And I don't even know what he said, but I believed him—and so did half the Parisians on this train who opened up their wallets and gave him something. It makes me feel cynical that I was not that open-minded. I don't know. I did notice that the people who gave him something didn't make eye contact with him."

"Why do you think that was?" said Laurie. "Maybe a form of respect? I don't know, maybe they didn't want to embarrass him."

"You know what I was kind of reminded of? Édith Piaf."

"The singer?"

"Yeah, you know, 'The Little Sparrow'? I have one of her albums. And there's a song that she sings called 'Milord,' which I really like. In it, she pours out her heart to her audience—she's very sincere and emotional. But then again, I didn't understand the words. That's what I thought of as this man was talking. There seemed to be a truth just in the sound of his voice—it was like 'Milord' without the music."

Laurie squeezed his arm. "You're a romantic, aren't you, Jack?"

"Yeah, I guess..." he said quietly, his voice trailing off.

Soon they were in the open-air square just in front of Notre Dame's west entrance. Jack looked around. "I don't know where all the tourists are, but the lines are pretty small, so we're in luck." They filed into the church via one of the three massive wooden doors. Once inside the small vestibule, they proceeded through a smaller wooden door and were standing at the very west end of the central nave.

Laurie was awestruck; she had never before seen such beauty in a mere building. She looked up at the high vaulted ceiling and just stared. Lowering her gaze, she looked down the naves to the transept, which cut across the axis of the building, giving it the shape of a Latin cross. Beyond the transept on either side were the deep stalls for the choir, and at the very end stood the high altar.

"Do you want to light a candle?" Jack asked as they walked down the side corridors of the cathedral.

"Yes, I would."

"Here," said Jack as he handed her two francs.

"What, you have to buy the candles?"

"Laurie, don't tell me you're surprised—you're in a Catholic Church here. Now take these." She put the coins into the slot of a small wooden box and picked up two candles. They weren't big, maybe four inches tall, but they were surprisingly light. She looked at one of them upside down and noticed that there were four vertical air chambers inside. She lit both candles from the flame of one that was already burning on the table. She stepped back, closed her eyes, and lowered her head.

Jack walked over to the nave and sat down on one of the many chairs aligned in rows there, where he lowered his head. A minute or so later, he stood up, removed a handkerchief from his back pocket and patted both eyes.

He's thinking about his son, Laurie realized. She felt her own eyes well with tears.

Jack replaced the handkerchief and rejoined Laurie in the aisle. "You okay?" she murmured.

Jack nodded. "Yup, I'm okay. Let's grab a beer."

They walked out of the church through the huge wooden door on the western façade. They turned the corner and walked east toward the small bridge to Île Saint-Louis, heading to Jack's favorite brasserie.

"Being summertime, I'll bet there'll be some entertainment waiting for us," Jack said.

"Where?"

"On the bridge, just up there—can you see it?" And sure enough, there was a crowd of people, maybe fifty in all, gathered around in a circle watching and listening to something. As they drew nearer, they could hear music; the rhythm was fast, the melody familiar, but European, not American, and it was setting the tempo for the young man performing in the center. He was wearing very colorful clothes—bright blue pants with suspenders and a horizontally striped red-and-white long-sleeved shirt. He had wavy brown hair and was constantly smiling as his eyebrows raised and lowered to the beat of the recorded music. The crowd oohed and aahed as he rode his bicycle around and around inside the small circle, both forwards and backwards. The crowd was happy—his act was a success. But it wasn't an easy chore, since the bicycle was only twelve inches high. Jack and Laurie left the circle before the performance was over, continuing their short walk over the bridge to the brasserie.

As they approached, Laurie couldn't hide her enthusiasm. It was a gorgeous spot with views of the Seine and Notre Dame. There were tables outside nestled under the trees, inviting the pair to sit and people-watch. Jack peeked inside through the open door to the semicircular bar in the front part of the brasserie, the restaurant being in the back. He saw the familiar antique zinc-plated beer tower perched on top of the bar counter. It was very large, over three feet tall, and had four spigots, two protruding from each side. Below each tap was a perch for the glass to stand on while the beer was being poured. Behind the bar and to the left of the silver obelisk, now with salt-and-pepper hair and sporting a pair of glasses, stood the man who had served Jack many a grand Mützig two decades ago. Jack wasn't sure that he would remember him, but it was worth a try. With Laurie in tow, he walked up and stood behind the bar. The barkeep had his back to Jack and was arranging coffee cups on a shelf on the back counter when Jack began, "Roland, Roland, *comment vas-tu, mon ami*?"

The bartender quickly turned around and looked to see who had called his name. As Jack and Laurie were the only ones standing there, there was little mystery, only surprise. It took a few seconds for Roland to speed through his mental Rolodex, but eventually his raised eyebrows and creased forehead disappeared and were replaced by wide eyes and a broad grin.

"Tres bien, Jack, tres bien! Et tu, comment vas-tu?" As the two outstretched hands found their way home and a robust clasp and handshake followed, Jack turned to Laurie and introduced her.

Roland nodded and smiled. "Enchanté, Madame." The reunion was a success. Jack and Laurie stood at the bar and had two Mützigs, one grand and one petite. Their French was not good, nor was Roland's English, but the communication was there and the good feelings were mutual. They exchanged a little bit of personal history, good tidings, and then they were on their way after about twenty minutes.

Once they were outside, Laurie turned to Jack. "That was so sweet. I'm so glad that I met him, and I'm so glad that he remembered you."

"Yes, I am, too, Laurie, I am, too."

In no time they were crossing the Rue Monsieur-le-Prince and gazing at La Polidor, truly one of Jack's favorite destinations in Paris. They were early and there was no line. As soon as she walked in, Laurie stopped and took everything in. She looked to the left and right, noticing the mirrors that went from the middle of the wall all the way up to the ceiling. The front windows, now located behind her, were adorned with various leafy green plants that provided an ambience, suggesting that the room was somehow alive. There were long wooden tables and chairs scattered throughout. Even though they were the first customers that evening, the setting seemed very warm, not at all cold or empty.

A very large, buxom woman with short, pulled-back blond hair soon approached. She was wearing a white short-sleeved blouse and a very short black skirt, and she immediately started asking questions in French.

"That's a good sign," muttered Jack under his breath. He held up two fingers in the air and said, "Deux, Madame, s'il vous plaît." The woman nodded, turned around, and walked over to a long table on the left near the wall that could seat maybe ten, placed two menus at the place settings facing each other, and walked away. "Is this okay?" asked Jack.

"This is fabulous! I just got here, but I can tell you that I already love this place. It is just what I imagined Paris was like in the thirties and forties. You mentioned before that Hemingway and Joyce hung around this place. I can see that now—a cozy gathering place for friends and comrades to join together and eat and drink."

"Well, it pleases me that you like it here," said Jack as he pulled his chair up to the table and unwrapped the silverware from his napkin, which he then placed on his lap. Before they even picked up their menus, a short blond waitress appeared. Smiling, she spoke in English with a heavy French accent. "Hello, my name is Peggy." She placed a small basket of baguette slices on the table in front of Laurie. "Do you care for some wine or something to drink?" The names and prices of the various wines that were for sale that day were written in white crayon on the surrounding mirrors, but the pair happily ordered a bottle of the house red.

"Do you think that it will be crowded here tonight?" Laurie asked, looking around.

"I bet it'll be packed in no time. They do things a little differently here than in the U.S. Instead of seating people around the room, they fill up one table completely before moving on to the next—or at least they used to."

Laurie nodded. "By the way, where are the restrooms? And don't point, Jack!"

Jack directed her discretely, and while Laurie was gone, the wine arrived and Peggy filled both wine glasses. After about five minutes, Laurie returned to the table and Jack stood up to greet her.

Laurie began to laugh. "Wow, it took a few minutes to figure that place out! I mean, are they kidding? It's just a tile floor with a hole in the middle and two places to put your feet!"

"I know--I've been here before. Welcome to Paree."

"Well, I've been to Paris before, too, but this is a first."

"Well, maybe you haven't been to the 'old' Paris before—it certainly is an experience, there's no doubt about that." He reached for his glass of wine and raised it in her direction. "To Paree, Madame."

"To Paree, Monsieur." The two glasses met in the middle of the table with a clink, and they each took a sip of wine. "Ah, that's nice," Laurie remarked.

"Yes, nice it is. A little young, but hey, we're in Paree."

Laurie put her glass back down on the table and reached for a slice of bread. "Now I am in Paris—I just arrived. I have a question, Jack. What are all those little drawers *for*, by the wall back there? They all have numbers on them."

"You know, I asked the very same question when I first came here. Apparently way back when, and I'm not really sure when that was, everyone had their own cloth napkin--I mean we're talking regulars here. And when they were finished with their meal, they would fold up their napkin and give it to the waitress along with a number and they'd store it for them in their own little drawer until the next time they came in to eat."

"Boy, that was a different era, wasn't it?"

"Yup," Jack nodded.

Behind Laurie's back, Jack could see the restaurant door open and a young woman walk in.

"Well," he said, "it looks like another customer has just arrived. Let's see if they plop her down right next to us."

The hostess proceeded to their table and placed two menus on the table right next to Jack and Laurie. While still standing, the new arrival removed her light shawl, placed it on the back of her chair, and sat down facing Jack. She looked to her left at Laurie, then across the table at Jack, and with a slight nod and a pleasant smile, said, "Bonsoir, Madame, Monsieur."

Jack nodded back. "Bonsoir, Mademoiselle." The new arrival was young and strikingly beautiful—Jack figured she was probably in her early twenties. She had long blond hair that was *up*, giving her a Scandinavian appearance, and her skin was perfect although she wore no makeup. Her deep blue eyes were stunning.

As Peggy approached the table once more, Jack and Laurie picked up their menus and started to peruse them.

"Peggy, may we have English menus, s'il vous plaît?"

"I am sorry, Monsieur, we have none right now, but we are getting new ones in a few days."

"That's okay," he said. He looked at Laurie and shrugged. "We'll muddle through."

"I am sorry to interrupt," the American across the table began as she bent forward, "but it appears that we're neighbors this evening, and since I live here in Paris, you will be my guests, and I'm hoping that you'll let me help you with the menu."

"Oh, isn't that nice of you," Laurie said.

Jack smiled. "Your mother has raised you well—looking out for the elderly and helping struggling tourists."

The young woman laughed as she threw her head back. "Yes about my mother, but I'm still looking for some elderly people to help." Looking down at her watch she continued, "And speaking of Mother, I hope that she's not lost again!"

"Is she joining you for dinner?" Laurie asked.

"Yes, she's supposed to. I waited outside for twenty-five minutes before I came in. I mean, it's really quite easy, isn't it? You get into a cab and tell the driver where to go. Unless…unless she lost the piece of paper that I gave her with the name of the restaurant."

"Oh, I'll bet it's just the traffic," Laurie suggested. "I'm sure that she'll be here any minute now."

"I hope so. Anyway, my name is Nicki."

"Hello, Nicki, my name is Laurie, and my friend across the table there is Jack."

"Enchanté, Laurie and Jack. It's a pleasure to meet you both."

Jack pushed his seat back. "Laurie, I always have the same entrée when I'm here, so why don't you and Nicki take a look at the menu while I'm gone. And Nicki," Jack said as he stood up, "is that short for Nicole?"

"No, it's short for Nicoline."

"Nicoline?" He paused as he was standing there. "You're only the second Nicoline that I've ever met. It's a beautiful name."

Looking up at Jack, Laurie asked, "Who was the first?"

"My Norwegian grandmother—Nicoline Christiana Holterman. Now, if you'll excuse me, ladies," Jack said, as he turned around and walked toward the loo.

After about five minutes, Jack slowly descended the steps from the back dining room. Laurie watched him pause by the small wood-and-glass display case where the owner watched over the cash register and his array of the evening's desserts. Their eyes met, and they both nodded. Jack reached for two restaurant business postcards and put them in his shirt pocket.

As Jack approached the table where Laurie and their new friend Nicki were sitting, he could see that the previously empty chair, the one awaiting Nicki's mother, was now occupied. He noticed Nicki's mother from behind, her long blond hair touching her shoulders, almost like a shampoo commercial. Long hair on a woman—nice, he thought, smiling. He circled around the sixteen-foot table to take his place next to the new arrival, first eyeing Laurie and then Nicki. He reached for the back of his chair, pulled it out, and was halfway seated when his eyes rose and he awkwardly plopped down onto his seat.

Laurie and Nicki were quick to notice his sudden lack of coordination. Nicki's mother turned her head slightly to her right to see who had made such an entrance and did an immediate double take. Jack's eyes opened wide as though he had seen a ghost. The two of them just sat there and looked at each other. Laurie and Nicki were now both staring at them. Seconds passed.

"Hello," she finally said, very slowly and sadly.

"Hi," was Jack's response—slow, soft, and tapering off to an almost whisper. A few more seconds passed, the four eyes seemingly glued together, hardly blinking at all.

"Hey, Mom, do you guys know each other?"

The woman paused. "Yes, Honey, we did. Or…we do."

Laurie's curiosity was now keenly aroused, but she was beginning to feel slightly uncomfortable, as though she were eavesdropping. She studied the three of them, wondering what she should do next.

"Jack, where's the powder room?" she asked, having been there just ten minutes prior and knowing full well where it was located.

"It's in the back, on the right," Jack replied, giving her the out that she was subtly requesting.

After Laurie left, the conversation did not pick up. Jack looked to his left, then the tablecloth, then slowly at the woman sitting next to him once more. "How have you been?"

"Fine, I guess. How have *you* been?"

"Fine, I guess."

Now Nicki was starting to feel uneasy. She stared at the bread on the plate in front of her but was afraid to say anything more.

"Jack and I used to know each other when I was still flying, before you were even born." She put her left hand on top of Nicki's right forearm and looked at her daughter softly. "Didn't we?" She turned her head around. "It's been a long time, Jack—a very long time," she said, her eyes again fixed on his.

He slowly nodded. "A long time, yes."

Nicki's eyes darted back and forth. Looking at them both, she could see her mother's profile, but she could see Jack Rheinstrom almost straight on. Laurie approached the table. This time, Jack did not move to rise.

As awkward as she felt, Laurie thought that she would at least try to make conversation. "No, you're right, Jack—that's not the Ritz Carlton in there." He smiled slightly, but Nicki and her mother weren't paying attention. When Laurie sat down, groping for words, Jack gestured to her and asked if they had been introduced.

"Well, actually, no," Laurie said. "She came in just before you returned and sat down."

"Well, then, Laurie, I'd like you to meet an old compatriot of mine at Trans Ocean. We used to fly together many years ago." Realizing what he had just said, he turned back to the woman in horror. "I didn't mean 'old' compatriot, I meant—"

"I know, Jack, you're forgiven."

"Anyway, um, Laurie, I'd like you to meet Katherine Moore."

"How do you do, Katherine? It's nice to meet you," said Laurie as she extended her right hand. They both shook hands and nodded at each other.

Just then the dinner waitress arrived at the table. Short, squat, and in her sixties, she was wearing a white apron and had her brown hair pulled back tightly. Her face was expressionless, and her pen and pad were ready to write.

"Et vous, Monsieur?"

"Madame, the other party has just arrived, and we need a few more minutes to decide."

With a scowl forming on her forehead, she looked at the ceiling, shook her head, and walked away.

"How long ago was that, Mom?" Nicki asked. Her mother did not answer, but instead stared silently at the white tablecloth in front of her, her hand gently supporting her face. Jack, also, did not talk. Laurie caught Nicki's attention. With exaggerated eyes and a slight nod, she motioned to the area of the back room. Nicki nodded.

"Laurie, could you show me where the ladies' room is?"

"Of course, follow me." The two of them got up and left the two statues sitting silently in their chairs. They hadn't noticed before, but there was now a queue for the loo, which they both agreed, in soft voices, was probably best.

"I know that we don't know each other," Laurie began, "and I'm not sure what's actually going on here, but I think you'll agree that they need a little time together."

Nicki nodded. "I've never seen her like this! She's normally such a strong woman."

"I'm sure that she is, Nicki, but you and I are kind of out of place here—by accident, of course. I'm not really sure what to do here, but let's just leave them alone for a few minutes and hide in this back room."

Back at the table, the air was thick with tension. "I can't believe that I'm actually seeing you," Jack began. "You have no idea how much I've thought about you, about us."

"I don't? How can you say that?" she quizzically asked. Their stares became intense and were fraught with a myriad of complex emotions.

"Where have you been?" Jack asked, his brow now creased.

"Where have *I* been? Where have *you* been?" she retorted.

"Wait a minute," Jack's voice rose. "I never heard from you for the entire two months that I was in the hospital—not once!"

"Well, first of all," Katherine's voice now also rising, "there were no visitors allowed when you were in the burn center, and the phone calls were hardly ever put through, and the times that they were, the nurse that answered the phone was, well, let's just say very dismissive if you weren't family.

"Well, as far as the hospital goes, I remember very little until I was just about to be released. I had enough pain meds pumped into me to kill an elephant. And when I did get out, I called your phone and it was disconnected, and when I sent you mail, it was returned as undeliverable. I asked about you, but no one had a clue—no one. What happened? Where did you go? I mean, you were my *world.*"

"I came here, to France." Her voice now calm and even.

"To France? Why France?"

"Well, Jack, my world kind of changed."

"Yeah, well, Katherine, guess what? Mine did, too! A lot's happened, Katherine, a lot's happened." Jack seemed to drift off for a few seconds. "Listen, I'm coming back to Paris in three days. Maybe I could meet you and your husband and take the three of you out to dinner. What do you think about that?"

"No—my husband is dead."

"Oh, Katherine, I'm sorry," Jack said, a look of pain on his face.

"It's okay, it was a long time ago. Anyway, I'm not sure of my plans. I mean that I might not be here on your return."

"I see," said Jack sadly.

* * *

The couple now stood directly across from each other, both motionless, staring down at the cobblestone sidewalk.

Meanwhile, Laurie took a moment to glance into the dining area to see what was happening. To her surprise, they weren't there! She stood there for a moment and then walked to the seclusion of the back dining room, empty and off limits to diners at this time of the evening. Nicki emerged from behind the glass door and walked straight ahead to join Laurie, without taking a peek. "They aren't there!" said Laurie.

"What do you mean?" said Nicki. "Is there another bathroom somewhere?"

"No, not that I can see."

"Maybe they went out for a stroll?" suggested Nicki.

"Maybe. Let's just go back to the table to wait for them and see what happens, okay?"

After they made their way back to the table, Nicki sat down but Laurie decided to keep walking and looked out the front window. She peeked outside, past the diners waiting to get in. Across the street, under a darkened arch and in front of a ten-foot-tall closed iron gate, were the two statues. They were standing just a few feet apart. If they had been talking, they were not now. Laurie saw Katherine Moore turn and begin walking back to La Polidor. She quickly scurried back to the table, sat down, and quietly mentioned to Nicki, "They're coming back!"

Katherine reentered, approached the table and flushed, began gathering her things. "Nicoline, we must go—now!"

"But we haven't even eaten, Mom!"

Katherine didn't respond. She took her sweater from the back of the chair, drooped it over her shoulder, tied the two arms around her neck, and glanced at Laurie.

"It was nice to meet you!" she said. As Nicki stood up, Katherine put Nicki's hand in hers, and they walked out the door together.

The waitress had just returned and was staring at Laurie. "Qu'est-ce que c'est? Are you eating, or are you leaving? Who is paying for the wine, Madame?" she barked with her shoulders hunched, her hands thrust in the air, and with an intense, quizzical look on her face.

Laurie stood up. "Un moment, Madame, s'il vous plaît, un moment." She hurried to the door, peered out, and saw Jack standing alone in the archway, head bowed, with both hands in his pockets. At this point, the neighboring diners were becoming curious.

"Jack," she called out across the street, "they need to know if we're eating or leaving!"

Jack looked up, crossed the street, and reentered the restaurant. "Let's stay, okay?" he said softly.

"Okay, if you want to but I'm really not that hungry anymore."

"You know, I'm really not either, at least for a big meal and it's starting to get a little bit close for me in here. Let's just finish the wine and the bread, I will pay the bill and we'll leave. Maybe we can stop at a little café or something on our way home—and then maybe, maybe I will have something to say."

"Scrappy, you don't have to—"

"Hey, I know that, but we're good friends, and I need a good friend right about now. Yeah, I need a really good friend."

"I have an idea, Scrappy—why don't I tell you about my exciting life? Wouldn't that be fun? And funky? And far out?"

Jack smiled. "You are a pal. I know what you're trying to do, but yes, of course, please do go on."

"Well, I've decided to start dating again! Oh, and while I think of it, while you were in the bathroom, I had a really nice conversation with Nicki Moore and we exchanged addresses and phone numbers in case she ever comes over to Boston or if I want to visit her in Paris. I don't know…would you like to have her contact info also?"

Jack thought about it for a minute. "Sure, why not? Who knows, it might come in handy someday."

"Good," Laurie said. "I'll copy it and give it to you later."

"Did she say why she was living in Paris?"

"Boy, you seem to be very interested in her! Isn't she a little young?"

"Very funny. No, you'll understand my interest when I tell you more about Katherine—which will be later. I can't do it now, I just can't."

"I know! I know! I'm sorry. Jack, I'm now just discovering that there is so much that I really don't know about you. I thought that I knew you inside and out, almost like my older brother."

"Wait a minute, Laurie, you do know me, and we are close, but you're going to have to wait until I'm ready. A lot has happened since we were so close. Twenty years is a long time, and there were some personal things that I've never shared with you, or anyone for that matter. So be patient with me, okay?"

"I'm sorry, Jack, I didn't mean to offend you. Did I? And if I did…." Tears now welled up in her eyes, and one ran down her left cheek.

"Laurie, Laurie, come on now, please don't do that. And, no, you didn't offend me, and now I feel like I'm the one who has hurt you! This is crazy. Let's start over, huh, Pal?" He leaned forward and reached into his back pocket. He pulled out a white folded handkerchief and handed it to her across the table. She took it, patted her eyes, blew her nose, and tucked the handkerchief into her purse.

"Okay, thank you. And you can have it back tomorrow, all spic and span, and ironed."

"Laurie, you don't need to—"

She raised her hand and stopped him. "As far as Nicki goes, she's a student at some prestigious art school here in Paris, I'm not sure if it's at the Sorbonne or not. Anyway, she rooms with three other girls in an apartment within walking distance from here and the Luxembourg Gardens. Is that near here?" she asked.

"Yes, it's just up the street a bit. We will walk by there when we go home tonight."

As the evening progressed, the glasses were refilled a few times, and the pauses in the conversation ceased. Jack stopped staring at the tablecloth, and it was as though he had taken a long yoga breath and slowly come back to life. He was focused once more, his easy smile was back, and he seemed at peace with himself. He raised his right index finger, leaned over the table toward Laurie, and looked her straight in the eyes. "I just want to say, and this will be all that I'm going to say on the subject tonight, at least for now, that at one time, Katherine was my…my *entire world*. And I know that it's not fair to say that and then bail on any questions, but I cannot, and especially here, open up that chapter of my life right now. Okay?"

"Of course it's okay, Jack! Of course it's okay. I'll be there for you when you do open up. You were there for me, friend—do you remember?" she asked.

"Yes, I do, like it was yesterday." They looked at each other, smiled softly, and nodded their heads together. "I think that I'm ready for the broom, Laurie, I'm shot."

"Hey, I completely understand. This has been an emotional evening for me as well. I'm sure that there's a lot on your mind, and there probably will be for the rest of the night. You needn't say another word tonight if you don't want to. Let's just walk home and make it an early night. Okay?"

"This is not how I planned the evening, Laurie."

"I know that."

"How about a rain check for our next Paris trip in three days?"

"You're on, but I'm not sure that I got the trip yet. It was on the open board, but the rundown isn't until tomorrow."

Jack paid the bill, left a large tip for the scowling waitress who was now purring, got up, and helped Laurie with her chair. They walked out of La Polidor together, made their way past the queue of diners waiting to get in, and resumed their walk up Rue Monsieur-le-Prince. After reaching the Luxembourg Gardens, they turned right and it was a straight shot home to the Holiday Inn, about a thirty-minute walk.

"Do you still want to come with me to the market in the morning?"

"I'm not sure, Laurie. If I'm not in the lobby by eight thirty, then go ahead without me."

"Okay. Good night, Jack." Laurie walked off the elevator onto the fifth floor.

"Night, Laurie, see you tomorrow." The door closed and the elevator ascended one more floor. Jack walked out, went down the hall to his room, and went in. He took off his shirt and trousers, lay down on the bed, and fell instantly asleep.

* * *

Jack was already on the bus, seated about halfway back on the right, when the rest of the crew boarded. Laurie saw him sitting there all by himself but decided on sitting in the front with Jane Farnsworth.

"How was your layover, Laurie?"

"Great, as always, Janie. How was yours?"

"Well, if I could afford it—which I can't—I could easily live here in this town. There is just so much to see and do!"

"This *town*?" Laurie laughed. "Yeah, me too. What's not to like?"

The weather was clear and the traffic was light on this August morning, and the bus made the trip to Charles de Gaulle airport in just less than forty-five minutes.

* * *

"Bonjour, Capitaine."

"Bonjour, Philippe," responded Jack as he approached the counter at the flight operations building. The two men stood there studying each other. "It's been over twenty years, but I think I know you."

His hand went forward. "Jack Rheinstrom."

A broad smile appeared on Philippe's face. "Oui, oui, Jack Rheinstrom. Comment va-tu, mon ami? It's good to see you once more. It's been a very long time. Welcome back."

Jack nodded. "Merci, Philippe."

"Here are your papers for flight forty-nine to Boston. We have had no delays at all this morning, and no more talk about fog. Mon Dieu, the fog! We are just now getting caught up from that catastrophe last week."

"Sorry that I missed it—that must've been fun."

"No, Monsieur, it was not."

Jack took the packet, turned around, and walked over to a large table with ten chairs surrounding it. He sat down and perused the paperwork, studying the details of the flight. Captain Black returned from the restroom and sat down next to Jack.

"I'll give dispatch a call," said Jack as he got up and walked back to the counter. "Philippe, may I use the phone for dispatch?"

"Oui, Capitaine Rheinstrom, une minute." He made the telephone connection and then handed the phone to Jack.

"Hello, dispatch, this is Captain Rheinstrom on forty-nine to Boston. Things look pretty routine to me, so I think I'll just go with your recommended fuel load, unless you know something that I don't."

"Hi, Captain. No, things are quiet—so I'll just give you the standard briefing. There is no significant weather, no turbulence forecast or reported at any of the three flight plan altitudes. In fact, you actually have a tail wind out there, around thirty west. Not much of one, but you hardly ever see one heading west. All three Nat Tracks are pretty much the same, time-wise. No ATC delays are expected, and the terminal area forecast for Boston looks like you'll have a perfect summer day when you get there—a few fair-weather cumulus clouds in the area, but nothing of significance. Alternate airport weather is also good. Do you have any questions for me, Captain?"

"Nope, thanks for your briefing—talk to you en route."

A white Air France minivan arrived at the remote flight planning building to pick up the two captains and deliver them to their airplane. As he was climbing the exterior stairs to the Jetway door, Jack looked down and saw second officer Bear Wagoner performing his preflight walk-around, the exterior inspection of the 747. Being elevated more than twenty-five feet above the tarmac; Jack had a vantage point and an excellent view of the nearby runway. He could see, but not yet hear, the airplane on takeoff roll. When Bear looked up and acknowledged Jack's return, Jack hurriedly pointed for Bear to head in another direction, and quickly. At that time, Bear was standing in front of engine number one, and it was blocking his view. But he took Jack's cue and hurriedly walked back to the tail of the plane. And when he got there and heard the thunderous roar of four afterburners rattling the ground and his entire body, he understood. He stopped and just stood there in "airman's awe" as he beheld one of the most beautiful sights in aviation history—a majestic white Air France Concorde, breathing four long tails of bright blue and orange fire, raising her nose upward and streaking back into her home in the skies. Both Jack and Bear stood there watching it until it changed into a speck in the sky. What a way to start the day, thought Jack. And it truly was.

The crew settled in and made their nests in the cockpit. The preflight checklist was completed, and the crew waited for the agent to appear with the final paperwork. When she finally did arrive, she seemed slightly out of breath but was excited to announce that departure would be on time, or possibly even a minute or two early.

"Bonjour, Monsieurs. They are closing the cargo doors right now, all ten non-revs got on, and we have meals for them. Here are your updated papers, and I bid you a good flight."

Bear suddenly interrupted, "We don't have the fuel slip yet!"

"You don't have your fuel slip yet?" she said with an alarmed look, her eyes widening. A quick call was made in French on her handheld radio, and she hurriedly left the cockpit, saying "I'll be right back." She descended the spiral staircase and went out door L1 into the Jetway. There, on the other side of the Jetway door, through the window, she could see the fueler in his bright blue company overalls waving his hands at her for attention. He was a relatively new employee, had apparently forgotten the combination for the Jetway door, and sheepishly surrendered the slip to the agent when she let him in. Back into the plane, up the staircase, and into the cockpit she came, now even more out of breath. "We are fine now, oui?"

"Oui, oui, we are fine now," Jack smiled.

"Au revoir, Monsieurs, au revoir," she said, and once again left the cockpit, went down the spiral stairs, and back into the Jetway. She looked at her watch, closed passenger door L1 electrically from the outside switch, and exhaled deeply. She retreated a few feet to the Jetway control panel, maneuvered it back away from the airplane, and stood there waiting to witness the actual pushback. In the cockpit, the crew had requested and received their overland clearance from air traffic control and had made intercom contact with the driver of the tug that was attached, via a tow bar, to the nose gear of the B-747.

An illuminated yellow light on the flight engineer's instrument panel suddenly went blank. "Door lights are out, Captain," announced Bear.

Jack looked to his right. "How about a push?"

Captain Black picked up his mike and pushed the transmit button. "De Gaulle ground, Trans Ocean four nine at gate two two, we have information Oscar, request pushback."

After a few seconds he heard the reply. "Bonjour four nine, reference a Lufthansa DC-10, left to right, when you are clear of him, you are cleared to push, tail south."

"Roger, cleared to push, tail south, TO forty-nine."

Jack was on the intercom talking to the tug driver. "Okay, we are cleared to push after the Lufthansa DC-10 taxis by, tail south."

"Oui."

The crew then completed the before-start checklist, which was followed shortly by the clearance, via tug driver, in the starting of all four engines. As they were taxiing out to runway two seven left, they completed the after-start, the taxi, and the before-takeoff checklists. They then stopped at the number one position for takeoff, waiting for the clearance from de Gaulle tower.

Captain Black had informed Jack during flight planning that he himself was going to be flying this leg to Boston, and that Jack would be acting as copilot, basically making all the radio calls and maintaining the paperwork and progress reports of the flight on the computer flight plan, but not doing any of the physical flying.

"Trans Ocean four nine, you are cleared for takeoff, runway two-seven left. Contact departure on one two two point seven when airborne," came the call from de Gaulle Tower. Jack looked out the windshield to the right to make sure there was no one on approach, pushed up all four throttles slightly, and with his left hand on the nose wheel steering handle, steered the 747 into takeoff position on the runway. He then looked to his right at Black. "You have it."

"Roger, I have it," Black responded. "Runway heading up to three." He pushed the throttles forward to just shy of the takeoff setting. The throttles were then fine-tuned to the exact value by Jack, the now copilot.

At the correct airspeed, Jack announced, "Rotate, seventeen degrees." Black slowly increased back pressure on the yoke, and the 747's nose began to rise. When it indicated seventeen degrees nose up on the attitude indicator, he held it there. The giant metal bird, now empowered by the wind under and over her wings, transformed herself from caterpillar to monarch, pulling her feet up and away from the runway. She was now back home, climbing into the blue sky above. The weather was perfect for flying—the sun was out, there was no haze in the air, and the sky was clear with the exception of some puffy white cotton balls that had to have been placed on the day's canvas by a landscape artist. The day was so beautiful that, once their actual flying duties were completed, the crew members spent a good deal of time just looking down at the countryside below. Majestic fields of yellow rapeseed, the Normandy coast, the English Channel, and the white cliffs of Dover—it was all there and all for the taking.

Bear finally put it into words. "You know, they actually pay us to do this."

"Easy, Bear, don't say that too loud," Jack quipped.

Jack made the announcements on the PA that late morning, and besides describing some of the interesting sites along the route and the arrival time and weather, he made certain that he announced the point where their Atlantic overwater portion would begin. "We'll be coasting out over Benbecula, an island in the Outer Hebrides chain, just off the west coast of Scotland." He loved saying that. He turned to the second officer. "I must go there someday, Bear, you know? Benbecula—doesn't that just say it all?"

"Well, yeah, I guess I know what you mean. It almost sounds Shakespearean, although it doesn't really have the clout of, say, Cleveland."

"Right!" Jack paused. "Bear, would you do me a favor while I'm putting the wind info into this computer? Listen up on the Shanwick Oceanic frequency for today's recording and verify the accuracy of our list for the Nat Tracks?"

"Sure, no sweat. Where is our copy?"

Jack went through the stack of the flight papers on his clipboard, found it, and handed a piece of paper back to Bear.

"Here, and thanks."

After about five minutes, Bear came back. "They all check, Captain, and the track message identifier is one seven five."

"Okay, then, I'm going to request our oceanic clearance. Back me up on VHF two, if you will."

"Shanwick Oceanic, this is Trans Ocean four nine, over."

A few seconds later, they heard "Trans Ocean forty-nine, this is Shanwick. Go ahead."

"Roger, Shanwick, Trans Ocean four nine is estimating five eight north, zero one zero west at 1345 Zulu. Requesting track Charlie, flight level three one zero, Mach point eight three, and we have TMI number one seven five, over."

"Roger, Trans Ocean forty-nine, three one zero is not available. You are cleared Nat Track Charlie at flight level three five zero, Mach point eight three, and to arrive at entry point five eight north, zero one zero west, no earlier than 1349 Zulu. Go ahead."

"Roger, Shanwick, standby." Jack turned to Bear. "Let's see here, we're at thirty-one now and we have about forty-five minutes before we get to ten west, and we have to lose four minutes on our ETA. Bear, when will we be light enough to go up to thirty-five? The computer flight plan doesn't have us doing that until we burn off fuel for almost another two hours."

"Well, we could probably go up to thirty-five right now as long as there isn't any turbulence up there. We're pretty heavy, and it's a little above our max altitude at this weight, but if it's smooth, then I think we can probably do it—it just won't be very efficient, fuel burn-wise, until we get lighter."

"All I know," Jack said, "is that if you wait until the very last minute to ask for an altitude change, something always happens! You either can't get through to the controller in time because of other radio traffic, or else someone grabs 'your' altitude ahead of you, and you end up being stuck at the lower altitude for the entire flight, sucking way too much fuel. Standby a minute, Bear."

Jack read back the oceanic clearance to Shanwick, then, switching back to VHF radio number one, initiated a call to the local ATC. "London, Trans Ocean four niner, over."

"Hello there, Trans Ocean forty-nine, what can I do for you?"

"First of all, have you had any ride reports on our route at three five zero?"

"Nary a one, Trans Ocean."

"Well then, requesting flight level three five zero at present time."

"Trans Ocean forty-nine," came a voice from the radio, "you are cleared to climb to flight level three five zero, call upon reaching."

"Roger, departing thirty-one for thirty-five, call when reaching, TO forty-nine."

Captain Black had been monitoring the radio and nodded his head as he pushed the throttles forward. Jack reached forward and pushed the climb button on the EPRL gauge on the forward instrument panel. He adjusted the throttles and then sat back in his seat. As the plane leveled off at thirty-five thousand feet, Jack called London and reported level, and then addressed his crewmembers. "And if you'll excuse me, gentlemen, my 'rented' French coffee has just gone right through me; I'll be back in a flash. Does anyone want anything? Have them put your meals on? Another coffee? Okay, no takers—see you in a jiffy."

Jack unbuckled his shoulder harness and seatbelt, slid his seat backwards, and as Black donned his oxygen mask, stood up, patted the second officer on his back, and left the cockpit. The upper deck lavatories were occupied, so he descended the spiral staircase to the lower deck. As he reached the bottom step of the stairs, he was almost standing in the first-class galley. There was a movie playing, and all the window shades were drawn down so that the picture was more visible on the screen. There was sunlight streaming through the small oval window in the service door. The galley itself was vacant. Jack noticed the serving trolley with an ice bucket holding a bottle of wine sitting on the top. The ice bucket was obviously not flat on the bottom for as the flight progressed, even with slight turbulence, the bucket rocked back and forth—but you would have to be watching to actually notice it. The half empty bottle of white Bordeaux was different; it was not rocking back and forth, but it was obvious, if you looked at the wine level in the bottle, that the airplane was slightly vibrating, because there were small ripples on the surface of the wine. Hmm, Jack mused, interesting little world there. I never noticed that before.

As he was waiting for the first-class lavatory to become unoccupied, he saw Laurie. He really hadn't talked to her since the previous night at La Polidor. When they made eye contact, Jack raised his thumb and his eyebrows. Laurie mimicked the gesture and nodded her head. Eventually Jack entered the lav and closed the door. Upon leaving, he retraced his steps to the galley and reached for the coffeepot.

Laurie interrupted him. "I'll get that for you, Jack. Cream, no sugar, right?"

"Yes, ma'am." As he was waiting and watching Laurie, he noticed the serving trolley slowly roll about three feet from where it had been stationed into the bulkhead wall and come to an abrupt stop.

"That must be a pain, putting up with that all the time."

"Putting up with all what?" Laurie asked.

"Having your rolling serving trolleys moving all the time."

"They don't in cruise, just during climb-out, when the aircraft nose is up. That's why we always make sure that the wheels are locked and the trolleys are put in their cubbyholes with the doors locked just prior to departure."

"So, they don't move in flight?" Jack asked, a sudden intensity in his voice.

"No. Why, is something wrong? Is everything okay?"

"Sure, everything's fine," he muttered and left Laurie with his coffee still in her hand as he quickly ascended the stairs. He put his key in the door handle and reentered the cockpit. It didn't take him long. "Jesus, Black, what the hell are you doing?" he exclaimed.

Black turned around in his seat as he took his oxygen mask off. "What?"

"Airspeed! Airspeed! For Christ's sake, *look at your airspeed!*"

They were cruising at thirty-five thousand feet and were supposed to be flying at .83 Mach, or eighty-three percent of the speed of sound as indicated on their Mach meter. But they were not flying at Mach .83, they were flying at Mach .65—slow, dangerously slow, and with a nose-high attitude of plus eight degrees, rather than the normal three degrees. They were mushing through the air like a speedboat not yet on the plane.

"Push the goddamn throttles up!" Jack yelled. Black appeared stunned and confused. Jack rushed forward and pushed the GA, or go-around, button on the engine EPRL gage, then pushed the throttles forward himself to match the called-for setting.

"The auto throttles screwed up—they were supposed to maintain our initial airspeed!" Black sheepishly whined.

Jack shot back, "Well, maybe you should spend a little less time in the simulator and the freaking training department and more out flying the line…*nobody* uses the auto throttles in cruise because they suck, they're horrible! Everyone knows that."

"Well, they're supposed to…" was Black's only reply.

"And *you* are supposed to *fly* the airplane, Black!" said Jack, practically shouting. "Now, thanks to you, we're close to a fucking stall! And we're still losing airspeed! We've gotta go down. We have to descend—we need to get some airspeed back. Bear, get up here and help me look outside. Descend, Black, descend now!"

"But we'll bust our altitude, and we'll get violated. London will violate us!"

"We don't have much time, Black. I can almost feel the nibble of the wing stall right now." Jack reached over and turned the transponder to standby. "There, I 'strangled the parrot.' It's off, now go down!"

Black lowered the nose to begin a descent while the two other crew members strained their eyes on the horizon and in the sky below, looking for other aircraft. Almost simultaneously a call came over the radio from London ATC.

"Trans Ocean forty-nine, Trans Ocean forty-nine, I've lost your transponder—recycle!"

"Roger, London, forty-nine."

Five seconds passed. London, who was regulating the in-trail traffic stream, called back. "Trans Ocean forty-nine, still negative contact. Recycle your transponder again. What is your estimate now for ten west, the overwater Nat Track entry point?"

"Roger, London," responded Jack as he returned to his seat and buckled in. "Standby." In thirty seconds, they had descended eighteen hundred feet and the airspeed was finally increasing. "Okay, bring her back up to thirty-five, but gently…gently." Jack, playing his part very well, called London and asked them if they had any radar contact yet with their transponder.

"Negative, negative! What is your estimate now for ten west?" a strained voice asked again. The engines were still at go-around power, which was limited to a maximum of five minutes. When they finally leveled off again at their assigned flight level 350, they were able to lower the nose to approximately the desired three degrees nose up. The plane seemed happy, although she was only flying at .80 instead of the desired and stipulated .83 Mach.

"We seem to have lost some speed here, London, and now estimate ten west at 1350 Zulu," said Jack as he reached for the transponder and turned the "parrot" from standby back to on.

In an instant came the frantic call from London. "Swissair thirty-five, Swissair thirty-five, make an immediate three sixty, an immediate three sixty. Acknowledge, *acknowledge*!" He was asking the Swissair flight to turn in a complete circle to regain correct spacing.

"Roger, London, Swissair thirty-five making an immediate three sixty."

Trans Ocean 49 and Swissair 35 were both converging on ten west at the same altitude and were too close to each other for London's comfort.

"So, you're reading us now okay, London?" Jack asked.

There was a longer than normal pause, then a brief "Affirmative" from the controller.

"Sorry about that London—don't know what happened there," Jack said. "I'll write up this transponder in the maintenance logbook and get it replaced when we get home. I don't want to do that to you again!"

Everyone who was listening on London's ATC frequency could feel the tension on the radio.

"Trans Ocean forty-nine, give your ten west progress to Shanwick. Out!" There was no recommended frequency, no "Have a nice flight," no "Cheerio," just a short, curt message. The London controller couldn't prove what he suspected, but he was obviously furious. Trans Ocean 49 coasted out and began its overwater portion of Nat Track Charlie.

There was no conversation in the cockpit for at least forty-five minutes other than the required position reports that Jack made on the radio; it was very quiet. Bear looked up from his small desk on the flight engineer's panel where he was entering numbers into the columns of the fuel score, the planned versus actual fuel quantity at specific points along the route. He looked at Jack staring out his left cockpit window and wondered what he was going to do, if anything. He then switched his gaze to the right, to Captain Black, who was staring out *his* side window, and asked himself the same question. And then he finally asked himself, I wonder if I should do something here? I wonder if London is going to file any complaint or paperwork against us, because if they both get violated, I'll get hosed, too.

He considered filing a NASA report, an anonymous confession of an aviation-related mistake that absolves the person involved from any wrongdoing. And maybe the others should, too? Bear didn't know what to do, but he figured he should at least note the particulars somewhere just in case. So he put his fuel score aside and began writing a narrative of the bizarre events that had just unfolded. When the flight was finally over and they were taxiing into the terminal in Boston, he was relieved—it had been the longest flight he'd ever experienced. The corrosive atmosphere in the cockpit had lasted the entire time.

After the airplane was parked at the Jetway and the checklists were completed, Bear remained in his flight engineer's seat, pretending to write something in the logbook, waiting for Black to leave the cockpit. When he eventually left, Jack and Bear just looked at each other for a couple of seconds and then both shook their heads. Bear was the first to speak.

"Jack, I put in for this next trip with you, the two-day Paris, because it was on the open board, but I'm not sure I want it now. Not because of you, of course, but because of him. This cockpit is not fun."

"I completely understand, Bear, not to worry. Flying is supposed to be enjoyable. You've done a great job, and I thank you."

"Wait a minute, Captain Rheinstrom, I'm not saying that I wouldn't take it, it's just that...well...just strike that last comment. In for a penny, in for a pound. I wouldn't sic that guy on another unsuspecting second officer—that wouldn't be fair. If I get it, I'll be with you."

Jack looked at him and nodded. "Thanks, Bear." He seemed distracted, though, or maybe just absorbed in thought. Bear observed his captain looking out the front windscreen and left-side cockpit window. Jack obviously didn't seem to be in any big hurry to leave, so Bear slid his seat back, unbuckled his seat belt and shoulder harness, and stood up. He then pushed his seat all the way in to its most forward position, closest to the engineer's panel, thereby giving Jack more room to maneuver as he exited the cockpit. He unstrapped his suitcase that was belted to the floor behind the jump seat and picked it up along with his brain bag.

"You coming, Jack?" There was no answer. "You okay?"

"Yeah, Bear, I haven't seen this sight for a while. I'm just going to sit here by myself for a moment. You go ahead without me."

"Okay, Boss. See you inside."

Jack looked out his left-side window at the Jetway. It hadn't physically changed, but he suddenly realized that it was the exact same Jetway that he had left from on the trip that ended up back in Boston on *that* Christmas Eve. His thoughts drifted back to that trip to Mexico some twenty years ago, and he lingered there; it was the first time that he had allowed himself to actually do that. He looked straight ahead at the terminal building, which appeared exactly as he remembered it. That wasn't here before, he thought to himself as he looked up and stared at the twin-pillared airport control tower, standing proudly 265 feet above the airplane-littered tarmac below.

* * *

When the phone rang, Jim McGarrity put his coffee cup down on the desk and reached for the receiver. "Hello, McGarrity."

"Hey, Jim, this is Bob over at the tower. You busy? Shall I call back?"

"No, I'm fine, in between projects. What's up?"

"I know that you're supervisor tomorrow, and I have a favor to ask of you."

"Shoot."

"I just got a call from the chief pilot over at Trans Ocean asking if we could possibly set up a tour of the new tower tomorrow for one of their captains, and I said yes. Can you free up one of your crew for a personal walk-through?"

"The *new* tower? You mean, the one that was built in '73, sixteen years ago?"

"Those were his words, not mine."

"Well, my wife is visiting her sister for the next few days so I have plenty of free time. I'll just show up an hour or two early and give him the tour myself. Have him meet me in Terminal C tomorrow at...no, wait a minute, just give me his phone number and I'll talk to him directly myself. What's his name?"

"It's Rheinstrom, John...no, make that *Jack* Rheinstrom. Thanks again, Jim, I knew that you would help." He gave Jim the phone number and added, "And let me know how it works out, okay?"

"Sure enough! Talk to you later, ciao."

* * *

At nine-thirty on Thursday morning, Jim McGarrity pulled into the central parking garage at Boston Logan airport, parked his Volvo on the third-floor level, and walked the ten or so minutes to the entrance of Terminal C, the Arrivals area located on the street level. He was early for the rendezvous and was about to make a phone call to his upcoming visitor when he noticed an airline pilot standing alone by the entrance doors. The figure stood out because he was in uniform but without the normal "caboose" of suitcase and brain bag on wheels.

"Captain Rheinstrom?" he called out.

Jack heard him, looked up, and then approached with extended hand.

"Mr. McGarrity?" he said, shaking his hand. "Thank you for making this special effort for me—I really appreciate it."

"Hey, it's nothing, and *I* really appreciate the free rides on the jump seat on your airline, so I really think that the thanks should go to you. Anyway, I thought that the tour could end up at the tower, but maybe you'd be interested in seeing our simulator."

"Your simulator?"

"Yes, we have a pretty sophisticated facsimile of an actual tower in Terminal E, just a short walk from here." As they strolled through the corridor connecting the terminals, Jim continued, "In the simulator, we have three very large TV screens, each one over fifteen feet tall, situated around the room. They portray the view of the outside world at Logan, from runways, taxiways, terminal buildings, and Jetways to even the Atlantic Ocean and the town of Winthrop just off runway two seven. And the interior is just like the real thing—everything from radar screens to desks and control panels, phone banks, and com equipment, you name it! We use it to train not only new controllers but also as a recurrent training tool." They ascended the escalator together, walked down a narrow hallway, and arrived at a door that Jim opened. "You practice simulated emergencies in the air, we practice them on the ground." They walked into the training room and entered the simulator.

The simulator instructor was alone and ever so happy to describe its operation to Jack.

"Look over here, Captain," he said, gesturing, "we have an airplane on short final." The TV reproduction of an airplane was small and not overly detailed, but it was definitely an airplane and it was moving and just about to touch down on the runway. Jack watched as it landed and rolled out on runway one five right. The instructor looked away and pretended to be busy with something on his desk.

"Wait a minute," said Jack, who suddenly noticed that the airplane had gone off the side of the runway at midfield and had flames emerging from its left wing amid a now rising plume of smoke. "It just crashed!"

"That's right," the instructor pounced, "you have an airplane that just departed the runway and you also have two approaching planes, one on short final also landing on one five right and another on approach to runway two two left—*what are you going to do*? And whatever that is, you'd better be right and you better do it pretty darn fast! Now, I really don't expect an answer from you Captain, that was just an intro to what we do here. We practice, practice, practice until we finally get it right and then the correct response to many emergency situations is ingrained as second nature in each student's thought process. And all events are realistic, and most are taken from real-life incidents."

"I see," said Jack, "very impressive and realistic, too—just like *our* simulator. It's interesting that all these years I didn't know that you guys had anything like that. I'm glad that Jim brought me over today." The three of them exchanged some war stories for about ten minutes before Jim looked at his watch and suggested that they move on to the tower tour. They retraced their previous walk through the corridors to Terminal C and the elevator to the Boston Logan Airport tower "cab." Upon reaching the tower level, they exited but still had to climb the three-level circular stairway by foot. They finally arrived at a large fishbowl, the eleven-paned, glass-encased control room with a commanding view of the airport, the taxiways, the runways, and farther afield the towns of Winthrop and Revere. One could also see the Atlantic Ocean, including Boston's inner harbor.

The off-going supervisor saw the two at the top of the stairs and approached them. "Morning, Jim. Is this your Trans Ocean pilot?"

"Hi," said Jack, extending his hand. "My name is Jack Rheinstrom and Jim here just showed me your simulator over in Terminal E—very interesting."

"Well, Jack, let me show you around our little nest up here while Jim signs in and gets his briefing. It's actually quite quiet up here this morning, which is fine with me, a nice change of pace. Any questions that I can answer before we get started?"

"Well, just an observation, but everyone except that fellow over there seems a lot younger than I expected."

"Oh, you mean the Old Man in the Mountain; he's our most senior controller, Alphonso Barba, and he's working local control. Basically, he's the tower operator that has jurisdiction on all active runways and airspace within five miles of the airport at or below two thousand feet. You'll meet him in a few minutes. As far as the other three men and two ladies that are on the crew today, you're correct—they are young. And it's all because of the PATCO strike in eighty-one when President Reagan fired eleven thousand of the thirteen thousand controllers after they refused to go back to work. We had to come up with a massive training program, and since controllers have to retire at age fifty-five, we had to limit the applicants to a max age of thirty-five. Here, it looks like Alphonso's free right now, so let's go over and have you meet him."

Alphonso Barba saw the two men approaching and signaled to his assistant to take over his duties. He was a handsome man, about six foot four, with grayish sideburns, soft eyes, and a very easy warm smile. Jack and the tower controller shook hands, exchanged pleasantries, and began the detailed tour of the facility. At first, Jack was intensely interested, listening to every word and keeping constant eye contact with his guide. But after about four minutes, Jack's demeanor changed. He began to look at the floor, just occasionally at first while nodding his head in agreement, and then he began to stare at it.

"Mr. Barba?" he finally managed.

"Yes, Captain?"

"May I ask you how long you've worked here?"

"Why, of course. Here at the tower? My entire career actually, thirty-one years. Why do you ask?"

"Would you do me a favor, Mr. Barba?"

"Sure, Captain, what is it?"

"Would you say something for me?"

"Say something? Sure, what do you want me to say?"

"Trans Ocean sixty-six, you are cleared to land four right."

Alphonso uttered the words, and his eyes opened wide in recognition. He stared knowingly at Jack, whose eyes changed suddenly, too, as they began to well up in soft tears. The instant and tight embrace followed quickly as the other members of the tower crew silently moved away from the two men, allowing them some private space.

"You have no idea, no idea whatsoever, how many times I've heard your voice over and over these past twenty years," Jack said slowly.

"Dear friend," said Alphonso, eyes also moist and full of emotion, "I have thought of you many, many times. I am just so glad that you lived, and I am thankful for finally meeting you."

As Jack left the tower that day, he had in his possession a phone number, a new friend, and one less layer to the long-buried mystery in his life.

* * *

Jack still had three hours to check in, and he was deep in thought as he started walking from the elevator in Terminal C to Trans Ocean operations in Terminal A. Suddenly *everything* came back to him in a rush, and he had to sit down and gather his thoughts.

What the hell am I doing, he asked himself. What am I trying to prove? He couldn't answer those two simple questions, so he asked them again and still came up empty. He had never noticed it before, even though it had been there since 1951 and was the first of its kind in the world, but he suddenly noticed it *now*—the doorway on his left and the sign, Our Lady of the Sky Chapel. He almost heard a slight buzz in his ears when he read those words to himself. I need to go in there, I need to talk with myself, but I *can't*. At least I can't while wearing this uniform. I am too emotional right now--it just wouldn't look right.

"Hello, Captain, are you travelling with us today?" said the American Airlines agent standing behind her check-in counter.

"No, miss, I have a favor to ask of you."

After twenty minutes, Jack Rheinstrom emerged from the Our Lady of the Sky with his mind made up. There was plenty of time to call out the reserve to cover his trip, and he knew he had to make the call.

His fingers trembled as he dialed the number. "Hello, this is Jack Rheinstrom. Is the chief pilot in today?"

"Yes, he is, but he ran down to the cafeteria just now and should be back shortly. May I help you?"

"No, but it's important that I talk to him this morning. I'm in the other terminal right now, and I'll come see him in less than fifteen minutes."

After going back to the American Airlines check-in counter and retrieving his uniform jacket and hat, Jack went into the nearby lavatory and once again suited up. He was relieved with his decision but still had a lingering feeling of emptiness inside; things just didn't feel right, but, as he told himself, it was what it was, and it was time to move on. As he left the American check-in area, he noticed a young mother sitting on a bench, combing the tousled hair of her five-year-old. The two were about ten feet away when the woman caught Jack's attention.

"Captain?" she asked.

Jack changed course and approached her. "Yes, ma'am?"

"Would you do me a huge favor, please?"

"Of course, what is it?"

"All my son talks about is becoming a pilot. Would you say hello and maybe shake his hand?"

"Well, of course I would. What's his name?"

"Nate."

As Jack bent over to get closer to the chap, the boy suddenly stood erect and produced a salute that would have made a West Point cadet proud.

A swift and sudden wind caught the pages of Jack's narrative and sent it instantly back about twenty-two years in the past. Jack was no longer in Boston; he was now on a layover in Bombay, India at the Taj Mahal Palace Hotel, built in 1903 and overlooking the Gateway of India monument and the Arabian Sea. It was 0030 in the morning, and he was waiting along with the rest of the crew for the bus that would take them to the airport for their flight back to Amsterdam. The bus had not yet arrived, and it was too early, without coffee, for him to engage in any small talk with the rest of the crew. In the lobby, outside of the area tastefully arranged with numerous couches and chairs, there was an open area by the towering plate-glass windows where he could look out upon the hotel grounds and the outlying harbor. Even though it was just past midnight, there was plenty of human activity to watch—there always was in Bombay.

As Jack was standing in front of the window watching the lights and sights in the distance, he suddenly noticed a lone figure in the foreground below, maybe forty yards in front of him. It was a little boy who was up much too late. And although it was pitch-black outside and he couldn't confirm that he had eye contact with him, Jack just *knew* that the little boy was looking at *him.* The two statues stood motionless across from each other for a good two minutes. It was long enough for Jack to silently wonder how and when this little mini-drama was going to end. He didn't have long to wait. The little boy slowly raised his right arm and performed a perfect salute. Jack instantly brought his feet together, almost generating an audible *click*, and returned the best and most important salute of his entire life. As his arm went down, Jack's eyes filled with tears. Why? He didn't know, other than the fact that this moment was one of the most beautiful ones he had ever, ever experienced, and he hadn't even seen it coming, hadn't had a clue. Wanting to save these few minutes forever, Jack executed a sharp left turn, à la his years of practice-marching in college ROTC, and left the window and the young soldier standing in the dark. Who was he? What did he see, other than a grown man in a uniform standing in front of a hotel window?

The instant replay of the Bombay vignette ended as abruptly as it began with Jack looking down at little Nate and returning his salute.

"Wow, where did he learn to do that?" Jack asked.

"His father was a Marine," was her somber reply.

"Well, once a Marine, always a Marine, as they say."

The little boy's mother wasn't looking up at Jack anymore; she was staring at the floor. It was suddenly an awkward moment, and Jack wasn't really sure how to proceed.

"Is he still in, or did he get out?"

"He was killed in a plane crash nine months ago."

Jack stood motionless for a moment, just thinking. "I'm sorry. May I sit down over here, or would you prefer that I just continue my walk?"

"Yes, please, Captain."

"Jack."

"Yes, please, Captain Jack."

"*Captain* Jack? No, really, it's just plain old Jack."

Their conversation was brief, but it was good for all concerned—the widow, the aspiring young Marine pilot, and for Jack as well.

On his way to Terminal A, Jack was deep in thought. The memory of the little boy in Bombay had merged with his encounter with the little boy in Boston. Their circumstances and differences were profound, but both boys had something in common—a dream, just like his own. Do I really want to say good-bye right now, or do I maybe want to taste the dream, taste the magic one last time?" He still had five more minutes to walk.

"Hey, Jack!" the chief pilot suddenly said, approaching him from the back. "Did you want to see me? Here, let's go into my office. We can shut the door and talk in there."

"Actually, sir," Jack said, patting him on the arm, "I think I'm all set."

* * *

During preflight activities, while the cockpit crew was settling in, head flight attendant and purser Heather Holland entered the cockpit. She was a gorgeous young woman of thirty-one, a cheerleader type both in history and in her buoyant personality—perfect for the job. Her thick chestnut-colored hair was stunning. In different light settings, it seemed to possess multiple hues, not just one color, and let down in a ponytail when she was off duty, it not only caught the eye of the healthy male, but was the envy of her friends and non-acquaintances alike.

"Hi, guys, guess what? We have VIPs on board!"

Jack turned around in his seat. "Oh, really? Good! Who?"

"Well, the Air France flight to Paris had a mechanical and canceled. We picked up a lot of their passengers, including the mayor of Paris and his wife, and the entire French National Soccer Team. How's that? And the really good news is that Air France had special meals prepared for them and for their crew, too. And they gave them all to us! So when was last time you ate foie gras on your crew tray on the pillow on your lap? Huh, Captain Rheinstrom?"

"You know, guys," Jack said, smiling, "this is going to be one hell of a flight. *On y va, let's go*!"

Heather, who had majored in French while in college, looked surprised.

"*Oh, mon capitaine, parlez-vous Francais*?"

"*Non, juste un peu.*"

"Okay, *on y va*!"

The crew felt that the trip was really starting well. The news about the special French meals and the VIPs spread quickly among the staff, and an almost universal festive mood spread throughout the cabin. The weather was good, the departure went smoothly, and they even got the most advantageous route that they had asked for—Nat Track Alpha. They were about three hours into the flight when Heather first received the intercom call from flight attendant Paula Stoner, who was at the most aft exit door on the left-hand side of the aircraft.

"Heather, we have a pregnant woman sitting in seat 44 D who is in a good deal of discomfort. Can you come back, please?"

As she was walking down the aisle, Heather's mind was racing about what the problem could possibly be. Hopefully, it was something simple like gas and not something complicated like early labor, as they had at least three more hours of flying remaining on their trip to Paris. After ten minutes, she contacted the cockpit.

"Yes, Heather, this is Captain Black. What is it?"

"Captain, we have a medical situation at seat 44 delta. About twenty minutes ago, a pregnant woman in her mid-twenties,

American, told Paula that she had pains in her stomach and that she was in her third trimester. She was really worried. I made PA to see if any medical personnel were on board, and two doctors came forward. I'll be brief here—this is serious! The three of us are just outside the cockpit, and the doctors say they need to talk to you. Do you want to use the intercom, or should I open the cockpit door?"

Captain Black thought for a few seconds. "Heather, I hate to delay this any longer, but if you could get the names of the passenger and the two doctors, I will confer with the company. In the meantime, I will talk to them on interphone. I just don't want to take any chances with this plane—Lockerbie was only seven months ago."

Black looked over at Jack and informed him of the medical situation in the back. "I'll talk to the two doctors and see what the story is. In the meantime, get a phone patch with the company so we can discuss our options, and get them to patch us in with the Mayo Clinic." Jack nodded and immediately picked up his mike.

"Shanwick, Shanwick, this is Trans Ocean three eight on five five upper, over." Jack paused and then continued. "Shanwick, Shanwick, this is Trans Ocean three eight on five five upper, do you read, over?"

Ten seconds passed by, but it seemed longer. The voice came through amidst the crackle of static. "Trans Ocean thirty-eight, this is Shanwick. I read you four by four." In the loudness and clarity scale, five by five is the best. "Go ahead."

Meanwhile, Captain Black was talking with Dr. Gwen Beard, an oncological surgeon from Boston's Dana-Farber hospital, on the intercom. "Captain, both the other doctor and I are in complete agreement as to the diagnosis for the patient. It has nothing to do with her pregnancy. We both believe that she has acute appendicitis. She's been getting increasingly more uncomfortable during the past few hours, and if the appendix bursts, she could die and probably lose her baby, too, if this is not attended to soon."

"How much time do we have?"

"How far are we away from landing?" Dr. Beard asked.

"Paris is about three hours from here, but we may have to hold when we get there, because the weather is not good."

"I don't know if she can make it for four hours; maybe so, but I don't know," Dr. Beard admitted. "Wait a minute, Captain, the flight attendant is asking for the phone."

"I have the names, Captain Black," Heather said.

"Write them down...no, never mind, just open the door, Heather, and let them in."

Heather retrieved the cockpit key from her serving apron, turned around to make sure there was no one behind her, opened the door, and followed the two doctors into the cockpit. By prearrangement, six-foot-four Bear Wagoner had retrieved the crash axe from its leather holder on the starboard bulkhead wall and had it in his hand, behind his back, as a precaution.

The two doctors stood in the cockpit as the door was closed behind them. Captain Black turned around in his seat to his left as Captain Rheinstrom turned to his right. Bear was standing with his back to the flight engineer's panel. Captain Black was officially in command of the flight since he was instructing, so he began the conversation and made the introductions.

"Hello, Captain, my name is Dr. Robert Howarth. I'm a GP from Newark, Ohio." "And my name is Dr. Gwen Beard," the other doctor chimed in, "surgeon at Dana-Farber Cancer Institute in Boston."

Once it became obvious that the strangers in the cockpit were indeed on a mission of mercy, Jack caught Bear's eye and nodded affirmatively. The second officer then took the crash axe, which had a pointed, protruding beak on one end and a razor-sharp half-moon blade on the other, and put it under his desk. He just then thought of something. He quickly opened his brain bag and grabbed an accordion-style clear plastic map holder and found what he was looking for—the Emergency Airport Locator Chart. It was divided into four separate areas: Pacific/Far East, Canada, Europe, and Latin America. The folded chart was a white-and-blue shaded map displaying the area covered, and it included selected airports listed in alphabetical order. Each had a number, a four-letter identifier, the latitude longitude, the MSA (minimum safe altitude to fly within twenty-five nautical miles), the runway direction, its length, its field elevation, and the appropriate local navigation aids for an instrument approach—basically everything that you needed in a dire emergency, and all in a nutshell. Bear was aware of the progress and position of Flight 38 as he was filling in the remaining fuel figures and the ATA, the actual time of arrival, on the computer flight plan after passing each waypoint.

"Captain Rheinstrom?" Bear asked, interrupting the doctor's introduction. "Captain Rheinstrom?"

Jack turned his attention from the doctors to the engineer.

"Look at the Locator Chart," Bear said as he handed it forward. "We're here," he said, pointing to an *X* marked in pencil, "and look at where Lajes is—it's less than four hundred nautical miles to the southeast of us!"

Jack looked at the map, then handed it to Black, who just glanced at it and handed it back. "Thanks, Bear. That's good."

The metronome of time ticked slowly for the assembled crew of five as they waited to hear back from dispatch and, more importantly, from the Mayo Clinic.

Suddenly the little yellow light on the overhead panel blinked on and off, on and off. Everyone jumped slightly at the first ring, and then they waited.

"I'll take it," Black said and pushed the yellow illuminated button to stop the dinging. He grabbed his mike, then pushed the transmit button. "This is Trans Ocean thirty-eight, answering selcall, go ahead."

"I hear that you have a medical situation," said the voice from dispatch, "and I have Mayo Clinic on the line. Go ahead and initiate."

"Mayo, we have an ill passenger," Black began, "but we have two volunteer physicians who have come forward. They're in the cockpit. I'll put on the overhead speaker and give them the mike so you all can talk to one another."

"Roger, standing by."

Both Jack and Captain Black reached overhead and flipped the on-off switch of the individual overhead speaker. Captain Black gestured to Bear to provide his microphone to Dr. Beard, which he did with instructions.

Dr. Beard looked nervous, perhaps suffering from mike fright. She took a deep breath, pushed the mike button, and began. "I am an oncological OB/GYN surgeon, and the other doctor is a family GP. We agree as to the diagnosis. The passenger is a twenty-seven-year-old pregnant Caucasian who is approaching her third trimester. She's been in general abdominal discomfort for the past few days but dismissed it as pregnancy-related. Upon examination—she is presently supine on a row of seats—we find that she has acute right lower quadrant pain that is increasing and becoming sharp and sometimes severe. If the area is gently pressed right above the appendix at McBurney's point, there's a resulting muscle spasm. She is presently shaking, experiencing chills, and presenting a temperature of one hundred point six. Upon palpitation, the abdomen is involuntarily guarded and rigid, which makes us both suspicious of peritonitis."

Captain Black raised his index finger. "Release the mike switch." He then picked up his mike and continued. "Mayo, thirty-eight, have you been able to copy all that so far, over?"

"That's affirm, over."

"Okay, Dr. Beard, continue."

She depressed the mike button again. "But what has us most concerned is the possibility of septicemia and SIRS, systematic inflammatory response syndrome, because not only is her temperature above one hundred, but she has an elevated heart rate of ninety-three in addition to a high respiratory rate of over twenty breaths a minute." She paused. "Over."

"Roger, thirty-eight, will need to consult. Standby."

Dr. Beard gave the microphone back to the engineer and approached Captain Black. "The bottom line is that we're afraid that without proper medical attention, she can develop blood poisoning and that will shut down her organs—period."

Jack was growing increasingly antsy sitting in the left seat, basically as an observer. He knew what he would do—and he would have done it about five minutes ago.

He addressed Captain Black. "We have extra fuel for the weather in Paris, so why don't we, since we're abeam Lajes, divert now? If the weather is poor there, or Mayo doesn't concur, which I can't imagine they won't, we can always divert back to the original plan for Paris. Again, since we're abeam right now, every minute that we go away from Lajes is another minute we have to fly back the other way."

"Captain Rheinstrom," came the stiff reply, "may I remind you that this is *my* decision and I will wait for the Mayo Clinic and then see what they recommend."

Jack exhaled deeply. And in a silent reminder of the critical nature of the passing time, he bent forward in his seat and pushed the button on the ship's clock that started the second hand of the chronometer.

"One other thing, Captain Black," Dr. Beard continued, "wherever we end up, or the passenger ends up, if our worst fears materialize, she will need to be put on a ventilator."

Trans Ocean Flight 38, Boeing 747, tail number N4713T, continued on its way to Charles de Gaulle airport at flight level 370. Traveling at Mach .84, it was gobbling up six nautical miles for every minute that went by, and so far, seven minutes had already elapsed since the crew had talked to dispatch and the Mayo Clinic.

"Captain Black, I think that the patient would be better served if at least one of us was with her, so I think that I'll go back," Dr. Howarth suggested.

"Okay," Black replied. And as the doctor turned around, Bear stood up, looked out the cockpit door peephole, and opened the door, allowing Dr. Howarth to leave.

Jack turned around in his seat. "Dr. Beard, while we're waiting, would you like to sit down on the jump seat? Or are you happy just standing there?"

"Why, thank you," she replied. Jack looked over at the second officer and gestured. Bear immediately arose and helped Dr. Beard with adjusting the seat height. He instructed her on how to pull the nearby hanging sweep-on oxygen mask over the back of her head and into position over her mouth if she needed to use it. He then went back and sat at his flight engineer's panel. The four of them just sat there and waited for the selcall chime. It had been thirteen minutes since Jack had started the stopwatch, or rather 156 nautical miles to return to the point where the plane had once been abeam Lajes.

"Captain Black, do you want me to use HF radio number two and maybe get some weather for Lajes?" volunteered Bear.

"No, dispatch will have all that info when they call back—*if* that's what they want us to do."

If that's what *they* want us to do? Jack repeated twice to himself as he gazed left out his cockpit window and looked at the moonlit ocean below. The tension in the cockpit could be cut with a knife—everyone felt it.

The selcall chimed as Jack's right hand shot up and pushed the blinking yellow button, his left hand grabbing for his mike. "This is Trans Ocean thirty-eight answering selcall."

"Trans Ocean thirty-eight, this is Shanwick Oceanic. We have a phone patch for you, over."

"Roger, thirty-eight, go ahead." The chronometer was showing twenty-three minutes had elapsed.

"Mayo Clinic concurs with the diagnosis, and we suggest that you divert present position direct to LPLA, Lajes Air Base. There is a health center listed in a town called Praia that is ten miles from Lajes, but they don't answer their phone, so maybe it's just a clinic. The main hospital on the island is in the city of Angra, and that's a fifty-minute ride from the airport."

"Captain Black," Bear blurted out, "there is a hospital *on the base*—it's a military hospital, but it's right there! I know because I was there two months ago on an Air Force reserve trip and my loadmaster got sick, and he was quarantined there. I've been there—I know it's there!"

Black nodded. "Dispatch, the second officer says there's a military hospital there right on the base at the airport. Call and check that out. We will be busy for a while here with the reroute. And how is the weather, over?"

"Well, there is a potential problem there, Captain. The terminal area forecast is CAVU—clear and visibility unlimited—for the next four hours, but there is a major system approaching from the southwest that will bring significant changes—marginal ceilings, gale-force winds, and cumulonimbus activity. How far away are you? I need an ETA when you can, and if it's going to be close, then we might have to cancel the divert. As it stands now, based on your last position report twenty-five minutes ago, and with favorable winds, and you have almost zero headwinds, you should be there in a little over an hour. That gives you some wiggle room—three hours. Anyway, standing by your ETA and intentions, call back when you can. Dispatch standing by."

"Thank you, Shanwick. Trans Ocean thirty-eight out. Oh, wait a minute, Shanwick, are you still there?"

"Affirmative."

"We're right on the borderline at four five north between you and Santa Maria Oceanic. We're requesting a medical divert to Lajes Air Force Base. Should I call them, or can you handle it?"

"Trans Ocean thirty-eight, you are cleared present position direct to Lajes Air Force Base, Azores, LPLA. Descend and maintain flight level three four zero and contact Santa Maria on six three four five upper sideband and call level with them."

"Roger, Shanwick, Trans Ocean thirty-eight is cleared present position direct Lajes, descend and maintain flight level three four zero and call level. We are out of thirty-seven and switching to Santa Maria on six three four five. Thank you for your help, Shanwick."

Black reached up and twisted a small knob on the front instrument panel until the numbers in the small window of the altitude reminder indicated 340. "Thirty-four," he stated aloud. Jack echoed "Thirty-four," disconnected the altitude hold function of the autopilot, slowly pulled the four throttles back about halfway, and began a gentle descent of five hundred feet per minute. The crew had plenty of time to prepare, so there was no sense of hurry. Black reached up to dial the new frequency into the number one HF radio. He turned the radio volume button down and then tuned the transmitter. Pressing the mike button once, he waited. There was a piercing, however now muted, tone that lasted for about three seconds, then stopped. He reset the volume control to its previous position and into his mike said, "Santa Maria, Santa Maria."

In the meantime, Bear was going over in his mind any pertinent facts that he could present to the two pilots to help them prepare for their upcoming destination, which was new to both of them. He had been there maybe twenty times in the past nine years, flying the Lockheed C-141 Starlifter, delivering cargo and passengers for the U.S. Air Force Reserves. He loved the island—it was old-world Portugal and his favorite trip.

"Captain Black, do you want me to use the other radio and get a phone patch with the Air Force command post there?" he asked.

"Yeah, that's a good idea." Black then turned around in his seat, directing his gaze at Dr. Beard. "When we know what we're dealing with, I'll get word to you and you two can plan accordingly. As of now, we will be there in less than an hour."

"Thank you, Captain," Dr. Beard replied. Black turned back around in his seat, made some annotations on the flight plan about what had transpired during the past fifteen minutes, and tried contacting Santa Maria once more—this time successfully.

Black pointed at the altitude reminder. "One to go," he announced as the 747 reached the thousand-foot level above the newly assigned altitude, FL 340.

"One to go," echoed Jack as he slowly pushed the throttles forward to the approximate cruise power setting.

Bear made contact with the command post duty officer at Lajes. He didn't want to interrupt Black, who was still talking with Santa Maria, so he covered all the bases that he thought were needed with a Major Jim Falardeau.

"Lajes command post, this is Trans Ocean flight three eight, emergency divert to your station. ETA is fifty-seven minutes. We are a Boeing seven forty-seven with three hundred thirty-seven passengers and a crew of eighteen. We have a medical situation—an American female passenger, pregnant, in her twenties, has appendicitis with possible serious complications. Do you presently have doctors and hospital staff that will be able to attend her?" He suddenly remembered and added, "And do you have a ventilator available for use? We are aware of the approaching weather system, so we want to make this turnaround as quick as possible. The passengers will not be deplaning, so there is no need for customs and agriculture, but the cockpit crew will need to deplane. The pilots need to flight-plan and get transportation to base ops. Will it be open? And do you have portable airstairs so they can deplane? I know that you handle military charters with civilian aircraft, so I assume that you do, but I need to make sure that you have compatible ground power units for aircraft use after we shut the engines down. We need to refuel—again, as quickly as possible, and I will help oversee that. Let me give you the telephone numbers of our dispatch in New York—they handle things like this all the time. Oh, and do you have the hospital medical personnel to be able to come aboard with a stretcher and remove her safely? And transport her to your hospital? Over."

Bear was ready to scribble down the responses on a piece of paper, but there weren't any answers—not yet, as Major Falardeau still had a lot of calls to make. This was an extraordinary night that was unfolding, not the normal routine for a midnight shift in a small situation room, on a small Air Force Base, on a small island in the middle of a very big ocean. Lajes didn't even have any scheduled inbound military flights for the next three days.

"Jesus," Falardeau muttered to himself as he put down the radio mike and reached for the base directory and the base landline phone.

As Flight 38 completed a two-hundred-degree right turn and proceeded direct to Lajes field on the island of Terceira, Portugal, Jack gazed out his left window, then forward straight out through the windshield. To the left he could see the moon. Oh, what a moon, he thought. Even though he had seen the moon rise many, many times over the years, a full moon always left him slightly awestruck.

That has to be a perigee, he said to himself. The moon was so big, so bright, so vivid, and so alive that he just couldn't stop looking at it. The Atlantic Ocean was almost seven miles beneath him, but the moon's reflection on the surface was like a painting—a sparkling silver tongue that urged the viewer to come visit, to gaze, and to stay.

After a few minutes of gazing at the moon and the beckoning sea, Jack stretched and leaned forward in his seat. Turning his head as far to the left as he could, he could see the number one engine hanging on its pylon, and also the outward top of the wing, shining like a sword in the moonlight. As he turned and settled back into his seat, he now faced forward and could see the distant, very distant ominous weather system that dispatch had warned them about. It was heading directly toward Lajes—and so was he.

Captain Black put the mike back into its holder by the side cockpit window, pushed the left headset muff back behind his ear so that he could hear, and turned around in his seat to face the other two crew members. "First of all," he said, addressing Bear, "what did you find out?" Bear relayed all the answers that he had finally received from the Lajes command post.

"Great," Black replied, "good job. I really don't have any more questions for them, so that pretty much covers that part. Dispatch has also been doing some coordinating with ATC, approach control, and has actually made contact with those on duty at the hospital. They have the necessary staff on call and will be waiting for us. The weather is okay now, but it is forecast to get worse. It's all due to the remnants from the hurricane-turned-storm Felix. It's supposed to get a lot worse about two hours after we land. I'm talking about severe weather here, but that shouldn't affect us; we should get in and out of there in less than an hour. We'll just refuel, get a new computer flight plan, file it, and vamoose. Wagoner, didn't you say that you're familiar with the base?"

"That's right," said Bear.

"Well, is there anything special about the place that I should know about? I don't like going into a place that I've never been before."

"No, it's pretty straightforward. I just got the weather from the command post. Winds are one six zero degrees at seven, pretty much straight down runway one five, and the sky condition is a broken layer at twenty-three hundred feet and another broken layer at twelve thousand, visibility more than ten statute miles."

"Well, that's pretty much what dispatch said, too."

"So, landing on one five," Bear continued, "which is nice and long, almost eleven thousand feet, the actual base will be on your left, so a left turnoff, and they said that there would be a 'follow me' waiting for us there."

"A 'follow me'?" Black queried.

"Yeah, it's just a pickup truck with a yellow flashing light and an illuminated sign on the back of it that says 'Follow me.' It will take you to the parking spot."

"Oh," said Black.

"Another thing," Bear added, "with it being so bright out there tonight with that moon, and the fact that the field sits on top of a huge bluff a couple hundred feet high, which is right at the end of the runway...I mean, there are a lot of factors at play here that could affect your landing. They do have a visual approach slope indicator, which gives decent guidance when the weather is good, but I would pretty much stay on instruments. What I mean is, don't go completely visual for the landing because of the possible optical illusions—you know, the night, the light, the bluff, the first time in there...."

"Good thinking, Bear, thanks," said Jack, who was looking over the instrument approach plate for the ILS runway one five,

Lajes Field, Azores, and who would be making the actual approach and landing.

"So," Black continued, "we'll be there in about forty minutes. Get Heather up here and we'll brief her. Normally in an emergency, I would be making the landing, but…." He paused and glanced at Jack. "Since this is just a precautionary landing, why don't you go ahead and take it."

"Okay," said Jack, nodding.

Trans Ocean 38 was handed off from Santa Maria Oceanic to Lajes Approach, who then gave them radar vectors to intercept the ILS, runway one five.

"Wow, I see what you mean, Bear," Jack said as the 747 broke out of the overcast at twenty-three hundred feet. He could see the runway lights straight ahead and the spectacular bluffs illuminated by the supermoon just ahead of them. Gliding over the runway threshold, the giant bird lowered itself gently down, smoothly transferring its entire weight from the lift of its wings to the waiting landing gear below.

"Spoilers," announced Bear. This confirmed that the lift-killing metal fences on top of the wings had automatically sprung to the up position upon landing gear wheel spin-up. The four throttles were now in idle. Captain Rheinstrom grabbed the four reverser control knobs and pulled them up and then back. The engine rpm's surged, and the engines roared as the reversers opened. The airplane shuddered and began to decelerate further.

"Eighty knots," the second officer announced. "Sixty," he said as Jack eased the throttles forward out of reverse and back into idle.

"There's the 'follow me' up there on the left," announced Bear. Trans Ocean 38 turned off the runway, the crew accomplished their after-landing tasks and checklists, and the plane taxied to the parking ramp, following the little blue truck with the blinking yellow lights.

The evacuation of the ill passenger went like clockwork. The stricken mother-to-be seemed stable and was even able to mouth "Thank you" as the medics carried her by the standing flight crew at the cabin door. She was placed on a portable gurney at the bottom of the airstairs and was then wheeled out to the waiting ambulance. While the two captains were waiting for somebody to show up and transport them to base ops, Jack found Laurie in the mid-galley.

"Hey, Laurie, how did things go for you guys?"

"Hi, Jack, pretty good, I think. Heather did an amazing job coordinating with the doctors and getting two volunteers to pick the poor girl up and deposit her on a row of six seats that we had converted into a kind of bed. But, boy, was she uncomfortable. Do you think that she'll be okay?"

"Well, she's going to be in a hospital with lots of doctors and nurses and medical equipment, and she's not at thirty-five thousand feet over the middle Atlantic. I don't actually know, but I think, I hope, that we got her here in time."

"Oh, and those doctors," Laurie continued, "were very, very caring and genuinely nice people. That girl is lucky to have had them on board."

"Where are the doctors?" Jack asked.

"We upgraded them to first class, and I just gave them some caviar that was left over from our meal service. I was saving it for the cockpit, but I'm sure that you guys understand."

"No, I don't understand!" Jack said, smiling as he touched her on the shoulder.

"They're sitting together now, in 4A and 4B."

"Thanks, I'm just going to add my two cents," Jack said as he turned and walked toward the front of the plane.

He approached the doctors and knelt down next to their seats. "Hello again, Dr. Beard and Dr. Howarth," he said quietly. "I have reports that you both did a great job, and I want to add my thanks along with those of the cabin staff and, I'm sure, the young woman."

"Well, Captain," started Dr. Howarth, "she has a good chance because you decided to divert the flight—the thanks should go to you!"

"Well, there's a lot of thanks to be passed about. We will be making a report of the incident, and the company will be contacting you about some form of quid pro quo—a thank you for being good Samaritans."

"Captain, we're not good Samaritans, we're *doctors*," he said with a furrowed brow.

"Yes, I know that," Jack continued, "but are you telling me that every single doctor would volunteer to get involved? No, you followed your professional heart—and soul, for that matter—and you came forward. I'm saying good for you, I'm proud to know you, and thank you."

The two doctors looked down, nodded their heads, and very softly whispered, "Thank you."

Jack stood up, and before turning around to leave, said, "How did you like my caviar?"

"*Your* caviar? I'm sorry, we—"

A big smile came over Jack's face. "I'm only kidding. We'd give you a lot more if we had it." He patted the back of Dr. Howarth's seat and went back to door one left to wait.

As the two captains emerged outside the forward cabin door and started to descend the portable stairway, Bear caught up with them. "I know that you guys don't know the recommended fuel load yet, but you might like to know what the command post just told me."

"And what was that?" asked Captain Black.

"They said that we can get fuel at the government price—it's like less than half of what we normally pay for Jet A!"

"Really?" asked Jack. Looking at Black, he continued, "Why don't we tanker it?"

"Tanker it?"

"Yeah, let's just fill it up to the max gross takeoff weight and carry the extra fuel with us to Paris. The weather there is iffy, and the extra fuel gives us more options, and if we can save the company a wad of money, well, that's a win-win! Why not?"

Black seemed unimpressed. He shrugged his shoulders. "Sure."

Jack turned and gave Bear a gentle slap on his back. "Good job, Bear."

The two captains continued their descent on the portable stairs that had been brought to the airplane's left side. Just as they reached the tarmac, a blue staff car pulled up to the airplane. A large figure, wearing a blue Air Force uniform and wheel cap complete with the silver "scrambled eggs" on its visor, emerged and approached the two.

"Good evening, or should I say good morning, gentlemen. My name is Colonel Rudy Zahorchak, Wing Commander here at Lajes. I am here to assist you and expedite your short stay here."

"Good morning, or evening, Colonel," Jack began, walking toward him and extending his right hand. "And thank you for rising so early to help us out."

"It's nothing. Couldn't sleep very well last night, anyway—the moon or something."

Captain Black just stood motionless in the background.

"My name is Captain Jack Rheinstrom, and that's Captain Jerry Black," Jack offered, gesturing. The two exchanged nods.

"I'll get right to it," the colonel began. "The meteorology department just updated the ETA of that system," he said as he turned to his left and pointed toward the west. The lightning flashes, although distant, were slowly becoming more visible and frequent. "And it should be upon us in...." He looked down at his watch. "About eighty minutes. We have enough time so that it shouldn't be a problem, but I'm sure that you want to get out of here as fast as you can."

"You've got that right, Colonel," Jack agreed.

"Why don't you two get into my car, and I'll show you the paperwork that they just faxed me. I've been working with your dispatcher in New York. Nice guy." The two captains got into the back seat, the colonel into the front. "Here's your flight plan to Charles de Gaulle with Gatwick as your alternate. The UK is wide open, but most of the central European continent has a real fog problem today, just as it had yesterday. If you sign the flight release, after you figure out how much fuel you want, I can fax it to Lisbon so they can start working on your ATC clearance. Anyway, here's your paperwork to peruse. I have two trucks connected and standing by so we can double-pump your fuel as soon as you decide."

Jack looked at Black and asked, "Fill it up?" Black nodded.

"Fill it up, Colonel, I think we can take somewhere around ninety thousand pounds."

"Done." Colonel Zahorchak gave the order over the radio.

Upon reviewing the en route and airport weather, the destination and alternate notices to airmen, or NOTAMS, and other important and relative information, Captain Black pulled out a pen from his breast pocket, signed the flight release papers, and handed them forward to the colonel sitting behind the steering wheel. Jack couldn't figure out why Black seemed so ill at ease and uncomfortable in Zahorchak's presence, but it did not go unnoticed by the wing commander.

Bear was making his preflight walk-around inspection and could see that on one of the two fuel trucks, the fueler, underneath the wing on his raisable platform, was disconnecting his hoses. Good, Bear thought as he looked to the western sky and the intermittent flashes of lightning. He could see, he could sense, that the atmosphere was changing—the humidity was increasing, the temperature was falling, and he could almost feel the electricity in the air. He lingered at engine number two, the one that had had higher than normal temperature indications on the constant speed drive compared to the other engines during the previous flight. He looked for any telltale fluid leaks on the cowling. He opened the small hatch on the engine cowling and peeked inside. With his flashlight, he could see the oil level; it was low, but above the minimum. Okay, he thought, closed the little door, and then latched it. He completed his walk-around, returned to the airstairs, and as he ascended, he looked again at the western sky. He then looked to his left at the military ramp where he had been just forty-five days earlier on an Air Force C-141 before disappearing inside the cabin door. As the wing commander stood there under the wing, the fueler from the second truck began to disconnect his hoses. Captain Black had already climbed the stairs and was getting settled in his right seat, leaving without so much as a simple "thanks."

"Colonel Zahorchak, I think that we'll get out of your hair now, but I just wanted you to know how much we appreciate your help and the performance of the men and women in your wing. The company will be in contact with you tomorrow, I'm sure, when the flight ops people are awake back in the States. And I think that the passengers, especially the sick woman, owe a lot to you. Maybe it was just fate that you were here, waiting for her, but everything worked out really well. Here's my card. I would love to continue our conversation sometime, either here, in the States, wherever."

"Captain Rheinstrom," Colonel Zahorchak said with an intense look in his eyes and a very firm handshake that seemed to linger, "it's been a pleasure, and I wish you Godspeed." He released his grip, withdrew his hand, and walked back to his waiting staff car.

Inside the command post, the phone rang. It was meteorology. "Major Falardeau," said the voice on the other end, "how is the seven forty-seven progressing?"

"Fine, I think. Why do you ask?"

"Well, this Felix storm is approaching faster than what I had previously thought. It's going to be here sooner!"

"How much sooner?"

"Well, I anticipate that the gust front could be here in less than forty minutes."

"Geez! Well, okay, I will check with them and pass on the info. When you say gust front, what are you talking about here?"

"Well, there's a weather buoy located just this side of the squall line, and it just recorded a peak gust of seventy miles an hour!"

"Wow! You said squall *line*—if they didn't make it off in, say, thirty-five minutes, could they wait it out and let it pass, and then take off after things settle down?"

"No way. This isn't just a squall line, this is a major depression that's been progressing northeastward from Bermuda and will be affecting us locally for probably two to three days. How many people did you say were on board?"

"Around three hundred."

"I hope they get out of here in time."

"Yeah, same here."

The call went out immediately. "Trans Ocean thirty-eight, command post."

"Thirty-eight, go ahead."

"I just got a call from metro—they said that the storm has picked up speed and that the gust front could contain seventy-mile-an-hour winds, and it will be here in about thirty-five minutes!"

"Hey, we're going as fast as we can!" Black assured him.

CHAPTER NINE

The airplane was buttoned up, the airstairs pulled away from the left front side, the passengers were seated and briefed, and the crew finished the appropriate checklist. Captain Black had requested an ATC clearance from Lajes ground control just five minutes prior.

"Ground, TO thirty-eight, we're about to start engines now. We'd like to taxi out to the approach end of runway one five and wait for our clearance there. We don't want to waste any time getting out of here."

"Roger, Trans Ocean thirty-eight, call when ready to taxi."

The airplane was parked on the military ramp facing directly west so that all three men in the cockpit had a very clear view of what was coming their way—and it was not good.

"Before-start checklist complete," announced Bear.

Jack nodded. "Let's crank 'em."

After the engines were successfully started and the before-taxi checklist completed, Black picked up his microphone. "Lajes ground, TO thirty-eight with information Alpha, taxi."

"Roger, thirty-eight, taxi up to and hold short of runway one five."

Captain Black acknowledged the instructions and asked, "Still no word on the clearance?"

"Standby, thirty-eight, I will check again."

The wheels had already been set in motion after Major Falardeau clarified how many passengers were onboard. The major, along with three others in the command post, were busy making contingency plans as to where they were going to house 337 passengers and a crew of 18, and how they would transport them and feed them—and for how long? Meanwhile, the B-747, loaded with two hundred thousand pounds of jet fuel and weighing seven hundred twelve thousand pounds, was briskly taxiing toward its appointed runway. As the plane came to a stop at the number one position for takeoff for runway one five, Jack pressed on his toe brakes and engaged the parking brake. Black looked at him and asked him what he thought.

"Well," he said, slowly rotating his head back and forth and slightly diffusing the pressure in the cockpit that had been steadily rising, "it's always *something*, isn't it?"

All three halfheartedly laughed and in unison said, "Yup."

They switched their radio to tower frequency and sat there and waited—and waited. Finally, a call came on the radio. "Trans Ocean thirty-eight." Black grabbed his pencil and picked up the clipboard, ready to write down the ATC clearance. "I'm still working on it."

The engineer adjusted his seat backward and turned away from his panel, now positioned close to the center pedestal halfway between the two pilots' seats, facing forward for takeoff. "What are we going to do if we can't get our clearance in time?" he asked.

Captain Black just sat in his seat, thinking. Captain Rheinstrom turned to his right and said, "Well, we're not going to do anything unsafe. We've got the squall line on radar—right *there*," he said, placing his finger on the actual radar screen. "It looks like it's about twenty miles away and is off to our right, and more importantly, it's not on our departure route. But if it's as fast-moving as they say it is, say forty miles an hour, it will be here in half an hour. What concerns me is the gust front, the strength and the direction of the wind. I don't know what the problem is with ATC; they said not to expect any delays with the clearance. Anyway, I'd say we have a window of fifteen minutes, give or take, if we get our clearance and the gust front arrives and is pretty much down the runway—but that's a big 'if.' If the wind is out of our crosswind limits, then we taxi back to the ramp, park, shut down, and wait. They were able to service all the lavatories here, but Heather said that the one in first class has an inop flush motor and was blocked off. They were able to get us more ice and they topped off our water, too."

Captain Black pushed his seat back on its tracks and started to unbuckle his shoulder harness and seatbelt.

"What's up?" Jack asked, looking over at him.

"I've got a problem!"

"A problem? What kind of problem?"

"A GI problem. Great timing, huh?" Black said.

"Okay, but just remember," Jack said, "that the first-class lav is inop. You're going to have to go back downstairs to the one near the mid-galley."

Just then came the radio call. "Trans Ocean thirty-eight, I have your clearance."

Black immediately put his seatbelt and shoulder harness back on and slid his seat forward. "Thirty-eight, go ahead."

The tower gave the clearance and Captain Black recited the information back to tower, who replied, "Good read-back. Trans Ocean thirty-eight, maintain runway heading, climb to five thousand feet, and contact departure. Cleared for takeoff runway one five."

"Roger, runway heading, up to five, contact departure cleared to go. Say winds."

"Winds are one six zero at fifteen, gusting to twenty-five."

They all looked at one another. "Let's get out of here," Jack said as he released the brakes and pushed all four throttles forward to just short of the approximate takeoff EPR. He dropped his right hand while Captain Black made the final adjustments, and then replaced his right hand back onto the throttles. The Pratt & Whitney turbofans responded with the roar of four lions as the airplane began to accelerate down runway one five. At one hundred knots, a gust of wind of over forty knots suddenly hit the right side of the lumbering 747, causing its right wing to rise.

"Whoa there, Nelly," commented Jack as he moved the yoke to the right, effectively putting more "down" aileron into the wind and lowering the wing.

"Rotate fifteen degrees," was Black's next callout. Jack slowly pulled back on the yoke until the nose was indeed pointing fifteen degrees up. The weight of the plane, just under the max allowable takeoff gross weight, was now being transferred from the landing gear and tires to the outstretched arms of the giant bird. The altimeter needle started to climb, and Black called out, "Positive rate."

"Gear up," Jack said. The command was repeated by Black, who raised the gear handle and then contacted Lajes departure.

"Roger, Trans Ocean thirty-eight, turn left to heading of zero four zero, climb and maintain flight level two seven zero. Looks like you got out of there just in time—Lajes just recorded a peak gust of sixty miles an hour."

"Yeah, that was a little too close for me," Black said, and then put the mike back into its holder. "Engineer, will you cover the radio for me? I can't wait any longer," said Black as he slid his seat back and unbuckled his belt and shoulder harness.

"Do you think that you have food poisoning," Jack asked, "maybe from that first-class fish meal?"

Black stepped over the center pedestal. "No, it's a sort of pH imbalance in my gut, my GI track. I had it a few months ago, took some meds, and it went away. Well, it's no fun and now it's suddenly back—and I will be, too, in a few minutes. You guys can finish up the after-takeoff checklist. Oh, and Engineer, I can't find my cockpit key—loan me yours. The cabin will probably be very busy setting up for their meal service."

"Sure," said Bear as he stood up, reached into his left pocket, and pulled out a small lanyard with a key on it. Captain Black took it and quickly left.

"Man, it sucks being sick on a flight," the second officer remarked.

"Amen," nodded Jack as the two of them finished their checklist and the 747 settled into its climb routine. Because the first-class lav was blocked off, Captain Black retraced his steps on the upper deck, descended the steps of the spiral staircase, then turned around and walked back to the four lavatories that were just aft of the mid-galley.

Flight 38 was switched over to Santa Maria Oceanic and requested a further climb to flight level 370. They also asked the center to accept primary radio guard, providing them with the ship's selcall code of JDBC.

"Roger, Trans Ocean thirty-eight, Santa Maria accepts primary guard. Climb and maintain flight level three seven zero and report twenty-five west. Standby, selcall check."

A dinging rang through the cockpit, the small yellow lights of the selcall receiver illuminating with each chime. Jack reached up and pushed one of the two lights, canceling the repeating chime as Bear responded on the radio. "Selcall checks."

The airplane was now passing 22,400 feet on its climb. Suddenly, in the cockpit, there could be heard—and felt—a very loud thump.

"What the hell was that?!" Jack exclaimed, turning around in his seat.

Just a few minutes prior, the cabin had been getting settled for the three-plus hour flight ahead. Bob and Dugie Turnbull of Clearwater, Florida were sitting in row 14, seats A and B, just aft of business class. Dugie was well into Chapter 3 of Tom Wolfe's *The Bonfire of the Vanities*, which she had bought in the airport bookstore in Boston. Bob was writing a letter to their sons, Alex and Rob, updating them on the progress of their long-awaited vacation and anniversary celebration to Paris and Aix-en-Provence.

Suddenly, Bob put his pen down and looked up as he thought that he heard something—a grinding or buzzing sound, coming from underneath the floor. His wife stopped reading and looked quizzically over at her husband. Suddenly, there was a loud hissing noise, and then a horrendous explosion.

Unbeknownst to the crew, the gull-wing-shaped forward cargo door had begun to slowly open from its normal closed, locked, and secure position. Air, with a force of 460 miles per hour, forced its way under the lower lip of the right-hand cargo door, and in 1.5 seconds—*kaboom*! The huge door and pieces of the aluminum aircraft skin and metal fuselage structure were ripped away from the right side of the airplane. An explosive rapid decompression and cabin tornado immediately ensued; the cabin pressure inside the airplane went from a controlled sea-level setting to twenty-three thousand feet in just over a second. The effect was an instant fog throughout the cabin, amid subfreezing temperatures of -22 degrees Fahrenheit. The passengers' ears popped, and life-sustaining oxygen uncontrollably exited from their lungs. Especially in business class and the section just aft of it, the noise was deafening. The plane's occupants could not hear, and they could not breathe. The oxygen masks that automatically dropped from the overhead panel didn't work, as the departing door had damaged the oxygen system.

Everything in the vicinity of the gaping hole that wasn't tied down was sucked out through that hole. The hole was huge, almost the size of two automobiles. Oxygen masks, glasses, books, handbags, papers, catering carts, and seats that had previously been bolted securely to the aircraft floor before it collapsed were gone. Seats that had had passengers strapped into them, seats 8G and H through 12G and H, had vanished. The man who had been seated in business class seat 9F, and who had not been wearing his seatbelt, was gone, his flapping seatbelt and the bent armrest suggesting the direction of his path. Some of the objects that were sucked out into the airstream were ingested into engines three and four, including, possibly, passengers.

The effects of the rapid decompression were experienced differently, depending on where the passengers were seated. In the very aft section of the airplane, the mayhem was much more muted than in business class, the scene of the actual damage. The cockpit also was spared the height of the fury, due to the fact that the cockpit door was sealed shut.

Back in the cockpit, the crew struggled to understand what was happening. "What the hell was that? I don't recognize that sound! What was that?" Jack frantically demanded.

"I don't know what that noise was either!" answered Bear. "The engine…it looks like we've lost number three!"

"Call the flight attendant—we're going down! Emergency descent. Put on your oxygen mask, Bear."

Jack was struggling with both hands on the yoke to keep the airplane under control, but he needed oxygen, too, so he quickly took his right hand off the yoke, grabbed the hanging sweep-on oxygen mask from over his left shoulder, and pulled the harness over the back of his head and over the top so that the mask covered his mouth. Then he inhaled, or at least he tried to.

"I can't get any oxygen, Bear! Something's wrong!"

"I can't get any…not getting any oxygen either!"

They both reached up and pulled the useless masks off their heads.

Breathing heavily, Bear announced, "Standing by the emergency-descent checklist. I've got the checklist, and, and…we're supposed to drop the gear…it calls for dropping the landing gear."

"No, I don't want to drop the gear. I don't know what systems we've lost, so, no! I've got the throttles back, speed brakes are out, we're descending and…where's the cabin altitude now?"

"It's reading fifteen!" This indicated that the actual pressure inside the cabin was at fifteen thousand feet.

"Well, that's breathable, and we're coming down like a manhole cover. Let's go through the procedure for one, uh, number three. We don't have any fire indications, do we?"

"There's no N1 indication—it's like the engine's frozen. And the power and exhaust gas temperature are both really low."

"Okay, we lost number three—let's shut it down. We sure could use Black up here, Christ!"

"Ready for number three?"

"Yeah, shutdown checklist, go ahead with it."

"Do you want me to start dumping fuel first?"

"Yes, go ahead, start dumping, we're really heavy. But wait...no, not yet. I don't know what we're going to do just yet. Let's just shut down number three."

As the 747 continued to descend to the life-sustaining air at ten thousand feet, Captain Rheinstrom and Second Officer Wagoner completed the engine-failure checklist.

"Bear, we've got a control problem here. We've got a hell of a control problem here. I've got almost full left rudder in on this thing!"

"Captain Rheinstrom, we've got a problem with number four engine, now—it looks like it's out, too!"

"What? Oh, great! Okay, what's the, uh, max EPR for numbers one and two?" Jack sputtered, asking about the maximum power setting for the two good remaining engines, both on the left wing.

"First of all, two hundred forty knots is your minimum speed to avoid a stall at this weight. Can you maintain two forty?"

"Yeah, just barely, but Bear, now we've got two engines out—start dumping the fuel or we won't be able to keep this thing in the air! We're too heavy for two out engines! Tell me when you've started dumping."

"I'm dumping now, and your max EPR is go-around EPR, one point nine eight."

"Okay, but I can't hold altitude! I've got takeoff power on this thing on both engines, and I can't hold altitude!"

Bear was shouting. "I was thinking about running downstairs to see what's going on down there because I can't raise anyone on interphone, but Jack, I don't want to leave you up here alone until things stabilize!"

"That's right. Don't leave now!" Jack pleaded.

A few seconds elapsed. "Well, you've got two hundred fifty knots now. That's good, and we're at seven thousand feet."

"Bear, go ahead and run down and see if you can learn anything, and find out how they're doing down there. Tell them we're descending because of a power issue, that we lost two engines, and that they should brief a ditch, although I sure as hell don't want to do that."

"Okay. You sure you'll be all right up here alone?"

"Yup, but be quick about it—and see where the hell Black is."

Bear got up, and just before he shut the cockpit door behind him, he remembered that he didn't have his cockpit key anymore, since he had given it to Black. So he grabbed his brain bag and placed it in the doorway as a doorstop, holding the door open.

As soon as he left the cockpit, he witnessed the severe damage immediately. He could see where some of the aircraft skin was missing on the upper deck. He could see frames and stringers, part of the aircraft interior structure, exposed. He scrambled down the circular stairs as fast as he could, almost tripping on the third stair down. As soon as he reached the bottom of the stairs, he saw senior purser Heather Holland. She was so relieved to see him that she almost cried, for it meant that the cockpit members were unhurt and still in control of the airplane. Bear made eye contact with her and pointed before giving her a thumbs-up sign to ask, "Are you okay?" She nodded. He then turned to his right and tried to take in what he was seeing. Heather watched as he assessed the damage; she saw all the color drain from his face as his mouth opened and his jaw dropped. She could read his lips as he muttered "Fuck!" He looked out a window to see the starboard wing and saw sparks and flames trailing from engine number four as far as the line of vision would permit. He immediately started up the stairs, and then abruptly halted. It was extremely difficult to communicate because of the roar of the wind, so with his hands cupped around his mouth, he shouted, "Have you seen Captain Black, Heather, have you seen Captain Black?"

"No!" she yelled back. "Why? Isn't he up there with you?"

"No," Bear yelled back, "he left to hit the lav on climb-out...find him and tell him that we need him up front, ASAP!"

Heather nodded her head vigorously, turned around, and immediately went aft. Bear scrambled up the stairs and back into the cockpit. "How are you doing, Jack? How are *we* doing?"

"Well, I'm maintaining two hundred fifty knots, but I still can't hold altitude. We're still descending, but a little bit less now. I see you're still dumping," he said as he looked back at the engineer's panel.

"Yes, but we've only dumped about twenty thousand pounds of fuel. And Jack, we not only lost number four, it's on fire!"

"What? What do you mean, it's on fire?"

"When I looked out the window to see the wing, I saw flames trailing out of number four."

"Well then, engine-fire checklist, and you're going to have to accomplish it by yourself! I'm using both hands and my left leg trying to keep this SOB upright. Tell me—what did you find out?"

"It's the right side! There are pieces of metal, and wires, and insulation just hanging and flapping in the wind."

"What do you mean, 'pieces'?"

"It looks like a bomb exploded—like Lockerbie!"

"And the fuselage?"

"Yes, the fuselage, it's just *open*!"

The gravity of the situation sent a chill through Jack. "How much of the right side is gone?"

"From about row 1R back to about—"

"Anybody...?" Jack interrupted.

"Some people are probably gone, I don't know."

"And Black? Did they find him? Where is he?"

"No, he's missing. They're still trying to find him."

"Christ," Jack said, shaking his head. "Are they preparing for a ditch?"

"I don't know. I can't talk to them on the interphone, it's out. Do you want me to go back down again and make sure?"

"Well, from what you saw, were people wearing their life vests?"

"From what I saw, yes."

"Well, Bear, I don't want to even say it out loud, because with a fractured and compromised fuselage, the plane would almost certainly break in two immediately upon hitting the water, but if I can't hold altitude...we're going in! I need you up here, but you have to, you absolutely have to have everyone prepare. Go, and come back fast!"

Bear's feet were moving so fast down the spiral staircase that he tripped again, but he caught himself on the banister. There were no flight attendants in first class, so Bear raced toward the back of the plane. There he saw Laurie, and the look they exchanged spoke volumes.

"Laurie, have they briefed a ditch?"

"What? I can't hear you, Bear!"

Bear repeated his question, yelling with all his might.

"Yes, yes—are we going in?" Laurie asked wildly, stark terror in her eyes.

"What?"

"Are we going in? Are we really going to ditch?"

"Laurie, I hope not, but it doesn't look good. I can't tell. We're losing altitude. We're very heavy on only two engines, and we can't seem to level off! If we ditch, it'll be in less than ten minutes or so. The PA is inop, so someone is going to have to be up in the cockpit with us until almost the last minute so they can relay the brace call to the crew. Okay?"

"Okay," she said, nodding determinedly.

"Still no Black?" Bear asked.

"No."

"Laurie, update Heather, and you can be the one to relay. We don't have too much more time to play with here, okay?"

Laurie nodded as she turned to seek out Heather. As Bear reached for the banister, he looked again at the big jagged hole with wires and tubes and pieces of metal hanging and swinging from the ceiling. He scrambled up the stairs and back in the cockpit.

"How are we doing? Any better?"

"Well, we're down to sixteen hundred feet and still going down at two hundred feet per minute. So what's that, eight minutes?"

"Laurie will be up here in a minute or two, and she'll be our interphone for the brace signal to the crew. Jack, you don't have your life vest on!"

"Well, Bear, you don't either. Put yours on and get mine, then hop into the right seat and take this bird for a minute. I'll put mine on, and...you might as well stay there, okay?"

"Roger."

Just then Laurie entered the cockpit with her life vest on, flashlight in hand, and a blank stare of shock on her face. "I'm here, Captain Rheinstrom."

"Good, thank you, Laurie. Hey, when we get out of this mess, the champagne is on me!"

"Thank you for saying that, Scrappy." She sat down in the engineer's seat and looked at Jack's profile. He could feel her looking at him and turned around in his seat. He didn't know if he would ever have another chance so he mouthed, "Love you."

She nodded, and with her heart racing and tears in her eyes, she mouthed, "Me too."

"Well, we're now at a thousand feet, and we're still descending at one hundred feet a minute. We're running out of time, Laurie. Have your crew start the brace call and strap yourself in. May God be with you."

"With you, too," she said as she quickly got up. "And you, too, Bear," she added on her way out.

"It probably doesn't matter, Bear, but why don't you terminate dump. No sense pumping fuel on the water when we, uh, make contact."

Bear jumped out of his seat, closed the dump manifold and switched the fuel pumps to the off position, then got strapped in again in the right seat. He thought of the passengers, tightly cinched into their seats, bent over and holding their feet. The flight attendants, also tightly strapped in, were yelling in unison, "Grab your ankles, keep your head down, grab your ankles, keep your head down, grab your ankles, keep your head down...." Jack and Bear, fervently searching straight ahead and downwards, could see the gentle waves twinkling from the reflected light of the supermoon. At any other time in their lives, the scene would have been beautiful beyond description, but tonight it was simply *unreal.*

"Bear, I tried contacting Santa Maria and Lajes approach while you were downstairs—no go." Referencing the 7700 emergency transponder code, he added, "We're squawking seventy-seven, but I don't think that they'll be able to read us at this low altitude." A few seconds passed. "We have to slow this thing down! If we hit the water at this speed, we'll be in a thousand pieces before we even come to rest. What's our stall speed at this weight, clean, no flaps?"

"When I terminated the dump just now, I checked the new weight. Stall speed is two hundred and five knots, but with that hole in the fuselage, and you putting in all that left rudder to offset the two working engines on the left wing, I wouldn't go below to two hundred fifteen knots, clean, no flaps."

"Well, we don't know what we're going to get when we put the flaps out, because some of the LEDs are indicating inop, right?" The LEDs, or leading edge devices, were on the front of the wings and provided extra lift when deployed.

"Right. When I tested them, I didn't get any green lights on the outboard ones."

"Bear, I don't want to be any faster than I have to be, and I don't want to stall it, either. So when we get below two hundred feet, we're committed. Let's start configuring, putting the flaps out, and slowing now, and see what we get. Then when we're below two hundred feet, we'll have no other choice."

"I know."

"We're supposed to ditch parallel to the swells and on top of the waves favoring the windward side, but I don't even see any real waves down there at all, do you?"

Bear, who was still sitting high up in his seat, looked forward, and then peered out his side cockpit window on the right. "No, it looks flat, like we could even water-ski down there. Boy, that huge moon sure helps."

"Okay, we're below a thousand feet now. Read off the altitudes for me."

"Nine hundred...eight hundred...seven hundred...six hundred...five hundred...four hundred...three hundred...two hundred."

"Okay, two hundred feet. Give me the landing lights."

"Roger." Bear reached up with a trembling hand. "Lights are on, standing by flaps, two hundred feet—standing by flaps."

"Bear, we've done everything that we could have. It's not up to us anymore."

Boston natives Roger and Annie Martin were sitting in seats 4A and 4B in business class, directly across from the gaping hole and the dangling wires and hoses. They had endured the brunt of what had happened that night. They were bent over, holding their ankles, their heads resting on the pillows on their laps. Terrified and trembling, they were praying and holding hands. "Grab your ankles, keep your head down, grab your ankles, keep your head down." After three minutes of the terrifying chant, and about 300 feet above the ocean, Roger had to look, he *had* to. He abruptly sat partially up, his left hand still holding Annie's, and he looked across the cabin and out through the gaping black hole. But it wasn't black outside anymore; he could now see the silver sea—it was close and getting closer. "Dear God," he whispered as he put his head back down on the pillow.

Back in the cockpit, Bear was doing his best to hold it together. "Two hundred feet, standing by flaps."

"Bear, you are already said that twice—no, three times."

"I did?"

"Bear, what's the wingspan? Do you remember? What's the wingspan of the seven forty-seven?"

"I think that it's around two hundred feet, maybe a little less, like one ninety or something. Why?"

"Bear, I think that we're in ground effect! We're in ground effect! *We're in ground effect!*" Jack's voice was now getting louder with each exclamation. He knew that ground effect, which occurs at the height above ground that is approximately one wingspan, decreases drag and increases lift. B-17 crews, their planes crippled and engines out, ran into this phenomenon coming back to England from bombing raids over Germany; it was like a cushion of air that, surprisingly, kept the airplane flying.

"You're right, Jack, you're right! We're not descending anymore!"

The two of them just sat there—the captain busy wrestling the controls of the shuddering airplane, the second officer with his left hand on the flap handle—staring at the instrument panel and the altimeter.

"Two hundred feet, Captain!"

"Two hundred feet, Mr. Engineer—two hundred feet! And Bear, you're going to have to help me here; my arms and my left leg are getting tired, very tired. I think that we're, uh, okay here at two hundred feet, and I don't think we're going to be descending any lower. We're not going to ditch, at least not here, and not right now. Can you take the bird for a while? It's going to take a lot of left rudder, you'll see."

"Roger, okay, I've got it."

"Roger, you have it. She's a bundle, isn't she? Are you okay? Are you comfortable with it?"

"Oh, yeah, she feels a lot like a Lockheed one forty-one, except, of course, for the rudder. I can see why your leg is tired."

"Okay, Mr. Copilot, we have to come up with a plan. Let me just think for a minute. We have a horrendous storm, what's left of Felix, approaching Lajes, and we can't go back there—it would be suicide. Besides the storm, we can't even climb high enough to make an approach, or get above the cliffs there. If we ditched, that would pretty much be suicide, too—the airplane would probably break in half. Now, assuming the near impossible, a successful ditching, we could have three hundred people in rafts in the water exposed to an approaching watered-down hurricane. So we can't go back, and we can't ditch here. In fact, no one even knows where we are. We have no options…we have to go forward."

"Forward? Forward to where? And how? On two engines, at two hundred feet in an airplane that feels like it could be coming apart at any minute?"

"Yes, on to somewhere, to Europe. The coast is only nine hundred miles or so away, and we have a pretty much full load of fuel. How much did you say that we dumped?"

"Only about twenty thousand."

"Okay, so we still have about…?"

"I'd say about two hundred eighty thousand pounds, but I can go back to the engineer's panel and look at the exact number."

"Let's speed up to the two hundred fifty knots that we were doing before, stabilize, and see what the resulting fuel flow is." Jack's brain worked through the math as he checked the INS, the inertial navigation system. It was about 1,355 miles to Paris, about five and a half hours, which would take approximately 170,000 pounds of fuel. "We need a hundred and seventy pounds of fuel to get to Paris," he informed Bear. "And you say we have about how much now?"

"Wait a minute, Jack, let me get the exact number." They transferred aircraft control, Bear got out of his seat, recorded the fuel readings, then returned to his seat, strapped in, and accepted aircraft control again. "A little over two hundred eighty thousand pounds."

"Well, that's over a hundred thousand extra—and Bear, you know what?"

"No, what?"

"If you hadn't found out about the cheap fuel, we wouldn't have taken the extra, and we might have ended up having to put her down!" They both looked at each other and nodded.

"Bear, the rest of the crew is probably hoarse as bullfrogs by now, so I'm going to go down there and call them off for now and give them the tentative good news." Jack left the cockpit, scrambled down the stairs, and went back to the main cabin to find Heather, the chief purser. It was a very strange experience for him, as he'd never before actually witnessed a pre-ditching drill, at least from this perspective—over three hundred people, all bent over. It reminded him of his first visit to a mosque in Casablanca, especially the repetitive, almost Gregorian-type monotone chant, again and again: "Grab your ankles, keep your head down, grab your ankles, keep your head down."

The rearward-facing flight attendants were erect in their seats, with their backs against the bulkhead. Jack found Heather at 2 left, second exit door on the left-hand side of the aircraft. She looked as though she'd seen a ghost. "Whaat?" she cried anxiously. "What's going on? Aren't we about to ditch?"

Jack was shaking his head vigorously. "No, Heather, not now! You can stop your brace chant. The airplane has leveled off, but we're only at two hundred feet above the ocean. I have to go back to the cockpit. Tell everyone that we are still in a very precarious position, very precarious, but for now, the situation is stabilized. And after you've briefed your crew and passengers, come up to the cockpit and I'll give you more details, okay?"

Her eyes were as big as saucers as she nodded. Jack turned around and quickly left, staring at the gaping hole before he ascended the stairway and returned to the cockpit.

"You okay, Bear?" he asked as he sat down and strapped himself into the left seat, sliding it forward.

"Yes, sir, nothing much has changed. I was just thinking—we're not going to try to go all the way to Paris, are we? I mean, isn't there somewhere closer we could land in Europe?"

"No, we're not going to Paris—that's too far, too populated, and too foggy. But, to where? That depends. We have to get there first, to the coast, that is, and stay in one piece. The weather forecast for the entire European continent is calling for widespread fog, from the western borders of Portugal and France all the way to Italy. Not good!"

"Then where are we going to go? What are we going to do?"

"I don't know—yet. But it seems to me that as we get closer to the mainland, even at this altitude or a bit higher, coastal radar will pick us up. Our radios will work, at least the VHF overland radio. I don't know what's wrong with the overwater radio, maybe a damaged antenna. It hasn't worked since the bomb went off."

"So, what you're saying is that we're limping toward Europe, but it's all fogged in?"

"Mainland Europe, the continent. The UK isn't under the influence of that weather system."

"So we're going to try to get to the UK? How far is it to, say, London?"

"Good question. Let's see, Gatwick." Jack punched the data into the INS. "Turns out it's about the same as it is to Paris. I don't see any other options, do you?"

"What about the Channel Islands, off France?"

"Well, that's a thought, but I think that their runways are pretty short, big enough only for a commuter plane. I don't know, but we'll look into it."

"I sure hope that this airplane stays in one piece. It's shuddering an awful lot."

"Bear," Jack said as he turned to face his copilot directly, "there is only one way to think about this, only one way. And that's in a positive way. There are close to three hundred and fifty people counting on you and me to make the right decisions. We have to stay focused, okay?"

"You're right. Sorry."

"Hey, man, this isn't easy, I know."

Heather suddenly appeared in the cockpit door, looking much more together than just minutes before.

"I can't believe that we're still alive, Captain Rheinstrom," she began.

"Well, Heather, we are, and I hope and plan to stay that way. But we have a lot ahead of us—I don't want to kid you, an awful lot. And you probably know, or have surmised by now, that Captain Black is gone."

Heather bowed her head and nodded. Jack briefed her on the present situation and the possible scenarios to come. He then received a full report on the status of the passengers and the one severely injured business-class flight attendant, who was almost pulled out of the plane. She was found clinging to a seat leg and was pulled to safety back inside the cabin by passengers and fellow crew. "How many seats, or if you know, how many passengers are missing?"

"Nine," came her solemn reply.

"Plus Captain Black."

"Plus Captain Black," she repeated.

"I don't want to even think about that—not now. Heather, check in with us every half an hour or so if you could, okay? I don't like not being able to communicate with you."

"Yes, Captain," she said, then left and went below.

Jack's left leg had been cramping up intermittently, so he took the opportunity to stand and do some leg stretches while Bear flew the airplane. As he was looking around the cockpit, he noticed a yellow light that was illuminated on the flight engineer's panel and asked about it.

"Oh, no!" Bear exclaimed, turning around in his copilot seat. "It's the number two CSD light that indicates low oil pressure. Jack, it's the only generator we have left! We left Boston with the number one disconnected by maintenance from the previous flight, and then we just lost the two generators on engines three and four that we had to shut down. What are we going to do?"

"Slow down, Bear. The first thing we need to do is get the abnormal procedure checklist out and go through it. Maybe the gauge is wrong; maybe it's giving us bad info. I'm going to get back in the seat and take the airplane so you can come back here and go through the your abnormal procedure for the indication. Go through it out loud so I can follow along, okay?"

They transferred aircraft control and Bear sat down in his second officer's seat in front of the flight engineer's panel.

"What is the actual CSD temperature, Bear?"

"Well, it's still in the normal range right now, but it's high, higher than normal. It hasn't overheated—yet. But I can't compare it to the other three CSD temps because all the other generators are inop."

"I see. Well, let's think here a minute. If we lost all electrical power, then...wait a minute, we still have the APU!" Jack's mind was racing. The APU, the auxiliary power unit, normally provided electricity and air-conditioning on the ground but can be used as a backup in the air. "Let's crank that up now while we still have a battery to do it with."

"Okay, I'll start it now," said Bear as he moved the APU switch to the run position to open the exhaust exit door. He waited a few seconds for the green light to illuminate, indicating that the door was indeed open. "Okay, here goes!" He flipped the spring-loaded switch from the run to the start position. Underneath the flight engineer's desktop and out of sight, Bear's hand was resting on his leg, his fingers crossed. "Come on, baby," he said as they both intensely stared at the exhaust gas temperature gauge. The rpm's rose and hesitated at the point where an ignition is introduced, creating a light-off with further acceleration and a successful start. But the rpm's stagnated there for about three seconds and then began to decrease, eventually falling back to zero. They both stared at the gauge in utter denial.

After thirty seconds of staring, Jack asked, "What's the starter duty cycle? How long do we have to wait before we can try it again?"

"Three minutes."

"Okay, let's wait three and try it again."

And just as they had feared, the number two start attempt was unsuccessful also.

"You know, Bear, they're not making this very easy," Jack murmured, shaking his head.

"I'm composed, Jack, at least somewhat, and I'm not losing it, but I need to know what's going through your mind right now."

"What's going through my mind? Well, I'm thinking that if the CSD and its generator go, we'll be left with only the ship's battery, which the systems' manual says is only good for about thirty minutes. We'll need to look up in your systems manual those items that are actually powered by the battery so we'll know what we really have left—*if* we lose our last generator, okay?"

"Okay," Bear replied, still staring incredulously at the lifeless APU instruments.

"And the INS's batteries are only good for thirty minutes, too," Jack continued. "But with the ship's battery, we can turn all unnecessary items off to conserve it and then turn things back on when and if we need them—" Jack was suddenly cut off in mid-sentence as the aircraft violently jolted and shuddered. "I'm slowing it down!" Jack exclaimed as he reached forward and pulled the number one and number two throttles back. In five seconds, the shaking stopped. "I don't think she likes two hundred fifty knots. We're at two forty-three now, so let's try that and see how that works."

"Okay, Jack, but what do you think that shaking is all about? What do you think is happening?"

"Bear, your guess is as good as mine. I've never flown an airplane in this configuration before except in the simulator, and that one certainly didn't have a hole in its side and unknown structural damage. Whatever happened or whatever caused that jolt has something to do with airspeed and the fuselage. Hopefully, we can just keep her going at this speed. And what I was saying before was that we can turn the ship's battery on and off if we actually get down to that scenario of no generators and no APU, but with the inertial navigation systems, it's a different story. If we turn the systems off to conserve their batteries, we can never reinitialize the units; we won't have the necessary reference position to input, to tell them where they are as a starting point. But at least we have them now providing course and ETE, estimated time en route info. Now, the winds might change between here and England, but we're only at two hundred feet and the wind here is a lot less significant than at a higher altitude. And as I was going to mention before, even if we could climb later, after reducing our weight due to the fuel burn-off, I don't want to go too much higher than this, maybe five hundred or seven hundred feet."

"You don't?"

"No, because if something happened to the fuselage later that made things worse, we might be forced to ditch, and we'd be descending from a relatively low altitude. But if we climb higher, say, up to two thousand or maybe three thousand feet, that's another story. Do you agree, Mr. Copilot?"

"Yeah, I see your point."

"Plus, at least right now, the ground effect is giving us our maximum lift, and we have plenty of fuel, thanks to you."

Laurie suddenly appeared in the cockpit, her color ashen, and a look of fear in her eyes. "What was that, Jack? Why was the airplane shaking? What does that mean?" she asked in a meek voice, her eyebrows raised, her forehead wrinkled.

"How am I doing, you ask? I'm doing great, Laurie. Why don't you go ahead and start the movie now?"

"Start the movie? Start the movie? Are you crazy?" she shrieked, then plopped down on the jump seat and started to sob hysterically.

"They're all waiting to die!" she managed to get out. "They either have their heads back staring at the ceiling, their lips moving in silent prayers, or they're holding hands, or arms, or each other, just staring at the floor." Her sobbing stopped and she began to nervously laugh. "Start the movie? Oh, God, that's great, Jack. That's really great! That really helped. Oh, thank you, thank you, Jack. Boy, I wish I could start the movie! Do you know what it is? It's *Frantic* with Harrison Ford! How funny is that, huh?"

Resuming her composure, she looked at Jack and then at Bear. "Can I do anything to help, and can I get you guys anything—anything at all?"

"Yeah, Laurie, a new left leg."

"What? A new left leg? What does that mean?" she asked.

"Bear and I have to take turns and spell each other. Our legs are getting tired from having to hold full left rudder in all the time." He turned his head around and glanced at her, saying, "We only have two engines left, Laurie, the two on the left wing, and they're at a very high power setting—they have to be, but that makes the airplane fly kind of sideways and we have to correct that by applying full left rudder with the rudder pedals. But don't worry; it's working and the rudder trim helps, too. It's not a pretty sight aerodynamically, but it's working."

"Are we going to be okay, Jack? Are we going to live?" Laurie asked quietly.

"That's our intent, Laurie. And by the way, any and all prayers are accepted. Most of all, we need a stiff upper lip—especially for them, our passengers."

"I'll try, Jack, I really will, you can count on me. You know, you guys need your physical strength. Don't you think that you should eat something? The galley ovens don't work anymore, but I had almost finished cooking the first-class meals—would you like to chew on a steak?"

"I think that you are absolutely right. Good idea—a good positive idea."

"Okay, I'll be right back. Oh, and what to drink?"

"Personally, I think I'd like a double, make that a triple martini, and I've never even had one before. Thanks anyway, we still have a bunch of water bottles up here in the cockpit."

Laurie returned shortly, delivered two cold steaks, gave Jack a quick neck massage, and returned to her flock below.

"You know, Jack," Bear observed, "we just both ate the same meal at the same time. That's against protocol!"

"Well, Bear, it's a good thing that the FAA isn't onboard. And if we both get food poisoning and suddenly die now, then I'm not going to believe in God anymore."

"Yeah, well, me neither. Jack, do you think that we should brief them about the possibility of losing all our electrics and all of our lights? I mean, emergency lights have independent batteries, but they won't last forever."

"Good point, although it will be light outside in a few hours. If you will take it for a while, I'll go down and talk to Heather and hit the lav while I'm down there—which I meant to do before we even took off. I don't know if they even work."

"Okay, Captain, I have it."

"Roger, you have it," said Jack as he slid his seat back, unbuckled his seatbelt, left the cockpit, and stepped down the spiral stairway. When he reached the bottom of the stairs he saw Heather standing in front of and staring at the galley, which was normally illuminated with many multiple function lights—blue, yellow, and green, indicating the status of the coffeemakers and the convection ovens. But the galley was now silent and dark; no lights were on.

Heather twirled around as though she'd been caught with her hand in the cookie jar. "Oh, Captain Rheinstrom," she asked, "How are things? Are we going to be okay? Is there anything new?"

Jack drew closer and put his hand on top of her shoulder. He then bent down to be close to her face and looked her straight in the eye. "Heather, you have to listen very carefully to what I'm about to say, and you're going to have to believe me and trust me, okay? Am I frightened? I don't think that's the right word. Maybe I will be later, but not now—I don't have that luxury. There are a lot of things to consider, and the copilot and I are doing the very best that we can to cope with the situation. What I know is that we have sustained some major damage from what, I still don't know—possibly a bomb like Lockerbie last year, but we're still in one piece, and except for those unfortunate souls that we lost, everyone is still alive."

Heather nodded, speechless. Jack went on. "We can't go back to the Azores because of a violent storm and weather system that is almost upon them. If you'll notice, we are flying very low, two hundred feet above the ocean. We're doing that because the wings have excellent lift there, and we need that extra lift because we lost two engines. That's the bad news. The good news is that we still have two good engines, and even though we're flying low and slow, we took on maximum fuel at Lajes, and therefore, even though we're burning fuel at a very high rate, we still have more than enough to reach Europe. A lot of questions have to be answered, and asked for that matter, but I plan to make it through this. Shortly, the batteries for the emergency lights will run out, and it'll be completely dark in the cabin. Inform your passengers that this has been anticipated and that in an hour or so, there will be sunrise, and there will be light in the cabin again. Have you discovered any more injuries, or anything you think that I should know about?"

"No, nothing, Captain. The people are quiet—quiet, praying, catatonic, and scared to death. May I ask you something, Captain Rheinstrom?"

"Sure, Heather, but it's Jack, okay?"

"Jack…will you give me a hug?"

He slowly nodded and, with tears in his eyes, took Heather in his arms and pressed her against his body. She squeezed back very tightly and lingered there for a few seconds. Her thick auburn hair was an inch below his nose, and he couldn't avoid smelling it. It had a wonderful scent; he hadn't smelled a woman's hair in over twenty years. His mind raced back to La Polidor, where he had been just days before, and his encounter with Katherine.

"How was that?" Jack asked with a subdued smile. He released her and stepped back.

"You have no idea, Jack, no idea. Thank you," she said as she turned around and went back to the cabin.

As Jack was halfway up the stairs, the airplane began to violently vibrate again. He froze in his steps and held his breath. After a few seconds, it stopped, and Jack hurried up the stairs and back into the cockpit.

"Are you okay, Bear?"

"Yeah, but what the hell do you think *that* was?"

"I don't know. Did you feel anything in the controls? In the yoke, or the rudder pedals?"

"Yeah, I felt it in the yoke, but it wasn't sharp, it was soft, if you know what I mean, and it didn't feel like a stall."

"You know, it might be some part of the fuselage skin flapping at times and disturbing the airflow over the wing. If it was damaged flight controls, they'd be permanently damaged, not hit or miss—do you agree?"

"Yeah, I guess. I just wish that it wouldn't do that anymore, you know?"

"Boy, do I! Are you ready for some relief at the controls?"

"Yes, sir, I am."

Jack sat down, buckled his seat belt, slid his seat forward, and assumed aircraft control again.

"You know, Bear, I didn't think that I was that hungry, but Laurie had a good idea. We're going to have to take care of ourselves physically as best we can, because this is going to be a long—" He stopped suddenly in mid-sentence. "Bear, that CSD warning light isn't steady yellow anymore—it's now blinking! What does that mean?"

"Let me go back to my panel and check the temperature again," Bear said as he got out of the copilot seat. "Jack, the temperature indicator has gone up. It's now just shy of the redline!"

Jack was thinking fast. "Bear, get out the book and read me the procedure for this. Do you have your flashlight handy?"

"Yes."

"I have mine out, too, but what about a spare? Quick, before you read that, check Black's brain bag to see if there's one in there."

Bear came forward to the copilot's seat and opened Captain Black's flight bag, nestled in a cubbyhole on the floor to the right of the copilot seat. "I got it! In fact, there are actually two in there."

"Great. Give me one and take the other one for yourself."

He retrieved them, gave one of them to Jack, and then went back and sat down at his flight engineer's panel. "Jack, if it hits the redline, which I'm afraid it's going to do, we're going to have to use the CSD disconnect switch. If we don't disconnect it when we're able to, without the oil lubrication it will overheat, self-destruct, and possibly damage the engine!"

"I was afraid you were going to say that, but we have no choice. Let's use the time that we have left to plan a course of action. You stay there and monitor the temperature, and be ready in case it goes into the red zone."

"Jack! I just thought of something!" Bear burst out.

"What?"

"If we shut down the CSD and lose all electrical power, then we'll also lose the fuel boost pumps for the engines. And if we lose the engines, we'll stall and hit the water like a brick! Maybe we should do a controlled ditch now and take our chances?"

"Hold on a minute, Bear. They're boost pumps, as in *boost.* The engines are mounted on the pylons, which are *under* the wings. The fuel should gravity-feed from the wings to the main engine-driven fuel pumps. We should be okay."

"You sure about that?"

"Did you ever fly the DC-10?"

"Just for about six months, when I was a new hire. Why?"

"Well, do you remember an emergency procedure about complete electrical failure? On the ten, the number two engine, the one mounted in the tail, will flame out with the loss of the electrical boost pumps, but engines one and three, on their pylons under the wing, will gravity-feed and run normally except at maybe max takeoff power. Do you remember that?"

"Yeah, I guess I do...well, anyway, I'm glad that you do."

"We don't have much time here with our generator. What we do have is a plane that is successfully flying, albeit on only two engines and at two hundred feet, but we have the luxury of extra fuel and therefore time to figure this thing out. Our INSs will work, they say, for thirty minutes on their internal batteries, so we have navigation for a while, a course to fly. Although, like for the guys in World War I, it will only be with our 'whiskey compass' once we lose the INS. And we'll have an idea about the ETA. The only big variables left," Jack continued, almost laughing, "are the weather en route at this altitude and what our destination will be. That's all! But, let me just say—so what? We're going to do it anyway. Are you with me, Bear? Are you with me?"

Bear worked to drum up some enthusiasm. "Jack—I really believe that you really believe, so yes, I'm with you, and I have to tell you that we are now at CSD temperature redline!"

"Okay, let's do it! Now, we have some important things to do and we have to do them right now. But before we disconnect the CSD, we need to get a present position *direct* to that waypoint on the chart, the one in the middle of the entrance of the English Channel, LIZARD. I'll fly, and you program the waypoint into the INS, and record the present time, the magnetic heading, the distance to destination, the cross track error, estimated time en route, and also the actual present winds. After you do that, run down to tell Heather that what we briefed about, the complete electrical power loss, is just about to happen. Make sure that she's already communicated that to the passengers. Then get back up here ASAP and go through the CSD-disconnect checklist. We'll lose our last remaining generator and will be in the dark until daybreak, but we'll have both INSs on battery power for a while and will keep getting updates for the course to the English Channel."

"Okay!" With renewed energy, Bear got out of his seat, left the cockpit, delivered the message, and then ran up the spiral staircase to return to the cockpit, flashlight in hand.

"Okay, Jack, here goes," he said as he completed the procedure and pushed the disconnect button. The lights in the plane and the landing lights instantly extinguished, and all was dark—save the August Sturgeon Moon, high in the night sky, the silver tips on the black Atlantic Ocean waves just two hundred feet below.

"Bear, what were the winds that you just recorded?"

"Okay, let me look here...they were three three zero degrees at thirteen knots."

"Okay, look down and remember in your mind that exact picture of the waves. The winds are three three zero, and we are on a course of zero six five degrees. If that site picture changes, if the waves change their direction or size, then we have to adjust our magnetic heading to compensate, okay? But that's not now, that's after we lose the batteries for the INS in approximately thirty minutes. Until then, we'll just follow the INS course. It may sound rudimentary, but I recall that the natives from Bora Bora found their new home in Hawaii by following a star and simply reading the waves. And, by God, we're going to do the same."

Bear was staring at the waves as instructed when suddenly he cried out from shock. "Jesus Christ, Jack!" Bear shouted. "Did you see that?"

"See what?" said Jack, his head snapping to the right.

"There was a sailboat down there that we just passed over—a sailboat, can you believe that? If we had been much lower, I think that we would've hit his mast! Can you imagine that? All of the stuff that we've been through tonight and survived, and then to find a needle in a haystack and hit a boat in the middle of the Atlantic Ocean!"

Bear slowly began to laugh, a hysterical laugh. He was slipping away, and Jack realized what was going to happen if he didn't correct the situation immediately.

"Bear, listen to me! Is your mother still alive?" he demanded.

"What?" Bear's face looked incredulous as he turned to his left.

"Is your mother still alive?"

"Well, yes. Why do you want to know that?"

"I was just thinking of mine and how important she was in my life. How about you?" Jack asked intensely.

Bear took a deep breath and remembered. And as he digressed about his mom for several minutes, Jack could see that his demeanor was returning to normal, and eventually he interrupted him and returned the conversation to the business at hand—a crippled airliner with hundreds of passengers over the Atlantic Ocean at night with no safe harbor awaiting them, no real place to go.

"Bear, I want you to record the INS route data every five minutes for as long as the batteries last. I just don't believe the advertised thirty minutes, okay?"

"Sure thing. Makes sense."

At exactly twenty-five minutes from generator shutdown and the subsequent loss of all electrical power, the INS batteries failed, just as Bear was halfway through recording the pertinent navigational data.

"Okay, Bear, how much time did it say we have left? What is our ETE to LIZARD?"

Bear turned his flashlight back on and looked over the information that he had just recorded on his clipboard. "Well, we have a thousand fifty-one miles to go, and at this speed with these winds, we have four hours and twenty-eight minutes left to waypoint LIZARD, and the heading remains the same, zero six five degrees."

"Okay, will you go down again and inform Heather of our latest information?"

"Sure, be right back. Do you want any bottled water?"

"Yeah, I sure do. My mouth is so dry, I can hardly swallow." They both nodded and nervously laughed as Bear again grabbed his flashlight. As he was leaving, Jack added, "And I need some relief flying this tank when you get back."

"Got it," said Bear, who then left the cockpit and the top deck to descend the spiral staircase to the main cabin level. But halfway down he stopped, turned his flashlight off, and leaned back, resting his shoulders against the stairway wall. Even though everything was pitch black around him, he closed his eyes and just stood there motionless. Jesus, four and a half more hours, he yelled silently to himself. Four and half more hours!

Below, Heather Holland was uneasy. The darkness throughout the cabin, the mysterious occasional flashlight illuminating from one of the other cabin staff, the roar of the wind just outside the gaping hole—all of this was creating a visual nightmare for her. She was scared before, but now she was unnerved. I have to go see Captain Rheinstrom, she thought. He'll make it better. She walked forward in the main cabin, just past the first-class galley, and started to walk up the spiral stairs, focusing the beam of her flashlight on the next ascending step. Suddenly, a large black trouser leg appeared out of the dark, and she screamed. Bear, whose eyes were still closed, was startled too, and he cried out. He quickly turned his flashlight back on, and seeing Heather, immediately tried to calm her.

"It's okay, it's okay, Heather. I'm sorry, I didn't mean to frighten you."

Heather had almost begun to cry, but it was only momentary,

during which time Bear put his arm around her.

"Sorry, Bear, I didn't mean to drop that on you. I was just startled there for a minute. I wasn't expecting to see anyone in the dark."

"Hey, this hasn't been easy for any of us."

"I'll be okay. Do you guys need anything?" she asked, sniffling and then blowing her nose into a napkin that she carried in her smock. "I was just coming up to check on you two."

"Well, I was just coming down to tell you that our course to the entrance of the English Channel is going to take us about four and a half more hours, at this speed and at this altitude."

"Four and a half more hours?" Heather asked desperately.

"That's right. We don't want to go much faster because the airplane doesn't like it. I'm sure that it has something to do with the damage that occurred to the fuselage. That's what we believe caused the shuddering that you felt a couple times."

"Okay," Heather agreed, nodding her head. "Yeah, I didn't know what the hell that was, but I was sure that it was going to be the end.

"I know. We didn't like it either."

"So, Bear, what happens in four and a half hours when we get to the English Channel? Where are we going to land? We're not going to ditch in the English Channel, are we?" Heather pleaded.

"No, that's the last thing we want to do. Our plan is to get to the English Channel in broad daylight and fly down the coast until we see the piers at Brighton. You remember those, don't you?" Bear asked. "They're very visible from the air and are pretty much due south of Gatwick. Anyway, we'll just circle there, creating quite a scene I'm sure, and wait for the RAF or the Coast Guard to intercept us and lead us to an airport."

"Why can't you try raising someone on your radio?" Heather asked.

"Because we don't have a radio or navigation—we have no generators left. We have no electrical power, zip."

"What do you mean, we have no navigation? How are we going to get to the English Channel?" she asked, her voice rising.

"Heather, we have a plan, and it's going to work. We have plenty of fuel, and we're going to get to the English Channel. It's just that another four and half hours in these conditions will be an enormous challenge for all of us—but hell, it sure beats the alternative."

CHAPTER TEN

At Royal Air Force High Wycombe in Buckinghamshire, United Kingdom, Air Chief Marshal Sir Alan Witkin opened the door and walked into the briefing room at Headquarters Strike Command. It was 0429 Zulu on Friday, August 4. Witkin's back was ramrod straight; his handlebar mustache was turned up at the ends, and as he made his way to the podium, his gait almost resembled a march. The seven officers assembled there, all junior in rank, rose to their feet and stood at attention.

"Seats, gentlemen," he quietly said as he stood on the slightly elevated stage in front of the situation board. He looked to the group, now all seated around a horseshoe-shaped table.

"First of all, I want to thank you for your quick response to this early morning muster. I will give you a quick synopsis, and then we have to move on it, time being of the essence. Here are the facts—we have an American airliner, a seven forty-seven, call sign Trans Ocean thirty-eight. The plane departed Lajes Air Force Base in the Azores last night at 0100 Zulu. It was on departure radar climbing through twenty-three thousand feet when it reversed directions and started a rapid descent. Lajes lost radar contact at about five hundred feet. They wanted to initiate a search and rescue operation immediately, but there was an intense maritime storm approaching and their one and only helicopter crew was not on Alpha alert because the Trans Ocean flight was in an emergency divert and there was no planned airfield activity for the base for the next seventy-two hours. Anyway, the presumption is that something went terribly wrong and the airplane crashed into the ocean. However, this is when it gets interesting."

Witkin turned around and walked closer to the situation board with his telescoping pointer in his hand, now fully extended and pointing at the ceiling. "An American sailor aboard his private boat transmitted that he heard a very loud sound of an airplane flying low overhead." With the back of his left hand pressed snugly against his back, Witkin quickly lowered his pointer to the map. "*Here* is Lajes, and *here* is the sailboat location. His report was relayed via satellite communication by a commercial freighter, some two hundred miles away. That time was 0130 Zulu, three hours ago. Now, we're getting lucky here. The point on the chart *here*," he said, pausing to point with his little silver sword, "is where a Maersk container ship reported hearing a very loud roar from a low-flying aircraft. However, the Maersk vessel did not actually see the aircraft. Now, if you connect these two points, you have a vector—and that vector is pointing to the entrance to the English Channel."

He paused to let his words sink in. "Because we don't have an exact time reported for the second report, we can't really calculate the plane's ground speed or get an accurate ETA. However, if you make a guesstimate based on rough figures, the plane should be arriving, assuming it's able to remain airborne, again, we don't have any idea what could've happened to the plane, but arriving sometime after 0600 Zulu. If—and I emphasize the word *if*—the plane is able to make it to the English Channel and we can intercept it, what are we going to do? I come to you directly from a phone conversation with Sir Robert Chisholm, who is with the office of the prime minister. I gave him the same briefing that I just gave to you, and I suggested that if we can intercept it, we could guide the plane northeast up the Bristol Channel until abeam approximately Kingswood. From Kingswood, it might be possible to lead it overland to RAF Fairfield. Fairfield would be an excellent recovery base given that their runway is one of the longest in the UK at almost ten thousand feet, in fact qualifying as a Trans Ocean abort landing site for the NASA shuttle flights. Fairfield also has specially trained emergency crews and medical personnel stationed there. However, the prime minister, with the Lockerbie disaster only eight months ago, does not want the possibility of another crippled airliner falling out of the sky and killing additional innocent townspeople below. Given these concerns, he has asked if there might be another airfield option, a safer landing spot that could be used--one approachable only by water. That is why, gentlemen," he said, stopping to peer at his audience more closely, "and ladies, we have decided upon RAF St Mawgan on the Cornish coast at the position *here.* Its runway is nine thousand feet long and an amazing three hundred feet wide."

Air Chief Marshal Witkin then turned around, collapsed his pointer, placed it on the podium table, and continued, "Royal Air Force St Mawgan is also the Strike Command's main base for maritime reconnaissance and search and rescue operations. We have time to accomplish the following but just barely. After the tasks are assigned, we will adjourn this meeting until zero six hundred when we will reconvene here, as an active command post. At that time, each of you will need to bring with you your direct communication link to your resource.

"Air Marshal Gamble, Trig, there are four interceptors, Tornadoes, from RAF Coningby on Alpha alert temporarily stationed at RAF Mildenhall—launch those *Tonkas* ASAP to a position midpoint to the Channel's entrance and have them set up a thirty-mile orbit, one flight of two at one thousand feet, the other flight of two at two thousand.

"Air Marshall Cook, Cooker, I want you to immediately launch the Avro search and rescue Shackleton from St Mawgan, coordinating with London control, reversing the airplane's expected approach course and try to find this incoming Trans Ocean thirty-eight. Also, again from St Mawgan, I want three Sea King helicopters loitering in that general area.

"And finally, Air Marshal Cathey, Bill, I want you to be the point man and coordinator for the assigned tasks, and report directly to me. Are there any questions?" He waited but was met with silence. "Right, well, there you have it. Let's get on it!"

As Air Chief Marshal Witkin stepped off the slightly elevated stage and started walking toward the door, the assembled officers moved to rise but were stopped. "At ease, gentlemen and ladies, I will be in the area all day." He opened the door and closed it behind him as he left.

* * *

Time: Local and Zulu—0455

RAF Mildenhall, Suffolk, England

The four RAF Tornado crews ran out of their alert facility, scrambling onto the waiting crew bus, and out to their nearby parked airplanes. The interceptors had previously been preflighted and all that was left to do was start engines, check in on their radios, and launch.

(Weasel One)—"Weasel Flight, *check in*—."

(In fast succession) "Two" (checking in)

"Three" (checking in)

"Four" (checking in)

"Mildenhall Ground, Weasel Flight, flight of four at the alert ramp, taxi—."

"Roger 'Weasel Flight,' Mildenhall Ground—you are cleared to taxi present position to runway two nine, taxi into position and hold. All traffic will give way to you. Contact Tower upon reaching the runway."

"Weasel Flight, go (radio) channel 2—."

"Two" (acknowledging)

"Three" (acknowledging)

"Four" (acknowledging)

"Mildenhall Tower, Weasel Flight, ready, in position--two nine."

"Roger Weasel Flight, you are cleared for takeoff, runway two nine, climb runway heading to 3,000, and contact Honnington Control on 365.5."

"Roger, Mildenhall, Weasel Lead—cleared to go on two nine, up to three, Honnington on 365.5"

The four Panavia Tornadoes had already lined up on the runway with 'Lead' in the center at the front of the formation and number Two 'staggered back,' just off Lead's *left* wing. On the *right* of Lead, also 'staggered back,' was number Three, with number Four just off and slightly behind Three's right wing. Weasel Lead raised his right hand in his cockpit for the others to see and made a 'spinning' gesture. He looked first to his left at Two, then to his right—Weasel Two saw it as did Weasel Three, who passed it on to Weasel Four. All four pilots then advanced their engine throttles to the *military takeoff power* setting in unison. When the subsequent 'okay' nod was passed all the way *back* to Weasel Lead, he made an exaggerated move *back* with his head until his helmet touched the headrest on the ejection seat behind him, then a slow exaggerated head nod *forward*. On that signal, the four "Tonka" pilots then each simultaneously pushed their two throttles all the way to the forward limit, injecting raw fuel into the exhaust section of the jet engine and lighting-off the afterburners. They released their brakes and their takeoff roll began, each bird now projecting a ten foot long, bright yellow-orange, pulsing sword from its tailpipes. When safely airborne, all four aircraft raised their landing gear at the same time on Lead's signal who then ordered, --

"Weasel Flight, go channel 4."

The response was immediate——

"Two"

"Three"

"Four"

"Honnington Control, Weasel Flight of four with you, climbing to three."

"Weasel Flight, good morning—we've been waiting for you. Turn right to heading of two six five; maintain 3,000, and I will be handing you off momentarily to London. London will then vector your flight to the AOR (area of responsibility).

* * *

At 0530 Zulu Trans Ocean 38, now at seven hundred feet above the waves, was continuing its odyssey toward the English Channel and was somewhere near LIZARD.

"I think that I'll take it again, Bear," said Jack. "Thanks for the breather."

"Good, you've got it. I feel like I've been rode hard and put to bed wet!"

"Roger, I've got it, and I couldn't agree with you more. I don't think I've ever really appreciated an autopilot as much as I do now—you?"

"I hear you, man, I hear you," was all that Bear could manage to say.

"So, Bear, I think that we've talked about the two-engine approach procedures enough, don't you? I mean, do you have any questions *at all* about what we're going to be doing?" Jack asked.

"No, Jack, no questions about what, only *where*."

"Sorry, Bear, can't help you there. But you want to know something?"

"What?" He turned his head from the vigilant scan out the front windscreen to look at his captain on his left.

"I think that there's someone up there pulling for us, I really do. It's a funny feeling that I have, but it's not a joke. I feel it in every inch of my body."

"Well, Jack, as my grandmother used to say, 'From your lips to God's ears.' I hope that you're right."

"I can see that the sky is beginning to lighten, Bear. That's a good sign, and it will relieve some our anxiety about not being able to see anything in front of us, only the waves below. And the light inside the cabin and outside the windows will be good for the passengers, too. And if we see any ships, we'll try to pass close by them so they can report our position. So continue to keep your eyes peeled, Bear."

"Do you suppose, Jack, that anyone thinks that we're still alive?"

"I don't know. I'm sure that when we dropped off radar when we got so low they might have started a search and rescue, but there was a hell of a storm approaching. I can't remember, but I didn't see any other aircraft parked on the ramp at Lajes, so it would probably be boats that would be out looking for us. So, to answer to your question, I don't know, and I really don't care right now about anything other than getting to wherever we're going, setting the parking brake, and going into a coma!"

The light, or at least the advent of it, buoyed their spirits along with those of the passengers, too. Heather Holland knocked on the cockpit door to announce her presence. Taking the cockpit key from her smock, she opened the door and walked in. She sat down on the jump seat and leaned forward, resting her chin on her two hands, her elbows on her knees.

"Ah, daylight—what a sight to behold! And how are my guys doing? Ready for a beer?" The light was obviously affecting her spirits, too.

"You know, guys, I've had a lot of time down there by myself, sitting in the dark, thinking about *things*. It's not over, at least not right now. I know that. And I don't know where we're going and if we are really, truly going to get there. But suddenly, I have this warm feeling inside of me, and it's a warm memory of all my past flights, all the Atlantic crossings, the times when the darkness of night is past. There's a new day dawning, a shower and warm bed waiting for me along with a nap, some shopping, and a great time with my crew at dinner. I hope it all continues, but if not, I look at how lucky I've been, how so few people on earth have ever experienced even *some* of the worldwide sights and sounds and friendships and experiences that I have been fortunate enough to have had. Lucky me, lucky me."

Jack turned to his copilot. "Bear, take it a minute."

"Okay, I've got it."

Jack twisted around in his seat so that he could face his purser directly, and in a soft and fatherly manner he patted her left knee.

"Don't give up, Heather—I think that we're going to make it. I can't promise you, but I really believe it. I know that there are only five hundred more questions to be answered, but hang in there." He gave her two more little pats, then retracted his arm and untwisted his body, relaxing again in his seat. Captain Rheinstrom took the flying duties back from his copilot, and the three of them sat there in silence for at least five minutes, just looking at the brightening sky and the big red ball rising in the east, lost in thought and reflection.

* * *

August 4, 1989 Time: Local and Zulu—0453

RAF St Mawgan
New Quay, Cornwall, England

Flight Lieutenant Peter Richards was asleep in his bunk at the alert facility. He was the aircraft commander of an Avro Shackleton, a four-engine, propeller-driven maritime search and rescue aircraft that was on standby duty, Alpha alert. He had one day left on his seven-day tour. The other crew members, consisting of the other pilot, the air engineer, the three radar observers, and the two coordinators, were still asleep in their bunks. The door to the darkened room suddenly opened and a flashlight-armed duty manager silently approached the bed. He gently shook Richards's right shoulder.

"Flight Lieutenant Richards, wake up—you've been alerted."

Richards jerked his head up from his pillow.

"You and your crew are to launch ASAP!"

As he scrambled to don his fleece undergarment "bunny suit" followed by the always challenging waterproof immersion suit, he was wondering what it was today—a pleasure craft? A freighter in trouble? An oil spill?

The crew bus was waiting outside, its engine running and headlights on. The rest of the crew had already assembled inside, waiting for their aircraft commander to arrive. While being briefed by Strike Command concerning the particulars of the mission, Richards tried to drink some of the black coffee that had been kept warm by the hot plate during the night in the ready room. He took one sip, then put the cup down, visibly frowning. I'll wait for coffee on the plane, he thought. With life vest and ditty bag in hand, he boarded the crew bus.

"Good morning, men," Richards began after climbing up the steps of the bus entrance. "To the bird, please," he said, turning toward the driver as the door closed. He then turned around and stood in the aisle in front of his seated crew.

"We have a high-priority mission this morning, one coming down from the prime minister himself. We possibly have a crippled U.S. airliner, a Boeing seven forty-seven that is limping, or 'maybe' limping, from the Azores to somewhere near the English Channel. The ETA, and again, this is going on a lot of assumptions is…." He stopped mid-sentence, looked out the front windshield and paused, then turned around. "I'll finish the briefing on intercom; let's get our preflight duties done ASAP and get airborne. Here we go." Richards led the group down the stairs and over to the waiting airplane and ground support team.

* * *

"Weasel flight, this is Neptune on channel 5, do you read, over?"

"Roger, Neptune, this is Weasel Lead, go ahead."

"Roger, good morning, Weasel. We just launched from St Mawgan and are now just abeam the Isles of Scilly, climbing to seven thousand. We will be flying the reciprocal of the inbound aircraft's estimated course. Is there anything new to report, over?"

"No, no, nothing is new. We have two sets of two, four overall, Tornadoes flying in two different thirty-mile orbits. Weasels One and Two will be at one thousand, and Weasels Three and Four will be at two thousand feet. And be advised, there are also three Sea Knight helicopters en route to our position who will be at five hundred feet."

"Copy all, Weasel, and for your info, we will be at seven thousand feet and maintaining one hundred sixty knots. I guess Strike Command is working with London on a discrete radio frequency and will be doing the coordinating."

"Roger that, Neptune—good hunting. This is Weasel flight, out."

* * *

"Well worth the wait, don't you think, Wallace?"

"What do you mean, sir?" replied the copilot.

"The coffee, man, the coffee!" said Richards.

"Oh, yes, sir. The coffee is good indeed."

"I mean, this could really jazz up even a honker stew! Did you get a chance to grab a cup in the ready room while I was being briefed?"

"No, sir. Not much time, you know."

"Well, I did and I nearly spit it out. Dismal, I say, dismal. It was like it was boiled all night long. So, this was worth the wait."

"I was thinking, sir...."

"Yes, Wallace, go ahead."

"Well, Strike Command recommended seven thousand feet for our search, and that will indeed give our radar more range, but I'm wondering if a lower altitude might be better. You know, the seas are up and the noise from the wave tops really do clutter the radar returns."

"So, what are you suggesting then, Flying Officer Wallace?" Richards asked, regarding the young copilot.

"Well, I don't know, sir, but aren't we looking for a plane that is supposedly flying quite low? Perhaps something like two thousand feet would...would be better?"

Lieutenant Richards thought about his copilot's suggestion for a minute, then announced, "Brilliant, Wallace, you take the girl, and I'll give Strike Command a jingle. But wait a minute, isn't Weasel flight at one thousand and two thousand? I'll ask for fifteen hundred to be safe."

"Roger, sir."

After a brief discussion, Strike Command concurred with the idea and the Avro Shackleton began a slow descent to fifteen hundred feet.

"Just about an hour to official daylight, Wallace. When it gets brighter, let's have the off-duty radar operator up here looking. Another set of eyes, you know?"

"Yes, sir, Lieutenant," the copilot replied, as he wrote a note to himself on his kneepad. "So, all we have to proceed on are two loud noises heard at night over the Atlantic and no visual sightings?"

"That's about it," Richards replied. "One a sailboat and one a container ship—but they weren't just faint noises, supposedly. On the contrary, they were both very loud and dramatic. They're looking for wreckage presently at the last known radar position near the Azores, but there is some wicked weather there hampering operations. We shall see," Richards concluded, upending his now empty paper coffee cup and peering out his left window. "We shall see."

At 0605 Zulu, an excited voice came over the intercom. "Sir, Radar One, I think I have something!"

"Roger, I'll be right back." Lieutenant Richards hurriedly unbuckled his seatbelt and shoulder harness and slid his seat backward on its seat tracks. He turned to his copilot. "You have the bird, Wallace."

"Yes, sir," countered Wallace as he bent down to reach the seat adjuster and then slid his seat closer to the yoke.

"Strike Command, this is Neptune, over."

* * *

"Weasel Lead, this is Two. I've got a visual tally on him; our bandit is ten o'clock low and closing fast. He's now passing underneath!"

"I don't have him, Two. Keep him in sight and assume lead. I will cross over beneath you, left to right. Do not lose him!"

"Roger, One, Weasel Two assuming lead, beginning left-hand one-eighty-degree turn *now*!"

The turn was sharp and the bank was steep, but the maneuver was a success as both Tornadoes were now directly above and following their prey.

"Weasel Lead, this is Two. I'm going to try raising him on the international emergency frequency." After repeated attempts, there was no contact made with Trans Ocean 38. Weasel Two stated that he wanted to resume lead, which, after a coordinated aerial ballet, he did.

* * *

"Oh my God, Bear!" Jack yelled.

"What? What? What is it?" Bear immediately responded.

"Look!" he said, pointing with his left hand. "I've got a fighter above, ahead on my left wing! They found us, Bear, they found us! We've been intercepted by, it looks like a British flag, the RAF!"

Bear's eyes widened. He looked to his right out the side window. "Jack, Jack, I've got one too, off my right wing!"

Jack nodded fervently. "I can see the pilots' heads, silhouetted in the airplane canopy. The forward pilot is pointing to his mouth and then his right ear. He must have tried to raise us on the radio! I'm going to respond with the no-radio signal."

Jack positioned himself close to his side window and moved his flattened left hand, palm inward, back and forth in front of his mouth, then the same hand back and forth in front of his left ear. Then he waited. The profile of the cockpit of the Avro Tornado is not particularly large, but Jack was sure that he saw the helmeted pilot nodding his head up and down in a very exaggerated fashion.

As Weasel Two took his position off the 747's right wing, he looked to his left and was instantly gobsmacked. "Weasel Lead, this is Two."

"Go ahead, Two."

"Nigel, you have to come over here and see this!"

"See what? What is it, Peter?"

"You'll see! I'll pull off to the right." With that, the lead Tornado moved to his left, dropped altitude slightly, and crossed over under the B-747 to take a position off the right wing.

"Blimey, Peter, what do you think? Another Lockerbie?"

"I don't know, Nigel, but it sure looks like a bomb to me. What else could it be? I can't believe he even made it this far. It was spot-on that we found him, but this mission is far from over. I wonder if he can actually make it to St Mawgan, and if he does, what onboard systems will he have left? And, hello, hello! Look at number three and four engines, Nigel—there's no heat, no exhaust coming from the starboard engines. He's only running on two engines, one and two on the left wing!"

"Peter, I'm going back into my position on the left wing and resume lead; you assume your position on the right again. I'm calling Strike Command with an update."

"Nigel?"

"Yeah, go ahead, Peter."

"Do you think that this Yank might know the HEFOE signals?" The acronym, standing for *hydraulics, electrics, fuel, oxygen,* and *engine,* referenced the signals used by pilots to silently communicate mechanical problems.

"Brilliant, Peter! I don't know. If he's ever flown formation in the military, he would. Let's find out."

Weasel Lead resumed his position above and in front of the 747's left wing. He looked back at the 747 cockpit and pointed to his helmet three times with his index finger. It'd been over twenty-five years since Jack Rheinstrom had flown fighters in the New Jersey Air Guard, but his knowledge of formation flying procedures had been permanently ingrained in his mind. One of those procedures involved cockpit-to-cockpit "no radio" communication procedures: HEFOE.

Jack stayed close to his left window and raised his left index finger, repeatedly pointing to his head. He then held up one finger for *H,* hydraulic failure. He pointed at his head again, this time holding up two fingers for *E,* electrical failure. He showed four fingers for *O,* oxygen failure, then finally five fingers for *E,* engine failure; the only system missing in the sequence was the three-fingered *F* for fuel failure, as they had plenty of that to spare.

"Weasel Two, these guys are in bloody trouble! I'm going to update Strike Command *again* because they're going to need to make a whole lot of contingency plans."

* * *

At Strike Command Headquarters, Air Chief Marshal Witkin was standing in front of the podium, again with the raised pointer in his right hand. He looked at his watch, then at the situation board.

"Good morning again, ladies and gentlemen. We have good news, and we have troubling news—good news first. We have found our chick and the Weasel Tornadoes are escorting him to RAF St Mawgan, along with a Shackleton, call sign 'Neptune' from Squadron Eight. ETA is thirty-four minutes from now, 0749 Zulu. The troubling facts are fivefold. Number one; the airframe is substantially damaged on the starboard side, forward of the right wing. Weasel flight suspects a detonated bomb blew a hole in the fuselage, big enough to accommodate two Volkswagen Jokers, to use their words."

He paused to advance the pointer. "Number two; the seven forty-seven only has two of its four engines operating. Number three, there is no direct radio communication with the aircraft. Number four, the pilot has indicated via hand signals that the plane has the following system failures: hydraulics, electrical, oxygen, and engine. The only system that does not appear to be amiss is fuel, so there is no immediacy requiring a rushed landing attempt.

"And number five—and this is the real sticker—*can* the pilot put his landing gear down, and *if* he can, will the compromised fuselage structure be able to withstand the different aerodynamic forces that will then exist? That was a question that originated from a Boeing engineer that we awakened in the U.S. during the night. And if we can get him on the ground in one piece, will he have the brakes to be able to stop, given the loss of their hydraulic system, although we don't know exactly which one or ones were damaged.

"The weather is good, the winds are light and variable, and the active runway at St Mawgan is runway three zero, which is over twenty-seven hundred meters long. There is a treeless clearway at the end, which should provide a relatively safe, or shall I say obstruction-free, avenue if need be. The three Sea Knight helicopters, in addition to the Cornwall Air Ambulance Service, will be in the area of his final approach, approximately where we think that he'll be attempting to extend his gear. In addition, there will be five ships from her Majesty's Coast Guard spread out along his final approach path. I must be honest with you; the situation is very troubling to me. I'm trying to be optimistic, but…well, let's just hope the best for those poor souls, all three hundred thirty-seven of them, and don't forget about the crew. For God's sake, they've made it all the way to the Channel."

* * *

Time: Local and Zulu—0731

The Celtic Sea

Trans Ocean 38 was flying over the water at seven hundred feet on an extended final approach course to runway three zero, RAF St Mawgan, twenty-three miles to the northeast of the Cornish coastal town of Newquay.

"Well, Bear, I think that we have briefed this and talked about the procedures more than enough. We're just about to cross the Rubicon, my friend." Jack paused and squinted out the window. "I can see a clearing way up there, one o'clock. Do you see it? And I've got some solid red VASI lights, too. Do you see them?"

Bear saw the visual approach slope indicator lights as well. "Yeah, Jack, I see them. Red over red, we're low."

"Yeah, I know that we're low. We'll just fly straight and level until we intercept the glide slope from *below*. Okay, Bear, our escort on my left just dropped his gear—that's the signal. That must be our airport up there, dead ahead. Get ready. Any last questions?"

"No, Jack. Let's do it!"

"Talk to me over a pint, okay?"

"Yes, sir, you're on!"

"Okay, Heather, it's your turn. You can go back now and start your 'brace' calls. Good luck, kiddo."

Heather got up from her jump seat and quietly kissed Jack on top of his right shoulder. "No, good luck to you, Captain. Godspeed."

"Bear, red over white on the VASI—we're intercepting the glide slope. Gear down, before-landing checklist…let's see what this girl is going to give us."

Bear reached forward and grabbed the gear handle with his left hand, pausing for a second with his head bowed and eyes tightly closed, then moved the handle to the down position. "Gear down. Jack," he said tensely, "we don't have any green gear lights because we don't have any electrics. I don't know if they're down and locked or not."

"Well, we can't make a two-engine go-around—we're committed to land!" Jack said. "Give me flaps one, then fifteen."

"Roger, one, then fifteen," Bear repeated.

"We're fast, Bear, and I'm not sure the flaps are working. Give me flaps twenty-five. How are we doing on the checklist?"

"Jack, the only thing that I can really accomplish on the checklist is placing the gear handle down. Everything else is just a guess because all the indicators are dead!"

"Well, then, just blow it off. That's the way it is."

"How does she feel, Jack? Do you have complete control?"

"She feels about the same—a handful. Anyway, at least it sounded like some or all of the gear went down. Can you see your engineer's panel from where you sit? Can you see any hydraulic system indications? Will we have any brakes?"

Copilot Wagoner quickly turned around in his seat to get a glance at the hydraulic system gauges. "Again, we don't have any electricity, so there are no warning lights. Everything looks normal from here, but I really don't know. I can't tell," he replied as he faced forward.

The airplane continued to descend, following the VASI glide slope.

"Looks like about two hundred feet, Jack…looks like about a hundred…looks like fifty feet!" These estimates were replacing the normal, electrically powered radar altimeter callouts. The airplane was just about to touch down.

As Jack slowly retarded the throttles of one and two to idle, Bear gasped; the aircraft nose veered to the left! Jack quickly corrected with rudder and aileron inputs. Was the gear down, and was it locked? They both held their breath and waited. It seemed like an hour, but finally the main gear touched down. Jack's right hand shot forward and grabbed the spoiler handle and pulled it back to the extend position, thereby raising the speed brake panels on the top of the wings and helping the airplane slow down even faster. His right hand then shifted to throttles one and two, which he then slowly pulled into reverse. Jack then moved his feet higher on the rudder pedals and depressed the toe brakes.

"They're working, Bear—the brakes are working!" Jack shouted.

"A hundred knots," Bear called out, reading the needle on the airspeed indicator. "Eighty knots…sixty…."

Jack slowly advanced throttles one and two, thereby taking them out of reverse thrust as the airplane eventually came to a stop on the runway. A conga line of fire trucks and ambulances quickly made their way to the beached whale, red lights flashing. Luckily, St Mawgan had the widest runway in the UK, three hundred feet, and that was indeed fortuitous today. The B-747, upon thrust reduction in the landing flare and with full left rudder trim permanently applied, actually deviated seventy-five feet left of centerline and close to the edge of the concrete runway.

The two pilots both took a deep breath, and with cheeks puffed out, slowly exhaled through their pursed lips. They sat silently in their seats staring straight ahead for at least a full minute. They then looked at each other and slowly shook their heads. Heather Holland came bursting into the cockpit; she could control herself no longer, and more importantly, she didn't need to now—this was her crew in front of her, not her passengers. She sat down again in the jump seat, face in both hands, and began to deeply sob.

"Dear God! Dear God!" Then, after about ten seconds, and as suddenly as it began, it stopped. Shaking her head like a wet dog emerging from a pond, she seemed to regain her composure.

"Okay, guys, are you ready for your crew meals now?" she asked, which brought forth teary-eyed laughter from both Jack and Bear.

"Okay, let's not do to *that* again, at least for a good long while!" said Jack as the three of them clasped hands over the center radio console.

"Heather," Jack began.

"Yes, Captain?" Heather replied.

"Heather, I'm not sure what the protocol is here. I don't know what you should say to the passengers yet. We're just going to have to wait for our ground handler's signals to figure out their intentions with us." He looked out at the runway. "Well, here comes a guy now, walking up to the nose with signaling batons. Let's see what he indicates." As they waited, Jack asked Heather how the passengers reacted to the actual landing.

"Well, it depends on where they were sitting. The ones in the front who had seen the actual hole and the missing seats for that long period of time were, for the most part, catatonic. The ones in mid-cabin were mostly crying or praying, and those in the aft, who really hadn't seen the damage, were cheering like fans at a football game or something—all in all, just unreal!"

"Don't mean to cut you off, Heather, but here comes a tug; they must have found a seven forty-seven tow bar somewhere. It looks like we're going to be shutting the engines down, and they'll be towing us in. Just tell the passengers to stand by, and we'll let them know what's going on as soon as we do."

"Okay, guys, see you soon," said Heather, who then stood up, touched them both on the shoulder, and scampered out of the cockpit, visibly different from the person who had recently walked in.

When the airplane was secured on the large St Mawgan concrete parking apron, the portable airstairs were positioned at the entrance door, 1 left, and three people approached to ascend them—a man in a military uniform, a man in a dark suit, and a uniformed woman. Heather gave the thumbs-up signal through the small window in the door, indicating that the door was now unarmed and safe to open. The door was then fully opened by the ground crew on the outside. The first one to enter the plane was Air Marshal Sir Robert Gerwig, RAF St Mawgan Commander.

"Who's in charge here?" he immediately asked.

Heather came forward, introduced herself, and informed him that she was the chief purser, head of the cabin staff.

"First things first, Ms. Holland—I need to know the medical needs of your passengers."

While the inventory of injured passengers was being reviewed and evaluated, the accompanying man in the dark suit went forward in the cabin, intending to climb the spiral staircase in first class to get access to the cockpit. His gait was brisk until he saw the gaping hole in the side of the fuselage, wires and debris hanging from the ceiling, and the eight missing passenger seats. He came to an abrupt stop and just stared at the scene with a visibly pained look on his face. After a minute or two, he continued his walk to the cockpit. He stood outside the door, which was now open, and peered inside.

"Captain," he politely asked, "may I come in?"

Jack and Bear turned around in their seats, where they had been sitting since engine shutdown.

"My name is Inspector Peter Beet, and I'm with the CAA, the Civil Aviation Authority, which is similar to your FAA," he said as he walked forward, extending his hand. "First, let me say how relieved we are, we all are, to see you. There are an awful lot of people who have been up all night worrying and wondering about you. I say, that gaping hole in your fuselage…my good man, you are very lucky to be here. Anyway, you might not be familiar with our procedures here in the UK in the event of an accident. I will not hinder you now with details, because you fellows need to get some rest and decompress, but there are certain regulations that need to be addressed."

Jack and Bear both nodded before he continued. "Number one,

we will provide you with a briefing room so that you can dictate a very short, say five-minute summary of what occurred. Then, and I apologize about this in advance, we need a urine sample from you, although you and I know that it's preposterous to think that there is any connection between those results and a detonated bomb. Then, we have arranged some quiet quarters with beds so that you and your crew can catch up on some rest. We've been in contact with your company, Trans Ocean, the FAA, and the NTSB. I know that your company wants to talk to you—the others can wait. Also, this event is a bombshell—please excuse the word, maybe poor choice and I'm sorry—but the news impact of your flight is colossal. From the UK to France to the U.S., all over Europe, people have been worried and have been trying to get any news at all of your well-being and your whereabouts. So again, let me just say how happy we are to see you and we'll do anything, anything at all, to help you cope and help you mend. Does that sound okay, Captain?"

Jack was overwhelmed. "Yes, Inspector Beet, thank you for your words. My name is Jack Rheinstrom, and my copilot here is Gary Wagoner. The only thing that I'm really going to say is that we lost a fellow cockpit crew member, Captain Black, who was sucked out by the explosive decompression along with nine passengers. We've been struggling to keep this airplane in the air for the past four hours, constantly feeling as though we were seconds away from death. We're both, along with the cabin crew, completely spent. *Exhausted* isn't even the correct word; it's more than that. I'll pee in the bottle for you, but you're going to have to wait for it, because right now, I don't have enough fluid in my body to spit!"

"I completely understand, Captain, and again I apologize. A British aircrew would have to do the same thing if this happened to them and they had landed at Kennedy."

Jack raised his right hand and waived it in the air "No, no, don't worry, Inspector. I understand. However, I would like to go back and check on my passengers."

"By all means, Captain Rheinstrom. I will be available to take you inside whenever you say. I'll go below now. If you'll excuse me," said Inspector Beet as he turned around and walked out of the cockpit.

Jack was the first one to get out of his seat. "Bear, you're not going to believe it," he said with a tired laugh.

"What, Jack?"

"Just try to stand up, man—just try to stand up! My body is just one big knot!" Jack bent over and tried to touch his toes, but his hands only got as far as his kneecaps. "I'll come back later and try stretching then. I have to go see the passengers first." With that, Jack Rheinstrom rebuttoned the top button of his white uniform shirt, tightened the tie around his neck, donned his uniform jacket and the hat, and walked out of the cockpit.

The debriefing went well, or as well as could be expected. Jack talked to the company and had a final request for Air Marshal Gerwig.

"I need to make an important personal overseas phone call," he told Gerwig, "and in some privacy, if I may."

"Certainly, Captain. Come with me to my office. I'm sure that you will find it to your liking."

"Thank you," replied Jack, and the two of them, the captain and the commander, ascended the stairs of Headquarters, St Mawgan, and walked down the hall.

"Captain Rheinstrom, I'd like you to meet my secretary, Philippa Wren. Philippa, this is Jack Rheinstrom. He'll be using my office and phone to make an overseas call, so help him if you can."

The secretary nodded, and Jack and the commander went into the room.

"I'm leaving now and will be available for you when you're finished. Just push this button here on the phone panel, and Philippa will pick up and make the phone call for you."

"Thank you, Air Marshal," Jack said. The commander nodded and quietly left the room, closing the door behind him. Jack pulled out the wallet from his back pocket and found the small piece of paper that Laurie Mills had given him after their encounter with Katherine and Nicoline at La Polidor. It contained the name of where Nicoline was attending art school. At this point, that name and Nicoline served as his only connection to Katherine, and he simply had to reach her.

"*Bonjour, L'ecole des Beaux Arts. Comment puis-je vous aider?*"

Jack began, "*Bonjour, parlez-vous Anglais, s'il vous plaît?*"

"Oui, yes, I speak a little…how may I help you?"

"My name is Jack Rheinstrom, and I'm calling from England. I have an urgent request. I'm asking you to locate one of your students there for me. It's very important!"

"You are a family member, oui, Monsieur?"

"No, I'm not, and I know that may sound unusual, but no, I'm a family friend, and it's imperative that I speak with her."

"And why is it so important that you speak to her, Monsieur? I'm sorry, but this is not in line with normal school procedures, so I must say no."

"Let me speak to your supervisor, please," Jack pleaded, trying to maintain any composure he had left.

"No, Monsieur, I will not, because he will give you the same answer. You must realize it is only to protect our students. You understand that, oui? Merci, Monsieur, and au revoir."

There was a click and the phone went dead. Jack looked at the phone that he held in his left hand, then closed his eyes and thought for a few seconds. He opened his eyes and put the phone back onto its cradle. Emotion overcame him. On the one hand, he was almost giddy being able to just walk again on terra firma—he was alive and had a future again. But the importance of the present moment was completely overwhelming to him. He had been thinking and rethinking in the back of his mind—when he wasn't busy trying to keep an unwilling piece of metal in the air—just one thought, and one thought only. He had promised himself that if he could somehow make it out of his unbelievable predicament, he was going to totally change his life going forward. But it was more than a promise that he made to himself, it was a solemn oath that he swore with everything that made him Jack Rheinstrom. He stood and walked out of the commander's office, passing Philippa Wren on his way out.

"Were you successful, Captain Rheinstrom?" she asked.

Jack stopped and turned around. He was so confused that he couldn't even speak. He just sadly and slowly shook his head. Philippa was not only an excellent executive secretary; she was also a very smart, observant, and sensitive person. Like a horse that knows its rider, she could sense how upset Jack was.

"Captain Rheinstrom, if you will have a seat outside in the waiting area, I will page Air Marshal Gerwig, and he will escort you so that you can rejoin your crew."

As Jack nodded and left the room, Philippa immediately paged her boss.

* * *

"What do you mean he *hung up* on you, Captain? Didn't you tell him who you were?" a frowning Air Marshal Gerwig asked.

"I didn't think that being an airline pilot would overly impress a Parisian receptionist," Jack replied, "and no, I didn't, although I really didn't even get a chance. He basically said that it was against school policies."

"Well, Captain Rheinstrom—"

"Jack."

"Okay, Jack, besides greeting you this morning, I had other official duties to perform at the behest of the French ambassador to the UK, relayed to me via the prime minister's office. There was a request that I greet and welcome the mayor of Paris and his wife. They were on your flight escorting the French national soccer team. He's a delightful chap and a very grateful one, especially when it comes to you. I say, do you think that the receptionist in Paris could find your student if the mayor asked him to?"

* * *

Jack was sitting at the commander's desk again, waiting for a call from Miss Wren. The phone rang and Jack picked it up. "Your party is on the line, Captain Rheinstrom."

"Thank you, Miss Wren." Jack was nervous—very nervous. He didn't really know why, other than the fact that this phone call had been long anticipated.

"Hello?" came the voice on the other end.

Jack swallowed hard. "Hello…is this Nicoline?"

"Yes, it is. Who is this?"

"We met a few nights ago when you were at La Polidor restaurant in Paris with your mother. This is Jack Rheinstrom. Do you remember me?"

There was a long pause—a pause long enough for Jack to think that he might have lost the phone connection. The voice that came back did not sound like the one that first answered the phone. No, something was different; he wasn't quite sure what it was, but it was different. She spoke very calmly and in a very soothing tone.

"Yes, I remember you. Mother told me all about you...Dad!"

If it's true that just one more piece of straw can truly break the camel's back, then this was that last piece of straw as far as Jack Rheinstrom was concerned. He could barely muster any words at all.

"What...what did you say?" Jack sputtered into the phone.

"Dad," said the soft voice again.

In an instant, thirty or forty vignettes of Katherine Moore flashed before his eyes. Inside, Jack Rheinstrom could be strong as he needed to be, but his mind and his thoughts were now exploding like a string of firecrackers. He didn't know what to do, didn't know what to say—he only knew that he had to hang up.

"Nicoline, please understand...please. I can't talk now. I'm going to have to call you back!"

"I understand, I really do," she said. "I'll be here when you want to call me back. I'll be here, waiting."

Jack Rheinstrom put the phone down into its cradle just in the nick of time. His shoulders were trembling as he sat forward in Air Marshal Gerwig's wooden chair, elbows on the desk, his face in his hands. He'd been through so very much that day. He was as tough as they come, but he had reached his limit. It began with a slight whimper, but the floodgates weren't strong enough—he broke down and began to cry.

CHAPTER ELEVEN

"What did the sign say?" An American tourist asked her husband.

"I'm not sure. It was in French, but I think I understood it—it said that it was *fermé* from fourteen thirty to sixteen hundred. I think that means that it's closed from two-thirty until four o'clock."

"Well, that's really weird, isn't it? It says here in the guidebook that it's open every single day from 8:00 a.m. until 6:45 p.m. Now you say that it's closed?"

"Yeah, but it doesn't look like the other people standing in line know about the closing either. Well, we only have to wait another half an hour and it will be open again, and I don't want to give up our place in line. And it's such a beautiful September day—you couldn't ask for a better one. So let's just stay here.

The woman was about to protest but was interrupted by the sudden tolling of Emmanuel, the thirteen-ton bell that sits alone in Notre Dame's South Tower. Five seconds later, the four smaller bells in the North Tower began to ring, just as the massive wooden doors of the Portal of the Virgin opened and a group of about thirty people began to emerge. The two Police Nationale BMWs were waiting just outside the gates, the lights on each side of their windshield fairings flashing blue.

The man turned to his wife. "What do you know? It was closed for a wedding. I didn't know you could get married there! Must be someone special."

Just then, the bride and groom emerged, the others following in tow. They turned to the right and began to walk down the center of Rue du Cloître-Notre-Dame, the two motorcycles with their flashing lights leading the way.

On the Pont Saint-Louis, a small trio was performing. There

was a young bearded man playing an accordion, another young man with long wavy brown hair playing saxophone, and an attractive young singer belting out heartfelt songs to the curious onlookers, of which there were perhaps thirty-five in all. When the woman first saw the approaching police and the following entourage, she looked alarmed and confused as to what to do.

When the procession arrived at Pont Saint-Louis, the two policemen stopped, turned around on their seats, and gave a deliberate hand salute to the group, especially aimed at the bridegroom. The lead motorcyclist made a call on his radio, and turning left, the two motorcycles both sped down Quai aux Fleurs back into the heart of the City of Lights.

As the bridal group began to walk across the bridge, the young singer suddenly stopped in the middle of her song and turned to confer with her accompanying musicians. She had recognized the man and wife walking behind the bride and groom; this was her chance, and she was going to seize it. She brought the onlookers closer into her court, enabling the group an easier passage. At just the right moment, she began to sing, and it was a song that every Frenchman knew, *Non, Je Ne Regrette Rien*. Her voice was raspy but had a wide range and was strong, very strong.

Right in front of her stage, the group stopped and listened. The emotion that she projected rang true and was a worthy tribute to the singer who had made the song famous when she sang it in 1960—Édith Piaf. Releasing her last note, the singer, Madeleine, extended her arms like bird wings and deeply bowed. Everyone clapped heartily and came forth with francs for the outstretched and upside down beret that the saxophonist passed around. Those on the outside either reached across their shoulders or simply handed the francs to the person standing in front of them. In addition to the tips in the beret, there was also a business card with a note on the back from the man that Madeleine thought that she had recognized—and she was correct, it was Claude Tombeau, the mayor of Paris.

"*On y va, j'ai soif*," exclaimed the groom, as his motioning arms urged the group forward. He then pointed with his left arm and announced, "Voila!"

There overlooking the Seine, with views over the bridge of Notre

Dame's South Tower, stood the Café La Brasserie de Île Saint-Louis. The name was written in white script on the red awning in front, which was just above the outdoor tables and behind the leafed-out plane trees.

Back on the bridge, a young man had broken away from the bridal party and was talking to the young singer. They were an interesting couple to view, she being barely five feet tall, and he six foot four. Since his mastery of French consisted of saying *Bonjour* and *Merci*, he was forced to ask her if she spoke English.

"A little," he thought she said with a heavy accent.

"I come here a lot on business trips," he was saying, when he was suddenly interrupted by a woman in the wedding party,

"Bear, come on, we're going to be late for the first toasts!"

"Okay, Laurie, I'll be right with you." He turned around to face the young singer again and looked at her directly. "Au revoir, Mademoiselle."

"Au revoir Monsieur." He hurriedly left, but with a telephone number scrawled in pen on the back of his left hand.

A French gentleman was sitting by himself at a table for two outside, under the shade of the plane tree. On the table sat a gray dimpled ceramic mug that contained a grande Mützig pale lager. He heard some distant laughing. Curious, he peered over the top of his *Le Monde* newspaper. They appear a happy lot, he thought to himself, and then returned to his paper. A minute or two passed and he again became interested as the group approached and began queuing up at the door, waiting to enter the café.

Mon Dieu! He said to himself as he reached for his backpack underneath the table and pulled out his cell phone. "Philippe?" he asked when his party answered, "Are you busy?"

"Non, Jean Paul—why? What is it? You sound excited!"

"You need to do something quickly, Philippe—quickly."

"What?" he asked.

"Contact Coach Broussard, if you can. I know he has a cell phone. Gather as many of the team as you can. And quickly, quickly Philippe, meet me at La Brasserie de l'Isle Saint-Louis—he's here!"

* * *

"You know something?" she asked.

"I know a lot of things," he responded.

"Well, you are one lucky pup. Yesterday, you were awarded the Légion d'honneur by the President of France, and then today you got to marry *me*!" she said, looking up at him with a contented smile.

"I really don't care about the award," he replied. "It was nice, of course, but it wasn't worth going through what I did to get it. Now, as far as *you* are concerned...my life is now complete. I love you, Katherine."

Her cocky smile was suddenly replaced by a piercing, serious look and one of complete adoration.

"If you only knew, Jack, if you only knew. It might take some time to convince you, Jack, so be patient, but you are everything, and I mean *everything* to me!" The sounds of the surrounding celebration in the dining room became muffled, slowly fading away. "I carry it around for safekeeping, Jack, but it really belongs to you."

"What does, Katherine?"

"My heart, Jack—my heart." She stood on her tiptoes, reached up, and slowly kissed him on his lips.

By now, the crowd had grown to over 250 people. Besides almost the entire French national soccer team, there were residents of the island, Parisian families taking their children for a weekend outing at the Berthillon ice cream shop, and there were, of course, curious tourists and onlookers.

Alain Broussard tried to open the door of the café, but it was locked. He knocked on the door, on one of the glass windowpanes. The bartender, Roland, wearing his white short-sleeved shirt with black bow tie, black vest, and white waist-level apron, came to the door but did not open it. He shook his head no and waved his flattened right hand across his neck, mouthing the word "fermé." Coach Broussard gestured with his right index finger for Roland to come outside, and then joined the outstretched fingers of his hands in a "please" gesture.

Jack had his arm around Nicoline, who was clearly in a moment of bliss. She looked up at him slowly, shaking her head.

"Happiest day, Dad—happiest day of my life."

Jack Rheinstrom looked down at his daughter, softly nodded, and then wiped away an errant tear. Roland approached them as they were toasting each other with their flutes of champagne.

"Roland, my good man, will you join us in a toast?"

"*Non, pas maintenant, Capitaine.* Will you and Katherine and the mayor and his lady come with me? S'il vous plaît?"

"Where are we going, Roland? " Jack asked.

"S'il vous plaît, Capitaine Rheinstrom, s'il vous plaît."

The four of them, with Nicoline and the bridal party in tow, followed Roland out of the dining room and into the bar area by the front door.

"They want you to come out," said Roland.

"Who does? And why?"

"Outside, in the front there, standing by the three young musicians, is the French national soccer team. You recall that they were on your flight, but afterwards they never got a chance to say thank you." Roland's voice was now pleading. "Go out, Capitaine, and see them—it would mean a lot to them."

Jack looked at Katherine, then at Nicoline, then at the mayor. As the door opened and Jack and Katherine walked out, hand in hand, the applause and cheering were deafening. But a forceful chorus soon replaced the collective applause en masse, with the singing of the conscience of France—their national song, "La Marseillaise." That day, the song was clearly sung with emotion and conviction; Jack heard the emphatic richness and timbre of the booming voices in the chorus and saw the serious expressions on their faces and in their eyes, many of which were moist with tears. Their voices rang loud and true, as if a much larger choir was present. The song would eventually be over and the people would soon be gone. But Jack's life was *not* forsaken—a new one had just been born.

The Rime of the Ancient Mariner

(Excerpts)

By Samuel Taylor Coleridge

The self-same moment I could pray;
And from my neck so free
The Albatross fell off, and sank
Like lead into the sea.

He prayeth best, who loveth best
All things both great and small;
For the dear God who loveth us,
He made and loveth all.

EPILOGUE

I have been fascinated by aviation since I was a child. The one facet of the subject that always held my keenest interest was that of safety. I remember buying my first issue of *Flying Magazine* when I was in the sixth grade and discovering a monthly column therein entitled "*I learned* About *Flying From That.*" It was always the first article that I would read. It was basically an avenue for pilots to pass on their lessons learned from their "almost" accident flights. Articles often echoed the well-known adage attributed to the British aviator Captain A. G. Lamplugh: "Aviation in itself is not inherently dangerous. But to an even greater degree than the sea, it is terribly unforgiving of any carelessness, incapacity, or neglect."

I was a flying safety officer in the Air Force for almost two decades and spent many hours studying accident reports. I remember very well the accident involving the United Airline's 747, Flight 811, that occurred on February 24, 1989. After reading the preliminary reports, I compartmentalized it in my mind as just another procedural error incident. I had no intention of ever putting any aspect of it into a written piece. That was until I read the front-page article in *The Wall Street Journal* published February 23, 1990, written by staff reporter Judith Valente. After that, the flight of UAL 811 took on new meaning, which remains with me to this very day. Ms. Valente has generously given me permission to reprint her article in its entirety, which follows this epilogue. I believe it not only accurately recounts the facts of the case but also provides a deep personal look into the lives of a lost son's parents and the unwelcome tragedy that then entered their lives. Ms. Valente's article is thought-provoking and questions a lot more than just the accident investigation. In the end, the actions taken by Kevin and Susan Campbell, for me, give a new meaning to the words *commitment, gallantry, courage,* and *love.*

"DEATH OF A SON"

Grief-Stricken Parents Devote Lives to Probe Tragedy of Flight 811

Why Did Jet's Cargo Door Fly Open Over the Pacific, Killing Nine, A Year Ago?

A $3,027 Repair Job Delayed

By Judith Valente, February 23, 1990

Susan Campbell will never forget the vision that woke her before dawn on Feb. 25, 1989. Sitting up in bed, the Wellington, New Zealand, housewife felt a strange sense of foreboding and beheld a "clear, clear" picture of her son, Lee, in front of her.

Sensing her anxiety, Kevin Campbell put an arm around his wife and kissed her lightly. Both went back to sleep.

The news came a few hours later. United Airlines Flight 811, en route from Honolulu to Auckland, New Zealand, had had an accident. Twenty minutes into the flight, at 23,000 feet, a cargo door had burst open, tearing a gaping hole in the fuselage of the Boeing 747. Lee Campbell was one of the nine passengers blown out the hole to their deaths.

The Campbells were devastated. At 24, Lee was the oldest of their three children. A scholarship student, he had recently graduated from college and was engaged to be married. He had just landed a marketing job with an import firm, and was on his way home from a business trip to the U.S.

Racked by grief, the Campbells groped for a way of dealing with his death. What they decided to do was extraordinary. In the months following the tragedy, Kevin and Susan Campbell embarked on a mission to determine exactly what had gone wrong with Flight 811.

In an echoing airport hangar in Honolulu, they photographed the mangled jet's interior and scraped off bits of paint from the outside as a keepsake of their son. In Washington D.C., they scrutinized metal pins and hooks recovered from the cargo door frame at the

National Transportation Safety Board. In their year-long quest, the determined couple examined over 2,000 pages of technical documents, and, with the help of a New Zealand university, even devised a computerized simulation of the incident.

They also spoke with 17 of the flight's survivors, including the captain and co-pilot, in an effort to reconstruct the events surrounding the incident. "I have never known any family to get quite this involved," says Ronald L. Schleede, who heads the safety board's inquiry into Flight 811.

As a result of their investigation, the Campbells have devised a theory on the causes of the accident—one that the government investigators now are studying. If correct, the Campbells' theory could not only help determine who is liable for the accident, but also force Boeing Co. to redesign the cargo doors on its 747s.

AMPLE WARNING

Researching the accident was emotionally wrenching for the Campbells. United, they discovered, had had ample warning of the problems with that jet's forward cargo door. According to maintenance records, United ground personnel had trouble opening and closing the door 12 times in the 2 1/2 months before the accident. But the airline's mechanics never pinpointed the reason for the failures.

Moreover, United admitted in hearings on the incident that it didn't inspect its 747s' cargo doors as frequently as federal regulations require. In retyping a Federal Aviation Administration order for distribution to maintenance workers, a United employee inadvertently omitted a phrase calling for certain inspections.

United, a unit of UAL Corp. and Boeing Co. declined repeated requests from this newspaper to discuss the accident. The safety board will know more in a few weeks, when the Navy is to try to retrieve the missing cargo door from the ocean floor.

Until the day of the accident, "life was settling down quite nicely," for the Campbells, says their 18-year-old daughter, Fiona. Mr. Campbell, 46, had retired from his car dealership. He spent most of his time rebuilding vintage cars. Their children grown, Mrs. Campbell, 43, had returned to college to study sociology.

NO BODY TO BURY

"The family was always everything to us," says Mrs. Campbell, a reserved, soft-spoken woman. Lee had become "such a good friend," she recalls. Tall, dark-haired and athletic, he was his father's partner at weekly squash games, his mother's confidant on family matters.

But everything changed on Feb. 25, when the Campbells awoke to a radio report on the accident involving Flight 811. "Susan looked at me with a look of sheer horror and said, 'That's Lee's plane,'" Mr. Campbell recalls. A few hours later, a United official called to say their son was missing and "presumed dead." Lee Campbell's body was never recovered.

At the memorial service, Mr. Campbell wore one of the suits his son had taken on his trip; Lee's luggage had been returned shortly after the accident. The Campbells parked their son's green MG sports car outside the chapel. On the altar, they placed mementos of Lee, among them a favorite tie with a piano-keyboard design on it, a pair of his trademark red socks and a Father's Day card addressed "To my Dad, who works so hard."

Five days later, the Campbells flew to Honolulu at United's expense to get a close-up look at the disabled jet. The visit drove home the tragedy. The jagged hole was 10 feet by 20 feet—big enough to drive a car through.

Flight 811 had reached a speed of 460 miles per hour when the door burst open. Because of the explosive decompression, the jet's interior looked as if a tornado had struck. The floor had collapsed beneath 10 business-class seats. Wires and cables lay exposed. Serving trays and drinking glasses were lodged in overhead bins. Most horrifying of all was the site of Lee's seat, 8H. All that remained were two broken legs.

A FOUR-MINUTE FALL

As they were leaving the plane, Mr. Campbell pointed to some dents on the wings. Mrs. Campbell whispered to her husband that she hoped Lee had hit the wing and was knocked unconscious before enduring the four-minute fall to the ocean.

In April, the Campbells returned to the U.S., this time to attend a safety board hearing in Seattle. The critical issue: Why had the cargo door's locks failed?

Safety-board investigators focused on two possible causes. One was that a baggage handler had failed to close the door properly; United's ground crew disputed that theory. The other was that some mechanical or electrical problem had allowed the door to open accidentally in flight.

A FAIL-SAFE DESIGN?

Boeing engineer James Fitzgerald explained how the doors normally work. Once the cargo is loaded, a baggage handler flips a switch, activating a mechanism that lowers the door into place. Two hooks in the door automatically grab the frame and pull the door flush with the outer skin of the fuselage. Eight latches then rotate around pins along the frame. Finally, the baggage handler twists a handle on the outside of the door, which causes eight locking arms to seal the latches in place.

Mr. Fitzgerald testified at the hearing that Boeing had known of problems with the doors since 1975. A number of airlines had complained that the electrical system occasionally malfunctioned, and that the locks, made of lightweight aluminum, were bending when the door was closed manually. In response, Boeing issued a bulletin advising airlines to reinforce each of the locking arms with an additional aluminum plate. United says it didn't find any problems with the locks on its 747s, and chose not to make the repair.

On March 10, 1987, an incident occurred that presaged the tragedy of Flight 811. Shortly after a Pan Am 747 took off from London, the locking arms and the latches on its forward cargo door failed. All that kept the door from blowing off were the two pull-in hooks. The Pan Am crew managed to land the jet safely.

A MANDATORY REPAIR

Subsequent inspection of the jet showed that most of the locking arms were bent and one was broken. Robert Dann, a Pan Am engineer who testified at the hearing in Seattle, said a ground worker might not have closed the door properly.

But Mr. Dann also said Pan Am had had difficulty with the door's electrical system several times before the incident. Mr. Campbell began to suspect an electrical malfunction was the problem.

The Pan Am incident prompted Boeing to issue a service "alert" in April 1987. It recommended airlines reinforce the lock sectors with steel plates, which would be stronger than aluminum. In July 1988, the FAA made the repair mandatory, but it gave airlines two years to do it.

SLOW TO FIX

Seven months later, when the cargo door blew off Flight 811, United had fixed only six of its 31 747s. (By contrast, Pan Am had modified all 38 of its 747s and Trans World Airlines had repaired all its 20.) Robert Doll, United's vice president of engineering, said at the hearing that United didn't believe the locks were enough of a danger to justify the cost of promptly repairing its entire fleet. Each plane would have been out of service for 15 hours, according to an estimate by Boeing, though the actual repair would cost only $3,027 per 747.

"The day after the hearings ended was a very sad day. We realized how unnecessary this accident had been," Mr. Campbell says.

While it was obvious *something* was amiss with the door, the Campbells still felt an urgent need to pinpoint exactly what had gone wrong. At the hearing, they had amassed thousands of pages of documents on the accident—airline service bulletins, FAA orders, United maintenance records. For four months last summer, Mr. Campbell, who has a background in mechanical engineering, did little else then sit in his living room overlooking the rocky coastline of western New Zealand and sift through the evidence.

INTERVIEWING SURVIVORS

He and his wife also continued to track down surviving passengers and interview them about their recollections of the accident. Sometimes they lost heart. Once, after talking by telephone to a couple that were seated behind Lee, Mrs. Campbell broke into tears in her husband's arms. "It's not going to make Lee any less dead," she sobbed.

Mr. Campbell found himself going back repeatedly to photos investigators had taken of the switch that activates the electrical mechanism. The pictures showed loose wiring and tiny scorch marks in the switch. Mr. Campbell became convinced that the photos showed evidence that the switch had malfunctioned. In his view, the switch had arced—that is, an electrical charge had leapt from one wire to another—in midflight, starting up the motor that opens the door.

United's maintenance records, which detailed electoral problems with the door in the 10 weeks or so before the accident, bolstered his theory, in his view. A dozen times, when ground-crew members tried to electrically open or close the door, it didn't work. "Things began adding up to an electrical failure," Mr. Campbell says.

FEARS OF A BOMB

He found what he believes is another clue in the transcript of the cockpit voice recording. At 2:09 a.m. Capt. David Cronin heard a thump and asked "What the hell was that?" Then, 1.8 seconds later, the crew heard what they thought was a bomb exploding. It was the door bursting open. Mr. Campbell speculates that the initial thump was the sound of the door's locks and latches giving way.

In September, Mr. Campbell submitted his analysis to the safety board in Washington. Once there, he discovered in the board's files a statement from passenger Roland Wilhelmy. About two seconds before the door blew off, Mr. Wilhelmy said he heard something buzzing. Mr. Campbell believes the noise was the electrical motor that opens the door.

Safety-board investigators say they aren't yet convinced. They also noticed the scorch marks, but they don't think an arc could have triggered the door's opening midflight. The door is designed, they say, so that power to its electrical system is cut off before the aircraft leaves the ground. Based on what Boeing has told them, investigators say four independent systems would have had to have failed for the door to open in flight.

The safety board believes a more likely scenario is that the door simply wasn't closed properly on the ground, or that the locks had been damaged previously. At 23,000 feet, the pressure differential was so great the locks gave way. But there are problems with this theory as well. An improperly secured door should activate a warning light in the cockpit when the crew begins to ready the jet for takeoff.

If the safety board's leading theory is proven correct, the United disaster will probably be attributed to human error. But Mr. Schleede, the investigator, says he hasn't ruled out the Campbells' theory yet.

"This guy has done his homework," he says. If Mr. Campbell is right, Boeing may have to redesign its 747 cargo doors. Mr. Campbell believes the electrical mechanisms that operate the doors shouldn't be built into the 747; he suggests instead the airlines keep such equipment for use on the ground.

A SCHOLARSHIP FUND

All the research has taken a toll on the Campbells. In November, Mr. Campbell was hospitalized for a bleeding ulcer. Fiona Campbell says her parents look "sadder, more tired" each time they returned from the U.S. They are beginning to put the tragedy behind them, though. Last week, the Campbells accepted a settlement from Boeing and United estimated by a family friend to be about $600,000. The companies also agreed to contribute $25,000 each to a scholarship fund in Lee's name. The Campbells decline to discuss the settlement.

In reflective moments, the Campbells say they feel their son had a strange foreshadowing of the bizarre fate that would befall him. After his death they found a poem he had written:

Waves hypnotizing me with green, beckoning fingers
A dream of space flight weightlessness
Air rushes past to fill a vacuum,
Progressive holes which must be filled

Lee had titled the poem "Was That Me?"

Ms. Valente's article in *The Wall Street Journal* was written forty-two days *before* the National Transportation Safety Board disclosed their ruling (NTSB/AAR-90/01) that the probable cause of the accident was "the sudden opening of the *improperly latched* forward cargo door [emphasis mine]," concluding that the door, possibly damaged previously, was somehow improperly latched when the airplane took off (human error).

But Kevin Campbell felt otherwise. He was convinced that everything pointed to an electrical problem in the door.

"Not so," countered Boeing, who concurred with the safety board in refuting Campbell's theory. A company spokesman added,

"The NTSB has very clearly ruled out electrical malfunction."

Months later in the same year, 1990, the U.S. Navy began a search and rescue mission to find the missing aircraft cargo door—and was successful. On September 26, and again on October 1, some ninety miles south of Honolulu in over fourteen thousand feet of water, they found it. The Navy recovered the two pieces of the cargo door, and after careful examination and analysis the NTSB *modified* their original analysis and probable cause. It *now* stated, "The door opening was attributed to a faulty switch or wiring in the door control system which permitted electrical activation of the door latches toward the unlatched position after initial door closure and before takeoff."

Had United 811's explosive decompression occurred minutes later, at a typical cruise altitude of say, thirty-six thousand feet, instead of on climb-out at twenty-three thousand feet, the results would have been horrific. The pressure differential would have been significantly higher, resulting in a much more destructive explosion, probably inflicting more damage to the 747's fuselage, but more important was the fact that the cockpit crew would only have had seconds, not minutes, to react to the sudden emergency.

The crew oxygen system had been disabled by the explosion, so when the cockpit crew went to don their masks, there was no oxygen waiting for them. And that occurred at twenty-three thousand feet on climb-out, where the time of useful consciousness or TUC is a generous five to nine minutes, and that is without a rapid depressurization—it's half of that, two to four minutes, with one. The TUC at thirty-six thousand feet, and including the effects of a rapid depressurization, is only twelve to twenty-five seconds! It actually took 811's crew fifty-three seconds to don their unusable oxygen masks. The only conclusion that I can draw is that, had the cargo door opened at cruise altitude, the plane and the passengers would surely have been lost, barring a miracle. At the time of the accident there were over 650 Boeing 747s flying around the world, mostly over vast areas of wide open ocean and all with the flaw that Kevin Campbell had opined about but couldn't prove.

Thousands upon thousands of air passengers are safer today than they were in 1989 because of a small family from Wellington,

New Zealand. Because of them, changes were made to the critically flawed doors and locks of the Boeing 747, potentially saving untold number of lives.

"I stand at attention, my hat is off and in my hand, in offering you a salute by dedicating this book to you, for I, along with the world of aviation—all the passengers, the pilots, and the flight attendants who ever flew on the Boeing 747—owe a debt of gratitude to you, Kevin, and to you, Susan, and finally to you, Lee Campbell. May you always rest in peace."

Respectfully submitted,
Gerry Hawes, January 12, 2015

Lee Campbell

AUTHOR'S NOTE

The interactions between the characters in the various settings in the book are fictitious, although the actual geographical locations are true. The major event in the story, the disastrous in-flight cargo door opening on United 811, was a historical event, as you know by now. I used the actual CVR (cockpit voice recorder) and FDR (flight data recorder) readings to ensure accuracy and authenticity in parts of the story. But there are two other actual accidents that had a role in the plot development; in particular, the Boston Christmas Eve crash. Those included the tragic "hard over" rudder accidents of two Boeing 737's; United Flight 585 approaching Colorado Springs, Colorado and USAIR Flight 427 approaching Pittsburgh. The toll on human lives of those two accidents was much higher than that of United 811, as there were no survivors at all.

I am a very lucky man. I realized my childhood dream and have enjoyed thirty-two years with my work desk being the cockpit of a U.S. airliner, specifically Eastern Airlines and Northwest Airlines. During my five years of active duty in the USAF, I flew KC-135 air refueling "tankers" before serving a combat tour of duty in Vietnam flying as a Forward Air Controller, or FAC. In addition, I flew the Lockheed C-141 Starlifter for twenty-two years in the Air Force Reserves, attached to the 732nd MAS (Military Airlift Squadron), McGuire Air Force Base, New Jersey—"Fly with the RAM." I have also, during the past five years, volunteered my time and personal aircraft, a Beechcraft Bonanza, to fly coastal patrols in New England for the U.S. Coast Guard (Air) Auxiliary.

It is my intent to share with you my love of the skies along with some interesting, at least maybe to some, insights into a unique lifestyle and profession. In the end, it is the safety aspect of the realm that must always be the main focal point, that which matters most in the future. It has to be; there is no other choice. It is true that one can be too cautious, however, there is never a case of one being too safe.

I thank you for coming along with me—I sincerely hope that you enjoyed your flight.

Sincerely,

GWH

ACKNOWLEDGMENTS

This book was an unintended journey for me. It all began in 1990 when I just happened upon Judith Valente's article on the front page of *The Wall Street Journal.* Her factual account and personal insight into the story made a lasting impression on me and I am indebted to her. I would like to express my appreciation to the Campbell family, Kevin and Susan, for allowing me to revisit a very painful time in their lives. And I would like to thank Jessica McAllen, reporter for New Zealand's national newspaper, *The Sunday Star-Times,* who first introduced me to the Campbells and who has been encouraging me during the entire two-year writing period. Accomplished authors Elizabeth Hawes and Nicholas Weinstock, and friend Elizabeth Kaiser have also been instrumental in their support and in the evolution of the actual story. And thanks to my wife Barbara who believed in me. Without the help of these very special friends, *Albatross* would never have been able to fly.